PENGUIN BOOKS

LAST CALL

Harry Mulisch was born in Holland in 1927 and now
is regarded as Holland's foremost author. His previous novel, *The Assault*, was made into a film which
won an Oscar for Best Foreign Film of 1987.

LAST CALL

HARRY MULISCH

Translated from the Dutch
by Adrienne Dixon

PENGUIN BOOKS

PENGUIN BOOKS
Published by the Penguin Group
Penguin Books USA Inc., 375 Hudson Street, New York, New York 10014, U.S.A.
Penguin Books Ltd, 27 Wrights Lane, London W8 5TZ, England
Penguin Books Australia Ltd, Ringwood, Victoria, Australia
Penguin Books Canada Ltd, 10 Alcorn Avenue,
Toronto, Ontario, Canada M4V 3B2
Penguin Books (N.Z.) Ltd, 182–190 Wairau Road, Auckland 10, New Zealand

Penguin Books Ltd, Registered Offices: Harmondsworth, Middlesex, England

First published in Great Britain by William Collins Sons & Co. Ltd, 1987
First published in the United States of America by Viking Penguin,
a division of Penguin Books USA Inc. 1989
Published in Penguin Books 1991

3   5   7   9   10   8   6   4

First published in Holland under the title *Hoogste Tijd*.
Copyright © 1985 Harry Mulisch Amsterdam.

LIBRARY OF CONGRESS CATALOGING IN PUBLICATION DATA
Mulisch, Harry, 1927–
[Hoogste Tijd. English]
Last call/Harry Mulisch; translated from the Dutch by Adrienne Dixon.
p.   cm.
Translation of: Hoogste Tijd.
ISBN 0 14 01.5601 1
I. Title.
PT5860.M85H6613   1991
839.3´1364—dc20   90–22207

Printed in the United States of America
Set in Imprint

These our actors,
As I foretold you, were all spirits, and
Are melted into air, into thin air;
And, like the baseless fabric of this vision,
The cloud-capp'd towers, the gorgeous palaces,
The solemn temples, the great globe itself,
Yea, all which it inherit, shall dissolve,
And, like this insubstantial pageant faded,
Leave not a rack behind. We are such stuff
As dreams are made on; and our little life
Is rounded with a sleep.

SHAKESPEARE, The Tempest, IV, i, 148–158

ACT ONE

1
The Invitation

The gong sounds three times, the lights slowly fade, and with the soft rustling of the curtain the musty smell of artificial life spreads across the scene. A petit-bourgeois living-room on a new housing estate. It is the first day of autumn, a darkly lit, stormy morning (but it is almost always windy in the polderlands) and a fat woman in her seventies throws a letter across the newspaper that her brother is reading in his armchair by the window. He picks the envelope from his lap and reads who it is from.

"The Authors' Theatre?" he wonders, and looks again at the address. She does not react; in her long dressing-gown which he detests intensely, she starts dusting the window-sill. As every morning, she takes a glass of sherry with her on her voyage around the room – in that always identical stage-setting, against the backdrop of their old age; starting at the wrought-iron table with the knick-knacks and the lace cloths on the glass top, then the diamond-shaped mirror above it, hanging against a batik drape and flanked by candle-like ornamental lights, and then through a forest of floor and wall lamps past the antique phonograph on the reproduction table beside the sofa, to the old-fashioned television set and the windows. Ashes drop from the cigarette that dangles between her lips; with her little finger she pushes the grey cone into the palm of her hand and lets it roll into a flowerpot, where she presses it slightly flat.

At the same moment her brother also uses his little finger. With three quick jerks he tears open the envelope and unfolds the letter. His hair stands out like inspired white flames around his forehead, which is supported by a forceful nose, two heavy eyebrows like

9

architraves, a wide mouth and a powerful chin. The entire panorama is as furrowed as that of a great actor from the past, for ever marked by the emotions of Hamlet and Lear, evening after evening, the pores of his nose and cheeks – so often gasping for air under make-up and grease – wide open. Undoubtedly make-up and grease are indeed the cause, but Hamlet and Lear he has never acted, unlike others of his family; nor even Rosencrantz nor Guildenstern; he was once a second-rate music-hall and variety artiste, somewhere on the fringe of the theatrical world, and the impressive furrows in his face are the result of countless grimaces.

After reading the letter he takes off his glasses and looks at his sister. He squints slightly. In his good eye (the left) there is something fierce, but in the bad one the blue iris blends into a ring of fish-like pallor, dissolving into the white. His sister still shows no curiosity; without responding to his gaze she passes in front of him, moves over to the sideboard, and starts working on the glass of a framed photograph: a dachshund lying in the grass like a small sphynx.

"Listen to this, Berta."

He puts his glasses on again and reads out the letter in a droning voice:

Amsterdam, 20.9.82

Dear Mr Bouwmeester,

As you probably know, the Authors' Theatre is a middle-sized company founded by a collective of playwrights. Our repertory consists exclusively of original Dutch plays and adaptations. For over ten years we have been the resident company at the Kosmos Theatre in the Nes in Amsterdam.

One of our members, Leo Siderius, has recently completed an important new play, 'Hurricane', which is about a great actor around the turn of the century preparing his farewell performance in the Amsterdam City Theatre. Owing to the cancellation of another production we are obliged (in view of subsidies dependent on a stipulated number of performances) to stage this play during the first half of the present season: the first night is scheduled for Friday 12 November, Short notice, but the play is not long and the intention is to stage it without an interval. The director will be Caspar Vogel.

Both the Committee and the Management of our Foundation would be honoured if you would – as our guest actor – take the leading part.

As you appear to have no telephone, and in order to save you correspondence, Mr Vogel and I will visit you, unless we hear from you to the contrary, around four o'clock on Sunday, for further discussion.

Hoping for a favourable response and fruitful co-operation,
on behalf of the Foundation,
Yours sincerely,
H. Michael
Business Manager

Uli (pronounced Ooli) Bouwmeester takes off his glasses again and looks at his sister with open mouth. There is now a slight quiver in his neck.

"They're taking you for a ride," she says without a moment's hesitation, as she picks a withered leaf from the fuchsia. Her fleshy face, still rosy despite her age, shows the striking features endemic in her family; in a history book her photograph would not be out of place, with a caption like *Krupskaya* or *Madame Blavatsky*. Through a genetic caprice her white hair, unlike that of her brother, is so thin that the pink skin of her skull is visible everywhere; at the crown the strands have been tied together into a bun the size of a pea. Her dressing-gown is a garment of truly suffocating banality; an indeterminate brown of an equally indeterminate shiny material, from under which the toes of her slippers peep as she walks; crimson with white nylon pompoms. To Uli this evokes unbearably an image of old age, which he scarcely yet feels in himself (except that everything takes more time and some things don't happen any more at all). When he complains, she entirely agrees with him and suggests he clear off to the old people's home where all the staff wear trendy white trousers and go about in plimsolls. And he might take a look at his own sandals dating from the year dot, and at his shabby knitted cardigan which on chilly days he wears under his shirt and whose saggy sleeves stick out from under the cuffs of his shirt. He no longer cares what he looks like, any more than she. Does he remember, duffer that he is, how elegant he used to be? (Yes, there was even a time when he would dance about the room with Berta on his shoulders and throw her up to the ceiling!)

Uli doesn't understand.

11

"Why on earth should they want to take me for a ride?"

"Well, what do you think?" Berta crushes the withered leaf in her palm with a crackling sound. "They need a great actor – and so they ask you. Are you a great actor? Your name is all they care about, nothing else."

"What name?" says Uli impatiently. "There isn't a single Bouwmeester left on the stage. That doesn't mean a thing to anyone now."

"Don't be stupid. They know nothing about you, or they wouldn't have asked you. But they ask you, without further ado. Why *you*, all of a sudden? I could perhaps imagine that they might want to talk it over with you, but no, hop, invitation. I'd watch out if I were you. They're up to no good. There's something fishy about it. How did they get hold of your address anyway?"

Uli raises his hand and lets it drop, limply, on his knee.

"It's unbelievable. Here I am, with a letter from the Authors' Theatre in Amsterdam, offering me a part, a leading part, to be precise, a leading part, here, here, it says so, and all you can say is that it can't be any good. Are you sure you're not jealous that they haven't asked *you*?"

"Authors' Theatre . . ." repeats Berta, " – there's another bit of nonsense. As if the audience didn't matter. I bet it's a bunch of those trendies drinking tea out of their left earholes. *Mouthing their lines like this . . .*" – she suddenly stands with her legs apart, feet turned inwards, arms outstretched, fingers spread, speaking these last words with an unnatural intonation while staring at the brown wallpaper with the yellow circles. "And then play leapfrog with themselves," she adds contemptuously.

It was no mean effort – although Berta (or rather Shirley Carola, her stage name when she was still on the stage) has seen such old-fashioned modern performances only on television – that is to say, forty-second extracts in Sunday afternoon arts programmes, in which the state of the theatre is electronically annihilated.

Outside, in the back garden, there is a yapping.

"Well, you do as you please," she says testily, lifts up the hem of her dressing-gown and leaves the room with her glass.

12

"Cow!" he calls after her – but not really angrily, more out of habit.

Uli is alone with the letter. He reads it a third time and peers at it for a while, glancing also at the blank back of the page, the way in which – in a reversal of circumstances – a castaway on a desert island examines a letter from the inhabited world, washed ashore in a bottle. Miracles still happen, he thinks. For years he has been vegetating in the direction of death, believing that no one knew he was still alive – insofar as anyone had ever known. Sometimes he doubts it himself. And now it appears that there are people in Amsterdam who are still aware of his existence. Somewhere in the inner city, in the Nes, where he so often appeared in the past (subsequently in decline as a theatre street, though in recent years on the up-and-up again), they had gathered together and decided unanimously that he should take the lead part in a play. Certainly not because of his name, but probably because of his age; there are few really old actors left in the Netherlands. All the parts are played by young people these days, just as you see only young people in the streets. On the few occasions when he goes to Amsterdam, once or twice a year, he never sees any old people. They show themselves only in photographs of villages in southern countries.

A splatter of rain lashes against the window. He lets the newspaper slide into the rack beside his chair, and rises with a groan. He turns out to be shorter than he seemed when seated. With the letter in his hand he stands briefly in front of the mirror and looks at himself – and still sees the person he has seen there for almost eighty years. He still belongs to the world, it has not yet turned away from him, apparently anything can still happen at any moment. He thinks he still looks quite good. He straightens his back, takes a deep breath and goes to the window.

The shrubs in the small front garden sway about as if trying to pull themselves out of the ground. Where fifteen years ago fishes swam and the wrecks of ships stuck out of the sea bed, a youth now whisks past in a black helmet, wrapped in the millionfold amplified sound of a mosquito. At roof level it would now have been

13

rough weather on the Zuyder Zee, fishermen would have struck the mainsail and battened down the hatches, while in the villages along the shore their wives in fluttering black skirts would have stood at the quayside in silence, a mumbled prayer on their lips. Faint flashes of lightning streak through the clouds; seconds later the strange, soft autumn thunder rumbles far away. The letter, now level with his navel, has made a breach into his past.

Honoured spectators! Let us enter. The die is cast.

2
A Passer By

For twenty years, holding a straw boater beside his ear, and in glittering costumes, he had made dancing steps and pulled faces in the back row of the chorus, in theatres with names such as Flora, Scala, Diligentia, Palace of Popular Drama, which had long since gone out of existence. In the thirties he occasionally managed to get a minor part in some lowbrow film, but without his name appearing in the credits. When the war broke out and many of his colleagues no longer showed up at rehearsals, somewhat larger parts came his way, with him having to conduct silly, comical conversations with chambermaids wielding feather dusters with which they tickled his backside, which he then hastily protected with his top hat. But he never managed more than modest parts in operetta; despite his famous name the public scarely knew him. Like virtually everyone else in cabaret (and not only in cabaret) he registered with the Chamber of Culture and continued cheering up audiences until 1943, even playing for Nazi organisations such as Winter Help and Front Fare – also after his Jewish colleagues had been deported and gassed – and finally even in Germany. In the following year all German theatres were closed (the end of the beginning of the end); he spent the last winter of the war in Amsterdam with his wife and dog, and in May 1945 he was arrested. His life had run aground for good. After a few weeks in the House of Detention he spent about six months as a kind of political detainee in a number of internment camps. He was never prosecuted, not having been important enough (perhaps the fact that he had a German mother counted as a mitigating circumstance) – but nevertheless, he was finished and that at the age of forty-one.

He appeared on the stage only once more. In the post-war years of poverty he came into contact, in a roundabout way, with a seedy operetta company consisting of the lowest dregs among variety artistes, playing before the workers in the recently reclaimed North-East Polder. In Flevoland, the even newer polder, in which he now lived, the memory of those days often came back to him. The antediluvian mud landscape, stretching from horizon to horizon, covered only in thistles, the scattered remains of boats and shot-down aeroplanes jutting from the surface. The camps of wooden huts, linked by long kilometres of straight roads, would one day become new villages, but for the present they were indistinguishable from the camps in which he had been interned in the summer of 1945. They were inhabited exclusively by polder labourers and soldiers of the War Graves Department, whose job it was to remove the bodies. Women and alcohol were forbidden in the area; perhaps it was thought that the men would therefore work harder, but the only result was the total blunting of their sensibilities.

With the dull gaze of animals in a zoo they watched him as, in one of their sheds, he interpreted, with fake moustache and goatee, the part of Count Lalou, constantly thwarted in love, in the operetta *Biarritz* set in the lounge of a luxury hotel, affordable only to the very rich. The count was old, though not as old as Uli was now; but at least it was a leading part. The operetta (a misdeed rather than a work of art) had been written, composed and directed by the manager of the company, who never showed himself again, having also a wholesale business in haberdashery to look after.

This tour of the reclaimed underworld was bearable to Uli not so much because of the twenty-five guilders he earned per performance as for the tender relationship which developed between him and the orchestra, consisting of one pianist, Barbara, who excited him beyond measure. It was not her handsome broad face with the cat's eyes, although that helped; it was her lean, bony body. She shaved her calves, but her heavy eyebrows, the down on her cheeks and her hairy forearms suggested that something quite

16

extraordinary was hidden under her clothes; a forest of hair, extending across her thighs and belly, as far as her navel and covering also a large part of her buttocks, which always made him drunk with randy excitement, making him wish he could leap at her from all sides at once. At night, in the back of a truck returning to their base camp, she would place her hand – capable of such rapid finger exercises on the piano – on the spot that is so grossly neglected by most philosophers. And then all was well again! There was at least something resembling happiness then, in that jolting darkness under the tarpaulin, and in the snugness of the grey horse blanket covering their laps.

In the morning they sometimes took a ride on the motorbike belonging to an engineer of the National Waterboard who was also stationed at their camp. With the scorching Barbara riding pillion, they spluttered through the pampas to the former island of Schokland, a narrow ridge with green trees, small deserted houses and a church, lost on the surface of a monstrous planet. The ancient wooden sea defences, still encrusted with mussels, now kept the wind at bay, the waves of awesome space. During those days he occasionally landed some minor part in a radio play, where his sonorous voice did well. Radio programmes cautiously listed him under a pseudonym which they had asked him to invent:

> *A civil servant – Frederik Rozenveld*
> *An SS-officer – Frederik Rozenveld*
> *A passer-by – Frederik Rozenveld*

His relations, with whom he had had no contact since the war, were not exactly enamoured of this choice. Frederik Rosenveldt was the founding father of the Bouwmeester dynasty – the highest theatrical aristocracy in the Netherlands – a great comic and slapstick actor of the eighteenth century who had given impetus to a complicated series of generations of comedians, ramifying like a river delta into dozens of actors and actresses and culminating in the great Louis (who ranked with Garrick, Talma and Moissi, and celebrated triumphs as Shylock as far as Vienna, Paris and Stratford-on-Avon) – and ending in the person of Little Uli, who bore a speaking, or rather silent, likeness to him.

17

Poor Uli. In the family chronicles the hero of this more than true history will not even be found in a footnote.

After his marriage he lived with his wife and his old dachshund Sebastian in a cramped apartment in a run-down working-class neighbourhood of East Amsterdam. He had little in common with his wife. Having been, at the end of the 1920s, an attractive chorus girl in the Bouwmeester Revue of Louis Junior, she changed within the shortest time into a frowzy slattern who pushed up her hair with two hands in the morning, stuck a few pins into it and left it like that for the rest of the day. Eventually her only remaining emotion was jealousy – and in that respect it was a good marriage, for Uli gave her every opportunity to indulge her passion. The only period during which she had no cause for jealousy was the time he spent in an internment camp; on the other side of a long table, amid a row of other women talking to their husbands, she once placed her hand on his, which immediately provoked a growl from the guard at the end of the table. This prompted Uli to remark that the man was probably jealous. The reason why he looked forward to her visits was that she always brought his dog with her – long dead now. Death had stacked itself high around Uli, and perhaps the only being for which he had ever felt a true, sublime, pure love was his little Sebastian.

One day, when the dog was still alive and on this earth, Uli went, after their walk in the park, into the grocer's shop opposite his house. There were no other customers and after some hesitation the shopkeeper suddenly disclosed that he knew who Mr Bouwmeester was; he had made a study of "the light muse" in the Netherlands between the wars. From the back room he fetched a scrapbook in which, without much searching, he found a programme with Uli's name on it, near the bottom of a long list: Willem Bouwmeester. Most of the names were followed by the signatures of their bearers, at which Uli's eyes briefly clouded. Clearly, no one had asked him for his autograph. His own archives had been confiscated at the time of his arrest, never to re-emerge from the vaults of the Law.

He looked up uncertainly and met the shopkeeper's servile gaze. Would Mr Bouwmeester be prepared to take on the direction of a comedy for the amateur group Enjoyment Through Endeavour, of which he, Gerrit Paap, was chairman? The choice had been fixed on *Pale Betsy*. He had already talked about it with his members and they would be honoured if Mr Bouwmeester, with his long, versatile experience, that is to say . . . in a word.

Touched, Uli accepted the offer. He had never directed anything, but it was true, his experience encompassed such a bottomless pit of nonsense, that not only the performance but also the rehearsals were highly successful. Admittedly, every antic had been shown before, in the twenties or thirties, but nobody remembered them and insofar as they were still used they gave the cast a sense of professionalism. Soon Uli received invitations also from other drama societies, the amateur theatre turned out to be a thriving underground network, and he began to love the artisan milieu in which he glittered as an authority from the great theatrical world.

After rehearsals, in the back rooms or workshops of members, the professional theatre was subjected to admiring scrutiny, whereby great actors were referred to familiarly by their first names. Seen Albert in *Richard III*? Maybe he wasn't altogether at his best in the second act, he played along rather too much with his opposite number, but his shortcomings were still better than the virtues of many others. And then Ko, they way he looked so moved, and that chin of his (his Habsburg chin, as the plumber said). And what did you think of Ank in that Greek play, what was it called again? *Electra, Gas and Electra* – that's a good one! A boring play, actually, but how in Jesus' name did she manage it, that eerie sob in her voice, maybe a bit overdone at times, but always magnificent. Uli was unable to join in much; he never went to the theatre.

The evenings usually ended with him being asked to talk about the past. Then he painted the picture they expected, omitting the animosity and the backbiting and the disappointments and the poverty and the wretched travelling and the malaise after the performance and the tour of Germany and his arrest and internment after the war; the philandering with the girls he hinted at with a little gesture and a greasy wink. Buziau, the great clown, one of the finest men he had ever known – still saw him regularly (which was not true, he never met anyone from those days). The great cabaretier Louis Davids, tragically deported to the death camps and much mourned, whose heart beat only for others, what a terrific colleague he had been. He remembered that one day, Lou . . . And then Johan Heesters: not only an operetta singer who even now had all Germany at his feet, but also a philosopher, a man who understood the art of living. Whenever he was in the Netherlands he phoned his old friend Uli and, over a bottle of Riesling in the Amstel Hotel, they would rake up old memories for hours on end . . .

All that effort and the leisure time that these sweet people sacrificed for one performance to entertain family and friends! Sometimes it almost brought tears to his eyes, and in due course a fire of missionary zeal was kindled in his breast. If there was no money to be earned with these ventures anyway, if it was nothing but sheer love of the theatre, then why not play something better than that trash from the catalogues published specifically for the amateur theatre? Gradually he began to use his influence to raise the artistic level, and from farces and tear-jerkers he moved on to real comedies. A few experiments with Noël Coward went off well, and he finally risked Molière. He adaped a translation of *Tartuffe*, edited brazenly like a genuine dramatist, added some jokes, and while directing, he sometimes felt as if he was rising above himself – as if those great Bouwmeesters, whose portraits hung in the City Theatre, were watching over his shoulder and helped him as he demonstrated how one greets a lady, with a dashing flourish of one's plumed hat even when one's legs are too short. Despite a number of cross-capers and the odd case of slipping trousers, the show was only moderately successful, but he did not care – on the contrary. In the mid-fifties he got Enjoyment Through Endeavour, on the occasion of its golden jubilee, to play *Mary Stuart*. By that time his wife was already seriously ill.

As a boy he had once seen Schiller's tragedy, with his famous great-aunt-twice-removed Theo in the title role, and she had unleashed such tumult in the audience that he could still remember it. Greta, Gerrit Paap's wife, was to play the part of the tragic queen. But during the rehearsals, at the peak of his development work among the lower classes, something malicious awoke in Uli Bouwmeester. Their broad Amsterdam accents, which in Coward and Molière he had disguised under sham refinement, he now left untouched, and felt a terrible urge to laugh welling up inside him. Mortimer was played by a new addition to the group, a motor mechanic from the garage on the corner, a weedy blond youth who even at the first rehearsal knew his entire part by heart, refused to be directed, but immediately after his first entrance put his right foot slightly forward, his right forefinger against his chin, cupped his right elbow in his left hand and spoke his lines with the speed of a machine-gun, without twitching a muscle. Moreover, he moved his lips synchronously with every word spoken by all the other actors; he had learnt the whole play by heart. When he appeared unable to unlearn this habit, and proved also in other respects unstoppable, Uli encouraged the others to memorise their lines in the same manner. Tempo, tempo! Time and again he had to assure them that this was how it should be, that the play demanded it, but they all remained doubtful (except the motor mechanic who stared wanly out of the window during the scenes in which he did not appear), but Uli's authority was so great that no one dared protest.

The jubilee performance was a catastrophe. They didn't even get as far as the beheading; as early as the second act the curtain came down for good. Greta Paap, agitatedly entangling herself in her hired robes, as exuberant as they were shabby; Gerrit, slurring his words as the Earl of Leicester, all in broad Amsterdam; Queen Elizabeth trying, with an excess of convulsive gestures, to keep up the tempo; gowns ripping, crowns rolling – and then of course Mortimer, stepping forward pale as death, cupping his right elbow and annihilating everyone and everything under his barrage of words. While tumult erupted in the hall, the suppressed fit of laughter finally burst out of Uli Bouwmeester, as an almost physical hurt, a thing that somehow no longer had anything to do with the show.

21

It was the end of his career as a director. The following day there was a brief article in the Communist paper about the sickening manner in which he, a third-rate comedian, had taken advantage of genuine working-class lovers of drama. It was a disgrace to treat people in this way. And since Communists have good memories, the paper added that little else could have been expected of a characterless collaborator who in 1943 . . . Incipient contacts with the student theatre, which would have meant a step upward, were hereby nipped in the bud. He had his name and photograph included in the dismal catalogue of an agency for extras, but there was never any call for him.

The death of his wife affected him less than the disappearance of Sebastian a few months earlier. She had taken the dog shopping and by chance Uli saw him suddenly running down the street, ears flapping, his lead trailing behind him. Uli opened the front door but by then the dog had gone. Outside a shop where dogs were not admitted, his wife had tied him to a metal ring and something must have occurred there; he had been let loose or had broken away, in his panic something must have happened to his brain causing him to run past his own house and thus vanish forever from Uli's life. In desperation he placed advertisements in the paper and for months kept roaming the streets asking if anyone had seen a small brown dog; at night he called out his name in the park, listened to the silence and wept like a child – holding in his hands the pale marrowbone with the imprints of Sebastian's teeth.

When his wife had gone too, he realised there was only one thing left for him to do: grow old. They had never had children, the only thing her womb had every produced was the tumour that killed her. Also, it seemed that, with the disappearance of her jealousy, his sexual fury rapidly declined; had he done it all for her? He now made a meagre living for himself by keeping the books, at his own home, for a small decorator's business. Until he was fifty he toyed with the idea of settling in Germany and building up a new life in the lively cabaret world over there, but perhaps because of that number, 50 – and especially after an operation on his gall bladder which one day had turned out to be full of stones – he no longer had the energy for such a step. From then on he felt he was sliding out of the world of the young into that of the old.

Through a chance meeting with someone in radio, or rather with someone who had moved from radio to television (television, the upstart, was run by second-rate radio people who had been shunted off by the top-notchers to the inane new medium) he was a few years later appointed as manager of a sleazy night-club. The Cellar was mainly frequented by small-time journalists, so-called photographers and other, even more disreputable riffraff who had been refused entrance to the proper artists' club at Leidseplein. The night-club had its premises in a basement by a narrow, remote canal in the former Jewish quarter; above it Uli had a rent-free flat. He had to run the club and supervise the two uncouth waiters who got drunk even sooner than the customers. The members thought it was funny, an authentic Bouwmeester in that lowly job, sitting on a stool behind a cash register, telling juicy anecdotes. It made them laugh, in fact they were always chortling underneath their outsize moustaches; they threw their too-strong arms around his shoulders and in that pose carried on laughing conversations with their friends – but it was the kind of laughter that easily vanished from one second to the next, and then violence might erupt and beyond it, perhaps real, dangerous villainy, so that Uli decided he had better submit to their whims. Once, two late customers (the waiters had already gone home) sat fooling about with a full ashtray, pouring whisky on the ashes and cigarette ends, and stirring the mess with plastic cocktail stirrers. Then they laughingly demanded a spoon and forced Uli to eat the contents of the ashtray and even to lick it clean. Uli was unable to sleep for several nights after that. This then, was what his life had come to.

From time to time an opportunity presented itself to take single ladies upstairs for an hour or so, or women who came to get drunk after a marital row. This became more difficult when his sister moved in with him, furnished the flat according to her taste and helped him with the management side of the job. She had to get rid of her cat, as he was allergic to cats. Berta was childless too. From her first husband she hadn't wanted any children, because they

23

would have interfered with Shirley Carola's career in the popular theatre – and this drove him to demand a divorce. Her recently deceased second husband, a boorish builder and whoremonger, already had five sons from previous marriages and wouldn't hear of it.

So life ran a more or less even course for some twelve years or so, until one day things went wrong again. Since Dutch soil does not consist of rock that can be drilled through, but of mud, the construction of a new metro line necessitated the demolition of buildings all along the proposed route, right through centuries-old inner-city neighbourhoods. After months of street-fighting between uniformed and un-uniformed youths, the ball and chain finally struck the house by the narrow canal, at the same time marking the end of The Cellar. The City Council offered Uli and Berta a terraced house and pocket garden in Lelystad, on an estate of brand-new dolls' houses. Of course, everything was brand-new there, the whole town and even the land on which it stood: the bottom of the sea. Nothing was nature, here, all was contrived by man.

This was where the evening of Uli's life began.

3
Further Discussion

On the appointed Sunday – it was calm late-summer weather –
Uli, from the moment he woke up, looked every so many minutes
at his watch, a silver-plated wristwatch with a lid that sprang open.
It was the only memento he still had of his father, whose initials
were engraved on the lid in artistic script. Throughout the
preceding days the invitation had not been out of his thoughts; he
had even contemplated phoning the Authors' Theatre to tell them
they were welcome to come a little earlier, but too much eagerness
might perhaps be detrimental. Every now and again he cast a
glance at the letter that stood propped up against the china deer on
the mantelpiece; an alien object that had miraculously appeared in
his house and was now present, like the pearl in an oyster. He
already knew the contents by heart, as if it was part of his future
role. Berta tried several times to make him change his mind, as if
she feared some calamity. When she did not succeed she stopped
speaking to him altogether.

"As long as you know I'm keeping out of sight," was all she said
that afternoon. "You'll have to make tea yourself."

"Suits me," said Uli. "Stay away by all means." He pointed at
the illustrated copy of *Privaat* she was holding in her hand. "Go
and read that rag of yours. Smack your lips at how the famous
grovel before the plebs."

"All right," said Berta. "You'd be only too glad if you were in it."

"Go to hell, woman."

Crossly she slammed the door behind her.

He had no intention of making tea; in the fridge stood a bottle of
champagne from the supermarket – well, sparkling white wine to
be precise, for the champagne had proved too expensive.

25

But when at last his watch pointed exactly to four o'clock, nothing happened outside, and half an hour later, still nothing had happened. In his good suit Uli paced from the living-room to the dining-room and back again. He assured himself that nothing was amiss, "*around* four o'clock", it said in the letter, they were simply a little late, had lost their way, were stuck in a traffic jam in Amsterdam; if they had still not arrived at five o'clock he would go to the neighbours and phone. Berta stuck her head around the door and sneered:

"Sucker! Sucker in the lead part!"

Uli heard her going up the stairs and felt again the misery of long ago, when he had set out the drinks and made up the fire but the lady did not come. All his fantasies of the last few days became brittle and crumbled away: the applause bursting forth, the curtain rising, suddenly letting the applause through at full strength, the lights going on in the house, revealing all those faces, far at the back, high up in the gallery, and he, hand in hand with his colleagues, stepping forward, then backward, the curtain falling heavily, drab-coloured at the back; the actors looking excitedly at each other, the ropes stretching, raising the curtain again, the audience on its feet, still clapping . . . Bravo! Bravo! . . . He stood still and looked at his watch. At five o'clock and not a second later he would phone.

Exactly when that moment came, a small black car pulled up, too fast, and stopped with a jolt in front of the door. At the same time a great weariness took possession of Uli; his feeling of satisfaction was perhaps more to do with his triumph over Berta than with the fact that his visitors had arrived.

Hidden behind the net curtains he spied on the two men as they got out of the car. One, with greyish blond hair and a pale face, looked very English in his brown check sports jacket, blue check shirt and regimental tie, in his hand a flat briefcase. It was a pity about the briefcase, but Uli noticed with approval that he was wearing dark brown suede shoes. The other man, the driver, made a less favourable impression on him. He must be the director, Caspar Vogel. He looked about thirty-five and was dressed entirely in black. Black boots with raised heels, shiny fake leather trousers, a black leather waistcoat and on his head a black hat, the brim of which could not be turned down and yet with a dent in the crown, something halfway between a bowler and a trilby. He took a bunch of flowers from the back seat and laughingly said something across the roof of the car to the first man, presumably H. Michael, who was slightly older. Overhead, Uli heard Berta's heavy tread; she must have been peeping out of his bedroom window.

The doorbell rang and in a fit of yapping the white poodle leapt out of his basket. Uli waited a few moments so as not to appear over-eager, but then Berta beat him to it. Making a dash for the flowers, no doubt. He opened the door to the passage but as the yapping dog tried to squeeze through the crack, he kicked the animal hard in the side so that it fell with its other side against the door; it did not squeal, merely looked up in surprise, as if not believing it could have been done on purpose. Uli was just in time to see "Mrs Bouwmeester" radiantly accepting the flowers – her wig (too full and too dark blonde for her age) on her head. Naturally, they thought Berta was his wife.

"Ah, good," he said, "my sister has already welcomed you."

His assessment of their identity proved correct. As he shook Caspar Vogel's hand (a rather chilly hand) he felt himself scrutinised like an object by those dark eyes; an impression not altered by the friendly smile, but he also noticed that the director had, in a fraction of a second, discovered his good eye.

"Quiet, Joost!" Berta called to the poodle as it barked and leapt up against the guests. "They're friends!"

"There was a road check by the bridge," Vogel said. "We almost got here late."

"Almost?" Uli let the lid of his watch spring open and tapped on the glass with the slightly too long nail of his forefinger. "You are exactly one hour late."

With raised eyebrows Vogel looked at Michael.

"Hadn't we arranged four o'clock?"

"I think," said the business manager with an apologetic smile, "you may have forgotten to put your watch back an hour. Winter time started last night."

Uli hit himself on the forehead, raised his hand briefly in the air

27

and opened the door to the back room. Slightly stooping, with a curious, loping gait, Vogel entered first. He unbuttoned his waistcoat, revealing a gigantic figure 22 on his black T-shirt. He did not take off his hat, but Uli dared not ask if he wished to put it on the hat stand, although he would have liked nothing better than to pull it over the man's eyes with both hands and then thump him on the skull with his fist. He beckoned them to sit down at the rectangular dining-table under the lamp.

"A cup of tea?" asked Berta, hiding her nose in the flowers like a girl in a colour-wash picture postcard of sixty years ago.

"Yes," said Uli with a traitorous smile. "You were going to make tea. Take your time."

When she had gone to the kitchen he opened a tin of long thin cigars of which only Michael accepted one. Meanwhile, Vogel was telling him about the wonderful journey through the polder, across the dyke, and Uli listened as if he was being personally praised. Then he asked the gentlemen to fire away.

As he had already mentioned in his letter, said Michael, a play had unexpectedly been cancelled, and adaptation of Grabbe's *Scherz, Satire, Ironie und tiefere Bedeutung*, made into a parody of the Dutch literary scene. An offended novelist who had got hold of the manuscript had taken it to a judge and managed to have the production blocked. Siderius' new play would be staged in its place.

"You must have heard of Siderius."

"Certainly," said Uli, although he hadn't. "Leo Siderius . . . But why me?"

Michael looked at Vogel who stopped rolling his cigarette and leaned slightly forward. In a soft insistent voice he said. "Because you are exactly the man we want. And now that I have seen and heard you in the flesh I am even more sure of it."

Uli gazed at him.

"Wait a minute . . ." he said. "Don't misunderstand me, I am most honoured, but how could you be sure before you had even met me?"

"Because I knew you from a photograph."

"A photograph? Of me? That must have been one from before

28

the war . . . or possibly during the war," he said hesitantly.

Vogel turned to Michael, who put his briefcase on the Persian table rug and took out a booklet. He opened it at a dog-eared page and handed it over. Uli went to the front room to fetch his glasses and halfway back saw his photograph among a row of others. He paused and looked at the faded cover. It was the prospectus of the agency with which he had once registered.

"How in heaven's name is it possible," he said, took off his glasses and held the booklet up in the air. "This is thirty years old. Where did you get it?"

Vogel leaned with one elbow on his crossed legs, while his fingers played girlishly with a strand of black hair that stuck out from under his hat behind his ears.

"You won't believe this," he said, again with that smile, "but I first saw that photograph when I was seventeen. At the flea market in Rotterdam. I used to go there when I was skiving from school, I already wanted to be a stage director then and I bought it at once, for ten cents, I think."

"What was so special about my face?" Uli asked, flattered.

He sat down and looked at the photograph again. The raffish face wore an insolent expression; the dark blond hair, greying at the temples, was stuck to the skull like a thick coat of gloss paint. *Willem Bouwmeester*. The brief curriculum vitae said remarkably little (nothing, in fact) about his activities during the war, only that he had directed plays for the amateur theatre, including some by Molière and Schiller.

"You can never tell why you are fascinated by a face," said Vogel. "I am full of faces I have seen at one time or another, in the street, or wherever, that I shall never forget. Men and women of all ages, children too. Sometimes it isn't even the face that suggests something to me, but the posture, a particular gait, something in the dress – not anything eccentric, because that is always boring, but the very ordinary things, such as a particular colour of socks, or the way in which someone brushes his hair from his face. Sometimes a little thing like that can be a kind of crack through which his soul becomes visible. Do you think that so strange?"

"No, not really," said Uli, his eyebrows raised. Caspar Vogel

29

kept nodding at him and laughing. There was something hypnotic about the dark eyes in his soft face – it was clear to Uli that these were people of a very different kind from any he had ever had dealings with before.

"As soon as I saw your photograph I knew that one day I would do something with you."

"Oh," said Uli, feeling a chill rising inside him, "so you are going to do something with me?"

"In a manner of speaking. While I was reading Siderius' play your face gradually came forward from all those others, and when I had finished it I was sure you were the person I had to have – if you were still alive."

"As for that, you've arrived in time. But how did you get my address?"

"Someone told me you had once been manager of an actors' club which was later pulled down. At the Council they told me where you had moved to and at Lelystad town hall they said you were still living here."

Uli tapped with his glasses on the photograph. "But it must have struck you, you with your sharp eyes, that I don't look quite the same any more."

"That has all been taken into account. You have aged in exactly the way I hoped."

Uli raised two fingertips to his temple in a military salute – the fingers slightly bent, in the manner of only very high-ranking aristocratic officers, in or out of music hall.

"At your service."

"That way of saluting proves to me I wasn't mistaken in your talents."

Berta entered with the bouquet of flowers in a milky white vase, holding it in front of her like a priestess carrying a sacred object – that is to say, like an actress portraying this. She had been drinking again. Uli now saw that the flowers were lilies, large white calyxes, and he thought, lilies? Surely you give those only when somebody has died? But of course this lad wasn't to know that, any more than he knew that his hat was an Anthony Eden, made fashionable before the war by Sir Anthony Eden. He had worn one himself –

but never indoors. Maybe the fellow was a pious Jewboy.

"Aren't they beautiful?" From one of the sideboard drawers Berta took a glistening card of tablets and pressed one of them into the water. "An aspirin," she said, "that will make them keep twice as long. My father taught me that."

"He must have needed quite a few aspirin," said H. Michael with a deadpan look on his face. "All those flowers he received after performances."

"No more than he deserved."

"Yes, yes," nodded Uli when she had left the room again, and looked from the odious flatterer to the figure in black. "You're awfully well informed, aren't you?"

"It's our job."

Uli felt more and more uneasy. They knew all manner of things, those two, but it was all from books, so really they knew nothing. It was as if the gloss of the visit gradually faded; something unpleasant crept in, though he would not have been able to say what it was. There they were, the one with his hat, the other with his briefcase, and all of a sudden they were holding his life in their hands. Rebelliousness awoke in him, as though he were being besieged; where did they get the nerve to sneak into his life like this?

"To the point," he said pompously, and more coolly than he intended. "That play by Siderius, tell me something more about it."

Michael put his briefcase on the table again and handed him a large book in a black plastic cover. It was a bound photocopy of the typescript. The last time Uli had held a script, it had been mimeographed on woolly paper, with ink-clogged Os and grey smudges along the edges.

Leo Siderius
H U R R I C A N E

His cigar between his teeth, he leafed through it. When ashes fell on it, he lifted the book with both hands, held it to one side, and blew a cloudlet into the room. He looked at Caspar Vogel over his glasses.

"It's all in verse."

"That only makes it easier to learn. That was why poetry was invented."

Uli looked at the *dramatis personae* and read the name at the top aloud:

"Pierre de Vries. Is that the great actor I am supposed to play?" And when Vogel nodded, 'But I am not a great actor at all. I was a variety artiste, a common entertainer."

"That is precisely why you should play him. An entertainer must be acted by a great actor, look at Pinter, but only a skilled entertainer can act the part of a great actor."

Uli looked at him pensively.

"Or perhaps he can't?"

"He certainly can. Especially an actor of that generation, when most actors did more acting in their daily lives than they do nowadays on the stage. And of course they didn't always do it all that well, without any direction, you understand? A great comedian, we should really say, a comedian of the old style. Surely you know what I am talking about, you must have known some."

Uli nodded. "They were the chaps who ordered a meal in a restaurant in a tone that made everyone else fall silent." He looked at the script again. "Pierre de Vries," he repeated. "Not a bad choice of a name." He took off his glasses and peered dreamily at Van Gogh's sunflowers on the wall. "We used to have Henri de Vries, he was related to me; as a matter of fact he was the son of Louis Moor, the son of Louis Bouwmeester Senior. And then there was Louis de Vries, but he was no relation. Did you know both his parents were deaf-mutes?"

"You can't be serious."

"And Bob de Vries, of course. No, Rob de Vries. All of them dead and forgotten. Nothing remains of actors. They vanish like . . . like . . . I don't know what. Like the echo of their words in the theatre. Imagine," he said, suddenly moved, "an auditorium at night, when everyone has gone, all those empty seats in the dark . . ." He took a pull at his cigar, looked at it and relit it. "At any rate he seems to be well informed, this Leo Siderius of yours. What kind of a chap is he?"

The visitors looked at each other.

"You tell him, Hendrik," said Vogel.

"A very interesting person, not very old yet. I expect you'll meet him some time. Although, you never know with him," said Michael, smiling with pursed lips.

"Say no more, I've heard enough," said Uli with a gesture as if brushing away a fly. "I've known enough madmen in my day. As long as it's a well-written play."

"That rhymes," said Vogel. "You're starting to speak in verse already."

As in a naturalistic play, too transparently divided into scenes, Berta entered with tea. Her chatter as she served the guests made Uli's vexation rise again. For sale for a bunch of flowers she was, the trollop, she could smell the stage again, that musty mixture of dust, sweat and rags, that suddenly came floating out of the past like a whiff of paradise. Uli noticed she had painted her lips – or rather, she had pencilled lips where there weren't any; and over her eyebrows she had drawn two irregular red-brown lines. If he cancelled the whole thing he would at least have the satisfaction of her disappointment. When she held out the bowl of chocolates in front of him, he turned away with a face as if they were dead spiders.

"Sit down, woman," he grunted irritably. "Give us a break. Let the gentlemen speak, for heaven's sake."

4
And Now the Play . . .

Hurricane was partly a play within a play. What could be more fitting than that: a parable within a parable? Mr Bouwmeester knew Hamlet's words, did he not?

> *"The play's the thing*
> *Wherein I'll catch the conscience of the King . . ."*

"Of course," said Uli.

It was not by accident that the name of Shakespeare was mentioned at this point, for it was a play by Shakespeare that played an important part in that of Siderius: *The Tempest*. In all likelihood his last play, the highly fantastical crowning of his entire *oeuvre*; its secrets had still not altogether been revealed and probably never would be. *The Tempest* (feebly rendered as *De Storm* in translation, as if we didn't also have the word 'Tempest') was the play with which Pierre de Vries, at the age of seventy-five, was to conclude his illustrious stage career: in the part of Prospero, naturally.

"Seventy-five?" Uli gave a brief snorting laugh. "A mere child."

For the third time Michael picked up his briefcase from the floor and took out a thumb-marked paperback which he held out to Uli as a "memory prop". Berta took it from his and passed it to her brother. With reluctance, as if it was now tainted, he took it and read the words on the cover:

William Shakespeare
DE STORM

"That will be a lot of hard work, I see," he said gloomily. And when Michael asked him if he knew the play, "God knows, I forget. If you knew how many things I have forgotten."

Strictly speaking, said Vogel, it wasn't necessary for him to have read it. The audience would find out no more about it than what there was in *Hurricane*: the rehearsal of two scenes, or parts of scenes. But an actor should always know more than he revealed – just as a good driver always made sure that he had power to spare. Actually, it would help him considerably when getting into his part; it was, after all, the play Pierre de Vries was constantly thinking about. Moreover, there were all kinds of hidden parallels between the story of Pierre de Vries and that of Prospero.

Prospero, the rightful Duke of Milan! As Mr Bouwmeester might remember, Prospero was a magician who lived with his daughter Miranda on a remote island in the Mediterranean. One-time Duke of Milan, but as such usually engrossed in supernatural studies, he had been deposed many years before by his villainous brother Antonio. On the island he now rules over the beastlike creature Caliban, son of the witch Sycorax, and over a number of good spirits whom he has freed from dreadful imprisonment by the hag. One day a ship sails by. Among the passengers are the King of Naples, his brother, his son Ferdinand, his court jester, his servant, and also the unlawful Duke of Milan.

With the aid of the serene spirit Ariel, invisible to everyone except his employer (and of course the audience) Prospero unleashes a terrible storm, the ship is about to perish, but by magic all the passengers reach the shore unharmed. Meanwhile, Prospero informs Miranda of her identity: Duchess of Milan. A little later she meets Ferdinand: the flame of love ignites. The other castaways, elsewhere on the island, think the young prince has been drowned, and the brother of the King of Naples, together with Antonia, now hatches a plot to kill the king. The jester and the servant, both blind drunk, meet Caliban and they decide to murder Prospero and seize power over the island. But through Ariel, Prospero gets wind of all this and he intervenes during the betrothal celebrations of Ferdinand and Miranda. Then all turns out well, the King finds his son, the scoundrels repent their misdeeds, Ariel receives his freedom and Prospero returns as

35

lawful duke to Milan, where great festivities are being prepared.

Uli narrowed his eyes.

"I hear you say it all, but I have already forgotten it again. Sorry. All I see is something like a fairy-tale, full of music . . ."

"Then you have picked up exactly what it is all about."

"Of course, you may think it's old age, but I used to be like this even when I was young. I was always far too busy watching, so I never had . . . what do you call it . . . a general view of the story."

"He doesn't even understand a thriller on television," said Berta, "I keep having to explain to him who's who."

"Yes, yes, all right. But I always know within five minutes who did it."

"That is true." Berta nodded from the one to the other while allowing Joost to jump on her lap. "Always the one you would least suspect."

"No, not him," muttered Uli. "Then it would be easy. Least but one." So much for Shakespeare. And now the story of Pierre de Vries, the actual play. That could best be seen as a kind of drawing-room drama with elements of a thriller, and Mr Bouwmeester would surely be able to follow it because his understanding couldn't be as bad as all that. It contained a fatal love story, set in the early years of this century, and, as in *The Tempest*, there were several intrigues in it. It was a historical play (in two senses, actually), most of the characters were actors, playing Shakespeare in the style that was customary in 1900. That was why the old Shakespeare translation by Burgersdijk would have to be used. Place of action was the Amsterdam City Theatre, and as already mentioned, there were rehearsals of scenes from *The Tempest* in it, though not all the characters were involved in those. Other important scenes were those between Pierre de Vries and his fifty-year-old friend.

"Fifty-year-old friend?" Uli repeated with a wry face. "What's this? He isn't a queer by any chance?"

"Alas . . ." Laughing, Vogel made a gesture that it wasn't his fault. "Of course nobody is supposed to know, but everybody does know."

"Christ," said Uli, pushing himself away from the table and

shifting in his chair. "Another one. I am slowly getting sick of all this homo-business. It's getting to be as if . . . Do you know why it is? Over-population. It's nature's own method of birth control."

"You mean," tried Vogel cautiously, "homosexuality is to be applauded . . ."

"Yes, yes." Uli gave him a penetrating look. "Are you a queer too, perhaps?"

"Not in principle . . ." Vogel began – but Uli cut him short.

"Leave it. Everyone must seek salvation in his own way, as Frederick the Great has already said. *Nach seiner eigenen Fasson.*"

"No wonder, he was gay himself. He even had something going with Voltaire, it seems."

"I dare say. But it sticks in my gullet having to crawl into the skin of an old queen. Not very appetising."

"That's a good one," said Berta, putting her forefinger into one of Joost's ears. "Would you not want to act a murderer either? Or a murderer, yes, but a queer, no? Then there must be something really wrong with you."

"The only thing that is wrong with me," snapped Uli (suddenly seeing a flash of burning Berlin before him) "is that you're my sister. Haven't you got anything to do? Shouldn't you be cooking dinner or something?"

"No."

"Just keep out of it from now on, would you?"

"In fact, Pierre de Vries is also a murderer," said Vogel.

Uli looked at him crossly and asked which of the characters were having a love intrigue.

"Well, that is very moving, actually. But what I wanted to say first is that an actor never crawls into the skin of a character. That is an old misconception. The character must crawl into *his* skin. After all, it is the actor who exists, not the character. As an actor you do not become another person, the other person becomes you."

Uli thought this was a good point. You could do something with that. There was clearly more underneath that hat than he had at first thought, but he didn't want to show his approval.

"And what about that love affair?"

"Don't you see?" Vogel continued. "In that sense there is something homo-erotic in all dramatic art. Maybe that is one of the things Siderius is trying to say."

"Quite likely," said Uli impatiently. This was nothing but lofty talk again, the hat clearly didn't want to tell him what it was all about. Uli continued to look at him questioningly.

"The love affair is really between everyone and everyone. Everyone wants to win someone over to himself, or keep someone to himself, and this leads to a kind of Gordian knot of Machiavellian machinations, lies, misunderstandings, abuse, including blackmail. You must remember that the trial of Oscar Wilde was still fresh in people's memories. When exactly was that again?" he asked Michael.

"1895 or 96."

"Well, anyway, you'll be reading it all." He looked at Uli. "All right, I know what you want to hear. Well then, the gist of the matter, the thing that sets everything going, is the *petit amour* between Pierre de Vries and the actor who plays Ariel. A youth of about twenty."

Uli put *De Storm* on top of the script of *Hurricane*, crossed his arms and said, "Gentlemen, I have heard enough."

An oppressive silence fell. If it is possible to giggle inwardly without it being visible or audible, that was what Uli was doing. He had nothing against gays and dikes (except when they promoted that tomfoolery of theirs into some sort of ideology) but he was using his supposed disgust chiefly to frustrate the negotiations, so that he could pull out decently if he wanted. It was getting too close to the bone. Of course, in the days when homosexuality was still something scandalous he had known of quite a few cases, but in addition there had also been in his own long life a certain occasion, forty years ago, when he was half his present age, something he had kept a secret from everyone, though not from himself, not even afterwards. With the stealthy pleasure of a voyeur (an auto-voyeur) he now looked back on it . . .

. . . and through the keyhole he sees the man with the pomaded hair coming out of his hotel and crossing the busy Potsdamer Platz, in a wide charcoal-grey pelerine coat, a white silk scarf loosely draped over his shoulders and a flat Egyptian cigarette between his lips. It is a cold February night, the last light falls thinly on the old buildings and the brand-new ruins. This is Berlin, at the beginning of his tour of Germany; for three years he had not been across the border, and with a feeling of release and happiness he walks in the new light, amid the different smells. (Yes, when hearing certain music – it doesn't have to be exactly Bach or Beethoven, preferably not, in fact; rather a song by Zarah Leander with her masculine contralto – he even feels immortal.) He knows he should not be here, but what harm does it do? He is a comedian and he doesn't meddle in politics, he does exactly the same as he has always done: entertain audiences! Moreover, he is, in a sense, at home; his mother was born here, as was his aunt who brought him up; he speaks the language fluently and virtually without accent. The night before, after the performance, he dined at Kranzler's with his uncle, Onkel Julius, railway official by profession but now also in uniform and, as he says, a member of the "Bismarck Jugend".

He pauses outside a cinema and tries to identify the photographs in the showcase. What film was it? *The Golden City? The Tiger of Eschnapur*, with the beautiful La Jana? He can't remember, but what he does remember is that simultaneously he saw in the reflection of the window a soldier standing beside him, looking at him in the glass, watching him. Uli turns his head away but the other keeps looking at his reflection. At that moment it is as if something shifts inside Uli, breaks through, topples, and turns everything upside down – a complete cascade, making him lose his bearings so that he no longer knows the way inside himself. He breaks out into a sweat, panting slightly as again he meets those eyes that look at him, insolent and frightened at the same time, and he no longer knows what to do. It is a frail-looking, blond youth of about twenty-one, not quite at home in the drab field-grey and the heavy boots (it will be twenty-five years before such footwear becomes the fashion in some homosexual circles). His face is pallid and almost pock-marked. Uli feels a desire closely bordering on rage, it is as if he is about to shit in his pants, hell, what is happening to him? Slowly, with trembling legs, and with an erection, for Christ's sake, he walks on, not daring to look back, but he knows they are already bound fast together. What next? He wants him, must and will have him, cover him with kisses and heaven knows what else – but where? Darkness falls quickly in the blacked-out streets; behind him he hears the boots on the pavement. Never before has it overwhelmed him like this, not only not with a man but not with any of those hundred or thousands of women in his life either (with the exception of the first). That it should be possible, the forbidden, this great foulness, far away in Berlin, that it should be about to happen! Or is he a provocateur? Is he under orders to test foreign actors for their wholesome-Germanic heterosexuality? But surely the Gestapo wouldn't use someone in uniform for that? Or is it precisely the uniform that does it? Taking off a uniform is quite a different thing from stepping out of an off-the-peg suit. Uli realises he is about to do something you can be sent to a concentration camp for – it is almost as bad as being a Jew or a Communist – and that in the heart of the Third Reich, with Hitler just round the corner in the Reichs-chancelry. At the same time he knows that nothing will hold him back, whatever the consequences. But where? His hotel is out of the question. The barracks wouldn't be possible either. To the park, the Tiergarten, that is close by, or with the U-Bahn to Grünewald, or the Wannsee. . . At this point, reality takes the decision out of his hands.

Awakening with a deep grumbling, the sirens begin to wail all over the city. This has a different meaning here than in the Netherlands, where the English fly peacefully overhead on their way to Germany and people walk out into the street to wave to the bombers – here it is in earnest. They have passed Braunschweig and perhaps also Magdeburg, which means they are on their way to Berlin; they will be here within fifteen minutes. The agitation of the sirens, unevenly rising and falling all around, the people suddenly running through the evening everywhere, the gun barrels on the roofs, being tilted against the still light-coloured sky, the approaching doom; all of it settles like an extra-voluptuous blob of whisked cream on the Mozart-Bombe of his excitement. Everything now happens at once, he could have screamed with pleasure. In the middle of a public garden, where bellowing soldiers are busy placing a long-barrelled gun in position, he sees people vanishing into an air-raid shelter. The oblong structure lies half above ground – without a seam the clipped lawn continues over the sloping sides and roof. He glances back before going down the entrance; after a couple of steps he has to make an S-turn past two short walls. On long wooden benches to the left and right, under the faint flow of a few lamps in metal cages, men in hats and women with shopping bags sit is silence; the spooky waiting-room of Doctor Frankenstein. When the soldier enters, Uli moves over to allow him to sit down casually beside him. The cellar fills up. The soldier, who is holding his cap in his soft white hands, moves up in his turn, so that Uli can feel the scorching heat of his thigh against his own. No one says a word, even the children are silent. The sirens die down in the depths of their own sound and in the stillness a new kind of time begins.

When even the central aisle is as crowded as a tram in the rush hour, the youth begins to speak to him softly. That he looks so different from other people, is he perhaps an artist? He says *"Sie"*, the formal mode of address, and at the moment when Uli hears his voice, everything changes. This is simply a lad who could be his son, he has made a mistake. Like a saucepan of boiling milk under which the gas is being turned down, his excitement starts to subside. In a low voice he talks about the famous Johan Heesters, a Dutchman like himself, although maybe you can't tell from his speech, in whose operetta he has a part, *The Gypsy Baron* (although the gypsies are also being exterminated these days) – it is a microscopic part, but be doesn't say that. And he? His name is Werner – Werner Hoffmann. Front line? No, thank God. He works as a courier for a department in the Kurfürstenstrasse, delivering dossiers by motorbike, that sort of thing. Tonight he is free, he had intended to go to the cinema. Uli doesn't ask what kind of a department it is; not until much later, after the war, when he is in trouble, will he realise that down there in that cellar he might have been in a position to work for the Resistance: blackmail the courier by means of sex, or perhaps still worse. Photograph the dossiers with a Leica and send them to London. He also deliberated whether he would simply make it up, pretend he had actually done it, but then his escapade would have become known and that seemed even worse than being locked up in a camp for a few months. In the end, he had the sense not to mention it.

Werner looks at him and smiles. At the same moment Uli feels himself floating again: whenever nothing is said, it comes back again. A few people raise their chins, listening. In the distance, the soft rumble of gunfire and bombs advances, the irregular ambling footsteps of a gigantic, destructive reptile, approaching from prehistoric times. Werner says nothing more, and Uli also feels afraid now. A moment later, the cataclysm is upon them, and it is more merciless than he had ever imagined. Waves of intermingling singing by hundreds of aircraft, quick-firing guns, loud artillery followed by the sharp reports of exploding shells, and then suddenly the whistling, shrieking descent of the bombs, thumping the earth with such force that the air-raid shelter leaps up and down like a farm cart on a country track. The lights go out and Uli grabs hold somewhere, and the youth grabs hold of him. As the surrounding buildings collapse, smoke and dust come spurting into the cellar; the wilhelminic dust of pulverising pillars and caryatids; by the entrance, shrapnel scatters, it is pitch dark and in the tumult it takes a while before Uli realises that Werner has grabbed him in the crotch and is squeezing him there. Good God! He in turn makes a grab and feels naked flesh, the soldier has unbuttoned his fly and it seems to Uli as if it is his own penis he feels, but numbed, as though before a medical operation – for until now, whenever he felt a penis with his hand, he had always felt his own hand with his penis at the same time. He needs no more than a few seconds to sink into a sudden, rising flood of steaming sugared water that disappears into the courier's mouth. With a scream not noticed by anyone, he sees during an immensely long time a shifting pattern of sliding geometric shapes, as in a painting by some decadent artist. His own hand is now wet, as if he had dipped it into a bucket of wallpaper paste. Sweating and still shaking he

42

gets up, seeks with his dry hand the boy's head and stokes him briefly through his thin, lank hair. With weak knees he pushes through the crowd towards the exit, he must get away from here at once!

Outside there is the suffocating night, aflame, frenzied, crackling, the firestorm, the shrieks of people and the sirens of ambulances and fire brigade, houses collapsing in towers of dust – he lets himself fall headlong in the grass: God almighty, what times were these!

The sparkling wine had remained in the fridge and when the members of the Authors' Theatre had left, Berta asked him why he had suddenly decided to decline.

"Because you were far too keen on it."

"I'm not keen at all."

"Aren't you? Why were you so eager then?"

"Because I didn't want you to do it just because I didn't want you to. I know you by now. There's something fishy about it, I can tell."

He looked at her with narrowed eyes. She had outwitted him this time.

"Then we're agreed for once," he said politely and looked out of the window. Across the road two women stood talking, both carrying plastic bags from the same supermarket. "I would have liked to go to Japan, though," he said absent-mindedly.

Berta looked at him in bewilderment. "To Japan?"

Uli said nothing. There was no wind outside. In the front garden not a leaf stirred in the velvety light. He sighed and suddenly started to sing softly:

> *Nur nicht*
> *Aus Liebe weinen,*
> *Es gibt auf der Erden*
> *Nicht nur den Einen. . .*

He stopped and looked for a brief moment into Berta's eyes. Then he slowly took off his watch and turned the big hand an hour forward, to seven o'clock. He looked out, reflected, and then turned the hand back two hours. It was five o'clock. The two men had not really been there at all, the visit was eclipsed – though on the table now lay the two scripts.

ACT TWO

ACT TWO

1
The Read-Through

It was a misty morning two weeks later when Uli took the bus to Amsterdam. The road, drawn with a ruler on a drawing-board, ran through the too great immenseness of a man-made world. To the left and right the fields and the lower parts of the young forestry plantations had become invisible beneath a white vapour that had taken the place of the water, in the way the spirit of a dead person still lingers in the house of mourning. Now and then, flocks of birds passed overhead on their way south, in changing patterns like the computer graphics between television commercials. Cars had their lights on, except a few, brought up too thriftily. On the long bridge to the former coast the mist cleared and with a sense of relief he entered the old land, where pricklier grasses and knottier willows grew and the houses and churches were older.

At the terminus he took the metro to Central Station, and walked up the Damrak. He hadn't been to Amsterdam for almost a year and he thought of the old days, when people used to say admiringly of Paris that you saw so many nationalities there. That was nothing compared with the situation here, with all these pizzerias, boulangeries, shoarmas, Wimpy bars and other exotic establishments. The Netherlands as he had known them no longer existed, perhaps still in the country here and there, but even that wouldn't last much longer, and it left him cold. He felt like a ghostlike apparition from a submerged civilisation, as he walked amid the bustle and the music that spewed out of the gaming halls and peep-shows, and looked at the outlandish faces: the Turks, Italians, Moroccans, Surinamers and other castaways, and then all those tourists, beggars, punks with green and yellow cockscombs, junkies staring immobile at their shoes; all of these in their turn had not the faintest idea from what epoch he hailed – but to this also he was indifferent. The world changed (at least on this side of the street, on the other side Berlage's Stock Exchange still continued to cast about itself a stern silence) as it always had done, and he would not have to witness it for much longer. He wanted only this one thing: to play Pierre de Vries. Beyond that he didn't care a damn.

In his worn papier-mâché briefcase still dating from before the war, was the script. He had read it and it was better than he had expected, even quite exciting in parts. It was set in 1904 (the year of his birth) and there was no question of blatant buggery or homo propaganda, though the swinishness constantly smouldered in the background, perhaps most of all in the sultry language of the verse. At one moment, drops of crystal were said to fall in the heart of the purest summer nights; at another, Pierre de Vries says to his sweetheart Max (who plays Ariel) that a certain Nocturne by Chopin rises as if in ecstasy, then to drop back moaning with pleasure. There were also several complexities that irritated him. (He had been unable to plough through *The Tempest*). At the post office he had arranged everything by phone and had not told Berta until afterwards. She meant well, it was all out of sisterly affection, that was clear from her crafty deceit that afternoon. For once he had had the decency to tell her so, and together they had drunk the bottle of pseudo champagne. With their last glass he had said, slightly tipsy, "I am very fond of that beastly sister of mine."

At this, her eyes had grown moist. "I only want to protect you. You're not so young any more, Uli. Think of all the stress there will be."

"Come, come. We'll see who's boss, Pierre de Vries or me."

With a glance at the place in front of the Royal Palace where the Punch and Judy show used to be, he crossed the Dam square diagonally. On the steps of the war memorial two Japanese stood photographing each other simultaneously – he himself must have been included in one of the photographs: an old man with a briefcase, in the background, in an album on the other side of the world. He turned into the Nes, where a slight gloom came over

48

him. Entertainment districts in the morning are as dismal as seaside resorts in winter. In the narrow street, he found the theatre in a building of which he had no recollection, but then it was twenty years ago or more since he had been here last.

The tall facade was covered in ornamental carving, all painted in glossy black, against which the gilt lettering of the word KOSMOS stood out in dreamy radiance. The box office was closed, but the double doors were open. There was no one in the vestibule. When he tentatively entered a curved corridor with worn red carpet, the walls adorned with framed posters, a long-forgotten emotion welled up in him: deserted theatres in the morning, at that hour not yet a festive assembly place for the public but the businesslike workshop of professionals moving about purposefully amid the plush and gilt, like priests in a closed church. How much he had forgotten! What was the point of it all, if you forgot it anyway – with total oblivion at the end. Yes, that was perhaps the most repulsive aspect of death, that even your memories would be wiped out.

"You must be Mr Bouwmeester."

He turned. In the curve of the corridor stood a girl in a too-large raincoat buttoned up to her chin. He reddish hair was done up in a large number of thin pigtails which she had bunched together and pinned up on top of her head.

"I've lost my way."

"Come with me."

Perhaps inspired by Siderius, he was reminded, by her clear, transparent voice, of the first thin coat of ice after a frosty night. She shook hands with him (hers was strange, warm but calloused) and said they had to be upstairs, in the foyer. When they were halfway up the stairs, a loud voice rang out behind them: "Willem Bouwmeester! It must be!"

A man held out his hand. Although he could be no older than forty at the most, his face was already marked by drink, at least he would have to have had a very eventful life to acquire such furrows without the aid of alcohol. His name was . . . but it slipped Uli's memory at once; only the girl's first name, Stella, still hovered in his mind. He felt as though he had come across it before, not long

49

ago. Between them, they took him to an oval room at the front of the building, where several people were already gathered.

At a trot that incorporated a little bow, Michael came towards him.

"Good morning, Mr Bouwmeester, welcome. So, after all . . ."

"After all, yes."

"You gave us a real fright. Don't you want to take off your coat?"

"Yes, no. Later, if you don't mind. It's still a bit chilly in here."

Michael introduced him to the others, but again Uli was too busy watching to remember all their names, Caspar Vogel rose to his feet behind a long table under a chandelier, and welcomed him, in his turn, to the Authors' Theatre, but immediately resumed his conversation with an Indonesian boy, or man, the set designer. An attractive, slim girl, the director's assistant, was taking notes. Actors and actresses, the property manager, the prompter, he would no doubt know who was who after a while; new people still kept arriving. Some names sounded familiar – from the papers probably; he also recognised some of the faces from television, perhaps from films, or from commercials for washing powders or life insurance.

He looked around. In the evening, in the interval, there would of course be rows of glasses and coffee cups on the table; on a side table gleamed a coffee machine with a cloth over it. All around the walls there were tall, spotted mirrors, separated by pillars half recessed in the walls – everything rather dilapidated and shabby, but it couldn't be more beautiful. Happiness flowed through him, A girl gave him a cup of coffee, he exchanged a few words with an oldish man, but he was present only in a different, detached way. How was it possible! He saw himself standing in this space, no longer as an outsider, a spectator of events, as he had been for at least fifteen years, but as part of them, as someone about to start work; he could believe it even less now than in the preceding weeks. He looked at Vogel – wearing his hat again, naturally. Vogel behaved differently from that Sunday afternoon at his house: he, Uli, belonged now. His T-shirt bore the number twelve today, he obviously possessed an infinite collection. And to him Uli owed all this. If that lad hadn't been at the flea market at the age of seventeen, Uli would now have been sitting by his window in the polder, waiting for his death. What had he been doing at the moment when Caspar Vogel, truanting from school, picked up that prospectus from a street stall in Rotterdam? Life is absurd, thought Uli – and he was grateful for it.

"You all know the play," said Vogel, "and what part you're playing. It's very simple in this case, actually. Let's –"

"Why isn't Siderius here?" a plump young woman with brown curls called out.

"Mr Siderius is unfortunately unable to attend," said Michael with mannered politeness.

"Oh, yeah, He needs a kick up the backside. Can't even be bothered to come to the read-through of his own play!"

"In my opinion we don't need him at all," said the man with whom Uli had spoken a few minutes earlier, and whom he suspected of being "his friend of many years' standing". "It's his play but it's our show."

"Hear, hear," said a young man Uli had noticed before. He was small and wore a sober dark-blue suit, like an old-fashioned diplomat, but he had combined this with white trainers. His face was completely crooked, perhaps he had had polio.

"I wouldn't be too sure of that," someone else remarked.

"With what right," called the girl with the curls, "does he always behave as if he were God Almighty? Every time we . . ."

"Okay, Olga," Vogel interrupted her. "How about getting started?" It's a quarter to eleven. We have only a month, twenty-four rehearsals. Far too few of course, but that can't be helped."

"Tell me first, then," said the man Uli had met on the stairs, "what the play is actually about."

Vogel burst out laughing. "The play is about an elderly actor who falls in love with a young actor who is engaged to a young actress. This constitutes a threat to the elderly actor's friend. Meanwhile, a third actor has taken a fancy to the young actress. He incites the old actor's friend to incite the young actor to blackmail the elderly actor, so that the elderly actor will begin to hate the

51

young actor. But the young actress tells this to the elderly actor, with unpleasant consequences for the elderly actor's friend. The third actor gets the young actress and the young actor gets nowhere at all."

Uli thought this was a good summary but the questioner was not satisfied.

"Yes, I'd got that far myself. That's for the programme notes. You know very well what I mean. Tell me the theme."

"The theme is the relationship between imagination and reality."

With ironic deference the young man curled the corners of his mouth.

"Listen to that! How very original."

All right, said Vogel, it was nothing new in itself, it had been a cliché for centuries, but *Hurricane* demonstrated that the artistic variations on this theme, from Shakespeare and Lope de Vega and Bidermann to Pirandello and Genet, were always enacted *within* the imagination. In fact, they were never about imagination and reality, but always about the imagination and an equally imagined reality – in other words, they were about an imagination and a second imagination, so not really about anything very special. In the last instance they contained little more than the old adage: All the world is but a stage, each plays his part and gets his wage.

"All the world's an aniseed ball," Uli blurted out before he realised, "each takes a lick and gets damn all."

Some, young enough not to have heard this variant before, like Stella, started to laugh, others nodded with raised eyebrows; only the actress with the curls fell into a fit of laughter, to Uli's gratification. First she leaned far back, breathed deep, and then lowered her head shriekingly on her crossed arms on the table, shoulders heaving.

But, Vogel continued imperturbably, there was another aspect to *Hurricane*. Of course, this play stayed within the imagination too, how could it be otherwise, but at the same time it seemed to be trying to reach across the frontiers of the imagination, to the real reality – like when someone licks the top of his middle finger and feels with a quick movement whether the iron is hot; he or she doesn't really touch it, and yet there is a very brief hiss. That was the point at which Shakespeare was introduced into the play. Suppose that someone was applying himself to the relationship between imagination and reality, in the sense that he *really* wanted to change reality by means of his imagination. Not by a roundabout way, but directly. Such a person would not only be a man of the imagination, of words, an artist, but at the same time a man of reality, of action. Such a person, said Vogel, was a magician. So there was Prospero – who was able to unleash storms and conjure up tables laden with food. In *The Tempest* all this took place within the imagination, and so, too, it did in *Hurricane*, of course, but because *The Tempest* operated within *Hurricane* (as did the masque in the fourth Act of *The Tempest*, but Uli hadn't read that) *Hurricane* moved, as it were, closer to the boundary of reality, so that it hissed briefly! You might say, said Vogel, that if you slid an infinite number of plays into one another, the most infinite of those plays would be reality.

"Thanks a lot," said the young man with the crooked face. "People have been working hard all day, they have been humiliated by their bosses, they have sat in traffic jams for an hour, and in the evening they think, come on, let's go to the Authors' Theatre, it's supposed to be very good. And what do they get dished up? Some sort of mathematical problem, with algebra, or abracadabra."

Everybody started talking at one.

"What do you want then," called out Uli's, that is to say Pierre's friend. "Consumer theatre?"

"Make them use their brains for once," said the man with the furrowed face.

"Their what?" enquired the young man in the dark-blue suit.

"Their brains. They do have brains, don't they?"

"That's what you say."

"Don't they, then?"

"Never noticed it."

"Haven't you, you git?" asked Olga, the girl with the curls.

"Leave him alone, he simply doesn't understand it himself, that's all, the twit."

"I think Paul is right," said a girl who had not spoken before.

53

"Truly great art is always very simple."

"Yes," said a third girl. "Read *Ulysses* and you'll see."

"Oh I say, Madam has read *Ulysses*," nodded the boy who had started the row and whose name appeared to be Paul.

"Or *Finnegans Wake*."

"Oh, Madam has read that too, has she? She'll read herself into the ground one of these days."

"Children, children!" said Michael soothingly.

"I'm not a child!"

"No, a woman disguised as a human being, that's what you are," said Paul with the kind of venom at which small men excel.

Uli began to laugh too. He got up and took off his coat. It was great here. The bickering meant nothing, it was merely the uncertainty of people who were on the point of changing, of transforming themselves, of letting the spirits of Siderius and Shakespeare take possession of them, and who, at the decisive moment, would have no support other than something they had not yet become. That point had not been reached just yet, but they were on the road towards it and they knew that that day, that evening, that hour, would inevitably come. This applied most of all to him, the lead player, but it was as if he had still not yet admitted this knowledge into his consciousness. Caspar Vogel calmly rolled a cigarette and the fellow who had provoked the row sat looking around with a pleased smile on the left side of his face. Stella had not joined in the argument.

It began to annoy Uli that he didn't know who was who. He pulled a bright yellow ballpoint from his inside pocket and asked the set designer, who was sitting next to him, to help him. He pointed at the young man with the weathered face.

"What's his name?"

The set designer opened Uli's copy of *Hurricane* at the cast list and silently put his finger under the third name. Uli glanced at it and said, "Yes, that's his name in the play. But what is his real name?"

"The same."

It took a moment before Uli grasped it. Siderius had simply skipped a stage and given his characters the names of the actors who were to interpret them. And why not? After all, he had written his play for this company. He peered at the cast list. There was one name that did not coincide with that of the actor:

Pierre de Vries (PROSPERO)
Etienne Post, his friend
Lucas van Geest (FERDINAND)
Max Oort (ARIEL)
Stella Middag (MIRANDA)
Trix van Rijn (IRIS)
Mimi Schipper (CERES)
Olga Kapetyn (JUNO)
Paul Musch, the director
A photographer, his assistant, stage manager's voice

The fact that he wasn't mentioned under his own name was logical: when the script was printed it had still not been certain that he would take the part. But shouldn't this be changed now? *Willem Bouwmeester* (PROSPERO). As Vogel was allowing everyone time to calm down, Uli asked him about it – in a casual tone as if he had known about the whole thing all along.

"Better not. As it is, people are bound to say we chose you only because of your name. Better not emphasise it."

You see, thought Uli. Berta was quite wrong with her insinuations. As Vogel resumed his speech (his introduction was intended solely for those present, he said, it was of no concern to the public, this was all backstage talk, only at the end of the process would such deliberations be raised again; in the reviews by the better critics) Uli turned again to his neighbour with a whisper. He pointed his finger at the name of Etienne Post, at which the man he had already suspected of that name was pointed out to him. Uli peered at him over his glasses. A rather subdued sort of fellow, by the look of him. The others he could identify without assistance; only Trix and Mimi blended into each other a bit. He felt as if he had to memorise a list of prepositions taking the dative, *mit, nach, nächst, nebst* . . . (as he never made a mistake with these, thanks to

55

his background, he refused to learn them at school, and failed German as a result). The only person he still had to identify was Max Oort – the Ariel with whom he was to have that nauseating, heart-stirring love affair.

"When you talk of the devil you tread on his tail," said the set designer, in his Indonesian accent.

The door had opened and in the doorway stood a young man of about twenty-five, with lank blond hair and glasses; his timid face looked startled in a pleasant way.

"Sorry I'm late, I had a dentist's appointment."

Vogel stretched out his arm.

"Max Oort – Willem Bouwmeester."

As Uli shook hands with him, he imagined that a silence arose, as if everyone had waited for this moment. Of course this lad did not look like Werner (now also sixty, Herr Hoffmann, respectable black hat with green ribbon on his thin grey hair, if he was still alive). Yet he thought at once of the sensual courier, and had a feeling as though some of the people in the room were aware of it. As the young man joined the group, Uli reflected that his Berlin memories must not be allowed to haunt him, he must use them solely for the understanding of his part, purely professionally.

Wiser perhaps as a result of the reactions, Vogel now spoke of more practical matters, about the style and the techniques of the production. Each episode would start with a tableau vivant, inspired by stage photographs from the turn of the century. These photographs – there was a pile of them on that table over there, lent by the Theatre Museum, were all that was left from performances of that time, everybody was familiar with them and they would form a stylistic link with the highly dramatic manneristic poses which he wanted them to adopt and hold for a long time, perhaps for a bit too long even, they would have to see about that. (All art of great quality went just a little bit too far.) The end of each episode would again freeze into a still-life, and then a blackout would follow, or a fade-out, it would depend. At certain moments a photographer would have to work with magnesium light, which made a wonderful bang, a beautiful white cloud and a roving after-effect that would drift about the stage in changing colours. As it wasn't the intention to turn the thing into a pastiche, let alone a farce, there would in each scene be a gradual de-dramatisation, but towards the end the acting style would gain in intensity again, so that a rhythm would develop. Sustained pathos there would be only in the two rehearsed scenes from *The Tempest* (culminating in the masque with the three spirits) as was evident also from the lines of Paul Musch, the director.

"Don't worry," said Paul Musch, yawning rather rudely. "I'll make sure everything will be very exaggerated. Do I have to wear a hat too?"

Vogel laughed. "That is a privilege reserved only for the truly great modern director. In your days directors had very little influence, so I'll have to deal with you firmly."

"I say," Olga called out, "you said you didn't want to turn it into a farce, but don't you think I'm too old and fat to be an airy spirit?"

Vogel pointed at the photographs on the table.

"Haven't you seen what such beings used to look like? Spirits don't exist, so why should they be young and thin? Yes," he said, and Uli saw he was suddenly inspired, "we're going to dig up all sorts of things with this production. All those things that have got lost in this century and have been buried beneath the sands over the last sixty years. Think of the masks in the Greek theatre, of the *expression* of those masks, and then think what is left of that now. At one time the total, turbulent and yet stylised presence of an emotion – and what do you see now? The ultra-cool raising of an eyebrow. And only because of one thing: technology – in this case, movies. Nowadays we are shown faces three by four metres in width, like the faces of Titans; a raised eyebrow travels half a metre and has therefore become just as expressive as a classical mask. But then actors started doing the same, and their power of expression was therefore diminished to the same degree as the face on the screen had become larger. The old style survived for a while in the much under-valued art of hamming, but even there we have lost our way. Just think how deep we have sunk, we can't even ham any more! That means only one thing: that we can no longer act. No wonder that the theatre is lying flat on its back. Yes, we are going to beat the cinema at its own game, the nightingale took lessons from the eagle. In the end, some people began to twig what was going on and tried desperately to get out, altogether, like Grotowsky and Artaud – and when that did not work out everybody sat down in the lotus position, contracted to a point and sank away for ever into nothingness. The perversity of it! There was that group recently that gave performances in loony bins and was proud of the fact that madmen seemed to show a reaction to their pranks. You bet they did! If you weren't nuts already you soon would be. That is why I regard this production as an expedition back into the time just before the great catastrophe. The distance from a Greek or an African or a Japanese mask to the acting style of someone like . . . like . . . Louis Bouwmeester – if I may say so – is smaller than that between Louis Bouwmeester and us. And now the moment has come to change all that. And why has that moment come now? Because people watch television now, television films; they go to the cinema only because new films aren't allowed to go straight on to video. But on a television screen the faces are *smaller* than those of real people. A film actor in close-up would in reality be as big as a church tower, and a television actor would at best be as small as a pygmy, but usually he is as small as . . . as a foetus. As if by magic the giants have been changed into dwarfs, and that is exactly where the theatre now has its chance. I don't quite know yet, but we'll find out. Not simply by going back to the year 1904, of course, that isn't how things work, television isn't a technical regression back to the cinema, but a progression from it. In any case there can be no harm in having a look at our colleagues from those days. Afterwards we'll see again. Perhaps we should also dare to think in terms of opera more, of music. One thing is certain at any rate: the theatre must become theatrical again, unreal – art!"

"Bravo!" called Uli, and clapped his hands. Laughing, everyone joined in, and Uli said, "We'll make it into an unforgettable show."

There were anxious cries of "Touch wood! Touch wood! Oh my God, touch wood!"

Disconcerted, Uli listened to the drumming of knuckles against the underside of the table top, with which the evil spirits were being banished.

Yes, if things went wrong *he* would be punished.

58

2
The Party

In the afternoon, after the read-through, Michael had taken him to his office where they had finalised the contract. He had also given Uli two complimentary tickets for the following evening. That came in handy, because Lucas had already invited him to an "inaugural" party that same evening, at about ten o'clock at his home – "at our place", he had said, without telling Uli who the other was, obviously someone from the group, and he hoped it was not Stella. The only problem was how to get rid of Berta after the show. He didn't begrudge her an evening out, but he had no desire to introduce her to his new friends, for he knew her, wild horses wouldn't drag her away again. He decided to tell her nothing, only that he would be late.

After the rehearsal he went, like the day before, with some of the others to the Tivoli, an eating-place-cum-bar further down the Nes. At half past four there was always enough room at the round table at the back, near the telephone and the door to the toilets.

"Beer, Mr Bouwmeester?"

Someone went off to get the order, for these days there was no service any longer in this kind of café, the young men and women behind the counter were indistinguishable from the customers; quite often they actually switched roles. As the café gradually filled up, they sat under the renovated gas lamp which was always burning, around a large ash-tray full of cigarette ends, and talked about the rehearsal, the subsidies that were in jeopardy, and about the shortcomings of other companies. Towards suppertime they left, but Uli did not mind staying behind on his own – on the contrary. Soon he would be going to see a show and afterwards he

59

would meet them all again. He enjoyed sitting alone reading the paper, ordering a schnitzel with too much fat, and being alive again.

At eight o'clock he strolled back to the Kosmos and gave his surplus ticket to the girl in the box office. It did not appear necessary, for the house was barely half full. He was annoyed to see that almost everyone was wearing ordinary casual clothes; jeans and baggy pullovers. People who did not dress up when they went to a play, he thought, had no feeling for the theatre. The play was called *The Killjoy*. In the programme notes he read that it was an adaptation (by Richter Romijn, a member of the Authors' Theatre) of a forgotten play from the early seventeenth century, *Philemon Martyr*, written in Latin by a German Jesuit, Jakob Bidermann. Where for God's sake had they dug up a thing like that? But then they had unearthed him too, they knew everything, those lads. The direction was again by Caspar Vogel; Paul Musch played Philemon, Etienne Post the "City Governor"; the others he did not know. He looked at the curtain. It had the purple-red colour of the cloth with which chairs used to be upholstered in his childhood. It seeemed inconceivable that in a few weeks' time he would be standing there himself.

The grotesque presentation, with all kinds of contrived gimmicky effects, was about a Roman actor who lived at the time of the persecution of the Christians. Philemon, a toper and a glutton, takes no interest in any religion. After desperate deliberations about the increasing neglect of the pagan gods, the city governor orders everyone to make a sacrifice to Jupiter. The cowardly Christian Apollonius is at a loss what to do: making the sacrifice is out of the question, but neither does he want to die a martyr. For a fee, he finds Philemon willing to take his place. With the irony characteristic of all drama, Philemon changes into Apollonius's clothes and sets off to make the sacrifice. But soon the irony of the irony is revealed: he is startled by the sudden appearance of an angel; further along the road other angels give him a taste of heavenly bliss, and, converted to Christianity, he prays to Jesus. Brought before the governor, he bears witness to his faith, but he is recognised as Philemon and reaps only amused applause for his impersonation. He persists until everybody collapses with laughter. At last he succeeds in persuading the public of his earnestness, and so he must die, but then Apollonius' conscience begins to prick, and he also reports to the governor. A pandemonium of miracles now breaks loose. Against a backdrop depicting scenes of hellish medieval torture, a soldier aims and shoots an arrow; suspended by two strings from the flies the arrow moves jerkily towards Philemon, makes a U-turn just before it reaches his breast, wobbles in the direction of the governor and bores into his eye. With their chopped-off but singing heads under their arms, the two martyrs are finally hoisted up to heaven, while the governor's eye is suddenly miraculously healed, resulting in his conversion and the abandonment of any further persecution of the Christians. Meanwhile the four legs are still dangling from heaven.

It was laughable. In fact, if you looked at it closely, all the plays staged by the Authors' Theatre were pretty crazy. Some kind of in-breeding, you might say. Uli wondered if he should go backstage to pay his compliments to the actors; especially Paul Musch, who had been very good as Philemon. After all, he was one of the group now. But on second thoughts it seemed a bit too pushy for the time being.

Lucas van Geest lived in a converted attic four floors up, with large windows on three sides looking out over the city. He had wrapped himself in a kimono; pulling the cork from a bottle between his bare knees he called out: "Make yourself at home!"

Uli laughed. That might not be such a good idea. Under the brown-stained boards of the sloping roof, held together by a complicated structure of joints, he saw a scene such as he had not witnessed for a long time. Vogel and his assistant Trudy were lolling on gigantic sky-blue cushions on the floor; Michael and Miss Wijdenes, the prompter, a lady approaching sixty, sat on a window-sill, glasses in their hands. Mimi crouched by the record player, surrounded by discs. There was one person he had not met before, Mr Caccini, the pianist; with his greying temples he looked more distinguished than almost any Dutchman. In the open-plan kitchen, screened off by a row of large indoor plants, Trix was preparing sandwiches, aided by Max. It struck him that they looked a bit like each other. Clearly then, Trix must be Lucas's wife or girlfriend, but when she turned to look for something in a cupboard he saw that Max showed her where to find it. So that was how the land lay. With satisfaction Uli reflected that for the present he wasn't yet getting senile.

"Well?" asked Vogel, looking up at him. "What was it like?" As well as his hat he was now also wearing sunglasses.

"I laughed a lot."

"Then it was all right. All seriousness begins as play and ends as play."

Uli nodded. "That may well be true."

"And that is exactly the trouble," said Trudy, in a tone as if she had something specific in mind.

Olga came up to him and asked if she could get him anything.

"A glass of beer, please."

"Nothing to eat?"

"No thank you."

Stella looked across Henk Aronds' – the set designer's – shoulders at an open picture book that lay on the floor. Uli felt a ridiculous flash of jealousy which he banished at once; he sat down at the antique round table on a straight farmhouse chair that didn't go with it and yet did go with it. In the centre of the mahogany top stood a marble bust of a young Greek god with curly hair and broken arms; on his left shoulder lay a strange little hand of a vanished person. It was so beautiful that in some way it formed the focal point of the room.

Olga put the beer in front of him and sat down beside him. "Do you know, you look exactly like my grandfather?"

Uli burst into a laugh. "Are you paying court to me?"

"Well, yes, I am a bit." She shook her curls as if she had come out of the water, and started eating in a greedy, almost voracious manner from the plate she had fetched. With her mouth full she held a forkful of salad up to him. "Want a bite?"

"No thanks. It tastes nice by the look of it."

She fluttered a hand beside her ear and said, "I want to get much

62

fatter still. Do you like fat women?"

She gave him a sultry bedroom look. Was she really flirting with him or was she pulling his leg? "Seed-begging eyes", they used to say in his day. Before he could answer, Paul and Etienne entered, their hair wetly plastered after a shower.

"What did you think of it, Mr Bouwmeester?" Paul called out, still in the doorway. "I saw you laughing."

"You were all splendid."

"If they hadn't been," asked Olga, chewing, "what would you have said then?"

"The same, of course."

"Then maybe it isn't true."

"I would have said it differently and he probably would have noticed. Anyway, what kind of a scamp are you?"

She shrugged her shoulders. "Never mind."

A moment later Etienne put a glass of gin on the table and sat down with them. With a discontented face he lit a cigarette and started grumbling about the public always failing to turn up. Things were bad in the world and even worse in the Netherlands.

"Aren't the Netherlands part of the world?" enquired Olga.

No, that was precisely the trouble. The Netherlands didn't even exist. They had only seemingly been wrested from the waves, the world didn't start until you got to Brussels. He was gradually becoming nauseated by the lack of culture here. It was because there had never been a court-culture, as for instance in France; art was the domain of the absolute monarchy, but the Dutch monarchy was nothing more than a petit bourgeois republic with a lick of gold paint. Wagging a finger at South Africa and El Salvador, and everywhere else where real problems existed, oh yes, they could do that all right, but as for going to the theatre, forget it. Everything was a question of morality and money, and even these were strictly separated by their confounded Calvinist hypocrisy.

"I think you're wet," said Olga. "And a typical Dutchman to boot. The Dutch always slate their own country."

"Shut up, you. What do you think, Mr Bouwmeester?"

Uli made a vague gesture. "How old are you?"

"Fifty."

"Then what is there to complain about? I sometimes think: oh, to be sixty-five again, just for once."

"Well, yes, of course you can look at it that way. Although . . . maybe fifty is worse than eighty."

"I beg your pardon, only seventy-eight."

"All right, seventy-eight. You have nothing more to worry about."

Perhaps someone should again have knocked three times against the underside of the table, for safety's sake. There was even a god standing on top of it. But Olga turned aside and called out to another corner of the room: "Are you starting up again?"

Clearly she had followed with one ear what was being discussed there, Paul blew her a kiss.

"Sweet darling of mine! In brief," he said provocatively to Aronds, but it was not intended for him, "it's the same sort of thing with newspapers. Women read the paper these days, for unfathomable reasons, but they still can't fold it up properly. You watch. Our old Jesuit got the drift of that pretty well, that's why he wrote a play with only male parts, for although women may unaccountably read the paper these days they still can't fold it up in the proper manner. That will take hundreds of years."

Amused, Uli got up to get another drink, while Paul got the altercation he wanted. In the kitchen, Max refilled his glass and asked him with a veiled smile whether he was enjoying himself.

"Very much," said Uli. "I rarely meet people these days. You have hauled me up out of a very deep well, did you know that?"

"And you'll never go back into it. You can't any more now."

Uli was silent for a moment.

"I don't want to think about that at all, what happens afterwards."

Max picked up his own glass, of white wine, and touched Uli's.

"To our everlasting collaboration." As he took a sip he continued to look at Uli and raised his glass again.

Perhaps in order to put an end to the squabbling, which not all the participants enjoyed, Lucas turned up the music, too loudly, pulled Mimi to her feet and started dancing with her. Aronds and

Stella also began to dance. Uli sauntered over to Michael and Miss Wijdenes. He cupped one hand behind his ear because he couldn't hear what Michael said.

"I suppose you can see what he's saying," he said to the prompter.

He couldn't hear her reply either, whereupon she went to the record player and after a moment's searching turned down the volume. She was clearly using the opportunity, for in her turn she now knelt down among the records and did not come back. Uli took her place on the window-sill and after looking around for a while, said, "Shouldn't Leo Siderius be here?"

"Take it from me," said Michael resignedly, without looking at him, "that Leo Siderius is never where he should be."

"Is he only where he should not be?"

"You could perhaps say that." He turned to Uli, "Was your sister unable to attend tonight?"

"My sister . . .", repeated Uli, "I thought this party was only for the performers."

"That is true."

Uli looked out of the window. Amsterdam glittered in the night as far as he could see; an almost full moon emerged from the clouds, vanished and reappeared. There lay his life. It lay drained away in all those streets and squares like a day's rain soaked into the ground, with only here and there a puddle as a reminder of its existence. Who remembered it? He hardly did himself. It seemed to him as if beyond the horizon, in the polder, he had been dead for many years. He was a kind of Lazarus risen from the grave when summoned. Somewhere thrown away in the distance stood his house. He saw the room before him, where Berta sat no doubt watching television, some mindless American serial about rich people. Perhaps she had fallen asleep, the poor woman, the snowflakey black-and-white images flickering on her sagging face.

He turned round and looked again into the warm room full of people and music. Richer than he, was no one. Paul was dancing with Miss Wijdenes; she laughed, which made her face look twenty years younger. For some reason Mr Caccini now blew a kiss to Uli. Vogel beckoned and pointed to the seat beside him. A little

65

ashamed of his stiffness, Uli lowered himself into the cushions.

The director said he had a feeling it had gone well that afternoon, at their first rehearsal. When Uli asked how he could be so sure that he could cope with the part – for there was no reason to think so – Vogel said he'd see to that. He was the one who decided what someone could do. Of course, certain conditions needed to be met, not everyone was capable of everything, but he could tell at a glance – even from photographs. His own talent lay perhaps in the fact that he had the courage to take his own intuition seriously.

Trudy stood up to find amusement elsewhere, and they talked for a while about talent and great actors. At the name of Louis Bouwmeester, Vogel said that of course Pierre de Vries was a very different type of man. In his daily life Louis Bouwmeester had been a spontaneous, emotional, somewhat plebeian man who in his spare time read only the trash of those days, such as . . .

"Nick Carter," said Uli, "Buffalo Bill."

"Precisely. But Pierre de Vries, on the other hand, is a fairly decadent grand seigneur who reads the symbolists."

"The what?"

"The French symbolists. A group of writers at the end of the nineteenth century. Mallarmé, Huysmans, Villiers de l'Isle-Adam, Maeterlinck, Villiers especially was a favourite of his."

"Of Pierre de Vries?" Uli looked at him in surprise. "Where does it say that?"

"It doesn't say it anywhere," said Caspar Vogel, taking off his sunglasses. "It's what I say, now."

"But . . ."

"No but. It doesn't say anywhere that he looks like you, either, or that he smoothes down his hair at a given moment. As an actor you have to try to get beyond the text which the writer has handed to you. The text is only a kind of concentrate, for you to supplement. You must try to catch hold of the entire world of which the text shows only a fragment. What do you think, for instance, would be Pierre de Vries' favourite drink?"

Uli took a sip and pondered. Not beer, that was certain. Suddenly he saw him before his eyes, somewhere in a dark, over-furnished room, very refined, in his hand a cut-crystal glass.

"Wine," he said.

"Red or white?"

"Red. Bordeaux."

"You think so? Could be. Where does he live?"

Uli laughed. The game amused him, but it wasn't merely a game. He couldn't just make it up as he went along; somehow or other a reality existed which could be retrieved. In his mind he hovered over the city, like a heron from the polder, spying for a fish in a canal.

"Somewhere by a canal," he said, "not one of the main ones, he isn't wealthy enough for that, but on a quiet side canal. There were far more canals then than there are now."

By the door Stella had been talking to Lucas for several minutes. He kissed her, she took her coat and waved. "Goodbye, everyone! I must be off." And just to Uli she said, "See you tomorrow."

"Bye, Stella, see you tomorrow." With a sense of relief he saw that Aronds was not leaving with her.

When he had seen her out, Lucas came to sit with them. He was a bit tipsy now. "Work in progress, I see."

"We are discussing the private life of Pierre de Vries," said Vogel. "Insofar as it has not been described by the author."

"Don't tempt me! I know an awful lot about that. Especially about that disgusting affair with Etienne. Of course Etienne was a handsome boy once, but after all those years there's nothing left of him but an empty-headed sponger who can keep his position with Pierre de Vries only by going to the dockside and procuring sailors for him. And then, of course, he gets his own back by all kinds of nasty manœuvrings and by hurting Pierre's feelings in public whenever he can, even though he is allowed to share in the maritime ceremonies himself."

Involuntarily Uli glanced at Etienne. He was still sitting by the round table, clearly reconciled to the Netherlands; he was leaning over to Olga, telling her something that made her laugh so uncontrollably that she seemed about to crawl across the table.

"But his study," said Uli, "where he has his books, no sailor is ever allowed in there."

"I don't know about that. All the way from the living room to his

67

bedroom the passages and stairs are strewn with sailor's collars, caps with ribbons, SS Johanna Maria, and those ridiculous flared trousers."

"That may be so," said Uli, "but when Etienne is still busy chucking the sea-food out into the street, he is already sitting in his library again in a silk dressing-gown and picks up a book by . . . what was the name again?"

"Villiers de l'Isle-Adam."

"That's right. And then he pours himself a glass of port. Port!" Uli repeated, surprised at himself. "That's what it was of course!"

"Very good," Vogel nodded. "Now we've got it."

When Max passed by, Lucas leapt to his feet, grabbed him by the waist and started dancing with him. Uli let his watch spring open; it was half past eleven, the last bus left just before midnight.

"I must go," he said.

He tried to get up but did not immediately succeed in shifting his centre of gravity far enough forward. Caspar was already standing, and pulled him to his feet.

"Stay a bit longer, I'll drive you home. It will be a pleasure."

"Don't be daft. You'd have to drive all that way back again."

Waltzing around with Max, Lucas called out to him that he could stay the night. But Uli did not want to stay. He was tired and preferred to get away.

3
Smoke Screens

After a few days it had become a familiar sight to the other customers at the Tivoli: the old man among the much younger actors and actresses of the Authors' Theatre.

"Beer, Willem?"

He had been completely accepted as a colleague and his age made no difference to them, but he didn't think it necesssary to mention that he was actually called "Uli". He had always hated the sound of it, an invention of his mother when he was little, and he was glad that this too could still be changed in his old age. He didn't say much at the round table (there was too much to say), but sat back comfortably amid the Amsterdam gossip.

When Caspar Vogel was not there, it was alleged that something very beautiful was developing between him and his new assistant, the attractive, long-legged Trudy. Wasn't he a fairy then? Come, come, Willem, keep up with the times! Very occasionally maybe, and so what? Who wasn't? Not Paul? Okay, not Paul. Paul was faithful to Trix. Anyway, it was better, said Olga, if his current girlfriend didn't find out about this business with Trudy; as far as she herself was concerned, she didn't care a monkey's. It turned out that she used to live with Caspar Vogel; now she had been married for a couple of years to a well-to-do art dealer who, thank God, spent a lot of his time abroad, mostly in America. This husband, in his turn had on occasion been seen with Mimi, coming out of the Hilton and quickly scurrying off to his Jaguar, or so Lucas reported, when neither Olga nor Mimi was present.

Uli drank his beer, listened to it all and at once forgot it again. It was always and everywhere the same. Everything whirled about like snowflakes. How often had he not witnessed these goings on, sometimes as a participant. In the twenties, in the thirties, forties, fifties, sixties (only in the seventies hardly at all), always different and always the same, so-and-so with so-and-so, and so-and-so with so-and-so, always different permutations of the same pattern, repeating itself endlessly like wallpaper around a room. And a hundred years ago it had been no different, and a thousand years ago, and two thousand years ago, wherever you went, whatever you read, masterpieces or trash novelettes, films, plays, always and everywhere the same tissue of people doing the same things all over again and thinking they were unique. Imagine you lived for ever! What a calamity . . . You might just as well be someone else.

No, it cannot be denied, at that table at the Tivoli our Uli was for the first time really old; and yet he felt happy, to belong to it all once more. This was paradoxical, he couldn't quite figure himself out, but that didn't bother him, though obviously it would have been better if someone had told him he was making a mistake: true reality does not reside in the whole, but in the details. A particular yellow circle on the wallpaper may repeat itself innumerable times, but that circle is at the same time in a unique way itself and not a different circle, though you couldn't detect it even with a magnifying glass. (Not to mention the beings who are not really on the wallpaper at all and who are yet perceived to be there by children or by people like Shakespeare.) And this was true also of Uli himself, sated with always and ever the same – this too had happened innumerable times before to old people and yet here it was the unique Uli to whom it was happening. To put it this way: perhaps the world might just as well not have existed, that is true; but this does not mean that in some way it does not exist. But such a person – who could have told him this (didactically forming a circle with thumb and forefinger) from the pale regions of thought, from where the world can recover some colour if it has lost its brightness, such a person did not exist.

Only when the conversation at the Tivoli turned to Stella (she was not present) was he suddenly no longer blasé and said he didn't think all this tittle-tattle was very nice.

"So suddenly," said Etienne, his eyebrows slightly raised.

Yes, so suddenly. Or perhaps not all that sudden. When he looked at her, during a rehearsal or in the café, he saw an ethereal being that he could not define. Then it was as if, in the background behind her profile, there was no longer the red-brick wall of the rehearsal studio, or the posters lining the café, but a wonderful garden, bathed in the warm light of the setting sun. And occasionally he also saw in her blue-blue eyes a look that confused him. Then he sometimes looked at his hand that lay on his thigh like a piece of broken tree bark.

Friday afternoon, at the end of the first week of rehearsals, when he was sitting next to her in the Tivoli, he asked if she would like to have supper with him.

"Isn't your wife waiting for you?"

"I live with my sister," said Uli, as if Berta wasn't waiting for him.

"We can order something here."

"I'd rather go somewhere different."

He would have preferred no one to notice, so it would remain a sealed secret between them, hidden in a shrine with an aureole around it, but when everyone got up to pay, she said slightly elatedly:

"I don't know what you're all going to do, but Willem and I are going to eat in town.

"Oh, là là!"

"How gallant!"

Smiling, Uli made a small bow, but he felt a bit unhappy. As he paid for his drinks he saw he had no more than twenty-five guilders on him, barely enough to have a meal on his own. But the discovery almost amused him – he'd have to see what happened.

"Won't your sister be waiting for you at suppertime?" she asked as they walked, in the falling twilight, through an alleyway towards the Rokin. She pushed her pink-painted bicycle along with one hand.

"I expect so."

"Shouldn't you phone her?"

71

"We don't have a phone." (But the neighbours did.)

She stopped. "Look, why don't we go another time, we see each other every day."

Now he could get out of it decently, and probably prevent a number of difficulties, but it was out of the question. He had invited her on an impulse, and it was now or never. Nonsense of course – had he fallen in love? The old man enamoured of a young girl? Up till now he had looked at her as an art object, a beautiful painting, but now that he was walking beside her in town through the hazy October evening, he felt deep down inside himself something quite different from aesthetic appreciation.

Emerging into the wide Rokin, he looked around and took a deep breath. It was a busy Friday evening, the campaigners hadn't yet succeeded in turning Amsterdam into a village, and when crossing the road – under a vast mauve cloud-filled sky of the Dutch school – he held her by the upper arm and almost jubilantly raised his other hand to stop the traffic. A boy stuck his head out of a car window and called out, "Getting on all right, grandad?"

"Where are we going?" asked Stella.

"You say, I'm rather out of touch."

She knew of a bistro in Rembrandtplein, close by, but all the tables were taken. The crowded eating-house (which had once been a haberdasher's shop if he remembered correctly) suddenly seemed to Uli the most desirable place on earth, and anyone who was not allowed in there was doomed. He looked around the square. Everywhere his memories lay piled up metres high. It was getting dark. In a narrow side street he saw in neon letters the word OSIRIS, of which the first "I" flickered on and off. Not having forgotten the demoralising effect of searching and dithering in situations such as this, he said, "Come on, we'll go in there."

"Are you sure it's a restaurant?"

The public didn't seem convinced of it; all the tables were empty. They went in. On the ceiling some dim light glimmered through a few open-work lanterns, for the rest everything was steeped in a profound twilight filled with soft Arab music: a woman's voice singing melancholy recitatifs followed by enthusiastic choruses, with strings and drums. By the bar, behind

72

a balustrade and a stuffed crocodile, a dark man in shirtsleeves looked up from his newspaper. When Uli enquired if meals were served he confirmed in a voice so deep that it seemed to come from under the ground. With a surly expression around his black moustache, he lit a candle on one of the tables and beckoned them to be seated, all of a sudden with the kind of warm smile born in sunshine that is unknown in the north.

"We'll soon find out what kind of a place this is," said Uli.

The wall panelling was painted with hieroglyphs, on touristy brass plates there gleamed the figures of gods, half human, half animal. Higher up on the wall hung dusty musical instruments and grubby, torn posters of pyramids and the Sphynx, temples, the golden face of Tutankhamun. Uli asked Stella if she had ever eaten Egyptian food, at which she turned her face aside with a quick movement and said, with the chin above her right shoulder: "No, Osiris" – at once acquiring, in Uli's eyes, something Egyptian herself: a reddish, archaic, transparent beauty. From her ears hung two artificial pearls like big drops on the point of falling. She looked at him cheerfully.

"Let us have," he said, randomly reading out a few names from the menu, "*mazza*, then *meshwyat menawaha*, and for dessert *baclava*."

He answered her look with a smile. That even the hors d'oeuvre on its own cost more than he had with him, filled him with a mischievous mirth which he recognised in himself but did not understand. Perhaps it was something to do with Berta who, on the other side of the dyke, was now letting two pork chops slide into the frying pan, doomed to a frizzled end. I am a dotty old man with a nasty character, he thought; but a moment later a bottle of Egyptian wine was standing on the table and he drank to her.

"To the performance, Miranda!"

"To the come-back of Willem Bouwmeester as Pierre de Vries!"

The wine was sweet, the Arabian bread hot, the mazza spicy and the music very different. Everything was clearly separated from everything else, only in himself was everything mixed up. He talked about the theatre, about the rehearsals, but it was only in a manner of speaking. Was he really in love with this beautiful,

73

good-humoured child? What on earth was he thinking of? When the conversation flagged he looked for a while at her pinned-up plaits.

"Red women are always possessed of the devil," he said, while all the red women with whom he had been to bed in his life appeared in his memory as one vague figure. "Yes, you'd better watch out."

He put one elbow on the table and rested his chin on his hand.

"I have nothing to lose any more."

"That's what you think. You're only just beginning."

He did not take his eyes off her (or rather, his eye; from time to time Stella looked into the wrong one) and said, suddenly rather moved, "Do you know, most men, when they see a girl like you . . . How old are you?"

"Twenty-one."

"Then they think, that girl could be my daughter."

"In *The Tempest* I am."

"You could even be my grand-daughter . . . My great-grand-daughter if need be. But I am thinking something quite different."

When he fell silent she asked, "What then?"

"That you could have been my mother." He looked at her uncertainly. Then he took a sip and said, "I am the son of an eighteen-year-old girl. Rather strange, don't you think, a man of almost eighty who is the son of a girl of eighteen? In my memory my mother is as old as you are."

"Maybe that's why you have lived so long. You're made of young flesh."

He rubbed his face with both hands. His mother had never become older than Stella was now.

"What are we talking about . . . As if you were interested in archaeology."

"I think," said Stella, passing the tip of her forefinger a few times through the flame of the candle, "it's all a coincidence. You are fifty years older than me . . ."

"I wish it were true. Almost sixty."

"But it might equally well have been the other way round. Me eighty and you twenty." She dipped her finger in the wine, briefly

74

stuck it into her mouth, and burst out laughing. "The question is only whether in that case you would also have been sitting here with me."

Uli leaned back and grabbled with both hands in his thick white hair.

"Let me think. As regards me, that would have been in 1925 and then you would have been born in . . ." He tried to work it out but she beat him to it.

"1845."

"There you are!" said Uli triumphantly. "Then you would have been Sarah Bernhardt or somebody like like. You can be sure that at eighty she still dined with young men of twenty." And the rest, he thought, but he didn't say that. "I have such women in my own family too."

"She still played Hamlet then, from a wheelchair."

The Egyptian, bringing clean plates, poured more wine and joined in the laughter. "Isse good," he grunted.

"Did she really play Hamlet from a wheelchair?"

"So you see, there's always hope. For me too."

"Look," said Uli, "You know things like that. I don't. I'm a nincompoop, I know nothing. That is to say . . . maybe it is a coincidence that I am older than you, but all the same, it is the way it is. Maybe you could have been older than me, but you aren't. Everything is the way it is and not otherwise." He took out his tin of cigars, opened it, offered it to her and asked, "Could you now, for instance, imagine that your mother was your daughter?"

But then something unexpected happened. Stella looked at the cigar, then at Uli, then back at the cigar, and suddenly her mouth twisted and she started crying. Startled, Uli asked if he had said anything wrong; at the same time his feelings for the girl welled up inside him like the tears in her eyes.

She shook her head. "Don't take any notice." With the ball of her thumb she wiped over her cheekbones. "It's gone already."

"Isse not good," said the waiter, placing a dish of grilled meat on the chafer.

Uli put his hand on hers, which was calloused like that of a cleaning woman. "You must tell me, or I'll go crazy."

"It's because of your cigar," she said, smiling with red eyes, pulling her hand away from under his. She served him and looked at his surprised face. "Yes, mad is bad."

"Tell me." There was a sound in his voice that compelled her.

All right then. Telling was salutary, so the psychiatrists said, at least when the listener was being paid; exactly the opposite therefore of what it was in literature. The best thing was always to tell everything. (*Always? Everything?* Certainly, he who is robbed of his dreams, who is constantly woken up by the mad professors as soon as he starts to dream, ends up mad. Has been scientifically established.) He had mentioned her mother hadn't he? When she was eight years old her father, out of the blue, had gone off with another woman who was in every respect the opposite of her mother, and who laughed till she cried at his jokes to which her mother used to respond with a face of cast-iron. Her parents were both fairly old (that is to say, they could have been Uli's children) and Auntie Ria was quite young, but who loved her father the most, her mother or Auntie Ria, that remained to be seen. But maybe in a marriage love shouldn't be too strong, it only led to trouble. Her father was a chemistry teacher at the Fishery College in Scheveningen, her mother was a nursery teacher in The Hague and Auntie Ria was nothing. Except, to her father she was everything. After her father had left – Stella visited him every Wednesday afternoon – her mother gradually began to go to pieces. There was probably more behind it, the same as whatever had led to the cast-iron face, and which might well be something to do with her own parents; she didn't know. According to her father, said Stella, everything had endless roots, maybe down to the beginning of the world. Everything was already present in the Big Bang.

"In the what?" asked Uli.

"In the explosion with which the world began."

"So your father thinks the world began with an explosion? Must be another of his jokes. What exploded?"

She did not know. Anyway, her mother became more and more quiet and strange. She spoke less and less, wandered about the house at night, smelt at the clothes her father had left behind and

76

for some reason or other began to find everything as if it were dirty. When she had peeled a potato she dropped it in the pan as if it were a ball of horse dung; she touched everything as if it were sticky, peculiar, alive. One afternoon, three years after her father had left, her mother gave her some money (guilders that she took from her purse as though they were red hot) and she was sent to buy a box of cigars of the brand her father always smoked. Was Dad coming back then? No, not exactly, but on the other hand, yes. It was in the middle of the summer and when Stella came back, her mother had closed all the windows and curtains. She, Stella, had to sit in her father's chair and light a cigar; her mother gave her a light. It was a short, fat cigar which she could scarely hold, and as she coughed and blew clouds of smoke into the darkened room, her mother sat by the table with her eyes closed, sniffing the old smell. When her mother started to cry, Stella had run out of the room, into the sunny garden, where she threw the cigar aside and, falling into the grass, wetted her pants and cried.

4
Pay-up!

"I can't eat any more," she said, wiping her mouth.

Uli put down his knife and fork too. He did not know what to say. Mechanically he felt for the tin of cigars, but put it away again at once.

"Have one by all means. My father was simply my first ever part. Maybe that is why I went on the stage."

"How is your mother now?"

"She's in a mental home."

"Do you ever visit her?"

"Never."

"And your father is in Scheveningen smoking cigars and making Aunt Ria laugh?"

"That's right."

Maybe it was partly because of the wine, but for whatever reason, Uli burst into a laugh.

"Love!" he called out, "Love!" He took a cigar out of the tin after all. "Did you know that as soon as I saw you I guessed there was something like that?"

"A *secret* in my life?" she asked, with theatrical emphasis, as she held the candle up to him.

"Yes, of course you can make it sound daft." He leaned forward, sucked the flame towards him and blew the smoke sideways through a corner of his mouth. "You can always make anything sound daft."

Stella put down the candle and said,

> *"Never till this day*
> *Saw I him touch'd with anger so distemper'd,"*

78

"I am sorry."

"No, no, you were right. Fact is, I never told anyone about it. Not even my father knows."

"But now I know."

"Yes." She took his hand and put her other hand on it. Two hard hands, out of keeping with the rest of her, with visible veins and bony wrists. "And now you were going to tell me the secret in *your* life."

Something flew to his cheeks, as if he were blushing, but whether that was so, whether he could still blush, he did not know.

"I shall have to think about that first."

Poor Uli. He looked at her and he saw that she saw something, but what could she see?

"Naturally."

She withdrew her hands and they watched in silence as the waiter cleared the table. They were still the only guests. But at the bar there now sat an Egyptian whom they had not seen enter – in an impeccable dark suit and gold cufflinks. Stella put her handbag on her lap and said, "I'd like to leave now."

"Leave?" Uli repeated in surprise, "There's still a dessert to come."

"I want to go outside." She put her chequebook on the table. "Do you mind if I pay?"

For one second Uli hesitated. He had completely forgotten about that.

"Out of the question," he said with an air of chivalry.

"Let's go halves then."

Of course that was even more impossible. He picked up the chequebook and put it in her bag. "Not at all, I invited you."

"Thank you, Willem, it was delicious. Next time I'll pay. Shall we go?"

He got up too and looked in the direction of the bar.

"You go. I'll have a coffee and sit and think for a while. Do you live near by?"

"Near the Zoo. I'll be there in no time, by bike, don't worry about me."

By the door he gave her a kiss on the cheek and heard hers as a soft little plop by his ear. He closed the door, swung round (tottering momentarily), and looked at the two men who looked back darkly and whose prisoner he now was, although they didn't know it yet.

Since nothing more came out of the bottle, he ordered another glass of wine. He let the lid of his watch spring open: nine o'clock. Plenty of time. The music and the hieroglyphs reappeared and it was as if the alcohol was now beginning to take effect. His eyelids no longer blinked but closed and opened slowly, while he talked to himself from time to time. A plateful of sweet pastry was put in front of him but he did not notice it.

Utter folly it was, what he wanted. But what did he want? Maybe not exactly to go to bed with her, but something like it, something in that direction. Suppose he did go to bed with her . . . It hadn't happened for at least ten years and she would be the last, that was certain. So far, the last one had been some slut in the Cellar, he had no idea who. But at the time he didn't know yet that she would be the last of that endless line. He began to laugh a little. It didn't often happen that someone knew it was the last time. You were run over by a car or you had a heart attack, or you had to move house to the polder, and then with hindsight a particular time turned out to have been the last. Or you had to go to hospital with cancer, and then maybe you did it once more, but then you'd always have the hope that it hadn't been the last time. It applied really only to suicides: one more screw and then: fini. There was no symmetry to life, because everyone remembered their *first* time.

He raised his head. His eyes saw the beaked figure of a god, but Uli did not see it. The first time . . . heavens, that had begun in this very neighbourhood – sixty years ago. He should have told Stella that! Look . . .

. . . there he goes, behind Rembrandt's statue, Uncle Karel, his father's younger brother, in plus fours, checked knee socks, straw hat, a white woollen scarf flung loosely over his shoulders.

"Hello, Uncle Karel."

"Hello, Uli, what are you doing out so late?"

"Just hanging around."

"Yes, I can see that. You should have been in bed long ago."

"What about you then?"

"Look here, young ruffian, when you're as old as I am you're allowed to gad about the streets. Aren't you supposed to go to school tomorrow?"

"Yes, but I'm not going."

"That's a fine thing. Well, all right, come along then."

And there they go, into the big world, or at least, into a blaring café-chantant where, on a small stage, legs fly up in the air, showing lacy knickers. Smoke, noise, bustle. Everybody knows Uncle Karel, who operates on the financial side of the theatre (soon afterwards he will introduce Uli into the world of cabaret and music hall). Waiters with long white aprons precede them with outstretched arm and clear a table on which, within the shortest possible time, there appears a bottle of champagne in an ice-bucket surrounded by four glasses, the other two of which are presently raised to the lips of two dancing-girls in glittering costumes, a moment earlier still infinitely remote in the transcendental world of limelight and spotlight, but now each putting a hand on the thighs of Uncle Karel and his nephew. Uli could shout for joy. A moment ago, a lonely boy in the street, not a penny in his pocket, now amid palm trees and glass and cast-iron pillars, the subject of family boasts and female admiration.

"My handsome young nephew, squints a bit alas, but the youngest shoot on the Bouwmeester tree. And still a virgin, aren't you, Uli?"

"Well . . ."

"Yes, yes, look, Suzie has an eye for these things, Suzie thinks you're a bit of all right."

The fact that Suzie is the most beautiful woman in the world, undoubtedly also still a virgin, and that he loves her and will marry her and never leave her, that is already no longer in question. She flings herself around his neck and kisses him and they roll off their chairs, are pulled to their feet, her tongue slips inside his mouth, while her hand goes upwards along his thigh, quite accidentally in fact, the slender fingertips of the artist now virtually, no, almost

81

completely at a certain place – and then Uncle Karel says suddenly, "All right, that will do. The bill, please."

The girls have suddenly vanished, and for a whole half hour he has to stand behind his uncle who has a host of things to discuss with everyone – constantly repeating to himself the address Suzie has whispered to him.

"Mind, Uli," says Uncle Karel outside in the deserted windy square, "not a word to your uncle and aunt about this."

"No, Uncle. Thanks for everything."

"And now, quick march, off to bed!"

But when Uncle Karel has disappeared round the corner, he runs, shivering with cold and excitement, to the address which he now keeps saying out loud, uninterruptedly, terrified of being struck by instant amnesia. A narrow street by the Amstel. After emptying his bladder against a softly hissing lamp-post, he goes to the door. It yields, and with his hand on a greasy rope, past bicycles and boxes of empty bottles, he climbs the dark stairs. On the landing a fat woman with pink bandages around her legs appears in a doorway, and asks who he wants.

"Miss Suzie, please."

"Fourth."

Past washing tubs, step-ladders and garbage bins, he climbs higher, from landing to landing, the stairs become steeper and finally change to a ladder. With his hands above his head he pushes a hatch open and smells at once that he is in her room.

She is lying in a wide bed, already asleep. On a little table in the corner burns a small lamp. She is lying on her back, her hands above her head, one breast bared, and as Uli looks at her something becomes totally disarranged in his brain, in the neurons perhaps (although in the twenties little was known about the nervous system). Whatever the reason, he is suddenly trembling from head to toe. Breathing deeply without taking his eyes off her, he sits down as far away from her as possible on the edge of a chair. Luckily, she is asleep, so he can wait until the tumult inside him has died down. The dark shadow of the hair in her armpits. He sees that her legs are spread underneath the blanket and he forces himself to look elsewhere. What poverty. The cracked wash-stand with little flasks and pots, and underneath it a strange, cylindrical instrument with a red rubber hose attached to it. Clothes over the chair, on the floor one shoe standing and another fallen sideways; above the bed, against the sloping roof, a reproduction of a painting: a naked young woman bathing, peered at by two lecherous old men.

When after five minutes his shivers begin to abate, he stands up, enveloped by the warm silence. Should he wake her now? The bare breast rises and falls; her closed eyes. It is impossible to wake her. Perhaps she doesn't even remember who he is, and will start screaming, and then the fat woman will beat him to death with a rolling pin. Everything is now totally different from what it was in the cabaret, so crowded and noisy. How beautiful she is. On tiptoe he approaches. The warmth that rises from the bed, the sweet smell. He presses his hand against his crotch and doesn't know what to do – but his other hand knows without consulting him and slowly alights on her breast, on that softness, with the hardness of her nipple exactly in the middle of the palm of his hand, between the lines of life and head. At the moment when he feels the message in the heart of his hand, his legs give way. On his knees beside the bed, anxiously watching her face in case she wakes up, his hand now disappears with outspread fingers beneath the blanket and glides over her body without touching it, a fraction above it, like a glider, a Zögling. When far away he feels some hair, his middle finger suddenly makes a strange, quick nod, and he touches something that . . . something unlike anything he has ever touched before! He touches something from another world, a paradise, which he did not know existed, a world in which there are such things to be touched!

He withdraws his hand and quickly gets undressed. Not all buttons allow themselves to be squeezed through the buttonholes by his trembling fingers; they produce soft little tocks at the other end of the room; his shoes also have to remain laced. Naked, his member upright like a spade which a farmer has rammed into the soil (so he can put a quid of tobacco into his mouth) he looks at her. She is still asleep – tired after her art and the champagne. On tiptoe he walks around the bed and on the other side slips cautiously

83

under the sheet, her warmth enfolds him. With bated breath, all the time watching fearfully whether he is waking her up, he edges little by little in her direction. As if something similar were happening in heaven, with even more jumping buttons, it begins to rain gently on the roof. When finally he lies close against her, he can suddenly no longer control himself; panting he clambers on top of her, oh, as long as she doesn't notice, as long as she doesn't wake up! At random he thrusts about with his tackle between her legs, something is wrong, dammit, there's something wrong. A moment later he feels how her hand leads the desperate guest towards the entrance – and at a stroke the two of them change into one loudly roaring and rearing legendary beast. In spasms it heaves and lurches all over the groaning bed, dragging sheets and blankets with it, the wooden headboard dips forward, the bed frame snaps and crashes to the floor, the headboard falls on top of them, but they notice nothing, nor hear the furious shouting of the neighbours below, for that does not take place in the world in which they have become the beast.

The shouting has died down by the time Uli comes to himself and looks dazedly at the havoc. He is wet all over, including his hair, as if he had just come out of the sea, even the panes in the skylight are misted over. Laughing, her head on her arms , half outside the tangled bed, Suzie lies looking at him. "I woke you up," says Uli guiltily.

"You didn't."

"What do you mean – weren't you asleep then?"

"Of course not, silly."

"Well done! avoid; no more!"

he muttered and wiped his eyes with a slightly quivering hand. His tears were the only fluid still left to him. He looked briefly at his wet finger and said with a melancholy smile at his glass, empty for the second time:

> *"We are such stuff*
> *As dreams are made on; and our little life*
> *Is rounded with a sleep."*

For the first time he felt he understood Prospero's words and –

because of the alcohol – much more besides, no everything, everything . . . He raised his hand.

"Bill, please!"

Clearly, they had been waiting for this signal, because the bill came at once. Feeling their eyes on him, he took out his wallet and searched with mounting amazement in all the compartments, he even opened the little lip and peered into the darkness of the interior. He laid the wallet on the table and started searching his pockets. This produced twenty-five guilders, which he put on the saucer. He got up, fumbled in the pocket of his overcoat on the coatstand, and made a gesture of being totally perplexed.

"Nothing money?" grunted the waiter, still standing by the table.

"I can't understand it – I am sure I had –"

"Not cheque?"

"Nothing. Yes, twenty-five guilders. And I am sure I had –"

The waiter raised a hand as if to say he had better be silent. He blew out the candle and went to the bar. Uli sat down again and awaited with crossed arms the outcome of the oriental deliberations. He would have liked to order another glass of wine, but daren't. The man in the bespoke suit now went behind the bar himself and turned off the music. The sudden silence had a chilling effect on Uli; in addition, a couple of glaring unprotected bulbs on the ceiling sprang into light, mercilessly revealing the shabbiness of the establishment. They're going to tie me up, torture and murder me, thought Uli.

"Have identity card? Proof?"

"Identity card . . . we don't have those in this country," said Uli with a curious kind of pride for someone unable to pay his bill. "That was only in the war, under the Germans. But perhaps . . ." He took out his wallet again, but there was nothing in it bearing his name or address.

"Then looks bad," said the waiter, "Not have?" – and fluttering strangely with his fingers he looked Uli up and down, until the fluttering suddenly crystallized in a motionless forefinger pointing straight at Uli's wristwatch.

Startled, Uli gazed at him. Now things were taking a turn he had

85

not foreseen. "That's an heirloom . . . it was my father's."

"Will get back. When pay."

Uli would have preferred them to phone the police, but as he himself had put them into a situation in which they would have to trust him in some way or other, he was hardly in a position to make demands now. With a feeling of humiliation, like someone being robbed, he took off his watch and saw how it left his hand and passed into that other, browner, younger one.

"Get back tomorrow."

Tomorrow it was Saturday, there would be no rehearsal.

"I don't live in town. Is Monday all right?"

The waiter consulted with the gentleman behind the bar; across the crocodile a brief, gutteral conversation unfolded.

"Boss say okay. Not later than two."

When Uli apologised once again, took his coat and was about to leave, there appeared on the face of the waiter – who held the door open for him, the watch in his other hand – that same sub-tropical smile as before.

"Nice girl," he said.

The injunction that he must not go back later than two o'clock Uli regarded as a penalty clause to which he was unwilling to submit, (after all, they didn't know he had known all along he could not pay) and he stayed at the rehearsal until half past four, then went to the Tivoli and strolled off to the Osiris at around six.

When he could not immediately find it, he first thought he hadn't paid attention properly, but a moment later he stopped with a shock. Even the name had vanished from the facade. Inside, only the wall paintings were left and the dismantled bar. The woman in the small stationery shop next door knew only that the removal van had left at about three o'clock. The place had gone bust. There was no-one there.

No, she didn't know where.

ACT THREE

1
Master and Servant

"Yes, Willem, very good," said Vogel. "Go on doing that."

"What?"

"The way you were holding your hands just now." He briefly rose behind his table to demonstrate. "Like this, level with your waist, slightly bent back at the wrists, fingers in that elegant position. Those are Pierre de Vries' hands, beautiful queenish hands. I'll let you have a ring, with an amethyst. A purple one."

Uli found it difficult to recapture what had apparently come all by itself a minute ago, but when he had got it once more and could do it consciously, and understood it, he never needed to be told again. He certainly did not need to be told that he should not exaggerate it. What mattered was that in the end everything became unconscious again.

"No, don't drum with your fingers, that's what amateurs do. Put one leg over the other. Cross your arms. And now wriggle your toes inside your shoe. No, only with that dangling foot, and a bit faster. Yes, like that, now you're sitting there being impatient."

"No one would ever notice!"

"That's what you think. The slightest movement has more dramatic force than the most profound aphorism that does not advance the action. You have no idea how they are lying in wait in the dark out there, those voyeurs; they see everything, and everything means something, even when your're sitting immobile. Very good, that. Turn your body into a work of art. You can come straight out of that with your dramatic outburst, with your beautiful bronze voice. The sound and the rhythm of the words are what matter most; that's how you convey the dark message, from

89

behind the content of the text. The literal meaning is only the vehicle of what it is all about. It mustn't be so that people might just as well read the play. You are acting the part of a great actor, who in his daily life plays the part of the great actor he is, with all kinds of reminiscences of other great actors in his gestures and inflections. They are the echoes of the Dutch heroic style, of Andries Snoek at the beginning of the nineteenth century, and the great Jan Punt from the eighteenth, maybe even of actors from the seventeenth, working with Vondel and Bredero. But he does this only when he is being observed. At this moment he is not being observed – except of course by the public."

A continuous lesson. Day after day the production was being slowly constructed; layer upon layer was carefully applied, as with the painting of an icon, details were added, nuances suggested, in every movement and every sentence, every word – or perhaps it was more the layer by layer uncovering of an archeological site, first with little spades, then with brushes, finally with water. It enchanted Uli. He had never experienced it like this before, and of his own manner of directing – years ago with the amateurs (some of whom would perhaps read his name in the paper, if they were still alive) – he preferred not to think at all. He had a feeling as if, during rehearsal after rehearsal, an ever finer-meshed net was being woven around him, a cocoon in which he had to pupate and change shape.

"Try this, Willem. Don't look the person you are talking to in the eye, but fix your eyes on the centre of his forehead – except when you speak as Pierre de Vries to Max and as Prospero to Miranda."

"What nonsense is that? I'm already cross-eyed as it is."

"Just try it. I think that will be very effective, both for you and for your partners."

Even after one week he no longer saw where he really was: in a bare space, a kind of gymnasium, on the floor a large sheet of brown canvas shaped like the stage. Obstacles were represented by strips of sticky tape, a few kitchen chairs and tables suggested the sparse Victorian furniture and the set pieces from *The Tempest*. Against the brick wall stood a piano on which Mr Caccini played from time to time. He would also do so during the performance, that is to say, during the rehearsals of *The Tempest*.

By the beginning of the third week they all had to know their lines, and would no longer be allowed to rehearse with script in hand. From that moment Miss Wijdenes prompted. Uli had found learning the text less of a problem than he had expected, and this, as Vogel had already predicted, was because of the more or less regular verse in which *Hurricane*, as well as the extracts from *The Tempest*, was written. In the evenings and during weekends he had done little else; if Berta wanted to watch television he went to his bedroom where he had the added bonus of being able to stand in front of the wardrobe mirror:

> *"Throughout my life you have exploited me,*
> *To you I was a play-thing, nothing more,*
> *An instrument of your purposes.*
> *My talent, so you thought, was really yours,*
> *While I did nothing but the drudgery,*
> *And all that ever mattered was yourself.*
> *You are a cipher thinking itself a muse,*
> *As well you may, with those brown velvet eyes.*
> *But think, Etienne, what will you do*
> *When presently the curtain has come down?*
> *You'll fall into a gaping pit,*
> *A hole that's in your soul."*

As he saw himself saying it ("You have to throw it out and at the same time hold it back, otherwise it won't work") it was as if that Pierre de Vries, there in the mirror, was a much more convinced and convincing person than this Uli Bouwmeester here. Uli was even a little scared of him, as if he himself was Etienne, although that was hardly possible.

The relationship between Pierre de Vries and his friend, gradually deteriorating as the first night approached, was seen against the dawning love of de Vries for the young actor Max, a situation cleverly constructed by Leo Siderius, Stella said it reminded her of two men on a beach at sunrise, engaged in a fight to the death, close to the breakers. When Uli heard her say this, he fell silent; this image, evoked in a few words by Stella, seemed to him almost

91

more beautiful than Siderius' whole play. Her remarks were also useful for his handling of his part and he could tell from the way Vogel looked that this had not escaped him either.

Everything was beginning to knit together. He had first read the play the way one reads a novel, forgetting that it wasn't an end product but a starting point; the looseness and openness of the text were necessary for the performance, the eventual work of art. Only with bad plays was there nothing for director and actors to do, bad plays were what they were, while good plays were precisely not what they were, but possibilities, suggestions, like musical scores. A concentrate, Vogel had called it. Even to those passages and moments that were, to Uli's mind, flat and unimportant, the director was able to lend a perspective or an echo. Early on in the play there was a scene in which Max Oort, hot and sweating from his at once artistic and clumsy antics as Ariel, drinks a glass of water. Pierre de Vries then says;

> *"Please leave a sip for me."*

When Uli said it with the stress more or less evenly spread, Vogel suggested,

"Why don't you say: 'Please, leave a sip for *me*'?"

The sentence suddenly cast a desperate light on the relationship between Pierre and Max; the water became their love and all at once Uli also knew at what tempo he should speak, and with what sultriness he should look at Max, as the water disappeared into his mouth. But when he was about to put accents above the words in this script, Vogel said,

"Don't bother. If you forget it, it doesn't matter."

In those weeks Uli learnt more about comedy acting than in all his previous life put together. Not only from Vogel's comments but also from the remarks made by Paul Musch, at the rehearsal of the rehearsal of *The Tempest*, in which he had to act Shakespeare in the manner of great actors of that time. Here is was the voice of Leo Siderius that was speaking:

> *"Prospero's island is the stage*
> *The audience down below, the sea."*

Everything was taken a step further here; it seems to Uli as if, in the last words of this sentence, he could hear the sea itself, Caspar Vogel, in his turn, had to explain not only to Uli but also to Paul how this idea should be understood – as a view of the theatre, in which Prospero, the magician, the master of change, became identified with the actor who was capable of unleashing emotional and intellectual tempests in the audience: turbulence in the auditorium, but also a soft rustling, or the high, unstirring silence above the sea on a summer evening in Greece . . .

> *"Although he, Shakespeare, never saw*
> *A sea except the North Sea, cold and grey."*

Mr Caccini had to improvise softly during these comments by Paul Musch (on a theme from Mendelssohn's Violin Concerto) and once he also did so during Caspar Vogel's comments, which led to a strange confusion, whereby Uli felt as though he were in a car, skidding on an icy road. But such confusions and skids were often intended by the author, and they became more clearly apparent every day, partly because he had given everyone (except Uli) his own name.

One morning, when Vogel told Stella to try and speak "like a white pebble at the bottom of a brook" it reached the point that she cried out "I'm going mad! This is impossible!", words that occurred exactly like that in one of her speeches in *Hurricane*, which Paul, amid general hilarity, immediately completed with:

> *"You're telling me*
> *To look at my own father like a whore!"*

And then, gravely, his own response:

> *"How often have not women in their dreams*
> *Slept with their fathers, Stella?"*

(In a classical pose, his right hand on his heart, left hand outstretched, middle and fourth fingers joined together; the words were, according to Vogel, a variant on a verse from Sophocles' *Oedipus Rex*.)

Uli did not join in the laughter, and he saw that she saw this. She always spoke like a white pebble at the bottom of a brook. Her reddish, pinned-up plaits. Neither had mentioned their supper at the Osiris again, as if something unpleasant had occurred there, but he had no idea what that could be. Actually, he had a feeling that she did not keep him at a distance because she didn't want to have anything more to do with him, but because he meant more to her than she liked. Nor did she know anything about the disappearance of his watch to God knows where – perhaps to Egypt – and he did not intend to tell her.

Of course Berta had noticed at once that he had lost his watch. As it was an heirloom not only of *his* father but also of *hers*, he had made up the story that after washing his hands he had left it in the cloakroom, from where it turned out to have been stolen five minutes later.

"Since when did you take your watch off when you wash your hands?"

"They were filthy."

"What with?"

"The floor. I had to crawl over the floor at the rehearsal."

This was true; in the final scene he did have to crawl over the floor. But the fact that at the age of seventy-eight he still hadn't reached the point that he no longer needed to lie (as if Berta were his jealous wife) did not strike him as odd.

"So now we don't anything left of Papa's."

"No," he said.

Towards the end of the third week, during the coffee break, Henk Aronds turned up with a model of the set. It created a shock in everyone. The moment had, of course, been carefully chosen by Caspar Vogel. The succession of rehearsals was by now acquiring an air of endlessness, as if it wouild go on like this for ever: everything becoming better all the time and more polished, but never culminating in a performance. Now, like the first day, there was suddenly a leap. Uli had assumed he would see something dark and cluttered, as he remembered the interiors of his childhood, with heavy furniture and plush curtains, draperies, carpets, vases of grey ostrich feathers. What Aronds put on the table was a snowy white set with a central design consisting of a maze-like construction of triangles, a kind of crystal, which had to serve for all the locations, corridors and stairways in the City Theatre, dressing-rooms, the rehearsal studio. Even the few grandfatherly armchairs were draped in white; only a single old-fashioned set for *The Tempest*, painted with dull green leaves, would lend colour to the scene.

At a stroke, *Hurricane* seemed a different play, not only to Uli. It lost the false naturalness that they had unintentionally allowed to seep into it in some dingy way, and by that same token it became once again clear, art, drama. The light that had suddenly been shed on it gave, that very day, a fresh impulse to the rehearsal, because everyone now had a clearer idea of the performance. But for the first time it also made Uli uncertain. Vogel had told him more than once that all was going well, especially in the scenes with Max ("Excellent, Willem, perfect; I've almost started having suspicions"), but soon it would be he and not Vogel standing there on that white stage, speaking those verses, watched by a house full of people. The leading part! He – who as a variety artiste had not even been asked to autograph the programme . . . At the same time his anxiety sharpened his eye for everything that might threaten him, and with this dramatic instinct he discovered something that had escaped even Vogel, yes, perhaps even the author.

It was a rather subtle and complicated point. He found it difficult to explain, but it eventually led to the greatest compliment he had ever received. After the first read-through the question had occurred to him (underneath the city, in the graffiti-daubed metro with the slashed seats): who was master and who was servant? In *The Tempest* Prospero was of course master of everyone and everything, ruling over both nature and people, and all kinds of other beings besides, such as spirits, of whom Ariel was the foremost. In the same way, Pierre de Vries was lord and master in *Hurricane*. He was the person giving a farewell performance of *The Tempest*, because he himself had decided so; he was the one who had founded the group ('The Dutch Theatre Company'); for the business side there was a manager (a certain Blaupot ten Cate, whose name was mentioned a few times), but he himself was the real leader. At that time, actors were still closer to jugglers and acrobats and other such freebooters than to the citizenry that watched them from up front. He knew what he was talking about.

"Yes," said Vogel, "fortunately that is different now, alas."

Nowadays, nodded Uli, they were really functionaries, like tax inspectors and policemen. But to the point. There were two things that were in conflict with Pierre de Vries' absolute dominion and that in a sense formed the core of the play and kept it moving. The first contradiction was that in *The Tempest* he had to obey someone who was in his service: the director. Of course Paul Musch made sure that the other actors remained no more than accessories, superior extras both in stage setting and in action but even so, de Vries was dependent on them. This strange relationship was expressed for instance in the scene in which Paul Musch was directing Stella as Miranda: de Vries interrupted them by imperiously snapping his fingers and asking something about his own part.

Paul, as always in smart suit and plimsolls, demonstratively cleared his throat. (For there was one thing of which Uli was absolutely incapable: he simply could not snap his fingers. No matter how many people, from Vogel to Mr Caccini, crowded around him to show him how to do it, with loud clicks like drumsticks on a wooden drum, all he was able to produce was a laughable, virtually inaudible little plock. At his suggestion, Vogel replaced the signal provisionally by "Hey Psst", which needed the approval of Leo Siderius, before he found out for himself and flew into a rage.)

The second contradiction was that de Vries' employee Max Oort – initially without wishing it or even being aware of it – had complete power over him, precisely by not giving in to his advances. This did not present him with any difficulties, for he was only interested in girls, especially in Stella Middag, to whom he was engaged in financially hopeless circumstances. If Ariel was the prisoner of Prospero, Pierre de Vries was Max Oort's. This dominated the entire play. Because the person who was keenly aware of this situation and wanted at all costs to put an end to it, was, of course, Etienne Post. He poured out his heart to Lucas van

Geest who then developed his diabolical plan. Out of love for Pierre, Etienne would try to persuade Max to exploit his power; he would have to blackmail Pierre with a public scandal, to get money, so that he would be able to marry Stella free from financial worries. The result could be that Pierre would begin to hate Max and that all would be well again between Pierre and himself. After that, he would make sure, by means of further blackmail, that the first blackmail came to nothing. He, Lucas, also had a stake in the affair: he was in love with Stella too, and if she found out what a dirty blackmailer her fiancé was, she wouldn't want to have any more to do with him, and then he, Lucas, could welcome her with loving arms. Out of love for Stella, Max gradually began to give Etienne's vicious proposal serious consideration, but half an hour before the opening of the first night, de Vries learnt the whole story from Stella, whose conscience pricked her. Pierre de Vries brought Max to his senses by warning him that he would lose Stella, and the result would not be marriage but imprisonment. Then, incensed, already half-dressed for his part, he returned to his own dressing-room, but when, a moment later, Etienne entered, tipsy and with a lopsided grin, his rage took on yet more dramatic forms.

"I thought you couldn't remember intrigues," laughed Vogel.

"Don't confuse me. This is how the plot fits together. But shouldn't there be another scene, in which those two powerful powerless men, Paul Musch and Max Oort, come to an agreement in some way? Wouldn't that clarify matters? It would also give more depth to Paul's role. I don't quite know how, I'm not a writer. The ending is very effective as it is, with that tableau vivant of Pierre de Vries in his dressing-room, maybe you ought not to touch that. But on the other hand, there might be scope for some sort of addendum, a kind of epilogue between Paul and Max, which would suddenly place the play in a new perspective: that of power relations."

As soon as he had finished speaking, he thought it was far-fetched nonsense. He shrugged his shoulders, but Vogel said: "Well, well, that is quite something, Willem. You rise above yourself, to true Bouwmeester-heights."

Uli threw a quick glance at Stella; when he read also on the faces of the others that Vogel had spoken only half in jest, something happened that had not happened for years: he blushed.

"Maybe it's all a load of tommyrot," he said, bowed his head and searched his pockets for cigars, except the pocket in which he kept them.

Maybe. But maybe not. At any rate it was worthy of top-level debate.

2
The Phantom Castle of the Night

Michael arrived with the message that Leo Siderius could receive them only on Sunday afternoon from ten minutes to three until twenty minutes to four. As he lived in Bijlmer – the latest, most south-easterly and most hideous extension of Amsterdam, so attractively begun. Uli was met at the bus terminus by Caspar Vogel, who was sitting in his small black car reading an English newspaper. His style of driving was quick-tempered, quite out of keeping with his calm bearing during rehearsals. Stepping on the gas, braking hard, bending forward over the steering wheel, looking agitatedly to left and right, he wriggled through the traffic like a toddler squeezing between the legs of adults in order to get a front line view of the ceremonial entry of St Nicholas. Uneasily Uli held on to the edge of the dashboard and listened to the sombre news that Michael had just given Vogel on the phone.

The day before yesterday, the Theatre Commission of the Arts Council had held a meeting from which it had been leaked that the survival of the Authors' Theatre was at risk. It was unbelievable! Just think, what they hadn't done over the last ten years. Who had tried, for the first time since the seventeenth century, to regenerate the art of play-writing in this country? They had. And who had consistently kept that up? They had. Sure, there was an economic crisis, everybody had to economise, but that didn't automatically mean that they had to economise on the arts, as was mindlessly assumed by everybody. Quite the contrary! What did the public want? Bread and circuses. So if there was less bread there had to be more circuses. Bread and circuses were inversely related, the arts budget ought to be doubled, as it was in France (it was, by the way, no coincidence that the Dutch theatre had never known better days than during the reign of King Louis Napoleon). But the political grocers in this land of pondweed would never understand that; to them art was frippery at best, you couldn't buy anything with it, you couldn't exchange it for anything. They were and remained iconoclasts, those cheeseheads. Admittedly, the last two seasons had been slack, they were in a depression, Bidermann wasn't doing too well either, and they had had some bad luck, as with that Grabbe thing for which the staging had been almost ready. And how had they coped? Within the shortest possible time Siderius had written *Hurricane* to fill the gap. What other company could have managed that? Any other company would have picked a Pinter or a Chekov off the shelf. It was even a kind of counterpart to *The Killjoy* by Bidermann-Romijn, because the authors were obviously spurring each other on to better and better achievements. And mark my words: now the fat was in the fire. You could be sure everybody was after the Kosmos, they couldn't wait to take over *their* theatre. Willem would soon find out what all the various cliques would have to say about *Hurricane*.

"What then?"

"Oh, anything. That the play is quite interesting as a celebration of dramatic art, or some rubbish like that, though only moderately so, but that the production is an impotent and reactionary attempt to breathe new life into an old style of acting, on a set copied from the German theatre of eight years ago, from photographs in *Theater Heute*, and that the Authors' Theatre is an outdated group that has had its day, and so on and so forth."

"And none of that is true?"

"Of course none of that is true. But then we're not a producers' theatre, and we're not a dramatists' theatre, not to mention the worst of all, an actors' theatre. Anyway, we'll see, maybe it will all blow over. The authors mustn't be forgotten either, they like to be involved sometimes." Vogel leaned forward and looked up, so that the brim of his hat knocked against the windscreen and briefly tipped up at the back. "At any rate, Siderius has sent us the right weather."

Grey clouds with jagged edges chased through a bright blue sky, one moment the sun was out, a moment later a squally shower hit the windscreen, shadows drifted about the colossal concrete buildings that were everywhere, fans of sunlight unfolded like pictures in a devotional book, and now and again a super-mundane fragment of rainbow appeared. "Grunder", "Fleerde", "Egeldonk", were the barbaric names of the nightmares to which architects, with hollow laughter, had here given shape. The apartment blocks looked like skyscrapers that, at the moment of being blown up and fracturing in two or three places, had been caught and laid flat on their sides. Vogel had visited Siderius a couple of times before, but the route was impossible to remember. After repeated enquires from solitary, recoiling passers-by, they finally found the "Grobben" complex where they had to be.

In the parking area (where , on television, cars returning from the yacht basin shriek around the concrete pillars and lethal shots are fired, but where now only a few black youngsters wearing headphones are roller skating) they took the lift. Its interior was covered with outbursts of typographical inspiration in primary colours, most of them the creations of two mentally sick scholars, Dr Smurry and Dr Funk.

"Waiting for the H-bomb," said Vogel as they walked along the windy walkway on the seventh floor, pointing with a curt movement of his chin at the concrete landscape over which all the seasons were present simultaneously, from the precise light of Jan van Goyen to the obscure glimmer of another Jan (*Jean*, actually) – Toorop. At a door without a nameplate he rang the bell. It was five minutes to three.

But even after three attempts there was still no movement. Within, the curtains were closed.

"Not again. I bet you he's in. Leo! Open up, for God's sake." With a key he tapped sharply against the window. "The idiot. Come on, let's phone from somewhere. He's obviously punishing us because we're five minutes late."

But when Uli, already by the swing door to the stairs and lift, looked back, he saw on Siderius' doorstep – where one would expect to see feet – a face peering at them. As they walked back, a virtually bald-shaven, boyish man got up, dressed in a ragged pullover, his filthy bare feet in sandals.

Caspar's name was Vogel, bird, but the bird's face was Siderius': a beak and two chilly blue eyes. Legs like stilts in tight woollen trousers. When Uli shook his hand he felt uncertain, as if not he but the other was half a century older. The writer looked into his bad eye and kept doing so – perhaps to punish him for the fact that he might have discovered shortcomings in his play. He behaved as if he had known Uli for years. Before letting them in, he took a step forward, tweaked the Sunday paper out of Vogel's pocket and threw it over the balustrade.

"No newspapers in my house," he said in a soft, husky voice.

The room into which they were shown had hardly been changed since the builders had left. Everything sounded hollow, the only furnishing fabric being the drawn curtains. Floors and walls of ribbed grey concrete, from the ceiling a bare bulb burning; a trestle with books and papers, and kitchen table with some food, that was about all. Above the trestle a poster had been stuck to the wall with sticky tape that had come loose along one side: a huge picture of Einstein waggishly sticking out his tongue at the photographer. On the opposite wall hung a large sheet of faded paper covered in a maze of red and green lines made up of dots, dashes, crosses and other signs and combinations. Uli recognised it at once as a sewing pattern such as Berta sometimes spread out on the floor on top of sheets of thin paper, following the lines with a toothed wheel on a stem, cutting out the resulting shapes, pinning them onto lengths of cloth, cutting and sewing – until another garment too hideous for words had been produced. There was one chair, but Uli was not invited to sit on it.

"Say what you have to say," said Siderius. He briefly rolled up his eyes as far as they would go, as if trying to make them turn somersaults in their sockets.

By way of introduction Vogel started to talk about the Theatre Commission of the Arts Council – but no sooner were the words out than Siderius pulled a face as if he had been struck by as many drops of vitriol.

"Shut up, I have plenty of other things to worry about. You sort it out yourselves. If that's what you've come for you can buzz off again."

"It could have drastic consequences for you too."

" Let Molly sort it out, or Jan."

Vogel made an inviting gesture to Uli, but Uli couldn't really remember what it was all about.

"I think you'd better explain it."

Vogel obliged promptly and lucidly, Uli listened with a feeling of pride, as he looked at Siderius who stood leaning against the wall beside the trestle. When Vogel had finished, Siderius said with an expressionless face, "What I have written I have written."

"There you are," said Vogel.

"You," said Siderius to Uli, "must do nothing else except humbly obey the commandments, just like Jesus of Nazareth. You are an actor. Until heaven and earth perish, not one jot or tittle of the law shall pass, until all has been accomplished."

With open mouth Uli started at him. The fellow was stark staring mad.

"That's more like it," said Vogel, with a laugh, "Was Jesus an actor?"

"Didn't you know?" asked Siderius; he looked genuinely surprised. "True, he once wrote with his finger in the sand, but that didn't amount to much. He played a part, that of the Christ – the only one to do so, actually, the others couldn't do anything except what they did, that's why his tomb was empty. He rose from the dead, but he didn't ascend into heaven, he went back to his company in the monastery where the author of the play was abbot. He became a gardener there and at a ripe old age he died peacefully in his sleep. That is the great chameleonic principle that dominates the world. You must have seen chameleons in the zoo," he said to Uli, "belonging to the highly philosophical family of salamanders, lizards, iguanas and other fairly eternal creatures? Now *they* are good at standing still," he nodded with a chuckle. "Their tails curled up like watch springs. Things are often the opposite of what people think. Did you know, for instance, that grass isn't green?"

"I beg your pardon?" asked Uli.

"Grass absorbs from the sun all the wavelengths of light except those of the colour green, it bounces those back. It doesn't want to have anything to do with those. So grass is red, orange, yellow, blue, indigo, violet, everything except green."

"Well, if you look at it that way . . ."

"An epilogue . . ." said Siderius, boring his gaze into Uli's bad eye – "do you know what is the epilogue of my play? Everything that happens after the curtain has fallen, until the end of time. Reality has never been anything else except a commentary on art, *Quod scripsi scripsi*. Gentlemen, it has been a pleasure." He pushed himself away from the wall and bent over his papers. Did he mean them to leave again already? Uli looked questioningly at Vogel.

"Take it easy," said Vogel, "we'll leave you your dignity, don't worry. But we're looking at it from a different viewpoint from yours, we have to make sure your play gets across to the public. At the read-through I spun them a fairly abstract yarn, a kind of interpretation, because we can't work otherwise."

"I'm glad I wasn't there."

"Your absence was indeed noticed. Why don't you drop in one of these days?"

"And that yarn of yours," said Siderius, ignoring the remark, "was about imagination and reality."

"That's your own fault."

"But that the so-called reality is in itself a question of imagination, that escaped you."

A grin appeared on Vogel's face. "I have to disappoint you. "

Uli remembered the hissing of the hot iron – how did it go again? These two gentlemen were crossing swords, as in a costume play. Siderius had just received an elegant touché and he now looked at his guests by turns, he wanted to say something but was still brooding on it, the movement of his eyes contained no seeing but thinking. Vogel, meanwhile, basked contentedly in his triumph; he repositioned his hat slightly, so that Uli (with a feeling as though it was indecent) caught for the first time a glimpse of his balding skull – that baldness that did not threaten him at all. What was he doing here, anyway? He in his grey suit and his grey tie in this bare apartment, in the company of a fellow in black with a hat on, and an eccentric in sandals with a mug like a fanatical monk talking rot. He had never known such people before, maybe they

104

hadn't even existed in his time, maybe they weren't people at all, but something much more monstrous.

"If you think there's something lacking, as you obviously do," said Siderius slowly, "how about adding something to the performance then, rather than to the text?"

"Explain yourself," said Vogel, with a broad gesture.

"Real reality, okay? Put something into your performance which doesn't act a part but which is really and completely itself."

"Gerda from the cloakroom, for instance."

"Oh no, she could never manage that, she'd immediately start acting too. Nobody could manage that."

"So?"

"So you must take an animal."

"Have mercy," said Vogel and clasped his hands imploringly. "Don't do that to me. Animals on stage, they wreck everything, I don't need to tell you that. One moth fluttering around a spot, not even Shakespeare can cope with that."

"And why is that?"

"Because it isn't art but reality. I'd rather have two rearing extras in a donkey suit than one real bluebottle."

"And what were you talking about just now? Weren't you talking about imagination and reality?"

"What's the poor beast supposed to do then, apart from jeopardising the performance?"

"The beast must be the escape route – the tunnel under the wall – to reality. The soil is nowhere so fertile as on the other side of the cemetery wall. The animal doesn't remain simply an animal on the stage."

Vogel gave him a long look. "Escape route?" he repeated. "What are you talking about? Whose escape? Where to?" And in a different tone: "What exactly do you want, Leo?"

"Aha, now you're talking. What exactly do I want?" Siderius raised one arm, and as his eyes swivelled up again he declaimed hoarsely,

> "Accoutred in the harness of a fiery light
> I'll batter down the phantom castle of the night."

"Goodness. Is that from your new play?"

"Those alexandrines," said Siderius scornfully, "were written two hundred and fifty years ago by Willem van Swaanenburg, whom you have never heard of, because you're a couple of useless knuckle-heads."

Were they both mad? Were they conspiring against him with some sick joke? Uli looked suspiciously from the one to the other. Something that he was unable to see through was being fought out here, while at the same time he had the dull feeling that he himself was the stake in this contest. Suddenly he felt a faint cramp in his stomach, perhaps from standing up for such a long time, and he asked where the lavatory was. To his surprise and relief there was paper. When he returned to the room and sat down in the chair, Vogel had already surrendered Siderius' beastly suggestion.

"What a privilege it is to be able to co-operate so closely with a writer," he sighed. He looked resignedly at Siderius, "And what kind of animal did you have in mind?"

"Well, look, you mustn't take it personally, but a bird would clearly be no good. I mean, a bird may be the highest there is, but a bird in a cage or a tame crow, they're almost actors themselves. No, let's keep it simple. Pierre and Etienne have a dog. So the dog represents the absolute otherness, the totally antipodal: namely, reality."

"We could take an emu," said Uli insolently.

Vogel burst into a laugh but Siderius gave him a measured look.

"You must understand, Mr Building Master," he said, "that if you enter with a dog on a lead, your task as an actor is far more difficult than if you were playing opposite your legendary relation."

"Anyway," said Vogel, "if you really wanted to batter down the phantom castle of the night, you'd have to *kill* an animal. Suppose you have someone cut a pig's throat or strangle a chicken or tread on a frog or swat a fly . . . it doesn't matter what. Then a live being dies a real death, his real and only death, and who has done it? The character in the play or the actor interpreting the character?"

"The one you can thrash for it."

"There you are!" Vogel made a gesture that the point had been proved. "In that thrashing the actor coincides with the character.

106

Then art has become reality and is therefore destroyed. End of civilisation."

"Sometimes," said Siderius to Uli with ironic confidentiality, "even quite intelligent people discover things you yourself had already forgotten again long ago, they're so self-evident. You yourself are already a long way ahead by then. Have you ever thought, for instance, why the Greeks knew the wheel but not the zero, and the Mayas knew the zero but not the wheel?"

"If I know what you're getting at I'm a bean."

"Beans," said Siderius. "Now there's another thing you've got to be careful with, according to Pythagoras. Probably because they make you fart."

"Look here, are you having me on, or what?"

Siderius went on looking at him pensively. Then, without transition, he said pityingly, "Poor character . . ."

Uli looked at Vogel. "Is he talking to me?"

"You never know with him," said Vogel. The unexpected twists and turns in Siderius' thought processes, like stones bouncing down a mountainside, did not seem to surprise him.

"That is the big question," said Siderius. "That is exactly what I am trying to find out. But in order to do so it is necessary for my –"

He was interrupted by a loud report in the concrete beside the window, but only the two guests, startled, looked in the direction of the curtain.

"What was that?" asked Vogel.

"They're shooting again. Don't take any notice. They always miss."

"They're *shooting* again?" Vogel repeated, his face tense. "Why the hell should anybody be shooting at you?"

For the first time, a real smile appeared on Siderius' face, a broad smile of large white teeth.

"Do you think I am not important enough to be shot at?"

"Oh, come on, Leo, be serious now. Where are they shooting from?"

"Who can say? I'll find out sooner or later."

"Shouldn't you call the police?"

The writer spat on the floor and spread the spittle with his sandal.

107

"Maybe it's the police that are doing the shooting."

"Go on," said Uli.

"Let's not talk about it any more. Where was I? Oh yes, the meaning of language."

Uli didn't think that was where he was at all, but he decided to let it pass. He would be glad to get away from here and never have to see this nutcase ever again.

"So you must try to find the rhythm of the whole play in every sentence, Mr Architectus. The words should not be your starting point but the play as a whole. The smallest unit is not the word but the sentence: that is the atom." Nodding, he looked at Vogel. "I think what I am saying now is not at all bad."

"Oh yes, you'd better write it all down."

"Do you know what is wrong with me? I don't listen to myself enough. If I did, I would be even more sensible than I am. As it is, I am one of the most sensible people I know."

"I always had the impression you were living here as a recluse."

"Each speech," Siderius turned to Uli again, "is a molecule; a sentence is an atom and the words are the protons and the neutrons in the nucleus. The punctuation marks are, of course, the electrons, any child would know that, and the letters are the quarks."

"Quark," said Uli, "my sister always eats that. Ghastly stuff."

Siderius shook his head. "You get everything mixed up. No that kind of quark, that's curds. Do you have a dog?"

"Me?" asked Uli, taken aback by the question. "Why? Well er . . . wait a minute," he said, "I do actually have a dog, that is to say, my sister has one. A right little monster he is, too, but I'm not having him bumped off for all that."

"No animals are bumped off in my plays. Who do you think you're dealing with? A peddler in emotions?"

"All right, all right. I don't mind. Better a dog that knows me, any day. But since you ask – who am I dealing with?"

Siderius raised one forefinger and said, relishing the words, *"Persona ad catastropham machinata!"*

Uli shrugged his shoulders. "I don't understand dog latin."

"Pity," said Siderius. "Otherwise you would have known that

108

tempus doesn't only mean 'the weather' and 'the tempest' and 'hurricane', but also 'time'."

"I can't see why you're shooting all that at me."

"We weren't going to talk about shooting any more."

"Well," sighed Vogel, "at least the dog is white. That's a lucky hit, anyway."

Siderius pressed the palms of his hands against his temples, as if he suddenly had a headache. The audience had some to an end. Uli got up and they took their leave, the writer, the director and the actor. When the visitors were already outside on the walkway, Siderius rolled his eyes heavenward and said to Uli:

"I intend to come to the first night."

"I am most honoured."

"Oh, by the way," said Vogel, "I nearly forgot." In a few words he explained Uli's digital problem, provisionally solved by "Hey Psst". Could they keep it that way?

Siderius stared at him for a long time as if he were dealing with a lunatic. "So you really think," he said finally, "that you can simply parachute a spondee into a mystery play of this sort, if you just happen to feel like it? Don't you realise the whole thing would be put out of joint? Are you really such a blockhead? It is in the *structure* that the secret is contained. Myths aren't just fiddle-faddle!" he exclaimed. "This project is a machine, a cyclotron in which everything, even the angström listens. Hey psst . . . How did you get that into your head! Oh la la, to be or not to be, that is the question – I suppose that would be all right too, eh, to your way of thinking? Rubbish you are, the lot of you."

"Come on, Leo, don't make such a fuss about it. I expect we'll have to say 'heel' to that dog of yours as well, from time to time."

"Nothing. Not a word. He must only *be* there. And for the rest, don't talk twaddle like a headless hen. I beg your pardon, don't let me insult poultry, at least they speak fluent English, *talk talk talk*." He took a step back and slammed the door shut.

All round them stood the apartment buildings like the walls of south European cemeteries. Uneasily, feeling himself to be a target, Uli looked about and said, "Let's get out of here. I'm dying for a beer."

3

A Wingbeat

That evening in bed (the house surrounded by the silence of the polder), the rehearsal and the characters and the words still would not leave him; he had to work hard even in his sleep. For a while he turned the visit to Siderius over and over in his mind, then he impatiently switched off his bedside lamp. Writers were crazy, that was proved by the fact that they had become writers in the first place.

As the contours of his bedroom loomed faintly in the darkness, he saw, mingled with them in the remembered neon light of the rehearsal studio, Vogel telling Paul how, as Paul Musch, he should tell Pierre de Vries how to say his lines:

"No, Paul, more politely, more cautiously, Pierre de Vries is God. Go on: 'This must' . . ."

> *"This must be said more solemnly, more gravely,*
> *Try it again."*

And then he himself, to Miranda:

> *"Tis time*
> *I should inform thee farther. Lend thy hand*
> *and pluck thee from . . ."*

". . . no, dammit, how does it go again?" he pulled a face, while Paul and Stella started laughing.

"Listen," said Vogel, "you are supposed to say: 'Lend thy hand and pluck my magic garment from me.' But you get into a muddle, that's to say, Pierre de Vries gets into a muddle and says, 'Lend me thy hand and pluck me from . . .' Try again."

He heard Berta slowly coming up the stairs with tired legs. He himself had not bothered to watch through to the end the old

110

dubbed American film on German television; in his head there was room for only one play: *Hurricane*.

> *"'Tis time*
> *I should inform thee farther. Lend me thy hand*
> *To pluck me from . . .*
> *No dammit!"*

"Good! Good!" called Vogel.

Stella began to laugh, this time as Stella.

> *"Stop*
> *That stupid cackle, or you'll get the sack,*
> *You third-rate baggage! Lend thy hand*
> *And pluck my magic garment from me!"*

Stella as Stella as Miranda helped him out of his imaginary magic mantle which at this stage of the rehearsals Pierre de Vries was not yet wearing (any more than Uli was wearing Pierre's clothes) – out of his talent, so to speak. Not present, yet present, the magic mantle slid from his shoulders to the floor.

> *"So!*
> *Lie there, my Art!"*

whereupon Paul Musch:

> *"Stay briefly in that pose*
> *And look down at the cloak. You are now*
> *A simple man again."*

"Okay, leave it there," said Vogel. "That was perfect."

Uli closed his eyes. Okay, leave it, perfect. Everything was going well. Thy hand to pluck me from . . . thy hand to pluck from me . . . my hand to pluck thee from . . . Vogel stood up. Coffee break. So much work, so much effort, necessary to perfect such a small part of any random play in any random theatre – first Siderius', then theirs. So much trouble, so much ingenuity, so much time, for even the smallest item. A fountain pen, a chair, a light bulb, the uncompromising, rusty part of a machine on a scrap heap behind a factory. How wonderful was professionalism. That was why vandalism was such a disgrace, professional vandalism most of all, warfare, wholesale demolition. You ought to be

111

allowed to destroy only the things you had made yourself, or could make yourself. Maybe many people today thought that things came into existence all by themselves, that they just grew, as in nature. In that case it would probably soon be war again. They were so stupid, they had no idea. (And Uli? What ideas did he have? Was he a tragic philosopher half asleep?) There was still that rushing of blood in his ears. Seventy-eight. No one knew what that meant. To yourself you hadn't changed but there were fewer and fewer things you could talk about; more and more often silence was imposed upon you. There was too much, you didn't know where to begin. Silence rose from the ground. Marsh gas. In the canteen, Stella, Stella Starlight, asked him if he wanted an almond cake with his coffee. Almond cake, Willem? Almond cake, yes please, how nice, and now he suddenly sees something rising, slowly, slowly . . . Clumping about on the landing, Berta flushed the lavatory and with a painful feeling in his head it went away, but then it was there again: rising stones, a slowly rising wall, grey, dripping blocks of stone, or is he himself sinking? He can see it through a round window, a porthole of course, just under the sill, by the heavy brass bolt, level with his navel, water alongside. Wait, the ship lies in a lock, on the Rhine, or are there no locks in the Rhine? (The journey up-river to the Pfaltz, from Mainz – where they had given a performance – to Heidelberg, navigating between the wrecks of ships and bridges, on either side, on the fairy-tale banks, smouldering cities that were linked by looped-together ferry boats lurching on the current; the water full of mines and unexploded shells, according to the fat steward, who looked exactly like Goering and was nicknamed "Herr Reichsmarshall", and yet – singing. *Nur nicht aus Liebe weinen* . . ., the girls in the cabins, looking up in mock surprise as they fastened a stocking to a suspender, Riesling, Trockenbeerenauslese on the stamping ship with the water rushing in the paddles left and right . . .) And then the arrival. Not a moment to spare. "Frederik Rozenveld!" Whipping round a corner and there is the castle. Massive towers and a flight of windows, at the far end of extensive geometrical gardens, in the dewy morning, but a moment later everything is becoming overgrown so that he cannot move forward in the dank and steamy undergrowth of shrubs and lianas and mouldy tree trunks. When all that has vanished – perhaps because Siderius slams down a shimmering aluminium aircraft case on the table, his legs are still stuck fast in the earth. Overture and beginners! Last call! Work to be done. But what? Which part? The Marriage. What marriage? he turns away with a grin: "Can't you make it, grandpa?" An unbearable weariness comes over him, he wants to sleep, but it is impossible in the heart-rending caterwauling that rises from the whitewashed courtyard. Stepping aside in order to evade passing shadows he tries to remember the text, but then everything slides into a heap like a game of draughts when some bastard suddenly tips up the board. After a laborious detour through the loft of a dilapidated house, bending his head to avoid age-old rafters through which the sky is visible in large cracks between the roof tiles, sinking up to his ankles in sticky bird's muck, he hears it again: "Try it again, Pierre." Is there no one who can help him – what is it all about? In a voice half speaking aloud and half whispering someone says, "A helper has just died in Ireland." A moment later he is outside, thank God, in a town square. By the plinth of the statue of the maritime hero flanked by bronze lions, a little girl in a green dress and white collar dances to the sombre rhythm of those words, like a doll, without bending her knees and with stiffly lowered arms. He wants to embrace her, but the doom that hangs in the air increases fast, as in the still moments between the first flashes of lightning in the rumbling violet clouds and the clattering rain. "Do something, Willem." Straining himself to the utmost, he sees a glimpse of the bar in the Cellar, the meal of ashes, the rattling cash register with the till jumping towards him, then Vogel pushes him forward through a clammy subterranean corridor at the end of which he is forced to turn, and hits his back resoundingly against a bolted metal door behind which something is waiting for him, something hideous that will destroy him . . .

He rose like a fish and woke up, but without opening his eyes. Exhausted he lay on his back, filled with anxious thoughts. Nothing, it all led to nothing. A life like a sagging garden shed, crammed with discarded junk, rusty tools, and at the end: a part with a part in it. The squib doesn't go off, lies hissing, and finally

113

produces a little plop. He was being used, Berta was right, but not in the way she thought; when it was all over they would drop him and forget him, and even if the performance wasn't a flop, it would be a mere incident, like a pig with two heads, at the fairground long ago. It would have been better if he had dozed off unnoticed here in the polder, forgotten almost by himself. What was he to do after the last performance? Surely life couldn't simply go back to what it had been before? Should he perhaps go straight to the Old People's Home with Berta? The future was like a road terminating abruptly at the edge of an abyss, such as you saw in photographs of landslides. He listened for a moment to an aircraft flying very high overhead (without dropping bombs), turned over on his side and heard the slow beat of his heart. Unlike so many people, he wasn't afraid of it; maybe that was why he had lived so long. He opened his eyes and saw Stella before him in the dark. He must put her altogether out of his mind. Once he had asked her casually if she'd like to come for a drink but luckily she had said that unfortunately she had no time. (Olga had invited him to drop in some time at her place, but he had not done so.) He tried to imagine he was the same age as Stella, and how an eighty-year-old man would go about courting her.

He switched on the reading lamp and got out of bed. By the door he turned on the big light, took off his pyjamas and stood naked in front of the mirror. A photograph from the collection of a mentally disturbed woman photographer. Once upon a time his hair had been dark blond, almost black; now this could be surmised only from his drab pubic hair which had lost its frizziness. His ancient, sunken mouth; what should be inside it was now grinning in the glass beside the bed. The skin of his face was still taut and healthy between the wrinkles, but his neck, his elbows, his knees, everything that had to turn and bend, hung about him like pallid rags. On his shins there were mauve patches, a beautiful colour in itself but not in those places.

"Well, what can you expect?" he mumbled.

Disgusting it was, ridiculous, it ought to be put an end to. He crawled back into bed, stuck one hand inside his pyjama trousers and clasped it around his penis – not because he had, would have or

114

wanted to have an erection, but more by way of comfort, the way one nurses a fledgling fallen out of the nest. He knew that in his room there was now that acrid smell, which he could not smell at this moment but which he always noticed after having been to the lavatory in the night.

No, the night is no friend of optimism. He knew that the sun, when it appeared above the horizon, would unaccountably chase away his gloom like the morning mist, yet this awareness had no influence as long as it was night.

Awareness – the weakest of all the forces.

"You look tired," said Berta at breakfast-time.

"I've been dreaming so much of late. They say sleep is refreshing, well, you can forget that. It takes me all morning to recover from all those dreams. I never used to dream."

"What did you dream about?"

He tried to think.

"I can't remember. All kinds of things." They had vanished for ever. No one would ever know.

(One moment. So the world does not consist only of visible events – seen or unseen – but also of that myriad of necessary dreams that the sun allows to exist on the shadowed side of the earth and drags without interruption across the surface of the planet, then, in the circumambulating morning, causing them to evaporate again like the dew. In the daylight, only art can preserve that nocturnal, pearly condensate. And in all the universe this takes place only on this one celestial body, in this one solar system. This by way of parenthesis.)

Uli bent over the newspaper, stopped chewing and said, "La Charlotte is dead. Lived till ninety-six."

"What! Was she still alive? Good heavens."

La Charlotte was a diva from a generation of actors preceding their own. Uli vaguely remembered meeting her when he was a boy; he had never seen her on the stage. He read in the obituary, which called her "the last of the great", that at the early age of eighteen she had been celebrated (as Puck). He wiped his mouth and passed the paper to Berta.

"Well," she said after reading the article, "at least Madame wasn't a flower broken in the bud. They used to say Papa knew her well."

Uli did not respond. Leaning back, his second cup of coffee in front of him, he looked at the poodle lying curled up in its basket, fast asleep. After a while he spoke.

"Look at that animal. Not much of a life, is it."

Berta looked at the dog.

"What's wrong with it? He's comfy enough lying there."

"Yes, just lying there all the time."

"What do you mean? Don't I look after him properly? Lots of people would be only too glad to have a life like his." She gave him a probing look. "Since when have you been taking an interest in Joost?"

With a jot the dog lifted his head and looked in her direction.

"Look how he reacts. You've only got to mention his name. The poor thing misses a lot in life, you can take that from me. What has he seen of the world? The house, the garden, a few streets, that's about it. A really big city, for instance, he has never seen."

"What are you waffling on about, Uli? You have to be off, you'll miss your bus in a minute."

"Yes," said Uli, looking at his wrist, but there was no longer a watch on it. He stood up. "I think I'll take Joost with me today."

Joost leapt out of his basket, straightened his front legs as far forward as possible, pushing his rump upward, then stretched his hind legs, dragging them along the floor a little way, shook himself, and come towards Uli.

Berta narrowed her eyes. "You're up to something, you are. Out with it! Were you thinking of letting him loose there, so you'd be rid of him at last, and then tell me he ran away?"

"Sometimes dogs do actually *pull* themselves loose," said Uli, half under his breath, suddenly with a faintly threatening look in his eyes. (Maybe Sebastian was still running about somewhere, trailing his lead behind him, in Tibet or China.)

As he stuffed his papers into his briefcase, he thought hard. He had to choose now; their own dog, but with Berta, or a strange animal. It was unthinkable that she would allow him to take the

116

poodle on his own, even if she knew what it was for; but as Joost's impresario it would be impossible to get rid of her at rehearsals. He couldn't really blame her, she too didn't have much left in life; but at the same time he was afraid he would be inhibited by her, who knew him through and through, watching everything he did. And it was all his own stupid fault. If he hadn't realised that supposedly profound nonsense about power and powerlessness, they wouldn't have gone to see Siderius and nothing would have happened.

"All right then," he sighed, "get your wig on, put that mutt on its lead and come with me. I'll tell you all about it on the way."

To say that Berta behaved as the dog's impresario was putting it mildly. She revealed herself as the terrible mother of a child prodigy (to be compared only with the widows of some writers) who has suddenly been allowed a chance to indulge her own ambitions through a defenceless creature. Immediately on that first morning she buttonholed Michael and insisted on a contract for Joost, including travelling and living expenses. The business manager smiled with pursed lips while his Anglo-Saxon refinement reached unrivalled heights. When he told Uli, during the lunch break, that his sister had quite correctly insisted on a businesslike arrangement with regard to the canine collaboration, the leading man wished himself a thousand miles away. It didn't take long before everyone knew about Berta's resolute action, but if Uli had thought he would therefore be a laughing stock he was mistaken; Lucas even came to congratulate him on the originality of his sister. At a stroke, the old woman was well on her way to popularity. That she called him Uli was also considered amusing, but fortunately no one copied her. He was the only person to notice the manner in which she looked at him when she found that here he was "Willem" to everyone.

The first two days of Berta's presence were still spent in the rehearsal studio, where she sat in a cane chair beside the piano, Joost on her lap. Vogel had not quite worked out for himself how the dog could best be fitted into the production. Together with Uli, he tried out a number of possibilities, each time to little effect.

"What would you say," said Paul petulantly, "if we asked Siderius to change the title – to *Hurricanine*?"

Only when Vogel tried letting Etienne be the main owner of the dog, did the idea begin to take on some form. The first few times that Etienne picked up the dog's lead, Joost braced all his legs and had to be dragged half strangled across the canvas mat, amid cries from Berta. Only with the aid of sausage fetched from the canteen by Trudy could a more convincing performance be coaxed out of him. At this turn of events, Uli reflected not without melancholy that they might just as well have taken any other dog, and that Berta's presence had therefore not been necessary. But such was life. In order to make a good impression, she even had Joost trimmed, so that he looked as if he had taken off a pair of pants and was left with only some ridiculous little knobs of hair on his legs and at the tip of his tail.

Everything else also went as it usually does in life. It seemed as though the merriment occasioned by all this messing about was not altogether untainted. Unlike authors (barring talented exceptions) actors are always prepared to laugh themselves limp, but the atmosphere of innocence that had prevailed hitherto showed signs of fading. This was not exclusively, not even chiefly, because of the uncertainty about the subsidy, in spite of all the discussions in the coffee room and at the Tivoli; (although the Theatre Commission had indeed returned an adverse recommendation to the Minister); no, the rehearsals had now entered their penultimate week and suddenly the day of the first night had come into sight, like death on one's fortieth birthday, even though it may still be a long way ahead. When Uli thought of next Friday, creeping closer like a snake towards a rabbit, he was sometimes struck by a sudden chill of anxiety, something like a large black wingbeat.

This was more than stage fright; it seemed not so much inside as outside him. Not that he believed in angels, he didn't believe in anything or anyone; no, he really *saw* something black beating its wings at the edge of his field of vision, but when he looked sideways everything was normal. No metaphysical crack in reality, nothing, Berta beside him in the bus, the white poodle on her lap, the people in the metro, arriving morosely from the Bijlmer, the rehearsal studio in harsh, positivistic light. Everything was shut tight.

118

4
Thespis' Chariot

On Wednesday the third of November the rehearsal studio also had become part of the past. When he and Berta entered that morning, they saw only a Turk or Moroccan with a vacuum cleaner. The canvas floor covering had vanished as well.

"Dunno."

Brother and sister looked at each other.

"It was only a dream," said Berta.

But it was simply that another leap had been taken, just like the time when Aronds had presented his maquette. New, white as the tip of an iceberg, they saw the structure on the stage as they entered the auditorium. Uli had not been back there since the evening he had seen *The Killjoy*, any more than the Pope visits St Peter's when he has nothing to do there. Only now did he see what the theatre, fully lit and empty, actually looked like. The woodwork of the smallish semi-circular auditorium was painted blood-red; over each of the five entrances burned the word EXIT. The most striking feature was the large sheet of canvas spread by way of ceiling above the upper circle. It hung as a celestial canopy, concave, painted with stars, moons and planets on an azure background, above the amphitheatre, lending it an air of mystery, perhaps precisely because it was so obviously a painted cloth. Above the proscenium, the red curtains of which were at present raised, there was a circle with a pastel-coloured painting of Atlas in it, carrying the earth on his shoulders. Uli pointed at it and said,

"Do you remember the coalmen with slit bags on their heads, like black monks but with bright blue eyes, and creaking sacks of coke on their backs?"

119

"I always thought," said Berta, "that the best thing was when they came out of the house with an empty sack and let it sail flat onto the pavement, always exactly on top of the other sacks. Never crooked."

"Yes," laughed Uli. "Good God, how old we are."

Slowly they walked towards the front. Only now was Thespis's chariot properly getting under way. (That is to say, during a performance it was standing still, of course, but for once the opposite was true; it would soon break the sound barrier.) On the stage there were technicians walking back and forth, whom Uli had got to know superficially but had so far had no dealings with. The stage manager, a greying man approaching sixty, with a large bunch of keys hanging from his belt, was standing centre-stage and called out instructions to someone high up on the bridge in the flies, whence came a muffled answer, unintelligible because of hammering in the wings. Aronds was walking around with a pot of white paint and a brush, touching up damaged spots, a technician was tinkering at a set piece from *The Killjoy*, lowered from the flies: the torture scene.

Like beings of a different order (who would presently be unable to retreat into the darkness) Max and Olga were strolling about the stage. There was no backcloth as yet. Among the piled-up props and other odds and ends by the brick wall, Etienne was talking to the property manager. As at the start of the first day, Vogel seemed to have no eyes for anyone. With Trudy, who wore a stopwatch around her neck like a medallion, he was sitting in the middle of the third row behind a lectern that had been rigged up for him there. He was busily rummaging in his papers like a small-time entrepreneur with insufficient staff. Berta sat down with the dog on the outer seat of the front row, while Uli, with a sense of excitement, walked to the temporary steps leading to the stage from the side.

However few these steps were (only five), in that short space of time his heart suddenly started to pound like that of someone unable to swim, who, on entering a ship, is welcomed by a smiling purser behind whose back fear lies in wait. When he reached the top, in the other world, he looked into the auditorium. With his

120

legs over the back of the seat in front of him, Paul was reading the morning paper. In a box by the side Michael sat talking to the bookkeeper. Stella was nowhere to be seen. The rows of empty, red-upholstered seats eyed him breathlessly. The balustrades of the balconies were decorated in relief with vases filled with flowers and linked by garlands. At the back, in the upper circle, someone sat leaning with his elbows on the balustrade, staring at the stage, his chin resting in his hands – perhaps someone who had simply walked in from the street; the sort of person, Uli knew, who always turns up in theatres; it was the rule. Perhaps it was always the same person. At that moment something strange blew past him again, as if everything was not only what it was but also something different. The closed space. The rows of seats like waves of a red sea under the painted sky. It was as if Aronds' white set, behind him, radiated coldness at his back.

It vanished when Vogel called: "Gentlemen! May I request silence?"

But it wasn't so simple. He called out once more, a little louder, but only when the stage manager asked the same question (with the kind of insufferable calm also found in hospitals, madhouses and police stations) did it become quiet. While Vogel announced that they would have a preliminary run-through so they could get used to the stage, the hammering in the wings started up again. The stage manager called out a name, whereupon a man with a hammer appeared and asked what was the matter. He looked into the auditorium, said "Oh sorry", and disappeared again. Through a side door Stella came hurrying in, apologised for being late and sprinted up the steps, briefly smiling at Uli. He smiled back but looked immediately at Berta, as if she was not allowed to see what she had of course already seen: his wife, stretching out a thirty-year-long tentacle of jealousy from her grave.

"Where is Mr Caccini?" called Vogel.

"Here," said the pianist, leaning forward over the *Corriere della Sera*, from one of the boxes above the stage which the authors had appropriated for themselves.

"Would you go and sit at the piano now, please? Is everyone here?"

121

"I don't think Lucas is here," said Olga.

"I beg your pardon," called out Michael. "Lucas sends his apologies for today, he is indisposed."

"Bloody hell, not again."

"Yes," said Paul, from the hall, "indisposed, I suppose that's one way of putting it. I reckon he's in some television studio, doing a commercial." And then, in a soft, cajoling voice like a psychiatrist, and with a nauseous smile on his lopsided face: "You see . . . what Jesus Christ was to mankind, Poopie is to your washing."

"Very funny!" called Max from the stage.

The laughter came mainly from the technicians. A stagehand tried to embellish the joke by adding something about a loincloth, but the moment had passed. Irritation hung in the air, but Uli knew that this was normal at this stage, Vogel clapped his hands.

"Beginners, please, ladies and gentlemen! Let's see how far we can get. Joop," he asked the property manager, "will you read Lucas' part? And can we have that thing out of the way?"

"It has to be ready for tonight," said the technician.

"I don't care a damn, you can finish it in the lunch hour. Away with it."

"My union won't stand for it."

"Then get yourself expelled, you twit. Up with it."

The stage manager nodded, the technician said, "Don't say I didn't warn you," but the piece was hoisted.

The entire stage setting, so clear-cut in the rehearsal studio, appeared to crumble in the new situation. It seemed to Uli as if he had learnt from a book how to ski and was now suddenly on the Schreckhorn – above the treeline where the sky is dark blue – being pushed out of the ski lift and deposited on to the dazzling ski slope: ravens hovering above, cawing, and then whoosh, down you go! Three paces in the direction of the window were suddenly three steps down a slope, on which he felt uncertain and wanted to hold on to something. But this was how it was supposed to be, Vogel called out from below, and it had been provided for – whereat the property man handed Uli a walking stick, an ivory one with a silver handle in the shape of a snake's head. There were constant interruptions caused by other problems, with the props and the slopes, projections, steps and dips in the glacier; each time Aronds was cursed at, he put his hands together in front of his forehead and made a little bow. Only Mr Caccini had no worries. He was sitting at ease improvising on the white piano that had been integrated into a grotto on the set.

Towards noon, after countless repetitions and minor modifications, everything began to settle down, so that by contrast the situation in the rehearsal studio seemed laughably inept. Even Joost, conservative as all animals and children, conquered his dislike of the zigzagging maze. In addition, the meaning of certain simulated actions, whose purpose had, on the canvas floor, gradually been lost, now became clear again – like a convulsive movement of Uli's (as though trying to catch a passing moth) that was meant to halt a toppling coatstand which turned out to be a rickety colossus on one leg, on which his magic mantle was to be hung. The same enlightenment also occurred in the tableaux vivants at the beginning and end of each scene; what had on the flat floor looked like groups of dummies in a fashion store, as Etienne had sourly remarked, revealed themselves as beautiful three-dimensional compositions, the effect of which Uli could judge from the faces in the house.

During the lunch hour a girl from the workshop brought in two posters. One, executed in old-fashioned characters was for the *"The Dutch Theatre"* for *The Storm, by W. Shakespeare, Farewell Performance of Mr Pierre de Vries as Prospero, in the City Theatre in Amsterdam, at the Leidscheplein, on Saturday the 12th of November 1904*. The other parts were printed in such small type that the director's name could be read only with opera glasses. When everyone had admired it, Aronds picked it up between forefinger and thumb of both hands and carried it to the stage in order to fix it to its designated place on the set. The second poster was for Siderius' *Hurricane*, presented by the Authors' Theatre, first night on 12 November 1982, Kosmos Theatre, and would be put up all over the city.

Pierre de Vries – William Bouwmeester

"Look, Berta."

"Yes Uli, I see it."

"If Papa could have seen that."

"You're not becoming sentimental in your old age, are you? Papa . . . you must be crazy. Better ask why Joost isn't mentioned."

The last episode – on the evening of the first night of *The Tempest* – in which *Hurricane* reached its dramatic climax, came up toward the end of the afternoon.

The dressing-rooms of Pierre de Vries, Max Oort, Stella Middag and Lucas van Geest in the City Theatre were located at different levels of the polar landscape. After a for-the-time-being imaginary blackout, the scene was one of white stools, make-up tables, coatstands and sham mirrors in the shape of gigantic splinters. Uli felt tired. In Stella's dressing-room she and Max started their scene in which Stella learnt that her fiancé – after his conversation with Etienne – intended to blackmail Pierre de Vries with his homosexuality. Love and crime! Extorting a dowry out of the old queen – and then away, on honeymoon to la bella Italia:

> *"Where in a gondola my song will be*
> *Both caught and freed beneath the Bridge of Sighs."*

Meanwhile Uli stared at the dull silver, and simulated, with the indecipherable gestures of an asylum patient, the donning of a wig. Stella recoiled from Max in horror and dismay, but he kissed her unconcernedly and went off to his own dressing-room, singing at the top of his voice.

"Not so loud!" called Vogel from below.

The spasms into which Max then fell meant he was getting undressed. Having checked that there was no one in the corridor, Stella – her right arm stretched out behind her, her left hand in front, as if having to grope her way through a thick mist – hastened to Pierre's dressing-room. Distraught, she told him what was brewing. She fell to her knees and Uli got up with a jerk, accidentally knocking over his stool.

"Bloody stool," he said, but Vogel called out:

"No, very good! We'll keep that in. Do it again."

This time, of course, the stool wouldn't topple, but after several trials he had found a way of tipping it over with his calf. Stella put her arms around his knees and begged for mercy, it had all been Mr Etienne's idea.

"What did you say? Vile serpents! Rats!"

He wrenched himself free (but he didn't at all want to wrench himself free from her warm arms around his knees, he wanted to sink down beside her and embrace her too and kiss her and let the theatre go up in flames so that only the two of them would be left) and ordered her to her dressing-room. In a moment the performance would start and she had to appear with him in Scene Two. By a different route he stormed – shouting "Just you wait! Just you wait!" – to Max's dressing-room where Max, dressed only in sky-blue underpants, stood examining himself in the mirror, in the pose of a sculpted Apollo (women and men loved him equally) and turned round in alarm. With all the authority he was able to derive from his voice and his position, Pierre settled his accounts with him – until the Apollo, who had imagined the one-way Pullman tickets to Venice to be already in his pocket, had been reduced once more to a paltry little Amsterdam actor.

Meanwhile, the stage manager (of *Hurricane*, here coinciding with the one of *The Tempest*) had already called out "Beginners!" more than once. Time was beginning to press. Back in his room, Pierre de Vries took a few snorting breaths in order to calm himself. Then Uli lifted Prospero's hypothetical magic mantle from the rickety coatstand and draped it around himself with mechanical movements while (simultaneous theatre!) Max dejectedly slipped into the flimsy garments of Ariel, Stella sobbingly put the last touches to her Miranda coiffure and Lucas would hummingly have dressed up in Ferdinand's brocade costume if he had not been indisposed.

"Gong!" called Vogel and imitated the sound. "Bong! Bong! Bong!"

On the Leidseplein stage the curtain rose and the first scene of

125

The Tempest opened: the shipwreck during the storm that afterwards would turn out to have been caused by Prospero with Ariel's help. The sound effects were for the moment improvised by the property man. "Boom-boom-boom, boom-boom-boom," he said rather uninspiredly, and, as if the theatre was possessed of a soul intent on reminding him of his inadequacy, at that very moment the hammering in the wings started up again.

"What the hell is going on now?" shouted Vogel.

Everybody dissolved in helpless laughter – Uli sat down for a bit in the white-sheeted grandfather chair – and waited until the man with the hammer appeared for the second time.

"Oh, I didn't know you lot were still here. Sorry."

"Boom-boom-boom, boom-boom-boom," the property man resumed.

Immediately at the start of this twofold (or rather threefold) imagined tumult of nature, Etienne, with Joost on the lead, had appeared in Pierre's dressing-room. Satisfied with the success of his plot with Max (contrived by Lucas), and in anticipation of the reception that was to take place after the mayor's tribute to Pierre he had already refreshed himself from the bottles put out in the upper foyer. Nothing further was said. As Max left his dressing-room and slowly, like a sleepwalker, set off for the City Theatre stage, Uli bared his teeth, his false teeth to be precise (alarmed, Etienne put down his glass), tilted slightly backward, fixed his eyes on Etienne's forehead and flew at him. While Stella sought comfort in the embrace of an absent Lucas, Uli, following a carefully worked-out choreographic sequence, put both hands around the throat of his long-time friend, pushed him to his knees, slid, amid the "boom-boom-boom" across the slumping Etienne, and held him in his grip until the vital spirits were extinct. Joost, who had already witnessed this scene a good many times, whiled away the time sitting on the floor with one leg raised, licking his scrotum.

"Right!" called Vogel, getting up from behind his lectern. "And now turn slowly for the tableau . . . yes . . . slowly . . ."

Like a conductor he steered the movement with which Uli rose to his feet in exhaustion, turned solemnly to face the audience, his right hand slowly clawing at his breast, his left hand rising tremblingly, his face contorted, then stiffening . . .

"Splendid! Hold it like that! Yes – stage manager . . ."

Hidden behind the set, the stage manager looked at his script and shouted the last lines at intervals, while Vogel now called out "boom-boom-boom, boom-boom-boom":

"It's time, Mr de Vries! Last call!
Please hurry, sir, no time to lose! Last call!"

5
Nostalgia

Two days later (the first night would be in a week's time), a precious rehearsal was cancelled. The board of management had called a general meeting to discuss what action could be taken to prevent the threatened liquidation of the Authors' Theatre. The meeting had first been planned for Saturday but it turned out that many actors then went to their second homes in the country. Uli, as guest actor, didn't really have anything to do with it; moreover, all organisational matters made him feel sick. In the past, when he had been employed at The Cellar, this had caused him enough headaches. But since anything was better than sitting at home in his chair by the window, he had gone to Amsterdam all the same. Of course, Berta came too.

In the foyer with the mottled mirrors almost all the actors had gathered together, including those from *The Killjoy* whom, for the most part, he knew only superficially. The administrative staff were there too, but none of the technicians had come. The director of the theatre made a brief appearance to wish them luck: a small, plump, jovial man, too young for his three-piece suit with chalk stripes – which according to Paul were drawn on it every morning by Michael – but clearly enjoying acting the big theatre director which he was and would remain, no matter what company was resident at the Kosmos. Lucas challenged him to stay for the meeting but he said laughingly that he was only a simple administrator who understood nothing about politics. He waved with a limp hand and closed the door behind him. This left an air of oppressiveness; the situation was grave.

Of the seven authors only those three that sat on the board of management were present. Together with the three members from the actors' group – Vogel, Michael and Trix – they were sitting at the short end of the foyer behind a row of tables pushed together. Uli had taken a seat behind Stella so that he could look at her plaits. Although according to the statutes (the "little white book") the board had no chairman, someone sat in the middle: a writer whose name Uli hadn't caught during the introductions but who was called "Molly" by everyone. Which was even worse than "Uli". Etienne had told him that Molly specialised in light-hearted comedies, which mainly kept the Authors' Theatre on its feet, though his recent adaptation of Grabbe had misfired. Around his head stood a nimbus of curly light-grey hair, an extension of which protruded from his open shirt. With a self-satisfied smile, apparently in the best of moods, he opened the meeting, whereupon Olga called out at once:

"Why aren't all the authors here? Isn't it important enough for them?"

"I don't know. Am I my brothers' keeper? You'll have to ask them. Maybe they're busy working."

"Exactly, there you are," called Etienne. "To them the Authors' Theatre is merely a plaything, a toy they can just as well do without. Writing you can do any time, but our entire social security is in the balance."

"I beg your pardon?" asked Molly. "What did I hear? Social Security? What does the honourable deputy mean? That he is not threatened by nuclear war?" He spoke in a hammering staccato, seemingly pleased that the term had been handed to him for the gobbling. "Oh no, that is not what the honourable deputy from the Land of Cockaigne meant. He meant that as an actor he has a fixed income which we writers have never had, and which if the worst comes to the worst will be replaced by state benefits consisting of eighty per cent of the last received wage. And that doesn't apply to us either. But you probably didn't even know that. Social security! What exactly are you? Artists, or a bunch of embittered petty bourgeois belly-achers?" He looked around defiantly, amid awakening murmurs. Within a minute he had succeeded in making the rift between authors and actors visible, or rather, to rip it

129

open. But he still hadn't had enough of it: "May I invite you for a moment to remember the Last Supper?"

"What about it?" called the actor who had played Jupiter in *The Killjoy*.

"It demonstrates how mankind is put together. One thirteenth part is all right, another thirteenth consists of the greatest imaginable scum. Seven or eight per cent is always fascist, anywhere in the world. You can quietly bump off every thirteenth passer-by, so long as you have a way of making sure he is actually the one you want. But eleven-thirteenths consists of soggy hangers-on, unimportant padding. Is that what you are?" Satisfied, he sat back while the hubbub around him became indignant.

"Molly . . ." said the balding author on his left without looking sideways, like a ventriloquist. He was clearly the more sensible of the two, and therefore the lesser writer, and better qualified to be in charge of the meeting. But he was not in charge.

"And I suppose you're Jesus Christ!" called out Olga.

Molly nodded. "Thou sayest it."

"It's enough to make you puke."

Now Michael straightened his back and said, "Look, ladies and gentlemen, this isn't getting us anywhere."

"All right, all right," said Molly complaisantly. "I should be the last to underestimate actors. After all, we live in a time when a superannuated old actor plays the part of president of the United States. Heaven help us!"

"What about the Russians!" called Etienne.

Did Uli imagine it, or had the writer briefly glanced at him as he spoke those last words? Molly couldn't help himself, things were getting out of hand, but he managed to save the situation in the nick of time, though only for a few seconds.

"Acting is a profession; being a writer is more complex. I wouldn't want to say it is a vocation, let's say it is a provocation. But if their social insecurity is a reason for my honourable colleagues to stay away today, then they in their turn are forgetting that the privilege of being free from constraints is also a kind of income. We intellectuals call that a psychological income. And especially the privilege to invent things ourselves instead of having

130

to learn by rote what other people have invented. Everything has to be taken into account in this life; especially, dear friends and fellow strugglers, the account that is presented when somebody has produced something really good."

Although he hadn't said anything funny, rather something terrible (how terrible he probably didn't even realise himself) he looked about the gathering with a grin. There was no possible doubt, he had the whip hand of everyone there; he was totally miscast as a chairman. After a moment's silence he invited Eduard, the writer on his right, to speak, lit a pipe and said nothing further.

Uli was informed by Lucas, who was sitting beside him and whispered into his ear, that the new speaker wrote sadistic plays, using the Middle Ages as a pretext. He was a slightly bloated looking man, with drab, dark-blond hair that changed its mind by the ears, turning into a reddish beard. When he started speaking, Stella turned round and asked not Uli but Lucas for a light.

It was as if the devil had a hand in it, said Eduard: in the last instance the Authors' Theatre owed its existence to the blood-spattering tomatoes that in the sixties – when the whole country was standing on its head – had been thrown at the establishment of the day in the City Theatre and that had eventually led to a complete overthrow of the government's policy for the dramatic arts. Did anyone remember what play was being performed at the time? No? Just as he thought. It was *The Tempest*, by his British colleague Mr Tremble-spear. Leo might be mad, as, for that matter, were all authors of any importance (the brighter the light, the blacker the shadow), but in writing *Hurricane* he seemed to have had a premonition, born from the madness of genius, that something was in the air, that a circle was being completed.

At this moment Uli sensed that Molly was looking at him again. When he met his eyes, the writer looked away.

But, Eduard continued, as Hermes Tremigistes had already said: the stars appeal but do not compel. The purpose of bad omens was to make sure that they did *not* come true. Pensively he rested his chin in his hand and went on:

"But if they don't come true because you saw to it that they wouldn't, can you still say they were omens? How can you prove

131

that according to such and such an omen this and that would have happened if you had not done so and so? People would think you were crazy, and they wouldn't know that in fact you had saved the world. Maybe the madhouses are full of people who have saved the world, exactly as they claim they have. Maybe they are really saints. Imagine that in 1889 in Braunau, Austria, someone had choped off a certain baby's head with a hatchet. He is arrested and says to the judge that he had deduced from certain omens that this child, if he had not been beheaded, would one day have sent fifty-five million people to their deaths. The man would have been put away for the rest of his life. True or not? Now I ask you: rightly or wrongly? Think carefully. Or let me put the question another way: are we sure we treat all child murderers justly?"

A baffled silence fell.

"What kind of drivel is this, for Christ's sake?" called the man sitting beside Uli, whom he recognised only by his voice as the actor playing the cowardly Apollonius in *The Killjoy*.

So in the end, control of the meeting was where it should have been in the first place: with the writer on Molly's left, whose name turned out to be Jan and who wrote naturalistic domestic plays. From that moment it was all done in a businesslike, competent, boring manner, just as it should be. From his inside pocket Jan took some notes, which immediately put him at an advantage, for the written word always represents power. The calm movements with which he unfolded the pages and smoothed them out on the table with the flat of his hand indicated that he wanted, first and foremost, quiet and orderliness. He read out the advice of the Theatre Commission, channelled the indignation, analysed it, formulated possible counter-arguments and drafted a plan of action to be addressed to the City of Amsterdam, the Provincial States of North Holland, and the Second Chamber of Parliament. Then a draft of a letter to the Minister. Spontaneous protest from the public to be organised: petitions, letters to editors, personal lobbying of politicians. Who knew whom? Who knew people who knew important people?

From time to time Molly peered at him out of the corners of his eyes (perhaps he knew the case was lost: from Tempest to

Tempest, over and out) and meanwhile Eduard was writing without interruption – maybe not so much a strategic plan for the rescue of the Authors' Theatre as a draft for a new one-act play about that sweet baby Adolfchen Hitler's murderer, whom the police had to protect from popular fury even in the nut-house – a play he would in due course offer to the new resident company at the Kosmos.

In the afternoon Vogel had to work the lighting at the theatre. Berta went with some others to the Tivoli but Uli was cramped from sitting in the smoke-filled foyer and felt he had heard enough talk for one day. He looked for Stella but it appeared she had already left. The weather was mild, still almost a late-summer day, and he decided to go to the City Theatre where there hung a portrait of Louis Bouwmeester as Shylock in the same melodramatic pose that he himself had to adopt in the final tableau of *Hurricane*. Vogel had given him a photograph of it, but he wanted to see it for himself. Yielding to an impulse, he asked the property manager if he could borrow the ivory walking-stick. It wasn't really allowed, but all right then.

Etienne, who never went to the café with the others, walked up with him, pushing his bicycle with one hand. He took a gloomy view of the Authors' Theatre's future prospects, but he didn't really care all that much, his children had left home and he was thinking of settling permanently in France. Away from it all, play boules with the locals in the afternoon under the plane trees. He had a little house in the Ardèche, a renovated farmhouse, and they could easily live there on his dole money and his wife's sickness benefit; she taught at an art college but had been declared unfit last year because of her back. So that was actually rather convenient. Besides he'd get a good price for his house in Amsterdam, even though the bottom had fallen out of the property market. There was a nice plot of land with it, in the Ardèche he meant, but he had also got his eye on a patch of ground belonging to his neighbour, a German cardiologist, which stuck like an odd wedge into his. Anyway, these weren't Uli's worries.

133

"No," said Uli, looking into his brown velvet eyes.

"What about you?"

"Me?" Uli let the stick tap elegantly on the flagstones and looked around the star-shaped Koningsplein with its traffic circling under the hazy blue sky; the flower market, the glass houses on the flat barges along the quay, the Mint Tower in the distance. "To me it makes no difference whether the Authors' Theatre closes down or not. It's my farewell performance anyway."

Perhaps this startled Etienne a little, perhaps there still lurked in him the illusion of immortality (in the Ardèche); a moment later he had mounted his bicycle and disappeared on the other side of the canal.

At the Leidseplein (which, divided by the projecting City Theatre, really consisted of two squares), street singers with guitars, white-chalked mime-artists and colourful bands of musicians with blaring amplifiers had promptly positioned themselves in the daubed porticoes in order to celebrate the sunny day. Four girls dressed in white played medieval tunes on violins and flutes, while a little distance away a wizened half-naked man raised a kerosene bottle to his mouth and, like a heretic, spewed fuming jets of fire towards the sky. The Middle Ages had returned. Around a tree, their backs towards it, stood a group of motionless men and women. Uli read on a banner: *Silence for Peace*. On the other side of the square another half-naked man threw himself face down on a bed of broken glass, and a leather-clad girl with bright purple tufted hair stood on his back. Uli inhaled the sweet damp smell of decay that came from Vondelpark.

The main entrance to the theatre was closed, but he saw people coming out of the side doors, which were normally never open. He went to look; a chalked scrawl on a school blackboard said that the entrance was on the other side. There (in the quieter part of the square), he was surprised to see a long queue of people waiting alongside the wall on which the sun shone low. They couldn't be queuing for tickets, for there was no box office there. Uli asked the people at the back – a distinguished looking couple such as you

134

seldom saw in Amsterdam these days (you'd have to go to The Hague for that) what was going on. In muted tones they said they had come to pay their last respects to La Charlotte. They had seen her where they were young, in La Dame aux Camélias.

Uli stood behind them in the queue. A little further down was the stage door. He now noticed that many people were carrying flowers. As he slowly shuffled forwards, he listened to the conversation of a group of young people, cheerful rather than sad, and gathered that they too were on the stage. Yes, he was part of it all now, Saturday week all these people would see his name in the papers, perhaps even his photograph. He would have liked nothing better than to raise his stick in the air and call out: "Ladies and gentlemen, here stands a Bouwmeester! The last of the great!" Across the street, in front of the Café Américain, a dark-skinned man was being questioned by two policemen. A constable leaned against the wall beside him, almost amiably, holding a passport in his hand. A second policemen stood facing him, one foot slightly forward.

Inside the building, near the cloakrooms, it was dark and no one spoke any more. Against the light coming from the exit on the other side, the silhouettes appeared black and threatening; they reminded Uli of a scene from a silent German film he must have seen more than fifty years ago. The procession narrowed, the waiting was long; after the couple had moved on, Uli went into the rotunda that had been arranged as a funeral chapel.

Enveloped in soft light and silence stood the coffin – always the same paradoxical coffin, present and yet not present, as if it was in two worlds at once. Four well-known actors and actresses kept vigil, so motionlessly that for a moment Uli could not believe they were who they were. He looked at the flowers, at the coffin in which the old lady now lay silent, and then again at them. One of them had his eyes closed.

Suddenly he burst out sobbing. It overwhelmed him, out of nowhere, like a gust of wind when you turn a corner. He quickly walked on, to the cloakrooms on the other side. The sobbing would not stop, more and more shockwaves welled up from depths in which he did not know his way and of which he was afraid,

135

because they seemed to have something to do with nostalgia – a kind of nostalgia for that which lingered in that rotunda. He could not go outside now, he put his hand on the smooth brass banister and climbed the stairs. On the top landing he leaned against the balustrade, waiting until he recovered. There was no one about. In the stairwell there were more portraits of actors.

It was thirty years since he had been here last, to a performance of *The Merry Widow*. Through two swing doors he entered a curving corridor that led all the way round the auditorium: an enlargement of the situation at the Kosmos. He blew his nose and slowly walked past the rows of absent actors and actresses who gazed at him from their frames, calm and self-assured, suspicious or vain, occasionally even timid, uncertain, sometimes breathless, frozen in mid-action – and everything was steeped in an ambiguous silence that was the silence of all those people down there by the rotunda. When he had completed a semicircle and had reached the stairs on the other side, he suddenly stood face to face with the portrait. He knew every detail of it, because of the photograph he had so often imitated in front of the mirror in his bedroom, but now that he saw it in reality, here in this place where it really hung, submerged in its heavy brown hues, it almost seemed as if it was Louis Bouwmeester himself who, with twisted mouth and sideways fluttering beard, clawed at his shirt and raised his left hand; a pose to which centuries of theatre history had contributed.

"It is closed here, sir." He looked into the face of a young attendant who beckoned him towards the stairs.

"I know," said Uli. "I was down there . . . with . . . that is my father," he said suddenly, pointing with the silver snake's head at the portrait.

From the way in which the attendant looked at the painting, it was clear that he was seeing it for the first time, and from the way he then turned to Uli it was equally clear that his own father was a very different sort of man. It was a mystery to Uli why he hadn't mentioned the real purpose of his visit, serious enough, here in this place. But the attendant, perhaps because the building was filled with reverence today, did not insist further, and disappeared through a door at the end of the corridor.

136

But what about Uli? If he went down the stairs here, he would join those who were still on their way to the catafalque, so that, for decency's sake, he would have to make the journey a second time. He decided to go back the way he had come; turned and saw, on the opposite wall, the portrait of La Charlotte. A grande dame, thirty or forty years older than the young woman he had once met – but at the same moment, the incident of which he had never thought again, appeared before his eyes: etched so sharply and poignantly and at the same time rising so miraculously from oblivion, that he had to grasp it at once lest it should evaporate like a dream.

With both hands he pulled at the doors to the auditorium, which first, in a sucking fashion, would not open and then suddenly yielded, but the night that then hit him in the face was too black. Quickly he walked to the stairwell and climbed a floor higher. In the deserted upper foyer he sank into a chair, deeply affected, and, covering his eyes with both hands, reflecting . . .

6
The Ring

. . . whereupon his father – tipsy but upright as a colonel – appears round the corner of a dark corridor and says, from his great height:

"I must talk to you, Uli."

Uli is lying on his tummy on the carpet, reading the captions under the pictures of Struwwelpeter to his little sister. Soft light hangs in the net curtains that are gathered with ribbons like a theatre curtain; millions of brutes and their victims are not yet born, from the workshops downstairs and across the street comes the clangour of the blacksmiths and coppersmiths who make more noise than will fill the city in times to come.

"I want you to do something for me. Coat on, cap on, come along."

"What about Berta?"

"Auntie is at home."

Although he must have got up to follow his father, in his memory he does not get up. What he sees is totally still: his father in the doorway, he himself on the floor, Berta trying to tear up the pages of the book. Then all of a sudden the scene has shifted: he and his father on a canal bridge, but again there is no movement. And then he himself in a hall with a bright blue painted ceiling and gilded leather wall-coverings.

How does one remember – no, how does Uli remember what he remembers of his eighth year: everything that lies before the watershed which is to be reached a few years later? As motionless images, tableaux vivants, between which his eye jumps back and forth, from image to image and back again, fixed in the aspic of what he knows, has heard, suspects, has added in his imagination – not in a sequence but in a timeless concurrence, the way one sees a painting. Is there not here a solemn duty for the narrator: must he not intervene and set the scene in motion?

"What about Berta?"

"Auntie is at home."

In other words: it is not *his* house, and he is not a colonel either. If the order or disorder of a life, or the order within a disorder, is hereditary (the narrative is at this stage twelve years away from the nineteenth century), then the student will here find proof of this meta-Darwinian thesis. Until the death of his much younger German wife (at the birth of Berta, now five years ago) he had been a variety artiste with a succession of travelling companies; but although Uli had been the cause of a shotgun marriage three years earlier, he, the widower, takes to drink, gets the sack. There are relations such as his younger brother Karel the impresario, who are eager to help him, but he is too proud, or perhaps too sad, to let himself be helped. Uli and Berta will later hear the story in dribs and drabs from various sources, though not all the dribs and drabs. While on his more sober days he plays smash hits with a singing saw in the colonnade outside the City Theatre, stubbornly returning each time after a constable has chased him away and finally landing in jail, the saw confiscated – the toddler and the baby narrowly escaping being sent to a children's home, because the sister of their dead mother lovingly takes them into her home.

"Auntie is at home."

Auntie is childlessly married to the window-dresser at the high-class "Maison pour Messieurs" in Kalverstraat. Uli remembers his foster father speaking disparagingly to visitors about his colleague the tailor who, at fittings, deliberately pinned the seat of the trousers to the customer's underpants, so that with a thousand excuses he was obliged to slide his hand inside the back of the customer's trousers from behind – and at this point his uncle would tap the palm of his right hand meaningfully on the back of his left hand, while his aunt Gertrud said "Pfui Teufel!". However, being brought up by this decent couple left little mark on their wards' lives; the tumultuous blood of Frederik Rosenveldt, the eighteenth-century comedian, had a far more decisive influence.

To everyone's amazement, after eighteen months the period of alcoholic mourning suddenly came to an end. Something must have happened, someone must have helped him, and now, almost three-quarters of a century later, in a big armchair in a too-silent theatre, his son suddenly understood who this person must have been.

Perhaps she heard someone whisper in the dressing-rooms that the fellow with the singing saw down there in the colonnade, just imagine it, was a Bouwmeester; she dropped a coin into the upturned bowler at his feet and started up a conversation with him, Perhaps. There was no one left who could tell the story. She, the twenty-two-year-old actress, must have pulled him, the drunk of forty-eight, out of the abyss and helped him to find work: with a company that shortly afterwards embarked on a tour of the East Indies, to boost the morale of the colonials out there. She herself also seems to have been in the Indies during this time, no doubt with a very different kind of company, not performing for the colonial police serving up-country, but to highly placed government officials, the top-brass among the colonial functionaries and wealthy planters, with the local sultan as the disdained guest of honour.

He now regularly sends home money for the maintenance of his children, and postcards from Batavia, Surabaya, Bandung – until suddenly there he stands in the living-room, bronzed, in a sweat-drenched linen tropical suit with threadbare elbows and frayed turn-ups. While his sister-in-law, shaking her head, darns the suit, the returned prodigal father tells wonderful stories about tigers and buffaloes, with Berta sitting on his lap and one of his arms around Uli's waist, dressed only in long underpants, but on his head once again his dull, mouldy-green Garibaldi.

But whatever happened between him and Charlotte, then not yet "La" – first in Amsterdam, later in the Indies – it comes to an end. She gets married, above her station, to a Count, a banker with a top hat and a carriage (perhaps in order to rid herself either of the shabby comedian, who is becoming more and more insistent, or of her love for him), and presently on her way to be "La" she becomes socially inaccessible to him. At this, he falls back into the misery from which she had rescued him; everything repeats itself, he starts to drink again, the payments stop and sometimes he doesn't show himself for months. One morning, coming home from school, Uli sees him leaning half-conscious against the wall beside a bar, taking one step towards the door and then one step back, his shoulders bumping against the wall, clearly not knowing whether he is going into the bar or has just come out of it. Uli would like to help him but daren't, and runs off . . .

"Where are we going?"

"You'll see."

So they must have gone into town, Uli perhaps waiting from time to time outside a tavern where his father quickly knocks back a gin; around him the rattling of cartwheels on the cobblestones, the clatter of horses' hooves, and, as they walk on again, his father muttering in a befuddled state about the isles of the Indies, about sultry nights with ominously swaying mosquito nets, the shrill cries of monkeys deep in the jungle, all of it, all of it pervaded by silent forces, soundless feet vanishing behind a palm tree, the walls sometimes unaccountably spattered with blood . . . And on the corner of the Heerengracht he points to the house where Uli has to collect a ring.

"A ring?"

"Just say: my father's red ring. She'll know." He lets the lid of his wristwatch jump open. "And don't stay away longer than ten minutes."

In the duffel coat made for him by his uncle he approaches the patrician house that looms larger at each step, walls clad with slabs of natural grey stone, in the gable a large coat of arms full of sculpted violence of lions and birds of prey and overthrown enemies of other races. He climbs the steps and pulls the bell. On the dark green door it says in beautiful white italic lettering: *Bentinck*. Waiting, he looks at his father leaning over the side of the bridge, spitting circles into the water; with deathly screeches the gulls skim over the canal under the bridge.

A servant girl with a lace circlet on her head and a white apron down to her feet precedes him through a fairy-tale marble corridor adorned with ornamental plasterwork and sculptures of angels hovering above the gleaming oak doors. Midway, a carved staircase of almost honey-coloured wood leads up. He almost chokes on his spittle, so beautiful is it all. (A world of superlatives!) With a

141

wink she ushers him into a huge room with a gilded leather walls. He takes off his cap and waits until it pleases the actress to notice him. In a lilac-coloured silk morning gown, her black hair loosely pinned up, she paces rapidly back and forth, ceaselessly rattling off sentences interspersed with "Goddammit!" and peering at the sheets of paper lying on the grand piano – and once letting out a dramatic wail in front of the gilt mirror above the marble mantelpiece, her gesture flowing seamlessly into a close inspection – with tilted head – of a possible blemish by her left ear. At that moment she sees him in the mirror, turns and comes up to him with outspread arms.

"Bubi! How lovely! Now I see you at last!" With both hands she takes him by the shoulders, turns him towards the light and examines him as though he were an image of herself. "How big you are already and how like your father you look. Come, take off your coat. What would you like to drink? Would you like a marble bottle?"

She pulls at a tasselled cord and with his hands on his bare knees he sits down in a low purple-red armchair by the window, to his one side a large potted palm, to the other a pier table with a gigantic vase on it, painted in pink and black with pictures of Chinese in wide robes. There is also a child's silver shoe on the table, the worn tip, the creases in the leather, everything of shiny metal. Outside, at the bottom of the garden, laid out geometrically as if a mirror were standing at the centre, glimmer the graceful pillars of a summerhouse in the shade of an old tree. Never before has he seen so many beautiful and costly things together. But of all of them it is she that is the most beautiful and costly. Her face is as pale as the sand in the hourglass on the sideboard in his uncle's house. The few loose hairs by her temple and on her neck, the singing vowel sounds when she says "marble bottle", with an intonation that at the same time makes it clear to him what a little boy he still is, liking marble bottles. But he doesn't care; at home he gets lemonade at best: marble bottles, that make it go prickly on your tongue, are far too expensive.

"Did you know that your father and I were very good friends? A long time ago, of course. If you knew how often he told me about you. He's very proud of you. Perhaps I know even more about you than you do yourself. You think that's crazy, don't you? But it's true. Once, when you were about four years old, somebody came to visit your uncle and aunt and told a very dirty joke in your presence. The only person who laughed at it was you. You roared with laughter and were sent to bed as a punishment. Afterwards your father asked you how it was possible that you had understood what the joke was about. You said you hadn't understood it at all but you laughed because no one else did and you were so sorry for that man. Do you remember that?"

"No, ma'am."

"You see!"

As she watches him sucking through his straw, he looks – while tasting the ice-cold drink – at the beaten gold ring on her hand, with a large deep-red stone.

"You have a little sister too, haven't you?"

"Yes, ma'am."

"What is her name?"

"Berta."

"Beautiful name. A bit German."

It is silent again. Now he must ask it, but he doesn't know how to go about it. He looks up at the ceiling, where more angels hover, in the light blue among white clouds. He is beginning to feel hot; what is he going to say to his father if he goes back without the ring? That she didn't want to give it to him? But then he will perhaps find out later that it wasn't true. Just as he is thinking that he will never manage it, she looks straight at him and asks softly:

"What have you come for, Bubi?"

He wipes his mouth on his sleeve and says:

"My father asks if you would please give him that red ring back. He said you'd know which one."

She stares at him, motionlessly, into his good eye. But to his horror he sees that meanwhile something is happening: water slowly fills her eyes, more and more, suddenly gushing out of the corners and pouring down her cheeks. Slowly, still looking at him but perhaps no longer seeing him, she takes hold of the ring with her other hand and twists it off her finger. Without giving it

143

another glance she puts it on the little table, gets up and goes to stand by the garden doors, with her back towards him.

"You'd better go now," she says.

He gets up too, puts the ring in his trouser pocket and starts putting on his coat. He succeeds in doing so, but as he puts his hand through the sleeve it accidentally touches, at the end of its movement, the Chinese vase, which totters and, while he tries to grab it with his coat half on, finally decides to shatter to pieces on the parquet floor.

Petrified, feeling the blood drain from his face, he looks at her back.

"I . . . it was an accident . . ."

She does not turn round. "Yes, you'd better go now."

He runs out of the room and down the corridor. On the way he realises he has left his cap, but going back is impossible, of course. The front door is open. The maid is leaning over the balustrade, calling out to someone below.

When he emerges into the open – his father stands watching on the bridge – he sees a man with a slit bag on his head like a pointed hat. From a handcart he takes a long slab of ice; in order to carry it he rams a large skewer into it and takes it to the tradesmen's entrance under the front steps. Under the cart stands a draught dog with hanging head.

When Uli – still dripping with memories – arrived at the Tivoli, the Friday evening bustle had already begun. Above the music he could hear the laughter at the back of the café. At the round table sat Berta like a guest of honour between Molly and Mr Caccini. Everyone was hanging upon her lips.

"Well, well. Here's my little brother the male lead! Where have you been?"

It was many years since he had last seen her in such an exuberant mood. He looked at her in disgust. With her wig now slightly askew from the drink, and her red imitation lips and her raw voice, she looked like a transvestite.

"Are you coming home?" he asked.

144

Scornful laughter erupted on all sides. Home . . . nothing doing! More beer! Lucas helped him out of his coat, Max pressed him into a chair that was being drawn up between Mimi and Olga (Stella wasn't there) and above their heads a brimming glass of beer was already approaching. But once he was seated and harmless, Pierre de Vries' walking stick between his knees, not even Olga paid any more attention to him.

"And then? What then?"

He did not listen. Slightly to one side and to the rear he sat in his chair like someone who did not really belong, like the chauffeur who was allowed to wait until the Countess deemed the moment of departure had arrived.

Before coming to the Tivoli he had made a small detour, past the house on Heerengracht. The exterior had remained unchanged, except that it was no longer the mansion of a banker, but had become a bank instead, the customers having to use the former tradesmen's entrance. He took a sip and wondered what in heaven's name had possessed his father. How had he got it into his head to saddle his son with such a task! Of course, he was short of cash, gin was expensive and gin a-plenty even more so, but what an idea to send a boy of eight on such an errand! Did this mean his father had therefore been an inferior, cowardly, contemptible character? Was that why Uli had buried the incident in oblivion, in order to protect himself against that insight, because he was, after all, his father? And anyway, how had he ever got hold of such an expensive gold ring with a ruby in it? Stolen? But that was less terrible, since it had been in the service of love. From love to degradation, that was how it had been.

Laughter broke out at the table. The end of the anecdote had been reached.

"Yes, Fausto," said Berta, blowing a thick cloud of smoke towards the lamp, "I have worn out miles of cock in my time."

The merriment reached a new pitch. Fausto. She called Mr Caccini Fausto. What the devil did that signify? Molly laughed with two rows of vicious little teeth that remained set tight on each other. His head quivered rapidly and in ecstasy, as if he was about to tear something up.

"Zhekrastche stoy spassiba!" he exclaimed in vigorous Russian, probably of his own invention. "And the higher things?" he asked. "Do you never think about the higher things?"

"The only thing I still kneel to," said Berta, "is the refrigerator, to get the sherry bottle out."

"Ah," said Molly in surprise, and looked around, his forefinger raised. Out of his inside pocket he took a black notebook. "This must be recorded."

"Now we see," said Olga. "That's how you people do it."

"Child's play."

Uli looked at his sister with emotion. At home he never saw her like this, but of course that was mainly his own fault. He would never tell her about that ring. He didn't know whether her father still meant anything to her, he couldn't remember her ever talking about their childhood, but it couldn't have gone completely. Nothing was ever completely gone, and she should be allowed to keep the image she had of him. Their mother had died at her birth, she had been the cause of her death, and God knows maybe there was something in her that considered itself its mother's murderer – just as it would also have been her fault that things had gone wrong with their father. God knows maybe something of that sort had smouldered in their father too, maybe he had let slip something of that sort, in one of his drunken states. But it was unthinkable that they should talk about it together – any more than you could talk to someone who was standing with the tip of his nose against yours. You couldn't even see such a person properly. He felt how under the table Joost put his head on his shoe. Although he disliked the dog, it gave him a feeling of warmth, not only in his foot; but he wouldn't be able to talk about it with Joost either.

And at that moment he knew with whom he should talk about it: with Stella, of course! It was very much like – but then quite different – her story about the cigar that her mother had made her light. *And so now you were going to tell me the secret of your life* . . . he could hear her say it now, in that literary imperfect tense that Dutch children use when they start playing a game: "I was the mother . . . you were the father . . ."

Indeed, Uli. Explain yourself further.

ACT FOUR

1
The Masquerade

Gold, ruby . . . but the sleep into which he sank again and again during the weekend, in his chair by the window, was of dreamless lead. Each time he woke, his eyes were burning so that he could barely keep them open. He groped for something to read within hand's reach, since getting up was for some reason impossible; not because he lacked the force to do it but because he had a feeling as if everything about his body was loose, as if his legs would be left lying in the chair if he stood up. After looking at the words and the sentences for ten minutes or so he dozed off again. Berta observed it all, of course, and he noticed she walked on tiptoe when he had his eyes shut, but he said nothing.

So he entered the last week. As if his constitution understood that from Monday such slackness would be tolerated no longer, he arrived fresh and fit at the Kosmos where, with incredulous pride, he saw his name on the new posters. Inside, everything seemed ready for yet another leap forward. There was no one in the auditorium; on the stage a few technicians were busy with the backcloth and they pointed towards the fire door in the brick wall.

Behind it, in the maze of narrow corridors and stairs, there reigned the agreeable hustle and bustle he knew so well. From the open dressing-room doors came laughter and chatter. Watched by a dresser, Stella was pacing up and down in the lamplight. She was wearing the kind of gown he remembered from his childhood: tightly laced around the waist, almost down to the ground, fur-trimmed, with lace sleeves; on her pinned-up hair a hat with feathers – everything in off-white, including the muff. As the dresser knelt down by her, she gave Uli a demure little nod that

149

was in keeping with her appearance.

"Magnificent!" he called out. "A dream!"

A bright red rose on her bodice provided the only colour. He glanced briefly at Berta, in order to include her in his admiration, but he did not like her expression.

"What are you looking at me like that for? Look at her instead."

"You're already doing that, you old lecher."

He looked at Joost who had clasped her calf in his front paws and with jerking hind-quarters wanted something about which he probably wasn't clear in his own mind – or perhaps he was trying to demonstrate that even in nature things were not always as natural and as normal as they might be. With his walking-stick, which he had not returned last Friday, Uli pointed at the optimistic canine enterprise.

"Look at that. You're randy as hell yourself."

"Don't be daft. So if Joost rides up against me, *I'm* randy, am I?"

"That's right. Got it in one. They can smell it."

"For God's sake," said Berta, and walked away, heedless of Joost's resulting tumble.

"Give my regards to Fausto!" Uli called after her.

Michael came up to him and said the television people would be coming tomorrow to make a recording for an arts programme, partly in connection with the threatened subsidy cuts. "They would also like to do a brief interview with you, not more than about three minutes. Do you mind? It would be important for the Authors' Theatre, of course."

Uli had to check himself. "Certainly," he said. "Why not?"

When Michael had moved away, his head spun. Television! Now everybody in the Netherlands would see him – and the first people he thought of were the customers of The Cellar who had so often humiliated him; they would sit in front of their sets and say, "Good Lord, isn't that that old barman of ours?" He suddenly felt like a rocket in a bottle, on New Year's Eve, the fuse already smouldering.

"Here stands a happy man, it seems."

Twirling a strand of hair that stuck out from under his hat,

Vogel introduced him to a gawky walk-on with sunken cheeks, who played the photographer in a tableau vivant at the Shakespeare rehearsal. Then he showed Uli to his dressing-room; in passing they had a glimpse of Olga cursing as she struggled with a costume like a net curtain fluttering out of a window. Vogel called Aronds and a moment later the three of them were inspecting the costumes hanging in Uli's dressing-room.

One was a sober lounge suit from around the turn of the century, trimmed with silk, of the same off-white colour as Stella's gown, as were the shirt, tie, socks and shoes. But the second costume, seemingly intended for a giant, hung, or rather stood, like a solidified explosion of all the colours and figures that Aronds had managed to release from the occult depths of his personality (or at least from the relevant reference books): gold brocade stitched with pentagrams, hieroglyphs, astrological and cabbalistic signs, snakes biting their own tails, triangles with eyes in them, and many other symbols – in an exuberant splendour of scarlet, saffron, bronze green, ultramarine . . .

Startled, Uli looked at the director.

"Words fail you, eh?" said Vogel proudly.

Aronds slightly readjusted the huge wide sleeves, and said, "I let myself be inspired a little by the Noh Theatre."

He clearly assumed Uli knew what that was, but Uli thought it meant "no theatre", another of those modern notions, like anti-theatre, hadn't they had that too?

"Am I supposed to wear that?"

"Sure!" laughed Vogel. "But try on Pierre de Vries' suit first." The door closed gently behind him, as if it were a sickroom; it was some time before the handle went up; presumably they were still talking to each other outside.

So, after all these years Uli sat down once again at an, as yet empty, dressing table. Above the mirror burned a chilly striplight; there were no windows. It was approaching ever closer. It was really true. He was alone with the clothes now. He looked at them in the mirror: they hung motionlessly. No wonder; there was no one inside them, only an earthquake could make them move, but their motionlessness was different from that of other clothes in which there was no one. Not that any of this was at all clear to him at that moment, let alone that he would have been able to put it into words (for that he has his servant), and yet he was aware that they hung there differently from the way his own clothes were hanging in the wardrobe with the mirror at home. Although these were his costumes, they were also not *his*: the one belonged to someone he had yet to become, the other to the person that someone would subsequently have to become. He listened to the voices and the hubbub in the corridor, and started undressing. Fortunately, the radiator was turned up, it was pleasantly warm in the small room.

Apart from the trousers, too long as usual (perhaps the tailor thought he had made a mistake when taking his measurements) everything fitted perfectly. Contentedly he tooked in the mirror and put the fedora on his head, a trifle too slantedly, as he always used to do, and stroked with the palm of his hand along the broad brim. The lime-green ribbon was now the only colour in his attire. He picked up the walking-stick, inspected himself once more from the side, first from the left corner of his eye, then from the right, gave a little tug at the lapels, smoothed the hair above his ear and stepped out into the corridor.

Applause broke out that lured the others from their dressing-rooms too. On all sides he saw looks of admiration.

"Eccolo!" exclaimed Mr Caccini who, coming down a narrow staircase, stopped in his tracks with outstretched arms. He himself was disguised as an archaic piano teacher (who had to make a living as a private tutor) with a foulard and a velvet Wagner beret – all in white, of course.

Uli leaned with his upper leg against his right hand which was holding the silver knob of the walking-stick, crossed his right leg in front of the left, poised the toe of his shoe on the floor and looked around with a crooked smile. There had been no need for Vogel to teach him this pose, for he knew it better than Vogel himself; it was self-evident. He tapped haughtily with one forefinger against the brim of his hat in the direction of Max who was also dressed *anno* 1904, also in white, but everything shabby, frayed, creased, a bedraggled bowler on his head. Then, with a rapid movement, Uli let the stick fly up between his fingers, caught it at the lower end, put it over his shoulder and blew a gallant kiss to Stella, who was now robed in the sky-blue, neo-classicist gown of Miranda.

"A dream," said Berta. While a dresser knelt by him and started pinning up the trouser legs, Vogel asked if everything fitted comfortably. Including his shoes? He must say if anything wasn't right, for nothing must be allowed to bother him during the performance. But Uli was already transformed by the costume.

"My dear boy," he said, "what are you talking about? Before you were even born I had already been and gone from the theatre."

Vogel narrowed his eyes slightly and did not quite know what to answer – or perhaps he knew only too well; but he controlled himself and said Uli had better try on the other costume now, so that they could start the rehearsal.

Back in the dressing-room Uli reluctantly took off the white suit. If on Friday it all went as well as it had done just now, everything would be all right. Standing in his underwear he hung the suit on the coat hanger. For many years he himself had never had enough money to buy such a fine suit, yet for someone who did not exist money was no problem, even the government contributed. What a crazy world. There was a knock on the door and the dresser asked (her forefinger probably still crooked and her face slightly raised) if she could have the trousers, so the alterations could be made straightaway. He opened the door a crack and held out the trousers, whereupon her hand took them. Angrily he threw a glance in the mirror at his old body – fifty years ago he would perhaps have grabbed that hand, pulled her inside and pushed her over the dressing table for a quick one.

Prospero's garments. First came the sandals and a simple tunic of dark-blue cloth to which the gold leather belt clearly belonged. Over it would come the colossal mantle. When he lifted it from its hanger he almost keeled over under the weight. Had they gone out of their minds? It was quite impossible! But at the same time he knew that it had to be this mantle and that nothing could be done about it. On the stage, during the final scene in Pierre de Vries' dressing-room, he would also have to put it on without assistance, so it was best to practise it at once. After a few trials he found a method; by standing in a particular posture, one arm in a sleeve,

153

and then quickly bending his knees, more quickly than the coat could fall, he ducked into it, under it, and then the rest was simple. He took the strange headpiece into his hands, a tall, bright red hood, stitched with silver thread, of an unyielding material, and examined it from all sides. Probably also "no theatre". When he had put it on his head, he was startled at his own appearance: here stood not a man but a mountain of symbols.

There was a knock again; before he could answer, Aronds had already opened the door. Uli was now almost a metre in width, and with tiny steps he made a quarter turn. He could tell from Aronds' face that he too had seen what Uli had seen, and it was as if even his back demonstrated this, for although he did not say a word, one person after another appeared behind him in the corridor. Uli began to walk, having to keep his equilibrium as if carrying a large pile of books on his head. From a corner, Aronds took a staff that Uli had not yet noticed, and handed it to him. The crowd parted, he was just able to get through the door. In the corridor he paused and said, "Well, thanks a million. It looks like . . . The Pope is nothing compared with this."

"Willem," said Vogel, "you have no idea how magnificent you look."

"I can't bloody act like this, can I! I can hardly walk."

"That is exactly how it should be. In that mantle you are a magician, you are burdened by your supernatural talents and powers. You mustn't try to eliminate the weight of that coat, but to exploit it. Resistance must always be converted into force – that is law number one."

"Yes, that's all very well for you, you won't be standing there, on stage."

"Let's try it. You'll see."

On the way to the stage the dresser followed him, carrying the robe. In his blue tunic he walked beside Stella, still in her virginal Miranda gown. He had not sought her company (she his?) but now that they were both here he suddenly had a feeling that there hung more between them than on the other occasions when they had been near each other. He tried to think of something to say but she was the first to speak:

"I wonder if there has ever been anyone on the stage with a career like yours."

The word "career" struck him. He had never looked at it that way; to him this part was an absurd incident at the end of his life, but of course, you could also – if you were young at any rate – see it was the crowning culmination of a "career". Smiling, he looked at her.

"To you, life is still a beautiful straight line, isn't it – a kind of staircase, going up one step at a time."

"And to you?"

He shrugged his shoulders. "I don't know. More the kind of line a toddler scrawls on a piece of paper."

"That can be beautiful too. To a mother that is very beautiful."

"A mother, yes . . ." He was silent for a moment and made a vague gesture. "I am not saying that everyone's life is such a mishmash, but mine certainly is. I hope for you that your life, when you are my age, will be a beautiful, straight flight of stairs when you look back on it. Something like . . . I don't know."

"The steps at the Piazza di Spagna. In Rome."

"I've never been to Rome."

"Well, what's to stop you? Why don't you go there, straight after the last performance? You've earned it. It will be spring then, and Berta would love it too, I'm sure. You can get trips for as little as a few hundred guilders."

He let her go through the fire door first. Against the red glow of the auditorium stood the tall rear wall of the set: a chaotic tangle of beams and bolts.

"Suppose we go there together?"

"Yes," she said, "that would be very nice too."

"Stella," he asked when she said no more, "when shall we go out for supper again? How about somewhere Italian? Then we can talk about our travel plans."

"I will give it serious thought." With a laugh she tapped briefly with her fingertips against his cheek, and turned away.

More even than by her reply, he felt put in his place by this gesture of hers. The touch burnt his cheek like a slap on the ear; the dirty old man, who had better not think he could tempt a young

155

girl to come on little trips with him. While all he had really wanted to do was tell her about La Charlotte and the ring.

Vogel suggested, now that everyone was in Shakespearean costume anyway, that they run through the rehearsal of the masque first, so that the photographer would get an idea of what was involved. In the afternoon this would be followed by a run-through of the whole play in costume.

The scene containing the masque – in the fourth act of *The Tempest* – was about two-thirds of the way through *Hurricane*. The writer had left it remarkably intact, with no more than two interruptions by Paul Musch. It was as if Siderius had held back here as though from something unassailable. Perhaps, Vogel had once suggested, this was because this scene occupied the same position in *The Tempest* as the whole play did in Shakespeare's work: an almost sacred jewel, more profound (and certainly more serene) than the play Hamlet had had performed in order to catch the conscience of the murderous king. Uli, on the other hand, silently agreed with Etienne, who said it was "pretentious twaddle"; as far as Uli was concerned, Vogel's interpretation was of the same order.

The director showed the photographer where to plant his tripod during the rehearsal and prepare the gigantic camera for operation. His assistant (Benjamin, the theatre director's young son) would meanwhile have to strew the magnesium powder on a tray on a cast-iron standard.

"Silence, please," said Vogel, seating himself at his lectern in the stalls. "We'll start immediately after the conversation between Max and Stella about their money problems."

When everyone had become quiet, except the actors muttering on stage, Paul Musch requested silence. When it had become quiet there as well, he announced that they would run through the masque. He helped Pierre de Vries into his magic cloak, put the hat on his head and handed him his staff and his Book. It was only at this moment that Uli saw the Book for the first time; until now the action had merely been mimed, like putting on and taking off

156

the cloak. It looked like a heavy folio, but it weighed nothing; painted polystyrene with the words *Monas Hieroglyphica* on the cover. Stella and Lucas nestled in stylised poses by a paltry set piece painted with green leaves. At a sign from Paul Musch, Uli, that is to say Pierre de Vries, that is to say Prospero, called out:

"What, Ariel! My industrious servant, Ariel!"

Promptly Ariel came floating across the white structure, feather-light, tripping on tiptoe, clad in a tight-fitting leotard, with gauze wings on his shoulders. With obvious delight Pierre de Vries looked at his boyish figure, while Uli saw with a little shock that Max was not wearing his glasses, which turned him into a much younger beauty. Prospero then raised his staff and gave Ariel the command to call up the spirits and create the vision: *"some vanity of mine art"*, the purpose of which was to impress on the betrothed pair, Ferdinand and Miranda, the existence of a physically and morally perfect world, from which premarital chastity also stemmed. With outspread arms, one leg lifted with bent knee, bowing forward from the waist, Ariel said in a high voice:

> *"Before you can say, 'come', and 'go',*
> *And breathe twice; and cry, 'so, so';*
> *Each one, tripping on his toe,*
> *Will be here with mop and mow.*
> *Do you love me, master? No?"*

> *"Dearly, my delicate Ariel. Do not approach*
> *Till thou dost hear me call."*

replied Uli gravely, while noticing with surprise how the thought of Rome had suddenly occurred to him again. Perhaps it wasn't even such a mad idea to go to Rome with Berta next year. Those steps. St Peter's. See Rome and die, he thought – no, that was Naples. Why? What was so special about Naples? Of course they could go there too, if they were in Italy anyway.

"Are you keeping your mind on it, Willem?" called Vogel. "*'Look thou . . .'*"

"Sorry," said Uli, and fixed his gaze on Stella and Lucas:

> *"Look thou be true; do not give dalliance*

157

> *Too much the rein: the strongest oaths are straw*
> *To the fire i'the blood . . ."*

While Pierre de Vries had his own ideas about this, Prospero impressed it on them, but Ferdinand reassured his future father-in-law – he, Lucas van Geest, the scoundrel who, in order to get Stella Middag, had hatched a loathsome plan that would be the ruin of everyone except himself. The magician called to Ariel to conjure up the spirits. At that moment soft piano music could be heard (to be replaced, for the performance at the City Theatre, by the Concertgebouw Orchestra, conducted by Willem Mengelberg in person), and Iris appeared. In ethereal tulle, adorned with long ribbons in all colours of the rainbow, Trix began to address the spirit of the earth, in a singsong voice:

> *"Ceres, most bounteous lady, thy rich leas*
> *Of wheat, rye, barley, vetches, oats and pease;"*

But Paul Musch interrupted her with a remark that, according to Vogel, "represented the only literary-historical verses in all dramatic literature" (perhaps he though the whole play was really a flop). In order not to make a second blunder, Uli forced himself to pay attention. Fortunately, he was allowed to sit down when the music began.

> *"Dear Trix, wait just one moment, and remember*
> *That you are Ariel."*
>   *"How so, me Ariel?"*
> *"My dear, mark this. In Burgersdijk's*
> *Translation, further on, Ariel says*
> *That it was he who acted Ceres."*
>   *"I*
> *Am Iris."*
>   *"Yes. In Shakespeare's text it says:*
> *'. . . when I presented Ceres'. To present*
> *Means introduce, but in another sense*
> *It means to act, to be another person,*
> *And also, to inform. Well, you announce*
> *Ceres' arrival, and you must be Ariel.*
> *Old Burgersdijk made a mistake.*
> *Ariel Ceres? Ariel the earth? What nonsense.*
> *That could not be. He is the rainbow,*

> *Connecting earth and sky. Iris,*
> *A being in between, which is both sun and rain*
> *Heaven and earth, Juno and Ceres, lightly . . ."*

For the first time Uli understood what the lines were about. Until now, he had let the words wash over him each time, his ears strained only for his cue: ". . . *Juno and Ceres, lightly . . ."*

> *"I say, director, how about us getting*
> *Down to work? You do your theorising*
> *In your own leisure time. 'Bilde, Künstler,*
> *Rede nicht.'"*

"No, Willem," Vogel interrupted him, "that sounded much too German again. Pierre de Vries can't do that. More of a Dutch accent please, more like a Dutch Minister for Foreign Affairs."

"Isn't it awful," said Uli, "that you're not allowed to be good at something."

"Yes, well, look here, that's what you're an actor for."

> *"Bilde, Künstler,*
> *Rede nicht."*

"Terrible, yes, that's much better. Paul . . ."

> *"But you can only 'bilden' if . . ."*

> *"Just tell her what to do. This kind of talk*
> *Is good for scholars, it's no use to us."*

> *"All right. Into your acting, Trix,*
> *Try to put just a little bit of Max.*
> *You, Max, where are you? – a bit of Trix."*

And as Iris resumed her hymn to Ceres, Pierre de Vries – having crept into Uli's skin – suddenly understood it too. That girl there was the boy he has in love with, Trix became maxified, Max trixified – and it was as though this fusion cast its perplexing echo back to Uli. He was no longer listening to the pastoral canticle. He felt as he used to feel when visiting the dentist (long ago, when he still had teeth) who poked about in his mouth, carrying out actions, bringing about alterations, while he himself saw only the sparse, embarrassed hairs on the man's lower arms, and had no

159

idea what was going on. He tried to concentrate again, but did not succeed. Yet, when Mimi entered, the heralded Ceres, garlanded with flowers, Vogel called from the stalls:

"Now you're really projecting it well, Willem!"

Of course, he mustn't just act Prospero, but Pierre de Vries acting Prospero – and at the same time, as he apparently did so, it was as though he was simply himself. Or was it perhaps like this, that he became himself because he acted Pierre de Vries who acted Prospero? He momentarily saw the shorn monk's skull of Siderius before him: there you had the dentist, doing invisible things in your mouth – with a white mask on, not in front of his eyes but in front of his own mouth.

Olga, the fat and yet heavenly Juno, had appeared as well in the meanwhile, in her hands a silver-coloured imitation harp, and the chanting changed into singing. A moment later Paul Musch decided to skip the dancing scene with the nymphs and the mowers, because the extras hadn't arrived yet (whereby Siderius had at a stroke saved the Authors' Theatre a considerable sum of money). Before they went any further, the photographer would take his picture. Although it was the first time, it went off well. He pulled his head away from under the white cloth, looked briefly, in silence, at the motionless tableau, and with a sweep of his hand whipped the cover from the lens. At the same moment Benjamin held a match to the magnesium, and a large, chalky white cloud rose up.

"Wonderful!" called Vogel. "Carry straight on!"

Dazzled, Uli stood up with a jerk.

> "I had forgot that foul conspiracy
> Of the beast Caliban and his confederates,
> Against my life: the minute of their plot
> Is almost come . . ."

But that was as far as he got. Burdened by the mantle and hat, he felt as if he was suddenly growing smaller. He began to sweat slightly, the Book slipped from his hand and bounced soundlessly down the set. With both hands he clutched the staff, forcing his eyes (his one eye) to see something across the fading explosion on his retina: the three girls, Mr Caccini, Stella . . . then they were

160

suddenly coming towards him, although he must already have been swaying earlier.

Of course it was all because he had stood up too quickly, and then that heavy cloak. Nothing to worry about. He could not remember having lost consciousness, and perhaps he hadn't; besides, he did not intend to think anything more of it. So many things had happened in his life of which he had thought at the time that surely this was serious, yet he was still alive. Fear, that was something for the young, for people who had nothing else to think about. Fear was something that took the place of real worries.

"Being afraid of flying," he said, "that's the same sort of thing. Just imagine, in the war people got into aircraft that couldn't only crash but that could even be shot at, too. People who are afraid of flying ought to be ashamed of themselves, for instance in front of all those air hostesses who get into those machines every day. Anyway, cycling is much more dangerous than flying. Do you know what it is, that kind of fear? Sheer luxury. When the English and Canadians arrived, in forty-five, with tanks firing and bombs falling and all the rest, do you think people were afraid of the war then? Don't you believe it. They leapt in the air for joy! That's how it is everywhere. There are people who are all the time afraid of cancer, but when their finger gets caught in the door they have suddenly forgotten all about cancer. You must be kidding! Soft, everyone has gone soft. I have been in bombing raids, what do you think, bang overhead – do you think I was afraid? Not at all. I was *alive*. Or take those people who have to live on social security and scream blue murder; they're all of them Rockefellers compared with people in Africa or India – and even compared with their own grandfathers or great-grandfathers. Honestly, I know what I'm talking about. I've gradually turned into my own great-grand-father, and I live on a pittance too, but I know how much worse it could be. The other day I saw a poor old sod on television, do you remember, Berta? He pointed at his car standing outside in front of his house and you'll never guess what he said. He said, 'If I have to get rid of my car as well, I'll do myself in, because there'd no longer be any point in living.' Just imagine it! Sixty years ago only

161

millionaires had cars and a hundred years ago cars didn't even exist yet. That's the kind of world we live in nowadays. I'm telling you, we shall see some very peculiar things. People are badly off, but if you ask me they'll have to become much worse off still. When they were really badly off, in the war, they were a lot more human. Give me the war any day."

"What are you drivelling on about?" said Berta. "Who are you actually talking to?"

"Anyway, I'll have another pint, before it's too late."

In the shrill light of the canteen, Uli, dressed in his blue tunic, looked defiantly at the faces that eyed him uneasily from all sides. He gave Stella a slightly agitated nod. Only Etienne nodded in agreement.

"Are you sure, Willem," asked Max, now wearing his glasses again, "you wouldn't like to lie down for a while?"

"Lie down? Me? Lie down yourself, man!" He looked at Vogel who sat a little further away, his back half turned towards him. "I say! Are we still rehearsing today?"

2
The Interview

After the rehearsal that afternoon he did not go to the Tivoli with the others, but when everything went well the next day, his malaise was soon forgotten, even by himself. The first night was now just three days away. Mircea, the Rumanian make-up man, came to do their make-up for the first time and Uli had a chance to get used to his two wigs. The first was Pierre de Vries', dyed much too black; the second consisted of Prospero's long grey locks. All the sound effects had now been recorded on tape, and when the static main light was replaced by the lighting programme, another new situation had arisen, already quite close to the real performance, except that everything kept going wrong because there was a new computer. But Uli knew from experience that much worse things would probably happen, especially at the dress rehearsal, which would mean the first night couldn't possibly go ahead, for that was how it was with every production. And yet the first night always did go ahead.

On that Tuesday everyone caught the fever. This was further reinforced by the press photographer who suddenly showed up on the stage in spastic contortions – standing, crouching, lying, constantly trying to remove the gigantic beetle that had lodged in his right eye. The photographer photographed the photographer (magnificent explosions!) and with the slow movements of a large fish in an aquarium the television cameraman was meanwhile wandering about the set too, his camera on his shoulder, guided across the slopes and ramps by a production assistant who held him by the waist, and followed by a sound man with headphones.

Some, especially Etienne, were bothered by all this activity, but

163

Uli felt enveloped and protected by it. It was how it was meant to be! Nor was he put off by the constant interruptions; if anyone forgot his lines he sometimes prompted them even before Miss Wijdenes in the wings. The whole thing reminded him vaguely of something – of the preparations for a party, far away in the shadows (all the world wars were yet to come), Christmas Eve at the house of his aunt and the window dresser from the Maison pour Messieurs, where he, Uli, a thick scarf around his neck, had to wait with Berta in the small icy cold side room where the sewing machine stood with which his aunt made a bit of extra money, and from where they listened to the mysterious, mounting bustle in the house. Footsteps going back and forth, soft talking, the pervasive dark smell of roast pork and red cabbage coming from the kitchen. It always took far too long, but finally, when they were shivering with cold, they were suddenly called; sometimes by their father, if he was there. In the living-room, now much warmer than before, the gas lamp above the festive dinner table had been turned off, and in the corner by the window stood the Christmas tree with the burning candles, gleaming baubles, festoons, glistening tinsel, the parcels on the red crêpe paper underneath. "Silent Night, Holy Night . . ." and, every year the same, the silver bird with the red tail hung upside down in the tree whilst, risen from fathomless mysteries, there shone the little glass trumpet from which came an eerie, high note when you blew on it . . .

"Ladies and gentlemen," Vogel called out at the end of the rehearsal, "even a first-class performance can still be spoilt if the curtain calls are untidy and clumsy. Let's practise those before we leave."

The curtain was not going to be used and in the last fade-out Uli had to ease his rigid final pose, stand up relaxedly and then bow. During the blackout immediately following, Etienne, murdered, had to get to his feet and also bow, letting himself be guided by Uli; after the second blackout all the others suddenly had to be standing at prearranged places, aesthetically scattered about the set – an effect that would in itself encourage more applause. None of this was new to Uli, except the fact that this time he wasn't standing near the backdrop, but centrally, at the highest point.

164

Expertly he made his bow, neither too short, nor too deep, and not for too long, to the silent, almost empty house. Only at the back, on the second balcony, a joker clapped briefly.

Immediately afterwards, television took possession of the stage. Props were shoved this way and that, the camera was put on a tripod and the production assistant went to sit in the white-sheeted gandfather chair at the top of the set, so that the lighting could be adjusted. Michael introduced Uli to an author he had not met before: Flip Mannikin, who under the pseudonym of Richter Romijn had adapted *Philemon Martyr* into *The Killjoy*. Uli had never heard of him, he didn't know anyone (Pierre de Vries knew everyone, of course). The writer had the weatherbeaten face of a yachtsman, or a roadmender, and with a jovial laugh he complimented Uli on his acting. He too was going to be interviewed; and Vogel was going to be asked about his views on stage-directing, and together with Michael himself, about the subsidy problem. Perhaps it would be best if Uli went first, then he could change his clothes afterwards.

"Actually," said the business manager cautiously, "you should take this personally, I mean, *not* take it personally, but it might be better if you didn't say too much about your political opinions."

"What do you mean?"

"Well, that the unemployed are Rockefellers, for instance."

"Aren't they then?"

"I totally agree with you, but there are a lot of people here who are glad they still have work. Besides, not everyone can cope with the harsh truth the way you formulated it yesterday. I believe that our main objective now is to cultivate goodwill for the Authors' Theatre. Much may depend on this broadcast."

With a quick movement, Uli grabbed him by his tweed lapels. "If I help you, will there be another part in it for me?"

He could tell from Michael's eyes that he hated being touched.

"We would be insulting you if we made it depend on that."

The editor of the Arts Programme, a notepad covered in scribbles in his hand, was, of course, another of those characters in jeans, with a fluffy little white shawl hanging round his neck. Why the hell must everyone wear uniform? If it wasn't a blazer it was

165

jeans. But he was friendly enough, introduced himself (Bram Polak) and asked Uli to sit in that chair up there. Uli put on his mantle and was immediately photographed again. While the cameraman joined him at the top of the set and scanned him with a light meter as if he was searching for radioactivity, or weapons, and when the sound technician sent a fishing rod with a microphone towards him, he suddenly noticed Berta in one of the boxes along the side; with Joost on her lap, she was talking to an attractive young woman. On the balustrade stood a cassette recorder.

Polak had gone over to the camera and the programme producer asked Uli to say a few words.

"What am I to say? Fellow countrymen! At last the hour has struck when –"

"Okay," said the sound technician.

The producer looked around and requested silence.

"Silence!" called Vogel.

Berta and her beautiful interviewer clattered out of the box and as silence descended (everywhere in the hall and on the stage eyes were fixed on him, including Stella's; she was sitting with her arms clasping her knees behind the camera on the floor) Uli felt how everything suddenly became tense inside him. Hundreds of thousands of people, who as yet knew nothing about it, would see him sitting here – people who had known him before the war, colleagues from the radio drama unit, the members of Enjoyment Through Endeavour, the rabble from The Cellar – something began to twitch in his neck, which he corrected by changing his position.

"Vision," said the producer.

"On," said the cameraman.

"Sound."

"On," said the sound man.

"Mr Bouwmeester," began Bram Polak in a voice that Uli suddenly did not recognise. "We have presently seen a few extracts from . . . Cut it boys, sorry about that."

The interruption did not last long.

"Vision on."

166

"Sound on."

"Mr Bouwmeester, we shall presently see a few extracts from Leo Siderius' new play *Hurricane*, which will have its first night tomorrow, played by the Authors' Theatre at the Kosmos Theatre in Amsterdam, in which you take the leading rôle."

Tomorrow? thought Uli – but just in time he realised that the programme would of course be broadcast the day after tomorrow, on Thursday. He nodded.

"A complicated play," said Polak, and waited for a response.

"If you're asking me whether this is a play for blockheads, then my answer is no. And as by far the greatest majority of mankind consists of blockheads, there are no more than a thousand performances in it." Uli laughed and flung one leg across the other. His tenseness had suddenly vanished, and instead he now felt to his satisfaction that the tension around him was increasing. "But you're right, it's all a bit crazy. Sometimes I think writers are crazy – the good ones, at least. Take a fellow like Leo Siderius now. Think of the things he makes us do, to follow his mental contortions. And yet we do it. Sometimes I wonder how in heaven's name it is possible that the figments of such a person's imagination can be realised – by means of very normal people, perfect professionals, like the dressmakers who have made this magnificent costume here. Actors are already slightly less normal, I do admit that."

"How is it then, that a lot of normal people will come and pay good money to watch it?"

"Yes, that is the craziest thing of all. It seems normal people need craziness too."

"Except the government, which refuses to subsidise this madness any longer with the money paid in taxes, mostly, as you would say, by blockheads."

"Precisely, there you are. Maybe the government is the craziest of all, because it doesn't understand that everybody needs craziness."

"And why is that, do you think?"

"I couldn't tell you. Maybe because the computers are in charge these days."

"The power of the government lies in computers?"

167

"I wouldn't be surprised."

"An interesting point of view. We shall come back to the financial problem of the Author's Theatre in a while, but now I should like to broach another subject with you. Mr Bouwmeester, you bear what is undoubtedly the most famous theatrical name in the Netherlands. Perhaps young people aren't so aware of this these days, but for at least a century, until about twenty years or so ago, there was a Bouwmeester to be found in practically every group and company. The Pierre de Vries, whom you play in *Hurricane*, has unmistakably the contours of the legendary Louis Bouwmeester – not where his sexual orientation is concerned, as far as I know, but in respect of his status as a great actor. You are the last branch on that tree. Director Caspar Vogel will presently tell us how he discovered you, if I may put it that way. My question to you is how does it feel to be in that position?"

"That is what I have been asked all my life, by everybody, and frankly, I am sick and tired of it. Look, to you I am a Bouwmeester –"

"Not only to me."

"To everyone. But to myself I am not a Bouwmeester at all. I mean . . . I simply am who I am."

"Willem Bouwmeester."

"That's what I am called, yes. That happens to be my name. But I am not the same as my name, am I? Ridiculous idea. Suppose my name was Hitler. Are you the same as your name, Bram Polak?"

Uli sensed he was entering dangerous territory – all the more dangerous because the camera continued to turn. He caught a worried look from Vogel, he saw Michael shaking his head, but what had he said wrong? It was true, wasn't it? As Polak did not reply, a heavy silence fell. This must be stopped, at once! He had seen this before on television, with a particular type of interviewer; they let their victim swim in the silence, hoping that he would commit some blunder or other.

"There is another thing," said Uli with composure, " and that is that you keep being forced to answer to your name. And so that is what you do, that's what you are an actor for anyway. But if you really coincide with your name, if, so to speak, you become even to

168

yourself a Bouwmeester, or a Jewboy or whatever, then you're lost. But if you are nothing yourself, or nobody, yes, then obviously it is rather handy if you're called – I don't know what – Count Bentinck or something, If you're simply called Jansen, then you really have been unlucky."

Uli did not understand why, but the atmosphere down below became more and more icy. Polak fixed his gaze on him again.

"Well, you are a colourful personality at any rate, I must say. *You* don't seem to be threatened by nobodyness. And you haven't taken a pseudonym either."

"Well, obviously, I don't intend to run away from my name. I can cope with it all right."

"How old are you, Mr Bouwmeester?"

"Seventy-eight years young."

"And yet in a sense this part is your debut."

"As far as the Grand Theatre is concerned. Certainly."

"What did you do in the past?"

"I have so many pasts. Which past do you mean?"

"Let's say, before the war."

All of a sudden Uli felt the threat of a terrible calamity – like someone who sees an iceberg looming up out of nowhere, right in front of his ship. How could he have been so stupid not to think of it, he should never have embarked on this interview!

"I used to appear in cabaret and operetta. Nothing worth mentioning."

"And after the war?"

"Nothing to write home about either," said Uli, breathing more freely again. "A few radio plays, a bit of directing of amateur groups."

"So it is really quite wonderful for you to have this opportunity now."

"It's spiffing, yes."

Polak nodded, scribbled on his notepad, whispered something that Uli could not hear, and fixed his eyes on him again.

"And yet, if I calculated correctly, in May 1945 you were only just over forty. Straight after the war there was a great demand for entertainment of all kinds. How is it that you weren't involved in

169

that at all?"

There it was. Frozen, Uli stared at him. His heart started to pound. What was he to say? The truth? Invent some fib? That he had been ill, weakened after the hunger winter? But not a word passed his lips, the eye of the camera glimmered with purplish iridescence, the microphone hung over him like the head of a snake. At the point where twenty or twenty-five pairs of eyes intersected, he was sitting on his throne as if it was an electric chair, and he felt how the catastrophe drew to its climax, second by second.

"Well, in that case may I refresh your memory? It was because from May till October 1945 you were in an internment camp. And the reason for that was that as late as 1943 you were still performing in Germany."

"In an innocuous operetta," said Uli hoarsely. "*The Gypsy Baron*. The case against me was dismissed."

"Still, it is a fact that in the middle of the war you still contributed to upholding the morale of the German people. And not only the German people," said Polak, looking at his notes. "On September the sixth of that year, for instance, you took part in a show for a battalion of Dutch SS men in the Barbarossa SS Junkerschule in Bad Tölz –"

"Have you gone out of your goddam minds!" Stella suddenly called out, rising like a swan flapping its wings for flight. "What the hell do you think you're doing?" She flung her hand in front of the lens. "What kind of bloody rotten trick is this?"

Uli stood up trembling, but still the general paralysis had not been broken. The programme producer looked around desperately and seemed unsure whether all this was good for his programme or quite the reverse. The cup of coffee, on its way from its saucer to Vogel's mouth, halted in mid-air; Michael, standing beside him, could perhaps himself feel that his face became paler than it already was. Max, in the front row, had put his arm around Trudy's shoulders and there it lay, like an out-of-place non-thing. Paul, in the middle of crossing the stage on tiptoe, for ever forgot where he was heading, and stopped in his tracks. Olga put one hand on the shoulder of the Bidermann-adapter and covered her eyes with her other hand. Somewhere in the wings the stage manager slowly crossed his arms; the property man, the dressmakers, Lucas, everyone froze on the spot – only the sound man, concentrating solely on the quality of the reproduction, looked about in surprise. For the rest, only little Benjamin did not have the faintest idea what was going on. With his nose in the open bottle of magnesium, he stood bewilderedly on the proscenium.

3
Discourse on Swan-Songs

Bram Polak took Stella's hand from the lens and said:

"There's no need for that. It hasn't been recorded."

He looked at his notepad and turned to the sound technician. "Would you wipe it from where Bouwmeester says 'it's spiffing'."

As soon as he had spoken, a commotion burst out. All the people who had been sitting in the auditorium came crowding on to the stage, someone knocked a chair over, Etienne darted forward from somewhere, looking as if he was going to lay into Polak.

"You bastard, taking on a man of eighty! Who do you think you are, coming here to act the judge?"

The excitement around him seemed to make Polak steadily calmer (there was little else he could do). He turned a page of his notepad and wrote something down.

"I'm not having myself called a Jewboy by someone who has entertained the SS."

"Cut it out, man! What kind of methods are those? You're just a shabby sadist, that's what you are. Do you know what I think of it? I think it's a . . . a . . ."

"Go on," said Polak, looking him straight in the face, "say it! A dirty Jew's trick?"

"Drop dead, man."

At this point Flip Mannikin alias Richter Romijn put his oar in. From his tone it was clear he was used to exercising authority somewhere, perhaps in a literary coterie, or at home.

"That's all very well, but you yourself started it by needling him about his name. It looks to me as if you were trying to provoke him."

"Not at all!" said Polak indignantly. "We only found out about it by accident, in the editing room, from some old cuttings, and I had no intention of using it. But when he started on about Jewboy . . . well, I'm sorry, but that jogged my memory. Odd, isn't it? Why do you think that might have been? Think about it, maybe you'll figure it out."

"But what did he say, anyway? That you shouldn't allow yourself to be forced into a role. That's precisely *against* racism."

"Is it?" said Polak. "Well, what I heard was Jewboy."

"But if you react like that, you're turning yourself into a Jew, Bram. That is exactly what the anti-Semites want."

"I *am* a Jew, for God's sake. If you can't feel the difference between a Jew and a Jewboy, then I don't give a cent for your literary talent."

The playwright made a gesture and said no more. None of the girls joined in the argument, not even Olga; it seemed as if Stella's outburst had made the women's standpoint sufficiently clear, and perhaps it had.

"What shit are you talking, man?" Etienne called out. He seemed to feel particularly involved in the subject. No one had ever seen him so agitated. "In forty-five you weren't even born yet."

"No, but quite a few people had died by then. You people don't understand the first thing about it, you're suffering from a damned serious form of virginity. Just like your colleagues in the war, come to think of it. Well, how about it, are we carrying on with it or aren't we?"

"Hang on a minute," said Vogel, putting his coffee cup on the floor. "Let's get this thing sorted out first."

With raised eyebrows Polak looked at him. "What is there to be sorted out? There's nothing on tape, I told you. Nothing has happened."

"Oh, hasn't it?" called Max.

"Nothing has happened, he calls it," said Paul to the television producer, in an attempt to involve him. But the man shrugged his shoulders and remained silent. Bram Polak was the star of the programme, the darling of the art-loving public; he picked his own

173

producers. They were dispensable.

Vogel raised his hands in adjuration.

"What has happened is the following: before you started we were a homogeneous group, working hard, not a cloud in the sky. Now, just before the first night, you have put a spoke in our wheel. You have revealed something we didn't know: that Willem performed in Germany during the war. You're not publishing the fact, but you have made it known all the same."

"And in doing so," Michael added softly, "you actually played a dangerous game. When you started, Mrs Bouwmeester was being interviewed in that box over there by a young lady from *Privaat*. We have been lucky, they've gone away, to the foyer I think, otherwise the entire country would have known next week what happened here."

"Jesus," said Polak.

"And whether that would have benefited the position of the Authors' Theatre at this critical stage is very doubtful indeed. There are people who are simply waiting for something like this. Let's hope it can be kept to ourselves."

Now the property manager turned to Polak: "I'm not at all sure who would be worse off if this became known – Bouwmeester or you."

"I would, naturally."

"And quite rightly too," said Etienne. "Isn't it about time for an apology?"

"You keep out of it. I have my own conscience, I don't need you for that. You, probably last of all."

"If you want the first night to go ahead on Friday," the stage manager stepped in, "you're going about it the right way." Although he said nothing more, the tone of his voice seemed to imply a whole range of further statements: that perhaps *he* alone could be the judge in this company of – as far as the war was concerned – scarcely born or not yet born people; perhaps he had been in the resistance or in a concentration camp, or both.

"Exactly," Vogel chipped in. "That is the only thing that matters. What are we talking about, anyway? It is forty years ago, and Willem tells us the case against him was dismissed. So we must

174

be bound by that too. He hasn't misled us either, because we didn't ask him anything – we could hardly expect him to mention it himself. Okay, it's not a pretty business, but it doesn't amount to very much either. When I think of war criminals, I think of something rather different from *The Gypsy Baron*. Here," he said, making a gesture towards Mr Caccini, "our maestro, he is also the wrong age, if I may say so, and we haven't asked him anything either. Maybe he played for Mussolini – who is to say?"

"Ah, il Duce!" called Mr Caccini, blowing two kisses towards the sky. "In the Palazzo Venezia! *Avanti, popolo* . . ." he began to sing, but he corrected himself: "Beg your pardon . . . *Primavera di bellezza!*"

This broke the tension momentarily. Lucas grabbed the production assistant by her waist and tried to dance with her, but the moment did not last long enough.

"If we had known about it," Vogel continued, looking up towards Uli, "we would have asked Willem to take the part just the same . . ."

But it did not escape Uli that Caspar, as he uttered these words, began to doubt the truth of what he was saying and that by the end of his sentence he was sure that he would *not* have engaged him. Poor Uli! Everyone seemed to have forgotten all about him. He was still standing in front of his chair, at the highest peak of the iceberg, listening to what was being said. Polak repeated once again that he hadn't spoken so much because Bouwmeester had *then* appeared in Germany, but because he had *now* used the term Jewboy – to which Vogel replied it was ridiculous to conclude from that that Uli was in any way an anti-Semite. If he *had* been, he would precisely *not* have used that word in this situation. He had used it in the old-fashioned way in which it was commonly used by his generation, before the war, even by Jews of that generation – just like the word "spiffing". "Can you imagine it, spiffing! If you'd been gay or something, who knows, you might have taken offence at that. God knows what you would have scribbled in those notes of yours then." Vogel looked up. "Willem, tell us, are you an anti-Semite?"

Uli looked at the faces that turned towards him. Everyone was defending him, but that was perhaps mainly out of self-preservation, in order to save the performance. Of course he wasn't an anti-Semite.

"How could I be an anti-Semite? I've worked together with Jews half my life." At the same moment he realised that this was the very argument an anti-Semite would have used. Everything was poisoned now. It was all finished.

The stage manager looked from Uli to Polak and back again. "I think both of you need a lot of forgiveness."

"It doesn't matter any more," said Uli, exhausted. He let the mantle slide from his shoulders to the ground, pulled Prospero's wig off with one hand and Pierre de Vries' wig with the other. "I'm going home."

In the silence that followed, the property manager said, "Now the shit has really hit the fan."

"*This is totally impossible, of course!*"

The man who spoke these words with tremendous authority was a new arrival on the scene: the director of the Kosmos Theatre. Somehow or other he must have got wind of what was going on, by intuition or telepathy – Uli, at any rate, had not seen him enter (any more than he had seen Stella leave). Short and stocky, in a grey flannel three-piece suit and a dark blue tie with white polka dots, he sat in his body as in an armchair. In a friendly voice he invited Uli to come down.

"Are there any more interviews to be recorded?" he asked Polak.

"That was indeed the intention, yes. But now –"

"Carry on then." And to Uli, "Would you come with me?"

The director's room was on the first floor at the rear, overlooking neglected gardens, with trees and shrubs here and there on which only a few withered leaves remained. Inside, everything was of a ruthless orderliness that nevertheless, because of the warm colours, was not sterile. The director, at most half Uli's age, pointed invitingly to the sofa and asked what he would like to drink. Uli said he could do with a brandy. In this peaceful room, what had happened suddenly seemed distant and fading. Ouside,

176

fast-moving purple clouds slid across the blue sky, making it appear as though inside the room the light was constantly going on and off. Uli felt numbed. On a long table against the wall lay stacks of folders, books and papers, all neatly parallel, the narrower always on top of the wider ones. In a corner by the wall stood a mahogany writing desk, diagonally facing the room, as befitted a director's office (the desks of subordinates are at right angles to the walls), a massive kidney-shaped piece of furniture, modern in the fifties and, after thirty years of hideousness, once again in vogue. The few objects on top of the desk were also arranged with mathematical precision.

The drinks cabinet turned out to be hidden behind a flap in the bookcase, another section of which was occupied by a stone relief of a small boy in profile. Before pouring out the drinks, the director held the glasses briefly against the light: he did everything very slowly, as if pondering something.

He placed the huge glass in front of Uli, offered him a cigar, hitched his trouser creases and sat down opposite him. He pulled up his right trouser leg a bit higher still, threw that leg over the other, tugged down his waistcoat with both hands and, with a smile, raised his glass of whisky.

Not everyone, he said, had perhaps been in a mood to appreciate it, but the way Mr Bouwmeester had stood there so motionlessly in his mantle at the top of the set had been a splendid sight, while down below all those past events were being stirred up again. He had suddenly been reminded of the great Kanetsu – that was a Noh actor he had seen in Japan. Perhaps Mr Bouwmeester wondered how he had come to be in Japan? Uli nodded. That was because he had studied art history for a brief spell. Why had he chosen to study art history? Would Mr Bouwmeester be interested in hearing about that?

The reason was that he had been intrigued all his life by the last works of great artists. He had a feeling that all of them, or nearly all of them, belonged to a universal set, to use a term of his son Benjamin; that was how children learnt maths these days, so that their parents would no longer be able to help them with their homework. What were the characteristics of this set? That was what he wanted to find out. Of course it was ridiculous to study art history for that reason, a waste of time really, but never mind, he didn't know that then. At the time he had still had a great deal of respect for the Academy of Art, he didn't yet know that study of that kind was intended for people who weren't aiming at something specific but something more general. If you wanted something specific you should simply go for it, and not for something different, you should go straight at it, chase after it, take short cuts, run across the fields, and that way you would learn more in a month than most students did in a whole year.

In monographs and other art-historical dissertations he discovered a great deal about the subject he was interested in, but it consisted chiefly of vague and rather half-baked waffle about serenity and completeness and perfect mastery. It was all universally valid in a way that was of no use to you; it wasn't an answer but merely the question all over again – while he had a feeling that there ought to be some sort of rule or law, also universal but at the same time very precise. Not in the same way as the natural sciences of course, but differently. Well, anyway, that was what he had been looking for. He would sit for hours on end in the Maurits House in The Hague, looking at Rembrandt's last self-portrait, while Rembrandt looked back. There were four elements, really: Rembrandt himself, his image which he saw in the mirror, and the picture he painted; of course only this last element still existed, but as a fourth, additional factor, there was he himself, the observer. He saw Rembrandt as Rembrandt had seen himself in the mirror, so that in a sense he became the painter at the moment he had applied the last brush stroke. What he meant was, there were the kinds of thoughts that went through his mind; in that way, from the inside, he tried to find out what was going on.

But where was the similarity between that amazing painting and, say, Richard Strauss' Four Last Songs? Or Beethoven's late quartets? Or between the last paintings of Picasso – which he had gone to see shortly after Picasso's death, in Avignon (in the Palais des Papes; sometimes no more than a few unerring strokes on the canvas) – and the divine *Oedipus in Colonus* by Sophocles? Or for that matter, Shakespeare's *Tempest*? "*Full fathom five thy father*

178

lies;" said the director, his eyes growing slightly moist, *"Of his bones are coral made; Those are pearls that were his eyes . . ."* That kind of heart-rending beauty. He could mention a whole string of works of art that he had gone to see, all over Europe – usually hitch-hiking, for he was poor then; a few times even as a stowaway, in a truck, on the way to some Dürer or other in Vienna, or a performance of Faust Part II in Hamburg.

It was as if all those final masterpieces had in a sense been made by one and the same man. What kind of man was that? Yes, that was the big question. It was a man standing on the threshold of death – although in one instance he was fifty-two, as in the case of Shakespeare, in another eighty-eight, like Sophocles; but it was as though those people were in some way or other already lit from within by death. What this inner light conferred was a kind of total freedom, a sovereign contempt for the rules of art, which at the same time formed the basis of those rules. A simplicity that had absorbed all complexity into itself, but that had at the same time risen above it. How should he express it? It was nature itself speaking. As Mr Bouwmeester knew, Aristotle had defined art as the imitation of nature, and this was usually taken to be a plea for the representation and therefore the duplication of nature: not the *created* but the *creating* had to be imitated. In that case music could also be included in Aristotle's definition – this thought suddenly occurred to him now. But where were we? In their last works, on the brink of death, great artists coincided therefore, so to speak, with nature, with the force that made bees carry pollen from one flower to another and that made the seeds grow; in short: with love. Anyway, that was what he had tried to say in his epoch-making book about the swan-songs of great artists, which, as Mr Bouwmeester had perhaps already realised, he had never written. Unfortunately he belonged to that most numerous contingent of people who want to write a book some time but never do.

And yet one day he had come upon the track of something. A detailed *ars poetica* that seemed to fit his subject exactly. It had been written for the theatre, more than five hundred years ago, in Japan. The author was Zeami Motokiyo, who had also, both as producer and actor, given Noh the form that it still had today. His system appeared to represent an entire philosophy compared with which the observations of Stanislavski or Brecht were mere child's play. In one of his numerous writings, said the director as he refilled the glasses, he had said the following:

"In every field, especially that of the theatre, there are the so-called secrets. This is because certain things increase in usefulness for so long as they are kept secret. But these secrets often look like nothing when they are expressed in words. But he who therefore calls them worthless is someone who has not succeeded in understanding the importance of the secrets."

The director had quoted these lines standing, slightly rocking on his feet, the brandy bottle in his hand, as if he were declaiming poetry. It was clear he had said them dozens of times before, to others and to himself, and that it was probably verbatim.

"In every field!" he repeated.

He sat down again and now crossed his left leg over his right. One of these secrets, he said, was called "hana", which meant "the Flower". It was a technique which, as Zeami put it, aimed at "the Bewitchment" of the spectator, whereby "yugen" was brought about – that was another secret; "Transcendental Phantasma", into which the spectator was transported. But all this beauty and harmony was still mere art. The "most secret of all secrets" was "kyakurai-ka": "the Returned Flower", about this he spoke only when he had reached a great age and then this concept also began to form part of those things they had been talking about just now. It had been Zeami's intention to bequeath it only to his son, but as his son died before him, he referred to it, but only so sketchily that the secret had in fact virtually remained a secret. Because he refused to reveal it, he was even banished by the Shogun.

The Returned Flower was a Flower that was no longer a Flower, a technique that was no longer a technique, an end stage of ineffable excellence which, according to Zeami (the director raised a forefinger) came only once in a lifetime, and about which nothing could be said except such things as: "In Shiragi the sun shines brightly in the middle of the night". The paradox even went so far that an actor in the highest but one stage always acted with absolute perfection, and would therefore deliberately, from time to time introduce something from his earlier, inferior style into his acting, which as a result became even better; but in the highest stage, that of the Returned Flower, he no longer knew, in a sense, what he was doing; the uttermost freedom of emptiness then prevailed. So then he was no longer nature in the shape of a man, as were ordinary mortals, but a man in the shape of nature, of the whole world.

Mr Bouwmeester was sure to understand that he wanted to know more about this. After all, "kyakurai-ka" was something that could perhaps be universalised. Off to Japan, therefore. In Tokyo and Kyoto (had it ever struck Mr Bouwmeester that the new capital and the old really had the same name: "Amsterdam" and "Damamster"?), evening after evening he sat in the Noh theatre where he once saw the great Kasetsu in a play by Zeami in which he, masked, seventy or eighty years old, played the part of a young girl – and so much with the Returned Flower that afterwards he, the director, in a taxi with a white-gloved driver, winding through the loops and spirals of the highways back to the Ginza in the centre, felt as if that whole gigantic city with its thunderous noise, its chinese-lantern-coloured neon-lights and its beribboned balloons, was now, through the performance, linked with that archaic world in which old men could become young girls in a way that even young girls could not.

Back in Amsterdam he got in touch with the Holland Festival, to try to get a Noh company to come over. He was successful but at the same time this marked the end of his search for the most secret of all secrets, because as a result of his proven organising abilities in the theatre he ended up on the art-managerial circuit, which finally brought him to this room and to this chair. That was how it had all come about. And now he did not want to bore Mr Bouwmeester any longer. There was just one thing he wanted to say in conclusion: the first part of his return journey was made in the middle of the summer on a rusty cargo vessel bound for Singapore. He had hoped to do some studying and writing on the way, but nothing came of it. After a stopover in Taiwan they sailed, without air-conditioning of course, in an appalling heat to Hong Kong; in the windless air the ship became a diabolical frying pan, and it was unbearable to stay on deck even for a minute. In Hong Kong he was able to witness how the body of a Chinese stowaway was lifted out of the freezer in the hold: covered with hoarfrost – you could have smashed him into a thousand pieces with a hammer. He had wanted to cool down for a moment, but the door had locked behind him.

Not until he was walking down the deserted corridor, still in his blue tunic, did Uli remember what had happened earlier. The director had wasted no words on it (except when he briefly mentioned the stirring up of past events); it didn't seem to interest him in the least. What he had said had descended on Uli like a shower of rain, a strange, incomprehensible lecture to which he had listened speechlessly – speechless especially because the story seemed to bear no relation to anything, he had expected some sort of moral at the end, relevant to himself, but there had been nothing of the kind. And yet he had a feeling that the speech had been, by some roundabout way, a response to what had happened, or a comment on it, at any rate it seemed as if it was now over and done with. At the time it had been unthinkable to him that the show could still take place, he himself especially had felt incapable of carrying on, but somehow or other there was no longer any problem.

Suddenly he stretched out his arms in front of him, as if there was someone to embrace (there was nothing and nobody) and he went to Michael's office. There was nobody there either. On the window-sill stood a bottle of sherry and a glass from which someone had drunk. He poured some for himself and sat down in the small armchair with the broken springs. In a room on the other side of the narrow street a boy wearing headphones was playing an invisible guitar, seemingly to an ecstatic audience of hundreds of thousands. When he caught sight of Uli – who raised his glass encouragingly – he drew the curtains.

A moment later Michael entered. He cast a timid glance at his visitor and sat down behind his desk.

"They've almost finished downstairs," he said. "It will go out

182

the day after tomorrow at half past eleven, so we can easily watch it after the dress rehearsal. I'll make sure there is a set, so we can all watch it together."

Before Uli could say anyting, Berta burst in excitedly with the dog.

"There you are!" Clearly she hadn't yet heard what had happened. "Guess who's going to be on the cover of *Privaat* next week. Well?"

"Me," said Uli. "*Proost!*"

"You'd be so lucky. It's Joost!"

4
Perspective

Berta had said, "It's all because of your damned cheek. Here you are, almost eighty, for God's sake, and you don't seem to have learnt a thing in your life. You still think you can say and do whatever you damn well like. You think that different rules apply to you. You! The actor! The leading man! They'll always forgive *you* everything, *you* can't put a foot wrong. It seems to me that you think nobody really takes you seriously, for when you do something it has to be different from when someone else does it, because you are a different kind of person, somebody special, somebody from a different world, a kind of angel or something. And do you know why that is? Because you yourself don't take anyone else seriously. You never did when you were young and now that you're old you do it even less. Besides, I don't think you understand much about people any more. You see a character in that kind of get-up they wear these days, with a week-old beard and a ring in his ear and you think: there's another good-for-nothing. But he might be a professor or a councillor for all you know. No doubt you thought: that young brat from the television, I can twist him round my little finger in no time. Well, I'm glad he twisted you around his little finger instead."

Uli peered at his long nails for a while before answering, "When I think of my life I feel like Marco Polo must have done when he came back to Venice. Nobody could imagine all the things he had seen and experienced, all those strange countries and peoples. Maybe they didn't even believe him. Maybe he didn't believe it himself any longer when he was home again, where everything had stayed the same. The same old Bridge of Sighs. I think he must have felt he had dreamt it all." Was everything really over and done with, as he had thought? The skeleton, having so unexpectedly tumbled out of the cupboard, had been quickly pushed back in again, door locked, as if nothing had happened. Perhaps nothing much had happened; it hardly deserved to be called a real skeleton, after all; more one of those oily plastic affairs like they use in schools. No one referred to it the following day. He had expected that a brief meeting might have been devoted to it, with a declaration by Vogel or something like that, but there was nothing of the kind. During the rehearsal he kept a sharp watch, but everyone seemed to have forgotten the incident, buried it under that other, much more important awareness, that the show had to go on at all costs. (Just as in the war, really.)

This was the last run-through before the dress rehearsal, the last time they played without an audience. When no one mentioned the incident, it gradually faded from Uli's own mind too, as if it had been no more than a part in a previous play (*The Gypsy Baron*) – although obviously, far away, somewhere outside his field of vision, it must have upset him, thrown him into disarray, like a fallen clock can still go on ticking but sometimes, suddenly, slows down or stops for a while and then starts up again. And Uli was such an old clock! A young person feels invulnerable, nothing can happen to him, the catastrophe occurs and after a moment's hesitation he steps across it and it has never taken place. But time will teach him that it did take place and that he was never invulnerable, at least that is to be hoped, because he is a human being and not an animal. Even the slightest mishap leaves dents and distortions, holes, just as a speck of dirt can pierce a rocket – a single word, a certain look out of the corner of an eye, a turned back; it is hardly heard or seen, one shrugs one's shoulders indifferently, but someone else, someone who is also oneself, later proves to have been wounded after all.

The problem is only this: how to convey this message to Uli? How can he be told, begged, ordered, to withdraw, now, at once, before it is too late; how can he be persuaded that the show must on no account be allowed to go on, that instead he ought to retreat behind the speed bumps to his little house in the polder and

185

abandon this unholy enterprise on which he ought never to have embarked? But we are powerless. He is out of our reach, he is caught in the depths of his story like someone living in a different era.

What exactly is at issue here? What have we got ourselves into? Perhaps someone will say that he who asks this question should be the very last to be allowed to ask it. If anyone knows the answer, it is surely he. Alas! The narrator and the listener stand together before the narration. They must cling tightly to each other, for they are equally vulnerable. The narrator is no more responsible for the narration than the listener, for the narration creates on the one hand the narrator and on the other hand the listener, in the way that the child causes the mother and the father to exist. The narrator is the mother, the listener is the father – and what is parenthood other than an uninterrupted state of shared agony?

The only person to mention it again was he himself – to Stella. They were waiting for their cues, side by side in the wings; he in Pierre de Vries's costume, she as Miranda, in her wig of long, loose hair.

"I haven't said thank you yet, Stella," he whispered.

"For what? For yesterday?"

"Yes, for standing up for me."

"Oh go on, I would have done the same for anyone. I simply lost my temper with that little twirp."

"I'd like to explain it all to you."

"What?"

"How it all came about, in the war."

"You don't need to defend yourself for my sake. The war is nothing to me."

"But if *I* feel the need?" And when she looked at him in silence, "Let's go and have a coffee afterwards. But not the Tivoli."

"All right, then. If you want to . . ."

Vogel had to intervene only a few times that afternoon. It had never gone so well before. Joost was a bit sluggish, but that suited everyone. At the follow-up Vogel said he hoped it wouldn't go even better at tomorrow's dress rehearsal, because that must be reserved for the first night. When Uli had already put on his coat, Michael came up and asked if he would like to come to supper, very informally, take pot luck. Mrs Bouwmeester had already agreed, Vogel would be there too. Of course it was all to do with yesterday, and he realised he could not refuse. Angrily he went to Stella who was still cleaning off her make-up.

"I'm terribly sorry, but I really can't get out of it. They must have thought that up in order to put me at my ease for tomorrow and the day after. Bloody nonsense. If you knew how sorry I am."

"Don't be silly, we'll see each other plenty more times. There'll be at least fifty performances if it goes like it did today. Anyway, I've got masses to do at home."

But in Vogel's car, with Michael, Berta and Joost in the back, he thought it was better this way. She didn't want to be with him at all, that was obvious from everything; it could only lead to disappointment. What did he want? He had once read in the Saturday supplement of a newspaper that in the Middle Ages syphilis sufferers went to bed with virgins because they believed this would cure them. It must be something like that – with his age being the disease.

Michael lived on the edge of Vondelpark, in a large house, as airy and empty as Uli had seen only in magazines. In the rectangular space filled with soft, indeterminate music, his heels tapped on gleaming, almost white marble; on the street side was a glass coffee table, a white sofa and two easy chairs; on the side of the park stood a round dining table, also marble-topped; apart from a few large plants and a case full of books and stereo equipment there was not much else. On the wall hung an old pastel drawing of an angel with a minute willie. It was all very beautiful, yet it repelled him, like a mausoleum; he would have preferred to turn tail at once.

Mortifyingly conscious of his scuffed shoes and grubby suit, he let himself sink into the white leather upholstery. Michael himself did not really fit into this environment either; it was chiefly the residence of Mrs Michael; in a salmon-coloured trouser suit and a smile that matched the marble, she immersed everyone in a cloud of civilities and good manners, like an ambassador's wife. A sullen-looking boy and girl in filthy plimsolls entered, limply shook hands and switched on the television. This was the moment for Mrs Michael's smile to be briefly eclipsed, only very briefly but so completely that the children switched the television off and trundled out of the room like a couple of imbeciles.

"You can go and eat at the Chinese," Mrs Michael called after them. "Sweet youth," she said to Berta. Then she took the glass of whisky out of her husband's hand and said, "No, Hendrik, your bladder is much too small for that."

Uli watched it all with ill humour. There was nothing for him here, but there was no chance of escape. On the glass table top lay several gleaming silver boxes; from a pile of art books he picked up the top one, put on his glasses and leaned back. The book consisted mainly of large plates, dealing with the development of perspective in painting. Fascinated, he looked at an old engraving of a voluptuous woman in the process of being drawn. Almost naked, she lay on her back on a table, her opened thighs facing the artist. In front of the table stood a frame divided into squares by threads. The artist's paper was divided into a similar lattice and in order to give his eye a fixed reference point he had placed a small obelisk in front of him, in such a way as to enable him to look exactly over the tip. In later pictures, people, landscapes and buildings developed out of fantastical, invisible and yet visible networks of lines, like spiders trying to catch the world.

What magnificent things there existed in the world! Things he had never heard of, or had always passed by without noticing. What kind of a life had he led, really? There must be so much more, of which he had no inkling, such as those things the theatre director had told him about yesterday. It was all to do with "culture", or not simply with culture but with what was behind it. Something mysterious, something that *also* existed but that was in the possession of a certain class of people, a small group that had perhaps no wish to see an awareness of these things shared by all. Or perhaps it was truer to say that it couldn't be explained, perhaps you could only discover it for yourself, when you were ready for it.

"Our guest of honour has retreated into the contemplation of

188

beauty," said Mrs Michael, briefly touching his shoulder with her long, red-painted nails. "Would you like to come and eat?"

Uli looked up. That book had just been lying there. Smiling faces were turned towards him. Another guest had arrived, a writer he did not know, also a member of the collective; Uli had shaken hands with him absent-mindedly and of course the man's name escaped him. Everyone stood up and Uli reluctantly put the book back.

"You'd rather go on reading, wouldn't you?" said Michael.

"To be frank . . ."

Michael took the book and gave it to him. "It's yours."

Uli stood with the book in his hands, not knowing what to say. Of course he had to decline the gift and then accept it after all; best of all he would have liked to kiss Michael on the cheek. Taking the book from him and putting it on the window-sill near the dining table, Michael pointed to the seat at his wife's right hand.

The table had now been set with a beautiful blue dinner service and delicately woven place mats. Berta appeared from the kitchen and said Joost didn't want to eat, to which Mrs Michael replied that he was clearly used to something better at home. The consommé was served by a woman of Berta's age, in a white apron; it was obvious that Michael did not have to work for a living, there were other means; or perhaps, thought Uli, this woman was Mrs Michael's mother, forced into servility by her heartless daughter.

Even during dinner Vogel kept his hat on. The writer, a man with bristly hair the colour of badly-polished silver, sat opposite Uli and was telling Berta about the genesis of the Authors' Theatre, in the late 1960s. Every now and then he had to pause for several seconds to conquer a fit of laughter. It was a complicated tale of intrigue and political machinations, phone calls, nocturnal rendezvous, hilarious press conferences, secret meetings in which Amsterdam city councillors and mighty bigwigs from a previous theatrical generation were involved, everyone leading everyone else up the garden path, playing off one against another, until no one could any longer comprehend the web of intrigue, rumour and lobbying that had resulted in the allocation of the Kosmos Theatre. They would have preferred the City Theatre, that was

189

what they had aimed at all along, but all right, the Kosmos was better than nothing. And even that was now in the balance. If the Authors' Theatre disappeared, it would mark the definitive end of the sixties, that golden age besides which the twenties were nothing. But that was life, nothing lasted for ever.

After this aphorism the author blew his nose, folded his handkerchief and, in order to put it into his trouser pocket, tilted briefly on to his right buttock. The story was worth writing a play about, he said. But someone else would have to write it, he himself was more interested in the theatre of cruelty – that is to say, metaphysical cruelty, and this wasn't really a cruel tale. It was more in Molly's line. If the Authors' Theatre was shortly to be axed by the kind of gentlemen who were currently in power, he could write a fine farce about it: by way of a farewell performance. Or as his first free production, because life must go on.

Uli listened without interest and ate his fish; even the colour of the food matched the interior. When the conversation shifted to the present government's policies regarding the arts (contrasting so shrilly with the situation in France) he no longer cared. If *Hurricane* became a success, maybe another company would remember him and give him an old man's part, but when he revolved this possibility in his mind he saw only a great emptiness. He looked at his wrist, but the watch still hadn't come back. Tomorrow at this time he would probably already be putting on his make-up for the dress rehearsal. As he took a sip of the platinum-coloured Alsace wine he looked at no one and no one looked at him. Perhaps they were afraid that yesterday's incident would raise its head again if they did, perhaps they thought he was silent because of yesterday, but that was not the reason. Gradually a strange mood descended on him, something that enveloped him like the warmth of a room when you come in from the cold. On the window-sill between a large wooden egg on a brass stand and an alabaster dancer with one knee raised high and arms outstretched front and back – lay his book. Behind it, beyond the darkened garden, was the park. Through his own reflection he saw a boy, in the light of a street lamp; a man, standing further away, strolled past the boy a moment later, stopped again after a few metres, and lit a cigarette.

The writer, observing Uli looking out of the window (writers always observe everything) turned and also looked out.

"Yes," said Mrs Michael, "we have continuous performances here."

Vogel raised one arm and declaimed in a solemn voice, "The demons are countless and of various kinds, and one of them is Eros!"

Uli put his napkin beside his plate and rose. "I must go," he said.

"Where to?" Berta asked at once.

He turned to Mrs Michael. "Please excuse me. I need to be on my own for a little while. Thank you for a delicious meal."

"There's a dessert to come yet, Mr Bouwmeester." And to the maid, who was taking the plates away, "What are we having again, Coba?"

"Strawberry Bavarois, Madam."

But Uli was determined. As he used to do on the stage, long ago, he kissed Mrs Michael's hand and walked round the table to say goodbye.

"I wish you success the day after tomorrow," said the writer. "We shall all be there."

Like a statesman, Vogel put both hands on Uli's hand. "Make sure you don't poop out, Willem," he said. "Dress rehearsal tomorrow."

"Thanks for the compliment. Me poop out?"

"Yes," said Berta, "and don't miss the last bus."

He gave her a nod and took his book from the window-sill. In the entrance hall Michael asked, "Are you feeling all right?"

"I feel strange, but not unwell. I feel as though I have to get in the clear about something. You understand that, don't you?"

"I certainly do."

Uli briefly put the book to his lips. "See you tomorrow," he said. "Good night. And don't worry about me, I'll be all right."

5
Stories

A chill wind blew. He put up his collar and walked along the deserted Vondelstraat to Leidseplein. Now that he had left they were sure to be talking about him. It was as if he could hear them.

VOGEL: It was very good of you to arrange this.

THE AUTHOR: But he didn't want to stay.

MRS MICHAEL [*to Berta*]: Is anything the matter with your brother, do you think?

BERTA: He's always been a bit funny. He'll be all right. Weeds never perish.

THE AUTHOR: We'll see about that, said the inventor, as he invented paraquat.

MRS MICHAEL [*viciously*]: Isn't it enviable, how writers always manage to hit the right note.

THE AUTHOR: A joke in time sharpens the mind.

MICHAEL: I'm a bit worried about him. Yesterday, after his conversation with Arend, it looked as if he had got over it completely, but it has obviously upset him.

BERTA: Uli upset? Don't make me laugh. But then, he is seventy-eight.

MRS MICHAEL [*amazed*]: Seventy-eight? I wouldn't have given him more than fifty-eight.

THE AUTHOR: Forty-eight!

VOGEL: When I think that at the end of the war he was as old as I am now . . .

THE AUTHOR: So now you know what's waiting for you.

VOGEL: Do you know why we don't understand a thing about the war? Because we know too much about it. We know far more about the war than people knew at the time. During the war you didn't know anything, you only heard rumours and lies. Think about it, we even know who won, and when. Nobody knew that then. All right, that seems like a platitude, but have you ever thought about it? We know things we ought not to know in order to be able to understand, and as for the emotions people had then, we've never felt a single one. That is why we must . . . [*he puts one finger on his lips*]. Now if Willem had human deaths on his conscience . . .

BERTA [*vehemently*]: Uli? Human deaths on his conscience? He, goodness personified? He was in the Resistance, he was! Bribed German messengers, photographed secret documents! The world never saw a more right-minded person! [*Suddenly impassioned, clambering on to the table*]: If by your Art, my dearest father, you have/ Put the wild waters in this roar, allay them./ The sky it seems would pour down stinking pitch,/ But that the sea, mounting to th' welkin's cheek,/ Dashes the fire out!

MRS MICHAEL: Coba, would you ask our guests if anyone would like some more Bavarois.

Like a great dish of light and movement the square opened before him. With a deep sigh, as if he saw it for the first time (or the last, but that is very similar) Uli looked at the bustle, at all the traffic, all those people in and around the crowded cafés and restaurants illumined by moving, variegated colours from facades and gables. The first showings at the cinemas had just finished, and under the gigantic billboards with their luminous heroes one crowd streamed out while the next already stood waiting. In the City Theatre, bathed in floodlight, it was now the interval; people with glasses in their hands were looking out of the foyer windows. Among the cars, parked criss-cross on the pavements, and past a burning litter bin, he made his way to a phone box.

Of the telephone book little more than the cover was still hanging in its place, the rest lay on the floor, in torn and trampled tatters. He bent down, and with the satisfaction of an explorer he found a half page with Stella's number on it. He put a 25-cent piece in the slot, but he might as well have held a stone to his ear; when he hung up, the coin didn't come back either. He could go to a café to make a call, but reflected it was probably for the best. He now had both her address and an excuse: if he phoned her she might say it was not convenient. He tore off Stella's number, put the smudged scrap of paper in his breast pocket, and went to the tram stop. The glass of the shelter was broken in a number of places, so that for several minutes the wind was able to assail him from various odd directions – almost in the way one draws a pentagram.

When after ten minutes a crowded tram arrived at last, he was unable to reach the entrance in the scrum, and had to wait for the next one. After a few minutes, the book clutched under his arm, he rode through ever quieter, more sombre neighbourhoods where he had rarely been, even in the past. The tram soon emptied and by the time he got off at the terminus he was the only passenger left. When he mentioned the address, the driver, without looking at him, pointed where he had to go.

Natura Artis Magistra. The golden eagles on the pillars by the entrance to the zoo had not changed since he had been here last, with his aunt and uncle. A moment later he came to a vast open area beyond which, on the other side of a canal, there rose a wall of warehouses and factories. In the weak light of the scattered streetlamps he saw nothing but chaos. Stretches of road and rusted rails disappearing into the weeds, overgrown remains of walls, wrecked cars, caravans, stranded boats, everywhere car tyres, tin cans, scrap iron. A dog barked, in a shed someone was welding; further away, in the middle of the wasteland, stood a brightly lit, colourfully painted shack from which muted thumping sounds issued; a party or a performance was in progress. Shivering with cold, he held the lapels of his coat pressed one over the other. It had to be somewhere around here. He glanced at some old delivery vans with smoking chimneys sticking out of them, and then he suddenly discovered a row of houseboats on the canal.

He walked towards them – and before he could distinguish the number he saw her pink bike on the poop deck of one of them. The curtains were drawn, but there was a light burning. Gingerly, holding on to the rail, he made his way across the gangplank to the door.

194

"Willem!"

He looked closely, but saw only surprise, not a trace of irritation or reluctance. Her warm, calloused hand. She had undone her little pigtails so that her hair now stood around her head in a rough, reddish mop. On bare feet she preceded him into the low, narrow room, where luckily it was warm. On the floor in front of the oil heater sat a little boy of about three, looking at a picture book.

Uli pointed at him and said, "Your son."

"This is Arthur. Arthur, get up and shake hands with Mr Bouwmeester."

But Uli was already kneeling by him and took the small, unresisting hand in his, the way someone finds a long-lost precious object. At a stroke everything had changed. He had expected to be alone with Stella. The existence of the child, his presence here (but not the man who must be presumed behind him) dissolved the folly that had stirred in him these last few weeks, and that might even have come about: the old man and the maiden.

"You got a funny eye," said Arthur.

"Charming little fellow, aren't you? What are you reading? Struwwelpeter?"

"What on earth is that?" asked Stella surprised.

"Well, you know, what's it called in Dutch . . . Peter Smudge."

But Arthur would not commit himself, he was more interested in the book Uli had brought with him, and he pulled it from under his arm.

"Out of the question," said Stella. "It's almost half past nine, you are going to bed."

"No I'm not."

"Yes you are."

"Silly poo," said Arthur, and opened the book.

Uli had just time to see it opening of its own accord at the picture of the artist and his model, but Stella took it out of Arthur's hands and resolutely pulled him up by one arm.

"Finished, done with. Say goodnight to Mr Bouwmeester and . . ."

Uli grabbed the boy around the waist, took him to a chair, put him on his knees and let him ride horsey, singing:

195

> *"Hoppa, hoppa, Reiter,*
> *Wenn er fällt, dann schreit er;*
> *Fällt er in den Graben,*
> *Fressen ihn die Raben:*
> *Fällt er in den Sumpf,*
> *Macht es Plumps!"*

At *"Plumps"* he opened his knees so that Arthur fell away with a yell.

"More!"

When after the second time a third time was demanded (bringing infinity into view), Stella put a stop to it. Laughing, she pointed at the ironing board and the piles of laundry, and said, above Arthur's screeches: "Make yourself comfortable and don't mind the mess."

It wasn't until she had said this that Uli noticed the mess – as if he cared. He took off his coat and sat down on the small seat beside a pile of ironed clothes and sneezed. In Mrs Michael's mausoleum they would now be sitting in the white leather with coffee and brandy, or an eau-de-vie – which would match the colour of the marble even better – but he was happy sitting in the chock-a-block houseboat, with stacks of dirty crockery in the small sink in the corner, while the rats were probably swimming beneath his feet. Nowhere did he see anything suggesting the presence of a man. Who was the father? Not Aronds, for sure, or the child would have been browner. He touched the corner of one of his eyes with his little finger, studied the moist speck for a moment and wiped it on his trousers. On the low table lay a collection of stories by Edgar Allan Poe. Then he saw, with surprise, a large doll, a Pierrot, reclining in the cusions on the divan (her bed, of course), whose melancholy eyes in the white face looked straight at him; Uli felt himself briefly hovering, like someone in free fall – if at that moment someone had suddenly torn the doll in two . . .

Stella entered and asked what he would like to drink: there was only wine but she could make coffee. The fact that she did not open the wine herself but handed him the bottle and corkscrew, filled him with pride, as if it were a sign of great confidentiality; this was how it had also been forty, fifty, sixty years ago. While she

196

put on a record, he boldly loosened his tie and told her about the dinner party at the business manager's house, but it didn't seem to interest her. She clearly didn't want to talk about yesterday's row either, nor did she ask him why he had come. With her legs drawn up she sat on the divan and raised her glass.

"To the day after tomorrow!"

"You can say that again!" He took a swig and asked, "What kind of audience will it be tomorrow?"

"I heard something about the upper years of some secondary schools. It's more a try-out than a dress rehearsal, really."

Her little toe curled up like a comma. The soles of her feet were covered with brown, here and there almost black, callouses, out of keeping with the soft skin of her calves and neck; her whole body seemed to move from hard extremities towards a centre that had to be proportionally softer and more yielding as the extremities were harder and bonier than in other women. For one moment his eyes widened, whereupon she lowered hers, and, with the nail of her little finger, pushed a bit of cork along the inside of her glass.

Resting his hand with the glass on his knee, he listened to the old music: two strange sopranos, accompanied by flutes, a cello and the virginals or something of that sort. He asked what it was. She handed him the sleeve: John Blow: *An Ode to the Death of Mr Henry Purcell*. Yet another thing he had never heard of. She told him that Blow had been Purcell's predecessor as organist at Westminster Abbey, and also his successor. Uli nodded, as if this were obvious.

"Those women sing beautifully," he said.

"They're men. Counter-tenors."

He was silent and tried to imagine men to go with those voices. Every now and then, when the melody took a lower turn, this was briefly possible; but immediately the clean-shaven jaws glided once more into the smooth heights of femininity. With admiration he looked at Stella: such remarkable records she played! He suddenly noticed that her eyes, in the lamplight, were not blue but green.

She laughed. "As an actress I should be glad I wasn't born a few hundred years earlier. In Shakespeare's time Miranda was acted

197

by a boy in drag. Maybe that has something to do with the theme of *Hurricane*, we should ask Siderius about that."

"There's no point in asking him anything," said Uli. He told her about his visit to the playwright, about all that nonsense the result of which was Joost and Berta, and again he looked into the eyes of the Pierrot. "That doll is looking straight at me. Very odd, that. I am suddenly reminded of . . . what was it again? At least ten years ago. I was sitting on a terrace in Lelystad and along the edge of the pavement they were putting up parking meters. Not at that moment, I mean, the metal tubes were already there, that the meters would be fixed to later. I was smoking a cigarette and . . . yes, I have been a chain-smoker all my life. Nowadays I don't smoke cigarettes any more. Not because I am afraid of getting lung cancer or something, I'm past those sorts of fears, but I suddenly couldn't do it any more, all that inhaling. Do you want to know why that was?"

"Of course."

"I can't remember when it was. One day I was smoking a cigarette, and then, while I was inhaling the smoke, I realised that it was really the same thing as if the whole room was suddenly pumped full of smoke, which you had to breathe. A moment later the smoke would be quickly sucked away and twenty seconds later there would be a new blast – and that would go on virtually all day long, year in, year out. It would drive you crazy, make you ill, true or not? Only when you were asleep would you have respite. Sometimes I thought that with such a room you could help people to give up smoking. I smoke cigars now, but I don't inhale those."

"A kind of homeopathic gas-chamber."

Uli started at the word gas-chamber – and only at that moment did he remember her story about the cigar her mother had made her smoke. He began to stammer something, but she said.

"Not a bad idea. You could become rich."

"Become . . . I'm not sure if I still want to become anything."

"Of course you do. As long as you're alive, you're alive. I think everyone should live as if he were immortal. Otherwise you might as well go and hang yourself."

"There's something in that."

When he said no more, Stella said, "I thought you were going to tell me something about parking meters."

"Parking meters?"

"Yes, about metal tubes that had been put up."

"Oh yes, of course." A bit shamefaced, he cast down his eyes. "So I was sitting there and that metal tube was standing at a distance of about four or five metres. My cigarette was finished and I was about to flick the butt away, like this," – he raised his hand and placed the tip of his middle finger on his thumb, with the other three fingers upright (the hand of a Buddha) – "and at the moment I flicked it, exactly at that moment, no sooner and no later, I was certain it would fall inside that narrow metal tube."

"And did it?"

"What do you think? I wasn't aiming, I didn't assess the force I was using, but with a wonderful curve it flew right into it. I don't believe I have ever felt so all-powerful as at that moment. That is how a magician must feel. Prospero. The crazy thing is that I didn't even intend it to happen, I simply knew it for sure." He laughed, and shrugged his shoulders. "Why am I telling you this?"

"You were reminded of it because Baptiste looks straight at you. Isn't it all simply a coincidence?"

Uli looked at the doll in its loose-hanging smock with the big buttons, shrugged his shoulders again and shook his head.

"Maybe. Although . . ." He took a sip of wine and asked, "Do you understand yourself Stella?"

She opened her mouth to answer, but at that moment there came a cry from the other room: "Mama!" She shut her mouth and disappeared with an apologetic gesture.

Uli leaned back and listened to the music, his hand on his book. The sound evoked a space, a mysterious hall, which could exist nowhere except by virtue of those sounds. An ode to Purcell, by Blow. That was another thing he hadn't known about. How many things he had missed! Now that the signs of this were coming through to him, his life seemed to become ever emptier, but at the same time it became filled with something to which he could not give a name and which he could not describe. He sneezed again, rubbed his eyes for a while and noticed he was breathing with

199

difficulty. Fine moment to catch a cold, with the first night coming up the day after tomorrow, but he was used to this – he knew he caught a cold only if he was out in the cold in more senses than one.

Stella stuck her head around the door.

"I'm sorry, Willem, you'll have to come and tell a bedtime story."

From a wooden bunk fixed to the wall at shoulder height, with a ladder of light-coloured wood leading to it, his head surrounded by an assembly of monkeys, bears, dogs and other animals, Arthur looked at him and said, "Aren't you old."

"Just you wait," said Uli, putting one arm on the blanket, which was warm from the small body; "your time will come. But for the moment you'd still like to hear a bedtime story, wouldn't you? What will it be about?"

"A little boy."

"Of course. And what is the little boy's name?"

"Er . . ."

"Arthur?"

"No."

"What then?"

"Pim."

"That's a nice name too. All right: Pim. And what is Pim going to do?"

"Go for a walk."

"Yes, that's what I think too. But of course, something will have to happen, otherwise it wouldn't be a story. What do you think that'll be?"

"He meets somebody."

"There you are. Who?"

"A cat."

"Just as I thought. What's the cat's name?"

"Minny."

"By Jove, so it is. Pim and Minny. Now it's getting exciting. They are on their way to . . ."

"A haunted wood."

"Now the fat is in the fire! Luckily, Pim has Minny with him."

"Minny isn't afraid."

200

"And Pim?"

"Not Pim either. They shoot all the ghosts dead . . ."

"But aren't ghosts already dead?"

". . . bang bang! Bang, bang! All dead. Bang bang!"

"Goodness me. That was in the nick of time. And then?"

"And then," said Stella, stepping on to the first rung of the ladder, "Pim went to sleep and had lovely dreams, because nothing bad could happen any more." She tucked him in and said, "Kiss Uncle Willem good night."

Arthur thought this was going a bit too far for the time being. Uli turned round and at that instant saw the cat, staring at him from among the toys on the floor. Its golden eyes held the merciless gaze of an extra-terrestrial being that knew no play other than practice for murder. He fled the little room and knew he could stay no longer, his sneezing was not caused by catching cold but by that wretched creature, which, naturally, was called Minny. He poured himself some more wine and looked at the script of *Hurricane* that lay open on the floor by the divan, covered in scribbles and red and green marks. When he sat down he avoided touching the divan with his hands, though he knew it was already too late.

"He's asleep," said Stella, closing the door softly.

Uli nodded. After a slight hesitation he said, "You called me Willem just now . . . To people who know me well, I am Uli."

She paused, then came up to him and gave him a kiss on the forehead, and he briefly put his hand on her hip. Then she turned the record over ("Now we'll have Purcell himself"), and, having resumed her previous pose on the divan, looked at him in silence for a while.

"What a scoundrel you are, Uli. Arthur says he wants you to come and tell him another story next time he's here. But you didn't tell him a story at all. He made it up himself from beginning to end."

"But he doesn't know that," laughed Uli. "I stimulated his creativity – isn't that what it's called these days?"

"Yes, yes. I think you aren't even capable of making up a story."

"Aren't I?"

201

"Go on, then. Tell me a story."

"And if you fall asleep too?"

"Too bad if I do."

"Uli took out his tin of cigars, lit one and blew the smoke in front of him. Should he tell her about La Charlotte and the ring? This was the moment – but at the same time the moment was past – superseded by the existence of Arthur."

"Once upon a time . . ." he said, without as yet knowing what he was going to say, "very long ago . . . In a faraway country . . . there was a houseboat. In it there lived a young woman with her little son. Nowadays houseboats can't actually sail. They don't have engines and they are attached to the shore by all kinds of cables and pipes, carrying electricity and water and telephones. They merely float; in the extreme case they can be towed away but that is quite a business. One day, an old magician appeared on this houseboat."

"Prospero," said Stella.

"No, not him."

"Who then?"

"I forget his name."

"Merlin?"

"Yes, I think that was the one. It would take too long to explain how it came about, but one day he was there and he thought: this can't go on, there must of course be a father somewhere, and the child probably lives in turns with his father too – for the mother, because of her work as a puppet-maker, is often away from home – and so the child doesn't really live anywhere. What is to be done? Merlin pondered a solution – but in spite of his advanced age he still underestimated his own magic powers, for even as he was thinking, his power was already at work. The engine, which wasn't there, started up and a moment later the boat moved off. The cables snapped, the gangplank fell in the water, and without anyone having to be at the helm, which didn't exist, the boat steered its way through the canals to the North Sea canal and at IJmuiden put out to sea. Even the magician himself was flabbergasted. After a few weeks' sailing in a southerly direction, with the colour of the sea changing from grey to blue, they arrived at a

202

sun-drenched island in the Mediterranean. Well, and that was about all, They lived happily every after, the magician, the mother and the child. Merlin became ever younger, the child did not grow older – and if they haven't died in the meantime, they are still alive now."

His breast rose and fell asthmatically, his eyelids thickened by the minute, and itched, but he knew he would only make it worse by rubbing them. He put his cigar away and looked at Stella, who sat biting her nails, her eyes closed. The voices of the counter-tenors dissolved into ever more melancholy melodies. Uli's breath squeaked, and in the manner of Pierre de Vries speaking Shakespeare's verse in the early years of the century, he declaimed

> *"Now I want*
> *Spirits to enforce, art to enchant;*
> *And my ending is despair,*
> *Unless I be reliev'd by prayer . . ."*

When she looked at him he saw her eyes were moist – and at the same moment so were his. He sneezed and scratched at his throat.

"What's the matter?" she asked in alarm. "You suddenly look like a Chinese."

"I'm allergic to cats. It will go away as soon as I'm outside. What time is it?"

"Nearly half past ten. Why aren't you wearing your beautiful watch?"

What possessed Uli? Why didn't he simply tell her the truth, instead of that fib about having left it in the cloakroom? Is he, ultimately, not worthy of our attention? (Even if that were so, it is now too late for that insight.) Unfortunately, Stella was more gullible than Berta.

"At the Kosmos? Who could have done that?"

"You can no longer trust anyone these days."

While he went so far as to say this (and it was now primarily intended for himself) in his thoughts he went even further: suddenly he saw the face of a stagehand who must undoubtedly have taken it.

"Have you any idea who it could have been?"

"No," he said, happily. He finished his glass and got up. "I'm

203

sorry, I really must go."

Stella helped him into his coat and said it was nice of him to have come. Next time he should phone beforehand so she could air and Hoover the place first.

"That wouldn't help."

She pressed a kiss on his cheek and suddenly looked at his temples. "Come into the light," she said, and pulled him under the lamp. He felt her fingers in his hair and then a sharp sting. "Look what I've found!" Triumphantly she showed him a hair, one black hair. "It's all coming back!"

Uli smiled. "Or maybe you've just pulled out the last one."

"What a pessimist you are!" She started laughing too, and rubbed her thumb and forefinger together so that the hair disappeared. "See you tomorrow evening, Uli. Thanks again for your visit, that was kind." And as she opened the door. "Wait, you've left your book behind."

6
Riddles

He drew the fresh air deep into his lungs and at once felt relief. The wind had died down; over the deserted wasteland there hung a chilly drizzle, so thin that it seemed to stand still in space. There was no one in sight, and the painted shack was dark now. In the distance the city hummed. As he walked across the stubble field without looking back, he suddenly heard an ominous sound which he was unable to identify. Only when it repeated itself did he realise what it was: a lion, and immediately afterwards there came the trumpeting of an elephant too. Then silence fell again. Still breathing deeply, he listened to his footsteps on the loose rubble and weeds. It was a long time since he had been so alone with himself. This did not arouse any clearly defined thoughts in him; it was more an awareness of existence, of being present. It filled him with well-being, so that perhaps he would have liked this field on which he was walking to be much larger still – reaching beyond the horizon; an endless nocturnal domain, strewn with junk and rubbish. How incredibly long had he been in his own company: Uli with Uli – all these years. He ran his hand over his face, it was streaming wet. Tomorrow at this time the dress rehearsal would be almost over.

After a few minutes he was once again walking on paving stones and asphalt, among houses. Across the square with the sombre, boarded-up synagogue, past highways rising from the ground, concrete buildings and the barren stretch where the new opera house was yet to be built (all made possible because of the mass murder of the original inhabitants) he walked in the direction of Rembrandtplein. He could have taken a tram to Central Station

205

earlier, and from there the metro to the bus terminal, but he first wanted to free himself of his intoxication, and in an upsurge of devotion he made a pilgrimage to the place where he had eaten with Stella. It was eleven o'clock, the last bus would leave shortly before midnight, he could catch it easily. From the bridge across the Amstel he looked at the gently rippling water. Because it was so quiet in the street, it looked as if even the black water was lonelier than usual. He did not believe in his death. Only other people could be dead, to the dead not even the living were alive. He felt a smile appear on his face, but perhaps this was caused by the wine.

In the dingy side street he again found it difficult to locate the house. Only on recognising the stationery shop did he realise that the vending hall beside it had taken the place of the Osiris restaurant. It was busy and noisy in there, a loudspeaker blared forth an inane carnival hit in three-four time. Like bachelors in apartment buildings, the rissoles, mince balls and rice fritters lay in rows, one above the other. He pushed a guilder coin into a slot and pulled out something repulsive; at the same moment the rear of the vending machine opened, so that he briefly looked into the eyes of a grimy youth refilling the trays. From the counter at the back, where the crocodile had stood, rose the vapour of frying oil.

"Hi, Grandad!"

"Still out and about?"

"Manage it, can you, on your pension?"

With dangerous familiarity a large hand was placed on his cheek. Three louts had designs on him, out of boredom, no doubt. All three were eating from plastic tubs full of maggots teeming in dollops of pus. He looked around, but whoever noticed what was going on, merely grinned or expressionlessly averted his eyes.

"Just about," he said.

By smiling calmly he tried to ward off the threat, and it looked as if he was succeeding. The hand went away and they carried on eating their supper, but remained standing face to face with him. When he made an attempt to leave, one of them took a step sideways, barring his way, a scrawny fellow with an old-looking face, a cap on his head (crowned by a red woollen pompom) and a large moustache that joined up with the hair by his ears; he was

206

wearing a red check jacket, and glasses of which one arm was held in place by grubby sticking plaster. The other two were a man of about thirty-five in a harsh blue tracksuit, with long wavy hair and a slinking, stooping back, and a straw-blond youth, too robust, whose shoulders began immediately beneath his earlobes and expanded to a width of almost a metre; in spite of the chilly weather he was wearing only a sleeveless white T-shirt out of which stuck two thick white arms covered from top to bottom with tattoos. This was the one who had put his hand on Uli's cheek.

"I have to be off," said Uli.

"No, you don't," said the man in the tracksuit. "You don't have to be off at all. We're having far too nice a time together."

Artiste though he might be, at this moment Uli felt the reaction of the bourgeois rising inside himself, that is to say the impulse to shout "Police!" But he didn't and when a moment later our hero was walking across the square between two of the men, he realised with incredulous amazement that he was actually being abducted. Swaying to and fro from sheer contained force, the bodybuilder strode along beside him, while Uli felt his own body shrivel up into something like a thread, such as sometimes hangs out of a sleeve. He knew he was protected by his age, but at the same time he knew that in the late twentieth century he shouldn't count on that too much. (He had lived through those few decades of West European history during which the streets had been free of robbers and murderers – at least in peacetime – but those days were now gone.)

In fact, he soon discovered he had landed in something not unlike a branch of business life. The fellow with the moustache, called Piet and clearly the leader, voiced the opinion that he was sure Grandad wouldn't mind earning a few "yellow-backs". Certainly, said Uli, but unfortunately he was not in a position tonight, as he had to catch the last bus home and had to make an early start tomorrow. Maybe another time. But Piet said it would be all right with that bus. In the small public garden, at the foot of Rembrandt's statue, he took a fistful of banknotes out of his breast pocket and held a twenty-five guilder note in front of Uli's face.

"No, honestly," said Uli, shaking his head.

The blond bruiser placed his feet wide apart and slowly folded his arms, a false smile appearing on his face. Uli's heart began to race, skipped a beat, and then went on pounding, audibly. There was nobody else in the garden; one lunge from one of those monstrous arms and the first night of *Hurricane* would have to be postponed for a good long time. What to do? At the corner of the square there was a police post, but it hadn't been in use for twenty or thirty years. He took the proffered banknote and Piet said,

"There's a good chap. Nothing to worry about. It's just that our regular grandad is off sick today."

Holding the money in his hand, Uli looked from the one to the other.

"What am I supposed to do?"

"Come along," said the man in blue. "We'll have a pint."

He pulled Uli along by a sleeve, to the bar across the street. Until about fifteen years ago it had been a well-known restaurant. The great variety artistes used to frequent it; he himself had often eaten there too, even a few times after the war. The marble walls, the paintings by the legendary owner, everything had remained unchanged, except that it had now become a bar. They sat down at a table; luckily the other two had not come with them.

"What time is it?" asked Uli.

"Only ten past eleven."

"I don't know what your plans are, but I have to be off in ten minutes at the latest. I live ouside town."

"Don't be daft. It's only a lark. My name's Bert."

He called the waiter and ordered beer. At that moment the bruiser came through the revolving door and walked past them without a glance. His arms were wet, the colours of the tattoos had become deeper, as if they had been varnished.

"That's Jopie," said Bert. "Terrific bloke, third Dan."

Uli became uneasy again. Fortunately, the customers in the bar seemed a reliable sort; not too young, by the look of them mostly up-and-coming businessmen, with reasonably respectable wives or girlfriends; most of them stood by the bar, glasses in hand. Jopie also ordered a drink, still swaying from one leg to the other, like an oil tanker unable to come to an immediate halt.

"There you go," said Bert, with raised glass.

208

Then Piet appeared. He glanced searchingly around and then asked politely if they minded if he joined them. Bert said it was all right. Uli put his book on another seat and was at a loss what to think. Something was being enacted here in which he apparently played a part. Jopie now leaned with one elbow on the counter and looked vaguely in their direction. Piet took off his cap and out of his inside pocket produced three matchboxes stuck all over with veined paper such as Uli remembered from old exercise books with hard covers; maybe they were used for keeping paper clips in, or rubber bands. Piet placed them upside down on the table, took a little ball from his pocket, put this on the table as well, and covered it with one of the matchboxes.

"Here we go," he said softly, but with a smiling face that was meant for others and seemed out of keeping with his tone.

He lifted the matchbox once again, to show that the little ball was still lying under it, and switched the boxes around a few times, very quickly, but in such a way that Uli could easily follow the whereabouts of the little ball. When Piet looked at him questioningly, he put his finger on the right box. "Okay," said Piet, and took out a twenty-five guilder note. Uli gathered that the same was expected of him; when he had also put his note on the table, the boxes were set in motion again. It wasn't difficult – but when he had again pointed at the correct box and had his winnings pushed towards him, Bert called out, just a trifle too loudly so that everyone could hear, "There you are, Grandad! All yours!"

People looked their way and at the third game – which Uli lost – general movement began in the direction of their table. To Piet this was the signal to step up the speed. In ever faster, more complicated interchanges, well-nigh impossible to follow, the matchboxes swirled across the table top, while the games succeeded one another more and more rapidly. In spite of himself, Uli felt admiration for Piet's nimble-fingeredness; he had the impression that it hardly mattered what he said; when he thought he was sure where the ball was, it wasn't there, and if he merely guessed, then it was. He won, he lost, but he won more often than he lost, which elicited fresh encouragement from Bert. Their table was now surrounded by spectators calling out hints; Jopie was one of the few still standing by the bar. When Uli had collected six banknotes, Bert pushed his chair back and said:

"That'll do, Grandad. Pick up your cash and skedaddle."

Of course this was an order. Uli put the money in his pocket and rose.

"Well, thanks a lot," said Piet bitterly.

Immediately, a merry, greying gentleman in a blazer sat down in Uli's seat, pulled a hundred guilder note out of his wallet, put it on the table and banged on it with the flat of his hand. His friend tried to pull him away so as to have a go himself; with the jolliness of older men out for an evening of fun, though not altogether for fun, they railed at each other, calling each other "Father" and "notary". When the notary started to play, Bert pulled Uli by one arm to the bar, making him stand between Jopie and himself.

"I really must go now," Uli said it softly; he realised he was under intensified supervision again.

"First we settle. Us two, I mean." But when Uli felt in his pocket, Bert said under his breath, after a quick glance at the barman, "Not here."

The barman was rinsing glasses over the brushes in the rinsing tub and acted as if he was trying to look simple-minded. Bert still made no move to leave. Another glass of beer was put in front of Uli.

"Look, I have to get to Lelystad. What am I to do when the last bus has gone?"

"Take a taxi."

"But that costs a hundred guilders."

"Money is no object."

Out of the corner of his eye Uli looked at Jopie's arm. It lay on the counter like an elephant's trunk, admitting an invasion of monsters from another world: green panthers with wide-open mouths and huge fangs, blue bats on the attack, female vampires, parrots driven to frenzy, fire-spewing dragons and among all these a host of other undefined mythical beasts thronging in the direction of his hand and the cheap fake gold ring on his little finger. From the gaming table, invisible because of the people around it, came laughter and shouting. It was gone half past eleven, he could

210

catch the bus only by taking a taxi now, and even then he should leave at once. Suddenly the blood rushed to his face. He must risk all: start shouting as loudly as he could, that he had been kidnapped, robbed of his freedom, was being used, had been made an accessory to a swindle, under duress. But at best they would try to calm him down, laughing as they plied him with more drink (how could he imagine such a thing, in their company, on such an agreeable evening!) and if things should get out of hand, there would still be that quick thump in the stomach.

"I want to go to the gents," he said.

Bert looked at him and twisted his mouth into a kind of laugh. "I'm busting for a piss myself."

While his guard pulled down his zip in front of a urinal, Uli locked himself into a cubicle. Although he had felt no urge before, he did now, at the sight of the toilet bowl. He put the book on the floor, lowered his trousers and sat down to pee (that way he could relax better, so it didn't drip afterwards) and he realised he was truly a prisoner now. Bert talked incessantly but Uli did not listen. Here was a chance to excape from that rabble; who knows what else they would get him mixed up in otherwise. Of course, Bert might fetch Jopie to force the door (he would simply pull it open, without even noticing it was locked), but it would still cause a disturbance and he wasn't that important to them. He took the twenty-five guilder notes from his pocket, including his fee, slid them through the crack under the door and said, "Here's your money, I've had enough of it."

The voice was silent. A moment later the notes disappeared. Footsteps. A door slamming shut.

Uli heaved a deep sigh. He stood up, arranged his clothing and sat down on the toilet seat again – which gave him a strange sensation: to feel the gaping closet bowl under his behind, but with his trousers on. To be safe, he waited a few more minutes. He could forget about the bus now, he's have to phone Lucas and Max for a bed for the night, which they had offered once or twice before. It bothered him that it was too late to phone his neighbours, although at the same time he felt that Berta's anxiety was exactly what she deserved for . . . yes, for what?

211

Dixieland music; all the tables were occupied. No one was waiting for him, and he cautiously looked round the corner of the L-shaped space to see if Jopie was still standing by the bar. He didn't see him, but was himself immediately noticed by the barman, who put down his napkin and came up to him.

"Follow me."

Without further explanation he took Uli through a door marked "Private" and showed him how to get to a back exit by way of the kitchen of the adjoining hotel. In bright neon light, among gleaming cooking stoves with rows of pots and pans above, Uli followed the escape route; two Turks, silently busy cleaning up, paid no attention to him.

The drizzle had stopped. Through a long alleyway with wet wooden fences to left and right, he reached a little gate opening out on to the street. It was still busy in town. A clock on the tower of a bank pointed to midnight. When a woman approached with a long-haired dachshund on a lead, he bent down and briefly stroked the animal. The dog rolled its eyes and bared its teeth.

"Be careful, he can be nasty at times."

"He won't do anything to me," said Uli. He was sure of it. In every dachshund all dachshunds were united, including Sebastian, and Sebastian would make sure none of them would ever bite Uli.

Now he had to make a phone call. He looked out for a phone box and then saw, pasted on an electricity substation, the playbill for the Authors' Theatre:

Leo Siderius
HURRICANE
First night Friday 12 November 1982
Kosmos Theatre

He let his eyes rest on it for a while.

Pierre de Vries – Willem Bouwmeester

It was really true. There it was. The day after tomorrow it would happen; the dress rehearsal was tomorrow. Now he must get himself a bed for the night, if he was to make a decent job of it. It

212

was only to be hoped that Berta would have the sense not to call the police, but she didn't so easily lose her head. He thought she had probably gone to bed.

7

Spectacle

Then he sensed he was not looking at it alone. To his left stood Bert and Piet, reading with him, to his right was Jopie's monstrous presence.

"Hurricane," nodded Piet. "You can say that again. Poxy weather today."

"That must have been a big number two," said Bert.

"Now don't be nasty. Grandad had lost us, that's all. He's been wandering all over the place looking for us, hasn't he? Well, here we are then, come along."

A great lassitude took possession of Uli; it was clearly meant to be. He meekly went along, this time to a large white bar full of mirrors and potted palms (apparently a convered garage) populated by fashionable young people whose clothing was in tune with the interior. Uli was given another glass of beer and the ritual of Jopie and Piet casually entering was repeated. As in Mrs Michael's house, Uli felt utterly out of place in his off-the-peg suit, and here also because of his age. Bert could just about pass muster in his jogging outfit, so could Jopie, but Piet in his working-man's jacket was impossible here. Everyone kept looking at everyone else at the door, but when Bert called out "Here you are, Grandad!" and "All yours!" no one made any move to join them. Only a few eyes glanced vacantly past them; for the rest, everybody remained as indolent as before. The matchboxes flashed about once again, and finally Bert addressed the public directly:

"He's won two hundred guilders already!" Looking all around, he raised his arm and pointed with lowered index finger at Uli's crown.

But no one reacted. At this moment Jopie lost patience. With an abrupt movement he whisked his beer glass from the counter, sending it crashing against a nickel table leg several metres away, and called out:

"Jesus, what a bunch of shitbags! God Almighty, go and crap yourselves! Bleeding wankers!" He stalked towards the door. "Come on," he said in passing, "Let's scram."

This still did not disturb the apathy of the clientele (perhaps not even the outbreak of the third world war would do that); they watched the departing men with empty eyes.

But now Uli had been given a taste of action. It was raining again outside, and as they walked through the streets Jopie continued his tirade; how he was itching to put the boot into that shit-hole and smack that bunch of pus-heads against the wall. That's what they needed, the screwballs, you had to break their bones for them, the bleeding pap-faces, he'd like to do them an injury. Bert chuckled to himself, now and then raising an arm heavenward. They hadn't demanded the loot yet; it was gradually being taken for granted that Uli was one of them.

It had become quieter in town, with scruffier people about. Whores were strolling everywhere; at corners they stood smoking in clusters, the fat ones together with the fat, the skinny ones with the skinny. Here and there, like phantoms, frail rent-boys could be seen in doorways.

"This place is swarming with arse-beetles," said Bert.

In two slow uninterrupted columns, cars passed by, each with a solitary man at the wheel, from time to time one turned off to a canal where it would wait till someone, bending low and looking sharp, opened the door. Uli thought of his bus, at this moment travelling far away through the dark polder – without him. The thought suddenly reconciled him to the fact that he was roaming about the inner city in the middle of the night. What did he have to lose? The dress rehearsal wasn't until the evening, and he could lie in tomorrow morning. Other men of his age had been tucked up in bed for hours in their suburban old people's homes, but he was still involved in some grotesque adventure, and the day after tomorrow, in a first-night performance, he would be playing the leading role. His name was plastered all over the city. No, a Bouwmeester wasn't beaten that easily. That would take a good bit more than this!

"Where are we going?" he asked defiantly.

It was as if his newly-rationalised reasoned zest for life immediately enhanced his power within the group. No one spoke, and Uli pointed to a bar on the other side of the street. In the narrow window, under the word MIGNON, stood a nurse, dancing on the window-sill, her snakelike movements apparently occasioned by inaudible music. Uli was at this moment alone in not noticing that she was a rather old-fashioned nurse, in a black gown that reached down almost to her lace-up boots, long sleeves, a long white apron narrowing at the waist, a stand-up collar, and on her head a starched white cap reminiscent of a sphinx's headgear.

As they crossed the road they had to pause midway for a police car which drove slowly past and which Uli could therefore have hailed but didn't.

It was jam-packed in the small bar, so it was not obvious that they had arrived together. The music was loud and of the sort that can be heard day and night on pirate stations; yet it scarcely rose above the uninterrupted din. Again Uli took the initiative. He pushed his way towards the back, where the crowd was even thicker, beckoning Piet to show his tricks. But halfway down the room his path was suddenly blocked by a middle-aged woman with black-dyed hair, piled up high; a pair of scissors flashed in her hands and before he knew what was happening she had snipped off his tie just below the knot. In triumph, to the cheers of the bystanders, she held up the two pieces. Uli could do little else but join in the laughter as she was lifted (hands shooting up between her legs) and pinned the tie to a beam on the ceiling. Like stalactites in a cave, hundreds of ties hung there, grown grey and dusty as the foreign banknotes with which part of the wall was covered.

At the far end of the bar, Uli ordered two whiskies and Piet could start his work. The interest was overwhelming. Within a few minutes there was such a jostling that those nearest the front kept being pushed forward over the dancing matchboxes, which prompted a tall fellow to turn round and enquire if anybody wanted his brains bashed in. Bert had no chance of getting closer, and Uli boldly took over his role by calling out himself that he'd already won one hundred guilders, one hundred and fifty: "Gotcha! All for Grandad!"

Then the moment came when he was brusquely shoved off his stool by the man who didn't want to be pushed around. He just managed to grab his book, before being expertly mangled through the crush to the back row where he found himself side by side with the nurse. She was wearing a white band around her left upper arm.

"You got yourself a nice bit of loot there, didn't you darling?" she said in a deep, somewhat rasping voice, while putting a hand on his shoulder and baring a row of large teeth.

"I certainly did."

She was about thirty and much too heavily made up. The pancake was cracking under her eyes, the nurse's cap covered the hairline. The warmth of her hand through his clothes on his skin made him feel uncomfortable, he was being pressed against her, against her full bosom (she was taller than he) and while Piet was now getting down to serious business, a thin man with a fanatical, hooked nose suddenly leapt up on the counter further along and shouted at the top of his voice that the Pope was a con-man and Christianity was "state occultism".

"They were dead right to crucify God for all the things he has done. It was an act of simple justice. There was only one person who understood this: Judas. Long live Judas!"

"We'll have another drink to that!" someone called out.

Perhaps it was somebody else who then tripped him up; as suddenly as he had appeared, he toppled again among the customers. Meanwhile – Uli could hardly follow it all – something had gone wrong with Piet as well. The matchboxes went flying through the air and blows were falling. Piet thudded head forward on the counter, grabbed his glass and smashed it against the edge of the bar. At this a general uproar broke out. Women screeched, a bar stool rose above the heads, and suddenly Jopie was there too. His white, decorated arms worked like pistons in Piet's direction, to the rescue, while at the same time he looked all around and called, "Where's the old geezer? He's still got the lolly!"

"Jesus, they're after me," said Uli, being shoved this way and that on the swell of bodies.

The only person who heard him was the nurse. She took his hand in her sweaty grip. "Come with me, I'll look after you."

Before Jopie or Piet could reach him, she was pulling him down a short flight of steps to the narrow toilets and then through a low door marked "No entry". She bolted it, took him by the hand and led him along as though he were a child.

In the sudden silence he followed her through a long cellar full of discarded furniture and crates of empty bottles. When they climbed a few ramshackle steps at the far end, a thumping and kicking could be heard against the door behind them. A hatch gave access to a sweetish-smelling (cocoa?) shed packed with canvas-covered stacks. At a trot they cut across to the other side, and a moment later, constantly switching lights on and off, she preceded him through a passage with frosted glass windows in metal frames, which led, through a steel door, to a small paved yard where a motorbike lay scattered in pieces. Uli deeply inhaled the fresh air, but not for long, for immediately he was indoors again, stumbling, steadied by her hand, and groping through all kinds of indefinable junk.

"Clever if they find us," she said, her voice leaping into a giggle. "What's your name, sweetheart?"

"Uli," said Uli, before he could say Willem.

"I am Sister Ariane."

"Where on earth are we? Where are you taking me?"

She started to sing:

> *"I need a lover that loves*
> *such a dangerous place to be . . ."*

Feeling as if he was dreaming, he was now walking on the white lino floor of a fitness centre or gymnasium. To the left and right were the instruments of torture that made people look like Jopie. Then they were going through a small living-room stuffed with furniture, where a fat man and a fat woman, both with their legs

218

wide apart, sat on a tasselled sofa watching a late-night movie on German television (two beautiful young people making love, half underneath a sheet: "Nicht doch, Günther!") – the heating turned up so high that the man was in his undervest and the woman in her bra. Ariane said hello but there was no response. Uli wondered if there would ever be an end to all this; he was now climbing a steep staircase with threadbare carpet, past a landing where a racing bike stood upside down, then a second staircase, without carpeting, and then a third. Exhausted, he waited while she opened a door with a key.

The room into which she ushered him was bathed in fierce, almost blinding, white light, like a photographer's studio. The interior contained a double mattress with churned-up bedding, a wardrobe with its doors open, a large mirror and a table on which lay the remains of a meal. On the wall, a black-framed drawing of a young woman, from the first half of the nineteenth century to judge by her dress and hairstyle; a record player and records, but nowhere a book or newspaper. The room was filled with music but, as at a funfair, there were all kinds of different music mixed together: from a back room there came the deep thrum of a double bass, like a corpulent man climbing an endless flight of steps; this was mingled with the violence of some heroic-tragic symphony on a record player below, which the neighbour above crowned with an off-key wail on a saxophone.

As if she had reached the end of her strength, his rescuer pulled the cap from her head, revealing a slightly balding skull that made her look alarmingly different, hitched her skirt up to her waist and let herself fall back on the mattress.

"Oof!"

She folded her arms under her head and, looking at him mockingly, drew up one leg and let the knee slowly fall sideways.

Uli froze. She wasn't wearing any knickers. Where her hairy thighs joined, there was not that which he expected to see, but neither was there the alternative (for surely it must be the one or the other, male or female, night or day, left or right, tea or coffee); what he saw was something terrible, something not of this world and which, if anything, resembled a crab.

In horror he clasped his hands together.

"What happened?"

"I'll give you three guesses. I had myself reconstituted," she said – or suddenly no longer she, but not he either; a transition, a twilight in-between, *l'heure bleu* . . .

Something broke inside Uli. Still with his coat on and still with clasped hands he sank to his knees, looking with moistening eyes at what was being offered to him there in the merciless light, that sign, exactly at the place where the doctors had somehow pushed the flesh into shape with their knives, in an effort to make it look like something, which wasn't this and wasn't that, except the image of a crab as it crawls diagonally across the wet sand towards the flooding tide.

"Casablanca," she said – as a veteran soldier might say "Stalingrad" or "Verdun".

The hard, woven sisal mat pressed through Uli's trousers into the skin of his knees, but it seemed to him that he must endure this pain. It seemed to him that this was the only thing that had so far been absent from his life, as if you had to live to the age of eighty in order to see what he was now seeing: this, *utterly different* thing, a third possibility, for which nature had made no provision and which was altogether secret.

Good old Uli! Now he would have to rise above himself, at this moment, his eyes fixed on this point in the world, this metaphysical navel, here in this glaring light, in a gradiose flight of thought (and now he would also have to reckon with a hidden camera filming the entire scene from behind that big mirror, operated by a shady cameraman with sideburns and a too-long cigar between his teeth, carrying out his task for the hundredth time: Sister Ariane and the Old Man – to be shown to scum from all walks and conditions of life, among whom there might be someone who knew him, or recognised him from the television) but this did not happen. And yet it did happen, had already happened, outside all thought and speech – although it is obviously absurd to say such a thing about a character in a story.

"You don't need to pity me, you know," said Ariane (Arrien before?). "It was the most wonderful moment in my life. Got rid of

220

that beastly thing at last." She looked at him and pursed her lips into a kiss. "Come to me, Uli."

That name from her mouth, more than the suggested kiss, increased his confusion still further. Groaning and slightly reeling, he rose to his feet; it took a few seconds before his knees had straightened completely. He took off his coat and lay down beside her. She put an arm round his shoulder, as if he were a child, and said:

"When I woke up after the anaesthetic the first thing I heard was the voice of the muezzin from the loudspeakers on the minarets, calling the faithful to prayer. Not bad, eh?"

Uli stared at the ceiling and listened to the cacophony. It was as if his whole life was emptying into this mystery he was now in. A sweet feeling flowed through him, or perhaps it was more like a smell, of blood maybe, which was not in this room but which he alone smelt because it came wafting from some distant corner of his life.

"Aren't we cosy like this, together?" With one arm under his neck she hugged Uli a few times so that he could feel there was something amiss with her bosom. "What kind of work did you use to do, Uli?"

"I was in the theatre. Still am, actually. I feel as if I've only just begun." He turned his face towards her and, even without his reading glasses, saw her coarse pores through the make-up. It did not fill him with revulsion, nor the contrary either, it merely added to the total incomprehensibility of everything. "And you? What do you do for a living?"

"Nothing. I got out of it. I live on social security."

"And before you got out?"

"I worked at the university, as a researcher. Arabic." She lifted her behind and pulled her skirt down a little. "That makes you look up, doesn't it? Oh yes, I was a very learned man. Tell me, what do you do in the theatre?"

Suddenly something cleared in Uli's head, as it does with someone who has dozed off without noticing. He sat up. "I must go."

"So soon? How boring. Let's play a record, and I've got a bottle

221

that needs finishing."

Uli got up and took his coat. "I've got a dress rehearsal tomorrow evening – no, tonight already. I really must be off." From his pocket he pulled the wad of banknotes, took out four and handed the rest to Sister Ariane who remained where she lay on the bed. "Here you are, for you, buy yourself a ticket for the first night. Friday at the Kosmos."

She laughed and took the money from him with a slow, coquettish movement. "Pricey ticket."

"It's the money those crooks handed me. I'll keep the rest for a taxi. Without you I wouldn't have had it."

"What kind of play is it?"

"You'll see. Bit complicated, but I expect that'll appeal to you. It has something to do with Shakespeare's *Tempest*."

She raised the hand with the money:

> *"Before you can say, 'come', and 'go',*
> *And breathe twice; and cry, 'so, so',*
> *Each one, tripping on his toe,*
> *Will be here with mop and mowe:*
> *Do you love me, master? no?"*

When Uli looked at her in amazement (with his own, now following line on his lips), she said:

"Give me a kiss, darling."

Uli lowered himself to his knees, on the mattress this time, and cautiously pressed his lips on hers, or was it his – but whatever it was, at this last kiss, in a sudden outburst of passion (or what must appear like passion) arms were flung around his neck and a tongue slipped into his mouth, money fluttered through the air, he slid backwards and tried to open his mouth to gasp for breath; at once Sister Ariane pushed him away, with resolute force, as if he had been the one to start the attack.

"You'd better bugger off now," she said when he was on his feet again. Without looking at him further, she made a movement with her fingers such as small children make when saying bye-bye.

Uli nodded. He left the room, struck by the thought that in a moment, as soon as he was outside, Jopie, Bert and Piet would be standing there again. He searched for a light switch; when he

222

could not find one he groped his way down the stairs.

Still he saw her gesture before his eyes. From primeval times the memory came to him that his mother – pregnant with Berta – had sometimes said *"Winke, winke"*, whereby she took his wrist and shook it so that his hand waggled involuntarily. Three-quarters of a century ago that must have been . . . and then it was as if at every step down the stairs he descended into another memory, or at least into another fragment of memory – like an archaeologist suddenly seeing potsherds sticking out of the ground – into something that must have happened a few months or weeks later . . .

. . . somewhere in a theatre with his father and mother? Clothes. A coat stand? A dressing-room? He, hidden among the clothes – on all sides soft, hard, coloured cloth

. . . confusion. What is happening? People everywhere

. . . his dog (the toy one), the sand-coloured dachshund with the floppy ears, without which he cannot go to sleep, pressed against him. Oh dog, eternal dog, friend, security

". . . a doctor! A doctor!"

. . . everything surrounded by night, robes – loosely floating somewhere, within a sphere, after the world has perished.

. . . the hand, that closes her eyes. No, that is later

. . . she screams

. . . His father, still with his make-up on but already wearing his bowler hat, beside himself, being restrained by gigantic acrobats in tight-fitting jumpsuits, with Kaiser-Wilhelm moustaches, "Berta!" A cat walks

. . . a wall with flaking paint, like the scales of a fish; it has existed all this time, he has carried it with him, that wall, all through his life, everywhere

. . . Hoppa, hoppa, Reiter, wenn er fällt, dann schreit er

. . . his father shouts, his mother pants, shouts. There she is. He does not see her face, she is lying with her legs towards him, on a couch, her knees (between which he was born too) apart. Everything soaking wet, someone has spilt something

. . . also blood, on the Smyrna upholstery, on the floor. How terribly the stork has bitten her

. . . with both hands she tries to hold something back that is coming out of her, a large thing that splits her apart in the crotch far too wide

. . . and will any moment fly out like a cork: like the cork in his popgun – and which later (when, shortly before the first world war he is with Berta and his Aunt Gertrud in Berlin, to meet their grandparents and their uncle) will reappear, to his bewilderment, when in the Sarrasani Circus he sees a man flying out of the mouth of a cannon, with a thunderous bang, right across the vast space to the net on the other side

. . . whoops, a somersault – music, applause

. . . a baby! Been put in there by the stork! A girl in a tiger skin (the tight-rope walker?), her hands covered in blood, holds the head of a baby which emerges like a bolt through a nut

. . . he looks, puts his teeth into the dog, while his trousers become warm and wet, but no one takes any notice of him

. . . what does the man in tails (the conjuror?) say, suddenly appearing, one hand on the door knob, the other on the door post, leaning forward into the room? That the doctor is ill? Cannot come

. . . his father curses, pulls himself free, is grabbed again by the acrobats. All that blood, not to be staunched: a fountainhead

224

. . . the baby begins to cry, then his mother becomes silent

. . . the slender juggler in his costume the colour of old white-of-eye puts his ear on the breast that has become calm. Hidden among the props, a small boy sees, in the shiny black hair, the white skin of the parting, straight as a shaft of sunlight

. . . was this how it happened?

. . . someone closes her eyelids. The ventriloquist maybe? On account of his power of speech, possibly.

ACT FIVE

1
Preparation

"What has happened to your tie?"

He was only just awake. Fully dressed, he lay on his bed, looking at Berta with large eyes. He touched his neck.

"You must have cut if off while I was asleep."

She shrugged her shoulders, put tea and a rusk by his side and asked no further questions.

"As long as you feel all right tonight."

His body was like a block of wood. Immobile he lay back, not knowing how to stretch his arm; normally he did it without willing it, but now that he wanted to, nothing happened. Only when he smelt the tea did it happen; just to be sure he quickly sat up on the edge of the bed. His body was stiff and unwilling, as if it belonged to someone else. After a few minutes he began to feel better. He ran the bath and undressed. Cautiously he lowered himself into the warm water and at once began to feel relaxed. Too much had happened these last few days. Above the water his toes were much larger than under it. As he moved his leg up and down he started to sing softly:

> *"Nur nicht*
> *Aus Liebe weinen . . ."*

At lunch he ate hardly anything and as the afternoon wore on, his restlessness gradually increased. He walked about the house, stood by the window, cast a glance at the script from time to time, watched a school programme on television (insofar as he was able to distinguish anything in the snowstorm on the old black-and-white set) and tried not to think of the previous evening. He also

229

had a constant feeling of having forgotten something. Berta said he ought to go out for a breath of fresh air and, although she advised it, he did. She asked him to take "colleague Joost" with him (she herself was already at the sherry); perhaps it would make him perk up a bit, he hadn't been out of his basket all day.

"Take him out yourself."

"I hope he's not sickening for something. His nose is all dry as well."

"Yes, the show would have to be cancelled."

It was cold outside. He walked to the town centre and had a cup of coffee in the square which had been named, not without some talent for the grotesque, the Agora. Almost physically he could feel Amsterdam lying in the distance, beyond the horizon. He could find no peace. It was as if he did not coincide with himself, was not actually quite inside himself but a few centimetres to one side; half an hour later he was on his way home again. Wearily he picked up the script once more, put it in his lap (although he knew it by heart) and looked with drooping mouth at instalment twenty-two of a programming course on TV. In a report on modern office practice which followed straight after, there were television screens everywhere, except in the director's room.

When at last he was sitting in the bus with Berta and Joost, driving through the senseless plain, it was as if a heavy snow shower was suspended on the horizon; between the darkening land and the purple sky hung a strip of bright light, as if the sky was being lifted from the horizon like a cheese cover, revealing a bright crack from which something incomprehensible might emerge at any moment. As he looked at it, with his papier mâché briefcase on his lap, he suddenly knew what he had forgotten – at Sister Ariane's: Michael's book on perspective.

It was now six o'clock. At the Kosmos there prevailed an activity different from that at previous rehearsals; the whole theatre was involved. The box office was closed, but Gerda was busy in the cloakroom, in the corridor the red carpet was being vacuumed by a foreign worker; two men were carrying a large television set out of

230

a delivery van into the building. Not until he saw this, did Uli remember the interview. It had vanished from his mind as if it had never taken place. In the auditorium and on the stage people were also busy. The seats were still unoccupied, but for the first time they radiated something expectant, as if in some way or other they were already connected with those who would shortly sit in them and who were at this moment still scattered about the city.

"Toi toi toi," said the stage manager as they walked past him.

Although it was still early, he had expected a certain bustle and excitement backstage, but there was a languid atmosphere, as if this was going to be the hundredth performance. Paul and the property manager were playing cards with a technician and the man who acted the part of the photographer; at the other table Trix and Mimi were playing a game of backgammon. With his legs on the dressing table, his chair tipped back, Etienne was sitting in his dressing-room reading an over-fat American paperback, recognisable by its cover as a sample of the sort that, thrashed out on a typewriter, is set at international airports, in the lobbies of expensive hotels and on the island of Crete – though not recognisable as such to Uli, since he rarely read a book. With Joost, who still did not seem to have recovered from his malaise, Berta went off in search of her Fausto; Uli – too tired to take off his coat – sat in front of the mirror in his room. With his hands in his lap he looked at himself, without seeing anything.

What was he doing here? He did not belong here. He should be sitting at home, in the silence, in his chair by the window, looking at the movement of the shrubs in the front garden. Suddenly nothing seemed more desirable than that; to be an old man in a chair who had never received a letter from a theatre company, but who pottered about the house in his down-at-heel slippers, between an ever more shadowy past and an ever more shadowy future, with only the furniture and the mealtimes and the lavatory and the snooze on the sofa as immovable fixities. Like an old racehorse afraid of a too-high hurdle he dreaded the imminent dress rehearsal, and then there was the first night tomorrow, and then a whole string of performances, also in other towns, and at night the queasy journey home, on the bus . . . what for? Maybe

231

there was some point to it if you weren't going to die, but if you died anyway, what was it all in aid of?

When long ago he had been in hospital for his gall-bladder operation, in a public ward, of course, an emaciated man had lain in the next bed, someone his own age, in the last stages of terminal stomach cancer. Right up to the day that they put around his bed the white screen behind which he died (with a daughter waiting sullenly and her husband strolling ceaselessly around the ward, chatting with the other patients and looking at his watch) he had been reading a book. Why? What use was it to him, to cram all that knowledge into his head when he was already on the slipway? After he had been wheeled away, bed and all, the book was left lying on his locker – like an object that had somehow become inviolable, sacred, awe-inspiring: Hölderlin, *Hyperion* (not that Uli still remembered this now – neither writer not title had meant anything to him – but that was what he had then seen, and so it must still be stored in his brain cells somewhere), *Hermit in Greece* . . .

Laughter sounded in the corridor, and he saw himself slowly looming up in the mirror. His coat hung open; from the breast pocket of his jacket there peeped something white, like a handkerchief. He pulled it out. It was the scrap torn from the phone book with Stella's number and address, pushed up by the nap of the cloth. He looked at it briefly, then rolled it into a pellet between his fingers. On a sudden impulse he put it in his mouth and swallowed it.

As if this gave him strength, he straightened his back and rubbed his eyes with both hands. It took a little while before his surroundings became sharp again. When things had fallen into place, he saw once again something white. An envelope had been propped up against the mirror. In elegant, calligraphic letters it said:

> *On the subject of Willem Bouwmeester*
> *(Short treatise towards further understanding)*

With raised eyebrows he took out the letter and read:

L.S.
At one end, nature enters man in the form of animals, plants and minerals, at the other end it leave as waste. The best is retained by the digestive system, after which the metabolism absorbs it, thus enabling the human

body to live. This also applies, *mutatis mutandis*, to the artist. At one end the world enters his mind and by means of a process of digesting impressions and mental metabolism is transformed into a work of art, whilst at the other end he produces a turd. This is all that is left for him.

Expressed as a formula:

artist – work of art = turd

No wonder that people keep a certain distance from the artist.

This applies to the creative artist, such as I. Now for the reproductive artist, such as he.

Everything that is going to happen is already in his head. The comedian has learnt his part by rote, every gesture he will make has been laid down, he knows what others will say and do, he knows the outcome. But there are two parties that know of nothing and that are linked to each other through this ignorance: the spectator and the character. To the spectator, the character is as free as he is himself; his future is open, everything is possible, nothing is inevitable (except, for the spectator, death; the character was never even born), but who hears and sees the spectator when he hears and sees the character? It is the comedian – that totally unfree person, subordinate to fate, the servant to inescapable predestination. Of all persons it is this insignificant famulus, this omniscient being, who has to demonstrate human freedom and give life to the naive character, and only he is capable of doing this, because it is impossible. Can we not learn something from this about the tragic nature of freedom? The first idiot acting Oedipus is more instructive than Oedipus.

I am speaking about masks now. (Speaking about masks is not altogether free from danger so that is why we had better keep this to ourselves.) It seems that it is only in masquerade that freedom, humanity, culture are contained.

And now for our devoted Architectus. He plays the part of someone who plays a part; he is given a second mask superimposed on his first – but this second mask, which overlays the human mask of freedom, is the magician's mask of unfreedom! Between him and Prospero a character must arise like a flash of lightning between a thundercloud and the earth: at the same time free and unfree, art and man.

I can scarcely await the outcome of this experiment. Tomorrow we shall know more (my excuse is that pain can also bring relief, like the crude cross pressed by a fingernail into an insect bite). Let us wish him a prosperous voyage!

L.S.

Uli stared at the letter. What kind of curious missive was this? Was it intended for him? He was referred to as "he"; "on the subject of"

Willem Bouwmeester, it said on the envelope. Perhaps it was meant for Vogel and someone had put it here by mistake. For a moment he had the uneasy feeling that something was going on behind his back, something sinister, but it was probably simply part of Siderius' general craziness. He stuck the letter inside the back of his script and took off his coat. As he hung it on the coat hook he briefly let his fingers glide over Prospero's mantle.

At that moment another author appeared in the doorway and looked at him with a savage laugh: Molly, one arm around Olga's shoulder, the other around Stella's.

"*Kraznaya pedzhalste kak smert vrozhinje!*" he called out, throwing his legs alternately up in the air.

His antics had the result (calculated or otherwise) that the general languor gave way to a mood of merriment which soon reached the canteen. The games were put aside and within half an hour every table was occupied by people eating from the plates piled with rolls that Michael had ordered. He announced that after the performance there would be an opportunity to watch television in the foyer; a cold buffet would also be provided there. This had actually been ordered for tomorrow, but never mind, they could have it twice. Beer and wine were drunk in moderation, everyone knew precisely how far he could go. No one mentioned the performance, only Vogel leaned forward to someone from time to time, for a last-minute instruction.

"In the final scene, Willem, after you have murdered Etienne, take your time, won't you. It's better to take a bit too long over it than not long enough." His T-shirt was emblazoned for the occasion with the figure 8.

"Right you are."

Now that he had eaten something, Uli felt better. He was sitting at a table with Stella, Aronds, the property manager, and Molly, who had lit a pipe and did not give anyone a chance to suffer from stage fright. While everyone was laughing, Uli leant forward to Stella and asked;

"How has Pim been since last week?"

"Pim?"

"Yes, your son."

234

"Oh, you mean Arthur." She looked at him quizzically. "Since last week? What do you mean?"

"Since I told him that terrific story."

"But Uli," she said, without taking her eyes off him, "that was yesterday. Last night."

He frowned. "Yes, of course," he muttered. "So many things have happened meanwhile . . ." But he didn't believe her. What nonsense. It had been last week. In order to prevent her from asking what were those many things that had happened in the meanwhile, he changed the subject. "What I meant to ask you – but of course you needn't answer if you don't want to: who is Arthur's father? Do I know him?"

"Hasn't anyone told you?" She looked at him in surprise, but through her surprise there still shone disquiet about his earlier remark.

"I didn't even know you had a child."

"How is it possible in this nest of gossip? Well, that's nice to know, anyway. Lucas," she said.

He stared at her with open mouth. Lucas? Max's friend? He looked at the table where they were sitting. With their knees against each other, Lucas and Olga were playing a children's game, singing and hitting the palms of their hands together, first straight, then crosswise, now on their knees:

> As I stood by a puppet stall,
> I saw some puppets big and small,
> I said, "Why are those puppets here?"
> "'Cos they are drinking puppet beer . . ."

As it kept going wrong, they sank shrieking with laughter into each other's arms, while Max watched with a tender smile, as if he were their mother.

"Are you being serious?" asked Uli.

"Sometimes things change," said Stella.

He was silent. It had all become too difficult to follow. Raising crumbs from his plate on the moistened tip of his middle finger, he tried to imagine them together, in bed, Lucas already thinking of Max. It was all far too complicated. And besides there was something wrong with the timing. There was something about

235

time itself that no longer squared, but of course Stella did not know this. She was too young, even though in a way she had already experienced too much. Something had been done to time, it had been tampered with, so that it kept going faster or, on the contrary, more slowly, with the result that everything had gone askew and no one could make head or tail of anything any more. He had once dismantled a broken alarm clock and put it together again, after which it ticked normally, although there was a cogwheel left over. After one hour had passed, the hands pointed at two hours later. A wheel was missing. It had rolled away somewhere, out of the world, and was now rolling in some other world, perhaps somewhere in the future, or five thousand years ago, in Egypt, where it rolled across the desert, grown to a height of a hundred metres, dazzling in the sun, straight towards the brand-new pyramids . . .

"Uli!"

Stella nudged him and he looked up.

"Yes," he said.

Most of the others had already got up. Suddenly there was tension in the air. Vogel called out that straight after the performance there would be a follow-up. That would be at ten o'clock at the latest so they would have an hour and a half until the television programme. Tomorrow afternoon everyone would in principle be free, unless there were some more i's to be dotted. As it would be tempting fate to wish them good luck (everyone knew that only a bad dress rehearsal resulted in a good first night), he stuck up two thumbs and said, "Worst of luck!"

It seemed to Uli as if he had briefly dozed off. With a dull head he went to his dressing-room, closed the door behind him and looked around irresolutely. He should now put on Pierre de Vries" suit, but he did not move and waited for something, without knowing for what and not thinking of anything. There was a knock at the door (this was several minutes later but he did not know that). Vogel entered, followed by Berta.

"Here we go then", said Vogel in a light-hearted tone that was out of harmony with the look in his eyes. Using the formal "you" he asked, "Are you happy to start?" Then, probably surprised at

236

his sudden formality, he switched again and added, "How are you feeling, Willem?"

"All right," said Uli, and took off his jacket.

Berta, who was holding Joost in her arms, looked at him sharply.

"You didn't have enough sleep last night. You ought to put your head under the cold tap."

The dresser appeared, and a moment later the make-up man with his little suitcase. The stiffness had gone and Uli enjoyed having everybody fussing around him. It must have been the same with Pierre de Vries and Louis Bouwmeester, always the centre of attention. While he was getting dressed, Vogel tried to cheer him up with some television director's stock-in-trade: that in a thriller no one should ever leave a room without first turning at the door and saying one last phrase, usually something doom-laden. He went to the door, put his hand on the handle and said, ominously:

"Is that the reason why you visited Gräfin Knödelblitz last night?"

And after his departure you always saw the person that had been spoken to make a quick phone call, beads of cold sweat on his forehead. When the person at the other end hung up, which almost always happened so that the line went dead, the speaker was guaranteed to look with surprise into the mouthpiece, which in real life nobody ever did.

Meanwhile Uli saw Pierre de Vries once again coming into being in the mirror: the actor acting himself in his daily life, never not acting – just a little too slick and elegant in his white suit. The door stood open and from the corridor people looked in from time to time.

"Damnation," said Vogel, pointing at Prospero's mantle, "What is that coat still doing here? That should be hanging on stage." He went to the door and bellowed, "Joop!"

He did not return. Uli thought of Siderius' letter but he could just as well show it to him after the performance. Mircea, the make-up man, who did not like talking, gestured invitingly at the chair in front of his open suitcase full of ingeniously arranged instruments, jars and paints. With his heavy, half-shut eyelids he looked very much like the leader of a gypsy orchestra. He pulled the wig with the dyed, too black hair over Uli's head, and as Uli felt the first damp but immediately drying layer being applied on his face with a little sponge, he thought of all those countless gypsies who, playing their violins by candlelight, had even bent over some woman friend of his, to let her melt in the deepest pools of the notes (meanwhile looking down her cleavage), while he, with a wordly smile, took a banknote from his wallet, folded it lengthwise and casually slipped it into the virtuoso's wide, embroidered left sleeve. Looking at Mircea in the mirror, as he had looked at barbers hundreds of times, he began to smile again. A waltz by Johann Strauss came to his mind ("*Ha, seht, es blinkt, es winkt, es klingt*"), and he started humming the tune softly.

"I don't know what's the matter with you," said Berta, "but Joost is definitely not well. His tummy feels hard and he still won't eat." She was still carrying him in her arms and kissed him on the head.

"I'm perfectly all right."

"Yes, yes."

Grumbling – how could Vogel think he would have forgotten – the property manager came to collect the magic mantle, and a moment later Henk Aronds appeared. Silently, by way of surprise, he lifted Uli's hand from the arm of the chair and slipped a ring with a large purple stone on to his finger.

"This was still owing to you."

Uli raised his hand before his eyes and stared at it.

"Look up a moment, please," said Mircea, as the sponge reached his lower eyelids.

"Does it fit?" asked Aronds.

Looking up at the ceiling, Uli checked with his other hand.

"Perfectly," he said. "You don't forget anything, do you?"

Going through the fire door he heard something unusual, as when you climb the last dune and the breakers of the sea are suddenly there. He walked round the black backdrop and past the set towards the front. Lucas stood bending down peeping through the hole in the curtain, and moved over to make room for him. "This

238

promises to be fun," he said.

For this one moment, the only time that evening, the roles were reversed. His walking-stick hooked over his arm, Uli spent some while trying to find the peephole among the curtain folds. He took off his hat and put his good eye close to the opening.

Under the dark blue canopy with the heavenly bodies, the stalls and circles were teeming with youngsters; they all seemed to be shouting at the tops of their voices to whoever was sitting furthest away. One boy was climbing up a cast-iron pillar to one of the balconies, paper darts sailed gracefully through the air or, misshapen, plunged in a helpless spin among the rows of seats; here and there in the aisles under the dress circle, young teachers were making calming gestures in a vain attempt to subdue the noise and rowdiness, but they took no further action. Near the front, on chairs in the stage box, Molly was talking to the theatre director; behind him a few other authors could be detected: Uli recognised Eduard and Flip Mannikin. Siderius was not among them. The stage box on the other side had been reserved for Vogel, but for the moment only Trudy was sitting there. With alarm he saw, coming out of the mouth of an attractive blonde girl in the front row (who had apparently caught his eye) a rapidly expanding pink balloon. He quickly let go of the curtain and turned round, before it had time to fill up the entire auditorium – then to explode with a thunderclap.

Having turned round too fast, he tottered briefly, but there was already a hand at his elbow. Whose it was he did not register. He was no longer being left alone, any more than the great Louis had been in the past. Presently the show would begin, and they were all looking at him now from the theatrical heaven: Louis, Frits, Louis Jr, Tilly, Lily, Wiesje and all those others, gathered under the bronze wings of Frederik Rozenveldt. Maybe all those children down there had been told at school from which family he stemmed – if the teachers knew, for they themselves were scarcely more than children.

All over the glacier, props were being hastily arranged. Like an exotic flower, Prospero's mantle stood at the highest point. It was indeed unthinkable that it should have been forgotten. Beside it were his staff and the polystyrene Book. With the musty smell of the curtain still in his nostrils, Uli went to the wings and stood, feet close together, looking at the fireman who was sitting in a chair reading a comic strip. He had completely forgotten that there were always firemen on duty, because theatres burn down at least once a century.

"Good evening," he said. The fireman looked up.

"Good evening to you."

As he said nothing further, Uli, no knowing what else to say either, walked aimlessly to the tautly stretched ropes by the wall, and looked up: in the flies hung bits of the sets of other plays. The stagehands were all dressed in white overalls; presumably in order not to be so conspicuous during the minor scene changes while the curtain was up.

Michael put a chair by him and asked him if he was nervous.

"If you mean am I suffering from stage fright – not a trace of it. This is not my first time, you know." He sat down and pointed with his ivory stick at the set, where Paul stood talking to Max in the cold light; muttering his text under his breath, Arthur's father was pacing up and down. "Doesn't everything look shabby in this wretched light?"

"That's the theatre for you," Michael nodded.

"What time is it?"

"Half past eight. We can start any minute now."

Accompanied by Vogel, Stella entered through the fire door. No, she did not look shabby, not even in this light. Laced in, her hands in the muff, on her head the hat with the feathers, everything white, she was a personification of light itself – but then of sunlight, as it shines on a wheatfield on a hot summer afternoon, motionless, in the fragrant stillness, with only the humming of the insects as a sign of the passing of time. A boy suddenly looks around with wide eyes and becomes immortalised. The immense world! But now it was an evening in November, the sun had set, and Uli had a feeling as if all those things were endlessly far removed from him, even though he now saw it all in the figure of Stella. He suddenly felt so moved that he had to avert his eyes from her.

240

"Attention, ladies and gentlemen! Beginners please! Opening positions!"

With his back to the curtain, his arms spread wide, the stage manager stood looking around. The din in the auditorium seemed at that moment to grow even louder, and Vogel had clearly had enough of it. He said something to the stage manager, who opened the curtain with both hands in such a way (like the entrance to an air-raid shelter) that Vogel could pass through the crack without making the stage visible to the public. Instantly, silence fell. Uli could hear almost nothing of what he said. He caught something about "consideration for the actors"; that this was not yet a real performance but a dress rehearsal, that what was enjoyment for some was hard endeavour for others. Uli pricked up his ears. Had he heard correctly? Enjoyment Through Endeavour! He burst into a laugh, with a goatlike, bleating squeal, so that Berta, who was giving Etienne some last-minute instructions about Joost – jerked round to look at him.

As Vogel returned through the slit in the curtain, the audience broke out into thunderous applause and foot stamping, out of sheer agreement with the request for silence.

There were shouts of "Encore! Encore!" and also: "Hat!"

"Start at once," said Vogel, "We'll bring them to heel, don't you worry. Get to your places, everybody. I'm going down there."

Uli, Stella, Max, Lucas, Paul and Mr Caccini took up their positions while the others withdrew into the wings. Pensive, leaning on his stick, Uli looked at the ropes, slung in a beautiful curve through the rings against the curtain (indicating the line along which it would fall later on), behind which the noise had resumed, though less loudly than before. Hardly an hour ago he had dreaded this performance as something insurmountable, yet now that the moment had arrived, he felt light, almost empty, and completely calm, as if he were standing at a tram stop waiting for a horse-drawn tram. He knew his text front to back and back to front; time was passing, it would go all by itself.

When at a stroke darkness fell, he closed his eyes and adopted his pose; his left hand on his heart, in his right hand the raised walking stick, like a monk allaying the devil with a crucifix.

2

The Dress Rehearsal

The gong was struck three times, the house lights dimmed slowly, and with the rustle of the rising curtain, the other, completely different world opened up; from it a fragrance of warm young bodies spread across the stage. Briefly the two worlds existed opposite each other in a common twilight; when the light intensified, making the faces in the auditorium invisible (except Vogel's, in the glow of the little lamp on his script) it became totally silent. Frozen in the tableau vivant – copied from a stage photograph of 1904 – Uli felt how he and his colleagues blended with the audience into one motionless body that was being lifted a metre above the ground. With his eyes fixed on the green illuminated word EXIT at the back of the house, he was aware how his own body participated in bringing this about, by an immobility that was nevertheless alive. Of course the performance should have consisted of only this: tableaux vivants, changing very slowly, scarcely perceptibly, hour after hour, without any text. Time paused, not only here in this building, but all over Amsterdam, all over the universe. It was up to Mr Caccini, the musician, to decide how long the spell could be maintained; when at last he struck a note (a drop of time falling into eternity) and began to play softly, a sigh went through the audience, hesitantly turning into a small ripple of applause. On all sides Uli sensed an easing of tension, in which there was at the same time a whiff of disappointment, that it could not remain so for ever. The evening had become almost unbreakable.

The performance was under way and everything seemed to go all by itself, as if not they, the actors on the stage, were using a text

242

to make a performance, nor that the text was using them, but as if it was the performance that, in order to exist, used both them and the text. Caught up in this, Uli felt as free as a yachtsman – sailing as he used to, long before the war, in a hired sharpie, united with everything; the helm and the ropes tightly in his hands, his youthful body leaning back overboard, his eyes fixed on the pennon and on the sails and on the glittering water all around, changing tack with a clatter, dodging a blow from the boom, but totally engrossed in the moment, without thought as to how it would be soon afterwards and already not remembering how it had been shortly before. The ever-changing moment (but changed in what respect? how could it change?) in which he lent hospitality to Pierre de Vries, offered him access to his body and to the world, whereby he, for all his alertness, existed in a kind of half sleep. Each thing glided into another. The insolent manner in which he, the actor celebrating his jubilee, treated Stella, the minor little actress, his beloved Stella whose mother made her smoke cigars, and his flirtation with Stella's fiancé, the beautifully made-up Max, queen of the first order – while he still invented new little touches as he went long, such as absent-mindedly pushing the new ring up and down on his finger, as he said,

"Please leave a sip for me."

The scene ran its course as though it were surrounded by plate glass windows, a space in which everything that happened could also be seen from outside, through everything that happened outside. With a full house, this rehearsal was totally different in character from all the previous ones. To Uli there was nothing new in this, of course – he had often been reminded of it when his wife died. Countless times – by her bedside in the hospital, on the way home, at home – he had imagined what it would be like after her death; but when she was no longer there, and all things were diminished by her absence, everything was different. He might just as well not have imagined anything at all, for he now discovered that it was not the living but the dead person who was dead. He had not bargained for that (the knife always strikes one in the back), and this held him for weeks in a spasm of grief for the woman he hated.

Slowly the light died on the tableau which concluded scene one. In scene two he did not appear, and in the darkness he shuffled on his crêpe soles down the slope towards the wings. There he felt hands on his shoulders and a chair being pushed beneath him; at the same moment he noticed how exhausted he was already.

"It's going splendidly," whispered Michael.

He nodded. Mircea carefully dabbed the sweat from his forehead and face with a paper tissue. How he wished he could lie down, full length, in a bed; he felt as if he could sleep for a hundred years at a stretch. Beside him sat Miss Wijdenes with the script in her lap. On the set and in the opposite wings, hurrying shadows were moving about.

The light poured down on the iceberg again and from the side he watched the romantic pose of the two lovers. Max looking up, arms hanging loose, the palms of his hands turned outwards; Stella with the red rose on her breast, half reclining on the floor, half raised against his legs, one pale hand reaching up to his shoulder. Because it suddenly reminded him of a monument on a tombstone, he averted his eyes and looked into the auditorium where he could see the authors' box and, just, the end seats of the first few rows. While Molly, with open mouth and eyes, awaited the end of the tableau, the theatre director sat looking at his watch. Below them shone the defenceless faces of two children, like Ferdinand and Miranda at that very moment busy discovering love: angels. And then, what he did not see (but what is visible): he himself, on his chair in the wings, between the light of illusion and the darkness of reality: an in-between person in an in-between realm: no longer altogether Pierre de Vries and not yet altogether Uli Bouwmeester; the stage there in the light not made of timber but of meaning, where Max and Stella were not only not saying their own words, but where their entire physical existence had changed, down to the last molecule: their flesh made dream, imagination.

The spectators were still well behaved. In the darkness their young brains, crammed full of figures and tests, were trying to integrate what was here being shown with what they themselves had already learnt about life, and about literature, which to them still coincided innocently; but of course they were also waiting for anything that might distract their attention (total concentration was too stupid, after all). The opportunity presented itself in the next episode, in which the relationship between Pierre and Etienne was portrayed, and the occasion for it was Joost.

When the light went on over the tableau, the two men were standing at some distance from each other: an indication of their situation. Joost was lying at Etienne's feet, his head resting on his forepaws – immobile and immortalised so that the students might well think it was a dummy. During previous rehearsals he had always been standing upright, impudently looking around, and thus, each time, providing a fine, natural disruption of the artistic design. When the scene began to move (and Molly, in his box, made a wide, enraptured gesture with both arms, like an ecstatic conductor at the return of the principal theme), Joost did not stir. Etienne, assuming he would go up and follow as usual, dragged him along the floor by his lead for a short distance, so that the dog keeled over, scrambled to his feet, braced himself with all four legs at once, was pulled further along in that posture, his collar making his ears flap forward over his eyes, and then lay down.

This was the signal for tumult to break out.

"You bastard, what d'you think you're doing!"

"Bully!"

Etienne gestured towards the wings and with narrowed eyes sought Vogel, who had buried his face in his hands, but then stood up and called out, "Right! That dog must go! Dog out!"

He said it with great determination, as if he meant the command to reach forthwith as far as Bijlmer, from where not even that art-wrecker in his concrete flat would be able to revoke it. Etienne peered into the wings again, whence, a moment later, Berta emerged.

First the recalcitrant animal, then Vogel's intervention from his stage box, and now the apparition of this grandma in her flowery dress (large purple blooms); the excitement was rising to fever pitch. Amid exploding applause she carefully lifted Joost from the floor and was about to carry him away; on her face could be read the intense disappointment that suddenly it had all proved to have

245

been in vain. But then, perhaps because of the ovation engulfing her, perhaps because it awoke something from the days when she herself had been on the stage – and there could be no doubt that this was the very last time – Shirley Carola swung round towards the audience and bowed. Not once, but twice, three times, four times – until Vogel had conquered his perplexity and shouted, "Will you get off the stage at once!"

Berta peered into the auditorium, searchingly raised one hand above her eyes and asked, "What's that?"

At this, the audience collapsed totally into helpless laughter. While here and there an individual was still sitting upright, wide-eyed and shocked into immobility by what was being wrought here, girls flopped shrieking against one another, boys yelled as they rose to their feet unleashing a rhythmic applause. Molly hung half out of his box, limp with laughter, the theatre director pulled him back by his collar, so that he toppled backward into Eduard's lap, was shoved into his own seat, and, beside himself with frenzy, screamed at the top of his voice, *"Tverskaya gospodin tovarich plazhrivrozavlenya!"*

Berta was still standing on the stage, the white poodle in her arms; God knows, maybe she was planning to do a little dance item, as an encore.

"Curtain!" bellowed Vogel.

The stage manager peeped round the corner and vanished. A moment later the curtain fell and the house lights went up.

And Uli? Where is Uli? In the confusion and the white terror on the stage no one had time to bother about him right now. First Etienne had to be calmed down. Ranting and raving, he flung his white hat on the floor (but everyone saw that this gesture did not come from his soul, only from a stage play or a film) and shouted that he was finished with it, he was going home, right this minute, for good, to the Ardèche, everybody else could drop dead as far as he was concerned. The property manager picked up the hat and started blowing the dust off it. Meanwhile, Michael was ordering Berta in a high tone to withdraw immediately to the furthest corner of the Kosmos and not to show herself again. She asked what was to be done about that cover story in *Privaat* now, but when she saw Michael's commanding finger at the end of his outstretched arm, she put her cheek against Joost's, briefly shrugged her shoulders in the direction of Mr Caccini, and walked away.

Just in time, because the next moment Vogel appeared, his face contorted with rage and even with his hat in his hand, so that most of the others saw for the first time that at the top of his head he was going bald in a mathematical, tonsure-like manner. Clearly, the situation was now very serious. He yelled furiously that that woman was even worse than the animal – where was she? And where was Etienne off to?

Etienne had almost reached the fire door. "I'm through."

"For Christ's sake, have you gone out of your mind? You stay here, damn you! This is a dress rehearsal, what do you think! It's just what they're waiting for at the ministry, that the show won't go on tomorrow!" And to Michael: "Ask Arend to tell that rabble out there that we're carrying on in a minute, but if they make so much as another squeak they'll be kicked out. So they can daub the walls at their leisure with their felt tips. He'd better talk to them from his box. And this is the last time I'm having that riffraff at a dress rehearsal. Next time we'll get the old people's home in, at least we'll be able to work in peace then."

As Michael went off to do as he was asked, Vogel put on his hat and looked around. "Where's Willem?"

It was Olga who discovered him, backstage, among some props from another play shoved together into a corner (parasols, a white-painted trellis weathered by sea air), without knowing how he had got there. He looked grey, there was alarm in his eyes. Vogel pulled out a deckchair and without first turning it into a kangaroo with twisted legs, he set it up. Uli lowered himself into it, cautiously, as if the dark-blue canvas was scorching hot from the sun.

Vogel crouched by his side and said that the things that were funny to retell afterwards were never funny when they happened; that only came later. Anyway, he did not have to teach Willem Bouwmeester that, he'd been in harness long enough. So perhaps the best thing was to laugh at it straight away. The way in which he then laughed was not his most convincing demonstration as a director, and Uli did not manage more than a wry twist of his mouth either.

"Do you remember," he said to Vogel, "we went to see Siderius because I had discovered something in his play that could be improved upon?"

"For heaven's sake, shut up."

"He gave us an earful, didn't he?"

"Stop it. It's all my fault. I should never have agreed to it. We're lucky it's turned out all right in the nick of time. Just imagine if this had happened tomorrow."

"Do you know, I had a letter from him this morning."

"A letter?" Vogel repeated. "You? From Siderius? When?"

"It was in my dressing-room earlier on, I'll show it to you. It was rather an odd letter."

"I don't doubt it. Would you like a drink? A brandy?" When Vogel looked up, Olga had already gone to fetch it. Vogel stood up and gave Uli a probing look. "Nothing is going to get us down, is it?"

"Weeds never die."

He kept his eyes fixed on Uli for a little longer. "That's the spirit. Now I must . . ."

With a limp hand Uli made an understanding gesture. On the other side of the curtain, in the auditorium, silence had returned, and he heard the director's voice, though without distinguishing his words. He would no doubt succeed in restoring order, perhaps he was telling them about the Returned Flower. He saw Michael's gesture before him again, banishing Berta (while only last week she had been a guest at his table); the way she had disappeared through the fire door with Joost. He opened his eyes wide and stretched his face, like someone waking up after having dozed off for a moment.

"Are you all right?" asked Olga, as she handed him the brandy.

The glass was smaller than in the director's office. He tried to gauge from her face how Berta was, in the canteen, for that was where she had gone of course; but he didn't want to ask. He took a

248

swig, which burnt his throat as it went down.

"A lot better, anyway."

But at the same time he felt as if none of this had anything to do with him any more – not the dress rehearsal, not the first night tomorrow, let alone the performances that were still to follow. Not that he was worried about them, as he had been earlier; it now seemed to him that it would go quite differently. How it would go – the property manager was once again standing, arms outspread, in front of the curtain – that was a mystery as yet unrevealed.

Helped by Olga (where was Stella?) he heaved himself out of the chair and took a step – cautiously, like someone who has been told that the ice may not hold.

3
The Dress Rehearsal (2)

> *"But think, Etienne, what will you do*
> *When presently the curtain has come down?"*

The two men, in a life-and-death struggle by the high-water line. It was going well. The audience never became as quiet again as it had been before the rupture in the performance, something restless and whispering lingered, like an echo, but Uli was not bothered by it.

> *"Prospero's island is the stage*
> *The audience down below, the sea."*

As long as Pierre de Vries stood in the limelight, Uli's fatigue was absent, although of course it must have remained somewhere, since he had not been asleep in the meantime, unless, who knows, playing a part is really a kind of sleeping or dreaming. Long, long ago – in 1943 in Berlin, during supper at Kranzler's, then as yet Unter den Linden – his Uncle Julius had told him, while spooning up his Mozart Bombe, how as a medical orderly in the First World War he had seen how soldiers, ripped open by bayonets in man-to-man trench warfare, went on fighting for several minutes before they died of injuries that should have killed them outright; and conversely, how it could happen that someone, seeing in the drumfire that his uniform and skin had been torn away by a splinter of shrapnel, looked into the pool of blood and fell down dead on the spot, even though he was shown to have sustained no more than a superficial flesh wound. Sometimes the soldier lived at the expense of the man, sometimes the man died for the soldier; everything was very, very complicated. Yes, war was a grand master, said his uncle, raising his glass of Spätburgunder, but only the Germans knew this – whilst artists, luckily for them, didn't know anything about it at all, for they had been exempted from service and were allowed to sing in operatta while others were dying. "*Zum Wohl, holländischer Neffe! Auf die holde Kunst und den Endsieg!*" And for the rest: "*Scheisse . . .*"

You don't need to know what you are in order to be it – perhaps it is even better not to know; to go back to Uli (for where are we going to end up if we go on like this?) who, as Pierre de Vries as Prospero, was rehearsing his scene with Miranda in which the magician reveals to his daughter her true indentity. Stella's voice like a white pebble at the bottom of a stream. Uli acted better than he knew; all those threads that during rehearsal had been woven together into a complex pattern – as Berta sometimes did when knitting: four, five skeins of wool around her feet at the same time, colours rising to her hands and, in the growing garment, all kinds of extra needles that were used in turn. In the romantic style of Pierre de Vries he portrayed Prospero's love for his daughter, and at the same time Pierre's revulsion towards Stella, engaged to the youth he was in love with; at least that was the situation during this first rehearsal, for by the time of the first night it would all have become different. Naturally, none of that would be shown, for the farewell performance would begin at the moment that *Hurricane* ended.

While he was acting, Uli felt as though he were saying goodbye to Stella. Her body, her face, her eyes so close and at the same time so far away. This was not only because she was saying words to him that not *she* was saying to *him*, but someone else to another, but also because she, like himself, now knew she was being observed: what was being observed hung around them and shrouded them like sulphuric acid coats the lead in a battery; it was not they looking at each other, but the observed looking at the observed, whereby the looking changed into the mutual blindness of the mask that forms the art of the theatre – and perhaps not only that of the theatre.

She helped him out of his imaginary magic mantle; the real one was not yet ready though already present, splendidly illumined at the highest point of the iceberg: an object belonging to the future. The not yet existing and yet already existing mantle slid to the ground.

251

"Lie there, my Art."

And Paul, a little later:

> *"You are now*
> *a simple man again."*

Yes, Prospero perhaps, but not Pierre de Vries, and Uli even less. Time passed and the performance proceeded through time like a ship through a canal in the polderland, sailing amid grass and wheat, vanishing and reappearing behind factories, silos, apartment blocks, now lit by the sun, then again in the shadow of the clouds. The tableau vivant, he, waiting in the wings, extinguished on a chair, then again sleep-walking in the limelight and in Fausto's music; he wiggled his toes inside his shoe, ostentatiously cleared his throat because he could not snap his fingers, held his hands with queenish elegance at waist level. In order to win Stella over to himself, Lucas suggested the intrigue to Etienne; and in order to win Pierre back, Etienne urged Max, in scene after scene, to blackmail Pierre, out of love for Stella, while in the meantime the rehearsals for *The Tempest* continued as if everything in *Hurricane* took place according to the classic unities of time, place and action – but then in a world in which the sun never rose or set, in the windowless cavern of the theatre, turning that world into a cubist, perspectiveless space, so that the action within it became open to whatever was possible or impossible.

It was now half past nine. Uli's *mise-en-scène* gradually approached the top of the structure where, for the rehearsal of the masque, he was to be helped into his mantle by Paul, would have the hat put on his head and the staff and Book handed to him. The old man's metamorphosis took place slowly and in a silence that communicated itself to the audience. With difficulty Uli held himself in equilibrium, and when Ariel – the prospective blackmailer – came tripping along in his transparent wings, giggles erupted everywhere, but that was not contrary to the intention. The magic enchantment of the three spirits, evoked for educative reasons for Ferdinand and Miranda, was respectfully listened to, but remained mere words, only tolerable to the young because of the music; and nobody understood Pierre's literary-historical elucidation addressed to Trix (about the identity of Iris, who was Ariel); when director Paul was told he ought to confine his theorising to his leisure time, there were one or two isolated hand claps.

Uli did not understand the applause, and in his confusion he again spoke the Goethe quotation in far too perfect German. A little later, when Fedinand asked if these were spirits, he lost his lines for the first time ever.

"Spirits . . ." hissed Miss Wijdenes.

> *"Spirits, which by mine Art*
> *I have from their confines call'd to enact*
> *My present fancies."*

Uli had long since lost all awareness of what he was saying. All the nuances he had built up during the rehearsals, with feeling and insight and practice, had become external – merely technique, professionalism. He himself had almost become superfluous; what was left for him was little more than emptiness and exhaustion.

Tableau! Benjamin, having for some time been watched by his contemporaries in a mood of solidarity, ignited the magnesium (Uli shut his eyes for a moment), which elicited fresh applause; the photographer took his picture, and with the white cloud like an old-fashioned ghost in a doorway, Prospero stood up with a jerk. The threatened attack on his life! His face contorted with rage, he struck the ground with his staff.

> *"Well done! avoid; no more!"*

Slowly the three spirits vanished, while Paul, with the script of *The Tempest* in his hands, called out:

> *"We hear a strange and hollow and confusèd noise."*

Miranda said she had never till this day seen her father touched with anger so distempered. Prospero reassured them all, Pierre de Vries positioned himself for his famous line, and Uli took a deep breath before the melodramatic delivery that came next:

> *"Our revels now are ended. These our actors,*
> *As I foretold you, were all spirits and*
> *Are melted into air, into thin air:*

253

> *And, like the baseless fabric of this vision,*
> *The cloud-capp'd towers, the gorgeous palaces,*
> *The solemn temples, the great globe itself,*
> *Yea, all which it inherit, shall dissolve,*
> *And, like this insubstantial pageant faded,*
> *Leave not a rack behind. We are such stuff*
> *As dreams are made on; and our little life*
> *Is rounded with a sleep."*

Uli froze in the tableau vivant that closed the scene. But in the slow fading of the light he suddenly heard in the loft a sharp metal click, immediately followed by a whistling sound, and then a loud bang behind his back. His breath halted; he was about to turn and look, but when he saw the audience still watching with fascination (Molly's face suddenly a plaster mask) he managed to keep himself in check. Behind him, there was something to be seen that was seen by everybody except by the people on the stage.

When the light had faded, there was no applause as after the other scenes. He turned round. In the dim glow emanating from the white set, he recognised the painted flat depicting the hellish torture scenes from the last act of *The Killjoy*. The metres-high monster was still swaying slowly back and forth in front of the backdrop. Uli felt he could not take much more. In the wings, he let himself be helped out of his mantle, his heart thumping.

"What a shambles it is this evening," said the dresser. "You see, you can never get away from human error."

He found his chair and let his arms hang limply by his sides.

"Something must have come loose," said Miss Wijdenes, turning over a page.

On all sides there were whispered consultations. The thing was stuck fast; the stage manager said the curtain should come down and the lights on, so the flat could be lifted from its cables. But Vogel, arriving even faster than last time, would have none of it. "We're not going to interrupt the show yet again. Let it stay, we'll carry on regardless. They seem to think it's wonderful anyway, the morons. Hurry up, action! I shall be glad when this is all over." After a glance at Uli he was gone again.

Although the Dante-esque paintings belonged to a different

254

play, they ensured the return of the attentive silence with which the performance had begun. (And perhaps this gave Vogel an idea: produce Noël Coward in Elizabethan costume. *The Gypsy Baron* with pictures of concentration camps in the background.) The play was drawing towards its close, but it seemed to Uli he had been here all his life and would stay here for ever, in this dark, ambiguous place. He hardly noticed Mircea dabbing his face and touching up the make-up here and there; Mircea had to put one hand under Uli's chin to make him hold up his head. Every now and then Uli closed his eyes for several seconds, and then gazed at the penultimate scene again, without really seeing it but experiencing it like a warm cross-wind, a scirocco blowing from the auditorium to the stage.

When the concluding tableau had been cut by darkness, the stage manager had to recall him from his absent-minded state.

"Only a little longer, Mr Bouwmeester. Then it's all in the bag."

Last scene. Time: the night of the farewell performance. Place: the dressing-rooms at the City Theatre in Amsterdam, at the Leidseplein.

The backdrop had been raised, so that the brick wall was now visible, with the cast-iron door leading to the stage where everything was being prepared for *The Tempest*. (There, in 1904, the curtain was still down, but the first guests, in tails and long dresses – decorations were being worn, of course – were already trickling in.) In the auditorium, only those who came to the Authors' Theatre more often were aware that the horror painting was not supposed to be hanging there.

Since they inevitably show things that are not supposed to be seen (the people in the wings, the reflection of the public), mirrors are forbidden on the stage, which, according to Shakespeare, should itself be a mirror; Uli therefore peered at the dull disc without seeing himself, while Pierre pulled Prospero's wig over his dyed hair. That Lucas was now hummingly putting on his make-up elsewhere, that Max, in Stella's room, hinted that their money worries would soon belong to the past, since, on Etienne's advice, he planned to blackmail Pierre de Vries with his homosexuality, just at this point when Pierre was defenceless, at the peak of his fame and the turning point of his life – Uli knew, of course, yet in some way he did not know it, and it was as if he did not hear it either, although it was being said only a few steps away from him.

He looked at the thin black scratches in the silver paint on the blind mirror: small capricious patterns that suddenly filled him with emotion. If he had not discovered them, no one would ever have seen them; their existence would have been totally pointless. One was in the form of a face in profile, like the caricature of a laughing man with an aquiline nose –

> *"Mr de Vries, forgive me that I . . . but*
> *There's something which you . . . I . . ."*
> *"Well, tell me then,*
> *What can there be of such compelling portent*
> *That you should come here at a time like this?"*

He had not heard her coming, nor had he paid attention to his cue ("*something which you . . . I . . .*"), but his answer came very naturally, as it came with Pierre de Vries, including the quaint, old-fashioned sounding "portent". After she had told him sobbingly what was going on behind his back, and had fallen to her knees imploringly, he stared at her in bewilderment for several seconds. Something seized up inside him in a terrible way. Someone intended to destroy him, in all seriousness. Destroy him, that was what they were planning to do, just as they destroyed Oscar Wilde a few years ago! He stood up with a jerk, his stool toppled over and Stella, weepingly, flung her arms about his legs.

> *"Have mercy! 't was not Max's idea.*
> *Mr Etienne's the one who thought of it."*

The scum! Rats, serpents they were! Filled with loathing he wrenched himself free; his head was in a whirl, as if the truth was dawning on him only now.

> *"Go to your room, you! Go, at once!"*

Beside himself he went to see Max, who was standing naked in front of his mirror and turned round with a start. For one moment Uli recoiled: he had not known Max would be wearing no clothes, would stand there with his organ vulnerably exposed in a circle of blonde hair like an exotic, flesh-eating flower; but then the sight of the beautiful youth only increased his rage. With bated breath the audience listened as Uli demolished Max utterly and completely, oblivious of the fact that there was an audience; the true audience was on the other side of the wall, in the sold-out house at the City Theatre in the year 1904.

When he had reduced Max from a radiant young god into a heap of human misery (the stage manager had already called out "Beginners" for the third time) he returned, still fuming, to his dressing-room where he had to take several deep breaths in order to calm himself. As soon as the performance was over he would give that louse the sack, and that slut too, they'd have to see how to scratch a living somehow, see if he cared. How did they get it into their heads! And then try and put the blame on Etienne! They'd find out who they were dealing with. With a quick jerk of his knees he ducked into Prospero's mantle, and at the same time there sounded, in the distance, the soft boom of the gong, three times. At the Leidseplein, the curtain rose for the first scene of *The Tempest*: the shipwreck.

In the muffled howling and thundering of Prospero's storm (produced by Ariel, the transcended stagehand – limp sheets of metal and other obsolete theatrical implements, that had to be shaken and turned), Etienne suddenly appeared in his room, in tails, a glass of champagne in his hand and with a broad, slightly tipsy smile. Uli pivoted on his heels and looked at him – and at that moment, in the way that lightning can, at night, illuminate the land and sea from horizon to horizon, all became clear to him as if by magic: there was something between him and Max! Those two were hand in glove! They wanted to trick him out of his money and make off with it together! So that was how it was.

And then it overwhelmed him. Night fell in his eyes, his lips curled inward, and without wanting or knowing it he flew at Etienne so that the glass was knocked out of his hand and smashed to pieces. At the same moment Max, in his transparent wings, had arrived at the rear wall and opened the fire door: at once the primitive tempest raging through the City Theatre was taken over by ferocious electronic thunder in the Kosmos; the door remained open. With the full weight of his mantle Uli fell on top of Etienne, his hand around his neck. Etienne tried to crawl away from underneath to say something (perhaps that it hadn't been his idea but that of Lucas) but he was unable to. When, a moment later, Lucas held Stella tenderly in his comforting arms (happy ending: the greatest scoundrel triumphant and rewarded, even though he does not yet know that the only witness to his villainy has just been put out of the way), movement ceased underneath the mantle.

Amid the deafening noise of the hurricane coming out of the loudspeakers, the audience gawped at the immobile scene: even the torture picture had finally come to rest. Uli took his time. Now he must get up slowly, turn round and take on his Louis Bouwmeester pose; but he took his time. When nothing happened, it was Vogel who – probably without realising that he was doing so – slowly rose to his feet in his box, his eyes fixed rigidly on the mantle.

"Get up now!" Miss Wijdenes called from the wings, but she herself was the only one who heard it.

A moment later the stage manager's voice, recorded on tape, with echo, boomed forth like that of an extra-terrestial being:

> *"It's time, Mr de Vries! Last call!*
> *Please hurry, sir, no time to lose! Last call!"*

But nothing happened. The tape ran out and the noise died down.

The silence buzzed. After a few seconds someone in the upper circle began to clap; others took it up. The applause continued to swell. After a while, the curtain fell.

vain, and this probably meant at the same time the death of the Authors' Theatre. The director met Vogel's eyes. He too had understood.

Etienne had got up and was sucking at a cut in his hand. Still shocked, he said he had never seen anybody look like Willem as he grabbed him by the throat. He seemed to have gone completely mad. The way he had squeezed as hard as he could; he, Etienne, had been taken unawares, he thought he was going to suffocate; but then all of a sudden Willem's grip had slackened and at the same time he had become twice as heavy, while his head had sunk on to Etienne's shoulder. He had whispered Willem's name, told him to get up for the final tableau, but there had been no response. As the curtain was up, he himself had also remained where he was, what else could he have done? He had felt like someone buried alive in a mass grave, like those people you read of in books about the war.

Mircea pulled the two wigs from Uli's head, and the electrician and the fireman helped him up, and out of his mantle, like a baby being lifted out of its pram. He was immediately made to sit down in the grandfather chair. The applause had died down; behind the curtain there was now the cheerful hubbub of the emptying house. When this also gradually faded, Uli tried to figure out what had happened, but something inside him resisted this, as if it was all over and done with now, put aside and for ever disposed of. Luckily Berta was there.

"I want to go home," he said again.

He stood up and his hand tremblingly sought the carved wooden arm of the chair under the white sheet. Everyone looked with shock at the shaky old man he suddenly was. Perhaps in order to break through this, to help him, give him her arm, Stella went up to him, but when she saw the look in his eyes which no longer had anything to do with her or with anyone else there, she faltered.

"I'll take you home," said Vogel. "You don't have to change your clothes, we'll take your things with us."

"I'll go and fetch them," said Olga.

"I'll get the car, then."

It had become quiet on the other side of the curtain. Olga in her tulle dress – Juno's colourful ribbons fluttering behind her – ran to the dressing-rooms and Vogel also left the stage, beckoning the authors and the director with a movement of his head.

Uli looked about him. Almost inaudibly he asked, "Where's my stick?"

The property manager disappeared into the wings and handed the stick to Mr Caccini, who passed it to Benjamin, after which, via Lucas, it reached Uli on the set. Between Berta and Michael he began the descent, step by step. In silence, a way was cleared for him. Molly, who had not gone with the others to the post-mortem discussion, was the first who managed to speak.

"You were fantastic, Willem. Absolutely brilliant."

Then he too had to endure Uli's gaze – a gaze that would never leave him again and with which, in some way or other, he would have to come to terms in the future, perhaps through writing a play or a novel, for in it he appeared to himself as an insect, as some disgusting vermin, while he wasn't that at all. Or was he? At the same time it sharpened his own gaze down into the microscopic: no one else saw the minute, ominous trace of silvery saliva at the corner of Uli's mouth.

Apart from Berta and Michael everybody remained behind on the stage, everybody was impatient to know what was to be done next. In the curved corridor with the red carpet (Gerda from the cloakroom, already with her coat on, slammed the flap of the counter down behind her and said good night; she knew nothing yet, and seemed not to see anything either) Berta said suddenly:

"Good God, I completely forgot Joost!"

At a trot, her fat stomach wobbling, she hurried back. As her hand reached the door ("No entry"), Olga appeared with Uli's bag and clothes. In the entrance hall Michael helped him into his coat; Vogel ran past and said he wouldn't be a moment, the car was just outside. Uli looked at Olga, perhaps he wanted to say something, thank her, but no words formed, it was as though he would never speak again. Olga began to cry, turned away and started walking down the corridor. When she met Berta, they gave each other a kiss.

"Just look at them. What a pathetic pair," said Berta, looking

261

from the dozy dog in her arms to Uli, who was leaning with one elbow on the box office till, his head trembling slightly. Beside him hung a playbill for *Hurricane*. "What a terrible evening. As for tomorrow, you can forget about that as well."

"Don't worry yourself about that," said Michael. "You've had your applause, at any rate."

A smile briefly passed across her face, as if she regarded it as a compliment, but when she looked at Uli again (it seemed as if he was trying to get something out of his pocket, without exactly knowing what) she stiffened.

Then she turned on Michael: "It's all your fault, you should never have asked him, I knew from the start it would come to no good. How did you ever get it into your heads! You've allowed yourselves to be carried away by . . . I don't know . . . by your sense of humour, I think."

Reversing with a screech, Vogel's car appeared and stopped abruptly in front of the entrance. A few of the teenagers, still chatting, sitting on their bicycles with one foot on the ground, applauded when they emerged.

Only when the car stopped outside the door of his house in the polder did Uli wake up from a state that had not been sleep but a lingering in a black, tough shadow, like the hollow underneath a folded bird's wing. He was sitting in the back, beside Berta, and was helped out of the car. Sleet was falling; he lifted his face: holy water. Watched by the neighbours, helping hands at his elbows, he walked through the small front garden. Inside, in the vestibule, it was suddenly dry. As he was being helped out of his coat, Berta said he ought to go to bed straight away, but he didn't want to. Silly poo. Horrid bed. He shuffled into the dark room – the smell of his things, the chair, the red, grown-old leather of his portable phonograph on the side table – and sat down on the divan. He bent down and laid his stick on the floor (that walking-stick, always vertical, now coming to rest full length: the ivory snake with its silver head could at last curl up and bite its own tail), drew up his legs, groaning a little, and stretched out with a sigh. Aah. All over now. He looked at the tunic covering his legs, the sky-blue turned indigo in the light of the street lamp, and then at the two men standing by him, Berta eased Joost into his basket, tucked the blanket around him so that only his head remained free, quickly went round the room switching on all the side lamps, and said she was going to make coffee. One of the men brushed this aside: they had to get back to Amsterdam at once, as Mrs Bouwmeester would surely understand, and therefore . . . Uli's eyelids dropped shut and he sees a table. The wet, smelly chopping block of a fish-monger's shop, on one side a hole into which the long knife shoves the slippery innards, shiny brown strands trailing all over the place. But what he is staring at (sixty, seventy years ago?) are the notches that have changed the edge of the thick wooden block into a set of rotten teeth; the marks left by the knives when chopping off the heads. The sharp teeth bite the air, no, they snatch strips out of the air in the fish shop, like fish do, with their tails almost vertically upright, tearing bits out of another fish, tugging ruthlessly – the table is itself becoming a fish . . . He opened his eyes and looked at the two men in his room. One of them was wearing a hat. They had sat down and were whispering to each other. What time was it? He raised his wrist to his eyes but he wasn't wearing his watch. Must have left it upstairs on the bedside table. In a continuation of the same movement he stretched out his arm and pointed with crooked forefinger at the television set. The man in the check jacket stood up and asked if he wanted to watch television – at the same moment the man with the hat had also jumped up from his chair. Polak's programme! Christ! That was all they needed! On no account must that be allowed to go out, he must phone the studio at once! Berta came in with coffee cups and the man asked if he could make a phone call. There was no phone but the neighbours were still up. The two of them left the room and the other man switched on the set. He asked Uli how he was feeling now, but looked sideways at the screen which remained dead and grey for several seconds. Why wasn't the programme allowed to go out? Here at last he was going to appear on television, on that glass screen over there, on which all the great personalities of the country and the whole world had appeared – at last everybody in the Netherlands would see him, and then somebody had to go and put a stop to it. Vaguely he remembered that something strange had happened, not long ago; something had come over him, had overpowered him, but he lacked the strength and the will to retrieve it. Anyway, that was all over now, it was as if he was slowly emptying, like a bath of dirty, opaque water. A soft humming filled the room, soon followed by the sound of police sirens and the screeching of car tyres. In the fluttering snowflakes four or five cars dodged into a side alley, drove into stacks of crates, dozens of policemen jumped out and surrounded a deserted factory, in which there was suddenly a sympathetic-looking but unshaven man who, on tiptoe, revolver in hand, stole furtively along a ramshackle gallery, holding a little boy by his other hand. Undoubtedly he had done the right thing, but the law did not allow it (at least not the law of this movie), he would die and the inspector would get drunk tonight. The inspector now approached him from an unexpected direction, across the roof, soon they would be face to face; as if she sensed it, the mother of the kidnapped child looked up from reading a letter and stared out of the window at the white horse grazing in the field, a present perhaps from the one who had still been clean-shaven then. The fragrance of mown grass! All those smells . . . What does he smell now? The musty cellar underneath the Maison pour Messieurs where, when his uncle switches on the light, the naked, sexless figures immediately stiffen in the postures they were in at that moment; their arms unnaturally contorted, they stare past one another, one or two lean against the wall, resting only on their heels, as if frozen. But they cannot fool him, he knows that as soon as he had gone they will resume their business – dancing slowly to the music of silence and darkness, very formally, with stiff and yet elegant movements. All those worlds. He felt himself floating away in corridors of shadows – and then there is a car drive through the polder to Amsterdam, in a westerly direction where the sun has just set – the horizon shoots upwards and he suddenly descends from a high mountain range, towards endless bays around a pink sea, full of purple, never-charted shores and islands . . . Well, they might as well forget about it. The porter had told him that only a lady announcer and the people from the newsroom were still at the studios; the technicians could do nothing without instructions, of course. Anyway, half an hour ago they'd had a phone call from Amsterdam, he'd been trying for ages to get hold of someone from the programme but it was no use. The man with the hat watched the little boy who was not sobbing beside the body of his benefactor, and he said it was on the other channel. The man in the check jacket bent forward and a moment later a little girl loomed up out of from the snow storm. She had had better luck in life; she was allowed to take a bite from a substance that would not take away her appetite, as her mother, cooking dinner in the kitchen and looking sideways over her shoulder, announced with a blissful smile, and then Lucas also looked up from his newspaper, and agreed with her. The two men stirred their coffee. On a planetoid a young woman, with long blonde hair that slowly rose and fell as if she was under water, floated barefoot across the beach, and Uli suddenly hears Sebastian squealing (Berta knelt down by the basket) and tries to find him in rabbit holes and mole runs into which he may have burrowed. But instead the dog he now sees a spinning top, a drop of blue wood; around the raised part he places the loop of the string, then winds it from the metal tip to halfway along the stem, not too loosely and not too tightly, so that a beautifully smooth sheath of string is formed, in one place with a slight swelling where the beginning of the string runs from top to bottom. Slowly he raised his arm (the men looked at it out of the corners of their eyes) and with a sharp click the top hits the paving stones, leaps up and then stands still for several seconds, spinning virtually motionlessly – until it begins to sway, ever faster and in wider circles, hits the paving stone with its side and rolls away in a sharp, irritated curve. Why has he never remembered this before, something so important; there have been opportunities enough, all those years in which he – taking it all in all – has been so bored. In Washington president Reagan showed himself reassured by the news from Moscow that the policies of the Kremlin, after the death of Leonid Brezhnev yesterday, would remain unchanged (the policies which until yesterday he abhorred and would abhor again tomorrow). All that movement. Bowling a hoop then; how by means of small taps left and right with a hoop stick he can keep the

265

movement of the hoop completely under control; but on a wind-less Sunday afternoon, suddenly overcome by the pointlessness of playing with a hoop, he picks up the stick and throws it vertically into the air, towards the grey sky, where, turning for a moment, it comes to a standstill, and then breaks to pieces on the paving stones. For a while he stares speechlessly at the splintered frag-ments, then bursts into a fit of laughter which ends when his aunt furiously throws open the window: "Have you gone mad, you rascal, you!"

"Mr Bouwmeester, we shall presently see a few extracts from Leo Siderius' new play, *Hurricane*, which will have its first night tomorrow, played by the Authors' Theatre at the Kosmos Theatre in Amsterdam and in which you take the leading role. A compli-cated play."

"If you're asking me whether this is a play for blockheads, then my answer is no. And as by far the greatest majority of mankind consists of blockheads, there are no more than a thousand per-formances in it . . ."

Uli saw Willem Bouwmeester sitting in the fluttering snow, dressed in a fantastic robe: he spoke, laughed self-consciously, relaxedly put one leg across the other – at that moment he sank to the bottom of the screen while at the top there appeared a second Willem Bouwmeester, a third, a fourth, ever faster, until it became a flickering cascade of Bouwmeesters. Groaning, Uli stretched himself and turned his face to the yellow circles on the wallpaper (Vogel sat forward with his elbows on his knees, again with his hands in front of his face, while Michael bent over the set and with Berta's assistance searched for a knob at the back) and Stella's address and phone number were already disintegrating in his intestines . . .

. . . and as it is beginning to snow even on their island, they re-embark and the houseboat glides still further towards the south, leaving Europe behind. With emotion he looks at Arthur, no, Pim, who is obediently sitting on the potty in his room. Small as he is, he has seen too much: his eyes have already been affected and they

266

must be healed by the sight of beautiful things; the starry sky and the Southern Cross, tropical sunrises, the faces of certain old people, works of art. But there is nothing of that description to be seen anywhere around. They must even have passed Africa already; before them on the horizon a high range of light grey vapour has appeared, flaring up occasionally in lofty streaks, now darting from east to west, now from west to east. Uneasily his eyes scan the desolate ocean. The water is changing too, it is becoming warmer and less transparent, its azure colour giving way to a milky consistency and hue. Here and there, sudden and extensive agitations of the surface can be perceived; these, he notices, are always preceded by wild flickerings in the region of vapour to the southward. The engine, which is not there, has cut out, and yet the boat's speed increases. The wall of vapour rises higher. Lightning flares up at its summit, its base divides, and a violent agitation of the water occurs close to the boat, so that everything – books, records, clothes, the crockery – slides from the tables and shelves. He takes Pim by the hand and they climb on to the roof; the heat having made it unbearable down below. Shortly afterwards, a fine white powder resembling ashes, but certainly not such, begins to fall over the boat and a large surface of the water. Fortunately, Pim is not afraid. Pressing the Pierrot against him, he points at a large white animal floating by in the water, but Uli, overcome by a sudden listlessness, averts his face. Perhaps everything has been for nothing. Could it be that he has made a terrible mistake, that he was not in any way able to bear responsibility for the child? He has come all this way and he has to face the fact that there is no chance of return. Continually and in vast quantities the ashy material is now falling around them, the range of vapour to the southward has risen prodigiously and begins to assume more distinctness of form. It can be likened to nothing but a limitless cataract, rolling silently into the sea from some immense and far-distant rampart in the heavens. The gigantic curtain ranges along the whole extent of the southern horizon. Desperately, Uli scans the sea, across which twilight slowly spreads. From the milky depths of the ocean a luminous glare arises that steals up along the bulwarks of the boat. They are nearly overwhelmed by the white ashy shower which settles upon them. The summit of the cataract is utterly lost in the dimness and the distance and yet they are evidently approaching it with a hideous velocity. At intervals wide, yawning, but momentary rents are visible in it, and from these rents, within which is a chaos of flitting and indistinct images, rush mighty but soundless winds. Tearing up the ocean. The boat is flung this way and that, he has to hold on tightly in order not to be thrown overboard. The darkness increases still further, relieved only by the glare of the water thrown back from the white curtain. He begins to sob. Gigantic and pallidly white, screeching birds fly continuously now from beyond the veil. In desperation, he forced a way for himself through the dense powdery ash towards the little boy; falls, raises his head. Pim! Pim! Where are you, my child? When he hears nothing, he lets his head sink forward in the ashes, and at that moment the boat rushes into the embraces of the cataract, where a chasm throws itself open to receive him . . .

5
First Night

At the other side of the curtain, the cascade of applause continues
unabated. His name is called. Motionless, exhausted, he stares at
the ropes, while softly repeating his last words, as if he was only
now becoming aware of their meaning:

> *"Now I want*
> *Spirits to enforce, art to enchant;*
> *And my ending is despair,*
> *Unless I be reliev'd by prayer,*
> *Which pierces so, that it assaults*
> *Mercy itself, and frees all faults,*
> *As you from crimes would pardon'd be,*
> *Let your indulgence set me free."*

"Curtain up!" calls the stage manager.

The ropes tighten in the brass rings and with squeaking jerks the
curtain rises, revealing the glorious gold and red of the full house,
bathed in electric light. Everyone is standing up, cheering him.

"Bravo!"

"Magnificent!"

He takes a step forward and makes a deep bow. When he rises
again, his eye passes over the radiant faces: the deaf old crocks in
the front rows, the regular customers almost all of whom are
known to him; everywhere, in the stalls and in the boxes, medals
are being worn, jewellery, uniforms; the amphitheatre and gal-
leries are filled with cheering young people. He sees countless
colleagues and other acquaintances from the artistic world –
everybody is here. In the orchestra pit, Mengelberg looks up with
a smile and taps with his baton on the edge of his desk; even the

269

usherettes in their little white hats stand clapping by the exits. He takes a few more bows, and moves a step back, and then the curtain falls. With emptying face he goes on looking at the two halves flapping one over the other; before they have come to rest they are already opening again.

So this is it; the end, the final execution. Perhaps the applause has always been what he lived for, yet at the same time he has always found these curtain calls embarrassing, for what is he really, other than a ridiculously dressed up fellow who ought to provoke volleys of laughter, as at a carnival? The *character* cannot say thank you, after all. It would be better if the actor first cleaned off his make-up and changed his clothes, but by then there would be little applause left to acknowledge. When the curtain has been raised for the ninth or tenth time, he forces a smile on to his face and wonders whether he should now spread out his arms to the wings, the agreed signal for the other actors to re-enter, but he wants to keep it to himself now, perhaps he will see no people at all for a long time to come. He glances at the royal box, but can see only somebody who is perhaps a lady-in-waiting; behind her in the shadows there is another person whom he is unable to distinguish. He makes a small bow towards the woman, who has remained seated and taps with a folded fan on her pearl-stitched evening bag while looking at him with the icy expression that certain sections of the aristocracy reserve especially for actors.

The curtain remains down, stagehands come running up from all directions and start carrying away the set pieces; the backdrop with the green foliage goes up into the air and makes way for a dark brown cloth with pillars painted on it, originating from the production of *King Lear* in which he scored a great triumph last year. Meanwhile his colleagues crowd around and congratulate him. Paul Musch grabs his hand with both his hands.

"You played like a god," he says passionately. "You cannot conceive how much you have given people. It is dreadful to think that this should be the end. Cannot something be done so that you may continue acting, farewell performance or no? You cannot sit at home all day and pass the time staring out of the window!"

"I am sure some way will be found. With time comes counsel."

Lucas rather boldly places his hands on his shoulders and kisses him on both cheeks, then looks at him with a strange smile, without saying anything.

Everyone is still in costume; the rough make-up on their faces, meant to be seen from a distance, almost hurts his eyes. He scarcely hears what they are saying – Alonzo, Antonio, Gonzalo, Trinculo, Stefano, Caliban, monstrously misformed and stuck all over with cardboard leaves. Stella has not come to him; in the corner by the fire watch she leans her forehead against Lucas's shoulder. She has quickly decided which side her bread is buttered, and who can blame her? Max has the good sense to stay away from him. He will have reason to be surprised. When the stage manager asks for attention and the actors withdraw into the wings, he observes the young lad with the gauze wings out of the corners of his eyes. He does not look straight at him, but knows that on his face there is still the despair that had been there throughout the performance; not a single time has he looked Max in the eye (not even at the last words addressed to him: *"Be free and fare thou well"*, only at his forehead so that in all their scenes Max had been trying to catch his eye like a cat a piece of string dangled in front of him.

"Mr de Vries!"

Ready to leave with the others, the stage manager points at the Victorian armchair now standing in the centre of the stage. He recognises it at once as the chair from Herzl's *The New Ghetto*, in which it was used six months ago. Surrounded by dozens of floral pieces and bouquets and even a few potted palms, it now stands there like a throne; with their sweetest faces the three spirits have taken up their posts behind it, Olga in the middle. When he sits down, still in Prospero's mantle, they make a curtsey; it is clear that they are enjoying their new role. To the right, just in front of the curtain, a lectern has been set up behind which the director of The Dutch Theatre has positioned himself; an over-refined man with silky blond hair and an almost too impeccable dress suit. He winks at Pierre – they have worked out the stage management of this evening together, but it is as though de Vries were now wearing his own face as a mask.

When the curtain rises again there is renewed applause, under-scored a couple of times by the Concertgebouw Orchestra with the sort of two-tone whoop one hears in a circus when the tightrope walker reaches the end of his rope. From the stalls, a heavy man with a greying goatee slowly climbs the steps to the proscenium and pauses there. On the left side of his chest glitters a gold star, and a broad, colourful sash runs diagonally across his starched shirt. Smiling, and looking at Pierre de Vries with slightly tilted head, he joins in the applause, though only with tiny, symbolic little claps, that would be inaudible even in total silence, and that therefore contain the message that the time has come to become quiet. When at last the house is hushed, the director says,

"Ladies and gentlemen! My name is Blaupot ten Cate, which is all I am going to say. The Burgomaster of Amsterdam will now speak to you."

Amid laughter and more applause he takes a few steps back-ward. Before the burgomaster reaches the lectern, a sombre, moustached man looking like the Paraguayan Ambassador to Uruguay emerges from the wings, places some papers on the lectern, and shuffles back. While the director sits down on one of the three chairs, the burgomaster clips a pince-nez on his nose, briefly glances at the papers and holds out an arm to Pierre de Vries.

"Grand maître!"

His broad gesture, his deep voice and the pause that follows, promptly elicit a fresh round of applause. When it has died down (for good) he embarks on his oration, which will be described in tomorrow's papers as "most witty", and "decidedly well-informed" (the moustached functionary will read this at his desk with melancholy assent) before returning to the real news of the evening. He reminds the audience that Pierre de Vries – "the last of the great" – made his debut at the age of eighteen in another play by Shakespeare, as Vortimand in *Hamlet*: that was in 1847, a lifetime ago – "mine, to be precise," he says and looks up in surprise, clearly deviating from his text which, equally clearly, he is reading for the first time. As he goes on to mention the highlights of de Vries's career, all the great roles in the world's repertoire,

272

4
Last Call

Whilst on the other side of the curtain the ovation continued unabated, people came running on stage from all directions, in white overalls, pullovers, Shakespearean costumes, Victorian dress. Cautious hands were put on Uli's back, lifted him up, gently turned him over. Everyone thought (feared? hoped?) the same: that maybe they were both dead; but then, still too shocked to move, Etienne spoke:

"I thought he was really going to murder me."

The stage manager, who had put his ear to Uli's chest, raised his head. "He's alive."

"Shouldn't we call a doctor?" asked Paul.

"What's the matter this time!" Berta called from afar. She clambered up on the set and knelt by Uli's side with her hands flat against his cheeks she shook his head, as if he were a clock that had stopped. "Uli!" she commanded loudly.

He opened his eyes and looked at her. His gaze roved past the standing figures around him and then returned to her.

"I want to go home," he said softly.

"Are you playing the fool or should we call a doctor?"

As his eyelids dropped shut again, he shook his head.

In the hope of another curtain call, the audience went on clapping. Meanwhile, the director and the authors appeared on stage.

"Everything is all right," said the dresser reassuringly.

The theatre director and Molly exchanged quick glances. Nothing was all right any longer. No one had died, but neither was there going to be a first night tomorrow. Everything had been in

259

from Sophocles to Gerhart Hauptmann, Pierre thinks of the misery behind the glory – of the countless farces and blood-and-thunder plays he has acted in, has had to act in, *The Two Orphans, The Hunch-back, Ben Leil or The Son of the Night*, the ghastly travelling, the performances in rural dumps on dreadfully cramped stages, *Oedipus Rex* on a set for *Friend Fritz*, the gruelling tours of the Indies. It has all been necessary for survival, but with dignified discretion none of it is mentioned now.

The burgomaster takes off his pince-nez and pronounces that after Pierre de Vries's departure Dutch theatre will never be the same again. He is therefore greatly honoured and delighted to announce that it has pleased Her Majesty the Queen to confer on him the title of Officer of the Order of Orange Nassau. Without averting his eyes from Pierre de Vries he pushes his pince-nez into his inside pocket, while the applause bursts forth, and holds out his other hand sideways at the exact moment when the infallible power mechanism propels the functionary from the wings to deposit the little blue box into his palm.

Pierre had not known that this was going to happen, although he had expected something of the sort (he had hope for a Knighthood of the Netherlands Lion). He stands up and the Authority of the State is now quite close, in whose short-cropped hair he can detect white flakes. When the decoration has been pinned on, he shakes hand with the burgomaster; he wants to steal a glance at the medal but it has already become unfindable among the signs and symbols on the magic mantle. Suddenly a laugh escapes from his chest; like a kind of burp, a laugh that has nothing to do with joy. Old comedian that he is, he immediately succeeds in deflecting it into something that from a distance seems to express pleasure and gratitude, but at the same moment he sees that the burgomaster is aware that it doesn't.

A moment later he is seated again, flanked by the three spirits, listening to the next speaker introduced by Blaupot ten Cate; the architect Berlage. In a casual tone which goes ill with his sharp, suspicious features, he says he will be brief, since everyone surely must be longing for the refreshments, not least the hero of the evening himself, whose merits he will refrain from extolling still further, as this has already been done sufficiently by the City Father and most of all by Pierre de Vries himself in this evening's performance. Moreover, as a simple architect, servant of the power of gravity, he has nothing sensible to say about the soaring flights of which the interpreters of dramatic literature are capable. However, he is speaking on behalf of the Society of Stockbrokers. The reason why these gentlemen have asked him may have something to do with the Stock Exchange he has built at the Damrak, which was handed over last year. The City Theatre, now exactly ten years old, is also a fine building, to be sure, though quite different. Anyway, he is glad to oblige them for the sake of his admired friend Pierre de Vries, and he hasn't come empty-handed either. He makes a sign towards the wings.

Promptly two uniformed attendants enter, carrying a painter's easel, which they put beside the Laureate. Two other attendants then place on it a large painting in a gold frame. Amid the applause Pierre looks at it as if he is seeing it for the first time, although he has posed for it for months. Painted in dark colours, in a grand, flowing style reminiscent of Frans Hals, it shows him in a monastic-looking study, bending over a heavy folio from which a glow as if of snow seems to rise, illuminating his ecstatic face.

Berlage raises one hand and waits until there is silence. From a piece of paper he reads,

"The Society of Stockbrokers regards it as a privilege to offer this portrait to the Society for the Foundation and Extension of the Gallery of Dutch Actors who have Demonstrated their Greatness in the City Theatre." He stretches out his arm towards the portrait. "Pierre de Vries as Faust!" Then he peers into the auditorium and calls out:

"Breitner! Where are you? Come forward!"

At the back of the house a man half rises from his seat and makes a few awkward bows to left and right before quickly sitting down again. Amid the polite applause for the painter, Berlage goes up to Pierre de Vries with wide open arms, embraces him and says:

"Adieu, Pierre. Much happiness in your second life."

When he has sat down beside the burgomaster, Blaupot ten Cate invites the hero of this festive evening to say a few words in conclusion.

After the embrace, Pierre has remained standing, but he does not go to the lectern. During the last few weeks he has prepared a speech lasting about twenty minutes; initially he had intended to plead for an improvement of the social position of actors, but as it did not seem to be in good taste to talk about money, it had become his own artistic testament; a plea for a more natural style of acting. He has learnt it by heart (without the slightest trouble; the range of text he has memorised during fifty-seven years reaches from here to the moon) and he could easily deliver it now, without notes. But he no longer wants to. It cannot be done any more.

"I thank," he says, "Her Majesty, Burgomaster Van Leeuwen, Henk Berlage, George Breitner and all of you."

He lets his head lean back a little and looks at the gigantic chandelier. The stillness becomes even greater, mother-of-pearl opera glasses are focused on him and he knows he can permit himself a lengthy silence. The luminous crystals are like the fragments of a suddenly frozen explosion. All those people in front of him and on either side in the wings, who are now, here in this theatre, for once not waiting to hear the words of an author to come from his mouth but for what he himself has to say. But everything is finished, broken, shipwrecked, it has all been in vain – only this grotesque performance still remains, for as long as it lasts. The lights begin to waver and he closes his eyes, so that two tears draw a glistening trail down his cheeks. A soft ripple passes through the audience. He has nothing more to say – and almost without knowing it himself, he says softly (but throwing his voice, so that he can be heard clearly even in the upper circle) and without the melodramatic booming of before:

> *"Our revels now are ended . . .*
> *We are such stuff*
> *As dreams are made on; and our little life*
> *Is rounded with a sleep . . ."*

Silence. Nothing else follows. With his head leaning back, his eyes closed, he stands there, immobile. Profoundly affected, and as motionless as he, the audience remains silent too; what an evening, what they are witnessing here is a historic moment, in their minds words are already being formed to tell the stay-at-homes about it. But now a problem is very rapidly developing. The first to realise this is Blaupot ten Cate; he straightens his back and looks uneasily at Pierre. A moment later the silence is suddenly broken by heart-rending weeping in the wings; some think they can recognise the voice of Stella Middag, the young actress who played the part of Miranda. Pierre de Vries still stands like his own monument beside the painting and there is no prospect of any change. In the eyes of the three girls in their ethereal gowns something like fear awakens, and a tremor of disquiet also passes through the audience.

This is the sign for Willem Mengelberg to intervene. The members of the orchestra, unable to see what is taking place on the stage, have been looking at him questioningly for some while – and now he points his forefinger imperiously at the leader of the orchestra, hisses "Mendelssohn", plays one stroke on an imaginary violin, hisses "E minor", sings "Pam-pa-paa-pam", and lowers his baton.

The effect of the first melting notes of the concerto is immediate and tremendous. The combination of the music and the tragic, motionless figure on the stage against the background of Greek columns, causes tears to flow everywhere; and when a moment later the orchestra joins in (from the way in which the maestro conducts, they all see the score before their eyes) the emotions are driven home with a sledge hammer. Ladies swoon, gentlemen's breasts heave behind decorations, it is as if the whole world is becoming liquid. Pierre still does not move – and now the stage manager takes the initiative and slowly, slowly, lets the curtain fall.

When everybody comes forward from the wings to congratulate him on his impressive *coup de théâtre*, Pierre looks around as if awakening from a sleep. He has not noticed that the curtain has come down for the last time; and only now does he hear the music which Mengelberg, on tiptoe and with one finger on his lips, is causing to die away, softer and softer – and shortly afterwards the chilly voice of the theatre director announces that only invited guests with *green* cards will be admitted to the reception in the

276

circle foyer.

"Will you hurry, Pierre?" calls Blaupot ten Cate. "And all of you too. Be quick! We mustn't keep the guests waiting."

Without a word Pierre goes through the fire door to his dressing-room. In the busy corridor he takes out the key and opens the door, but when a couple of walk-on actors go by (sailors from scene one) he closes it again, waits a few seconds, and then quickly enters and locks the door.

Etienne's body has already changed in these few hours. He is still lying in the same position, on his back, among the fragments of his glass and the spilt champagne, half under the make-up table, his arms strangely twisted like those of a window-dresser's dummy, wedged underneath his body; but his face has acquired the colour of a book that has lain open at the same page for too long. Between his lips his tongue is visible, mauve as a chow-chow's. Pierre feels his mouth filling up with bile, he turns away and just manages to reach the wash-stand before vomiting. He pulls the wig from his head, throws water on his face a couple of times and sits down panting.

What next? Run away? As in some cheap novel? Even if he managed to get out of the theatre, where to? He cannot even go home to fetch his money (a few thousand-guilder notes between the pages of *A Rebours*): the dressing-room would be forced open within minute. Anyway, what should he do in Belgium or Argentina, how would he make a living at his age? He looks at his face, covered in smudged make-up, and then sees the corpse again in the mirror – that body, which he has loved so many times in the last twenty-five years. He takes off the mantle and with averted face throws it on Etienne, so that only the translucent silk socks and the patent leather shoes with the silver buckles, bought together a week ago in the Maison pour Messieurs, are still visible. He feels nauseous, but has no regrets. He got what he deserved, the scum, the parasite. He, Pierre, was in love with Max too, he is the first to understand such things, but if the roles had been reversed he would never have betrayed Etienne in this loathsome underworld

277

manner.

There is a knock at the door.

"Pierre? Are you nearly ready?" Blaupot ten Cate.

"I'm coming in a minute."

"Everyone is waiting for you."

"You go ahead."

He feels time rising around him like a flood. Something must be done. At once. He looks at the folded razor with the tortoiseshell handle in his make-up case. He could cut his wrists with that; not across the arteries as amateurs do, but lengthwise, with a few firm pulls from the wrist to the crook of the elbow – as he has done so often, with the same movement squeezing a capsule of red paint. But he does not want to die. He can die later, any time. Call the police? Wait here until they knock on the door, just a bit too loudly? He has already let things go too far for that. But the longer he puts it off, the greater will be the scandal and the revulsion. Well then, let it be as bad as it can be.

He has taken his decision and it is as if this instantly makes him slightly tipsy. A laugh leaps out of his chest. Everything is as it is and as it is, it is now. He quickly gets undressed and starts to remove his make-up. The vomit (*Parfait de foie gras, Faisan à la Périgueux, Gâteau mille-feuilles Pompadour*: consumed at lunchtime at the Café Américain together with Etienne) lies stagnating in the wash basin; he looks around for something with which to poke it down the plug hole, but then, why should he care? He puts on his dress suit and slips the amethyst ring on to his finger. Finally he looks at himself sideways in the mirror, first from the left, then from the right, gives a little tug at his lapels and briefly runs the palms of his hands across the black, all too black hair above his ears. He thinks he looks well for his age.

As he listens at the door, his eye alights on the medal among the other symbols of the magic mantle. He unfastens it, throws his old medal away, and pins the new one in its place. Fragments of glass crunch under his shoes. With a brisk movement he steps into the corridor and turns the key.

A little further along, Blaupot ten Cate is waiting for him on the tiled floor. Everyone else has already gone upstairs.

"At last!"

As they turn the corner, his is called back by a dresser. She has her hand on the door handle of his dressing-room.

"You've locked the door, sir. I have to take your things to the costume room."

"Later, later," says Pierre with a charming smile. "I have a little secret in there."

"Well, if you think I'd steal anything," she says, in an aggrieved tone, "and I'd like to get home too, you know."

"On the contrary, my dear, you will join me in the foyer and drink a glass of champagne to my prosperity."

"Oh yes, that'll be the day!"

On entering the warm, crowded foyer he is greeted with applause. A gypsy orchestra is playing; it strikes up, in strange Magyar tones, "Long may he live". Here and there, a few well-bred voices join in. Blaupot ten Cate leads him to the far end of the room, to a table laden with letters and telegrams. At once a queue forms, to congratulate him. Accompanied by their ghastly wives in rustling silk and satin, whom they married no doubt for mercenary reasons, delegates, aldermen and councillors, with vacant, self-satisfied faces, file past, looking at him as though he were some second-rate vaudeville artiste, and he is glad when he can shake hands with the first of his colleagues; empty vessels usually (for professional reasons) but at least live people.

"The right Duke of Milan," says a handsome actor of about twenty-five. "I have come to pay you homage. I am just back from London and even there your performance would cause a sensation. The teacher puts the pupil to shame."

"Thank you, Eduard. It won't be long before it will be the other way around."

A young actress, still almost a child, kisses the purple amethyst on his hand.

"You pay me too great an honour," he laughs. "One does that only to the Holy Father."

"To me you are the Holy Father of the Dutch Theatre."

279

"You are a darling, Charlotte."

Some have presents with them, books, small objects into which much thought has gone, and which Blaupot ten Cate puts on the table behind him. Waiters go around with trays of champagne, and the mood heightens as the cigar smoke thickens but is kept in movement by fans like multicoloured ducks coming up from the water and flapping their wings. The brief conversations, the laughter, the turning in surprise to the next guest (each one a different fragment from his life) leave him no time to think of what has happened and is yet to happen; every now and again it appears fleetingly, like the taste of the bitter pip in the sweet berry, but whole minutes pass during which it is completely absent from his mind.

"Such a crowd, is it not dreadful," says a refined, balding man in his fifties, as they shake hands. "It was exquisite, Pierre."

"And that from the lips of an author."

The author, who seems to be lightly powdered, pulls the red rose out of his buttonhole and offers it. But when Pierre is about to take it, he holds on to the stem and looks at Pierre's hand with the ring.

"Curious. I see that our hands are of the same type." He lets go of the rose and fixes his gaze on Pierre for several seconds. "Am I wrong in supposing that you too are not unfamiliar with certain Uranian peripetias of life?"

Pierre smiles and raises the rose a little higher. *"Une fleur du mal?"*

The writer makes a small bow and says, *"Amusez-vous toujours."*

When after half an hour the queue of waiting guests is beginning to thin out, he glances around the room from time to time, where everyone is talking to everyone, but of course no longer about him. By the fireplace Mengelberg is holding forth to the burgomaster, with large gestures, no doubt trying to get support for his orchestra; blowing out clouds of smoke, the politicians sit together in big armchairs and discuss, across their fat stomachs, how the social democrats can best be kept out of government for all eternity. A writer and critic, with a nose like a plough and a neck like a bull, suddenly raises his voice and says to a pale round man who has had the audacity to speak to him:

"Be silent, sir, and begone! Your physiognomy displeases me."

Artistic life is taking its course, it no longer has anything to do with him. One of the last to approach him is a formidable old lady (of his own age) in black. He starts. With wide eyes he receives her kiss on his cheek.

"I thought it was a tedious play," she says stoutly. "Unbearably so, but you were magnificent. The crown on your life's work."

"Thank you, *maman*."

"Where are you playing tomorrow?"

"In The Hague, at the Theatre Royal. Deo volente, at any rate."

"I would have preferred to see you in an amusing comedy, but never mind. By the way, where has your secretary got to? I haven't seen him all evening."

Pierre pretends to look around.

"Perhaps he has gone home. He wasn't feeling very well. Even before the performance he had had too much to drink."

"Then things must be very bad indeed with my poor baby. An evening like this would have been the breath of life to him." She looks at him and takes his hand between hers. "It will be difficult for you, Pierre. You and I have reached the age of farewells, there's nothing to be done about it. You can always count on me. It's worst for bachelors and widows. Come and have tea with me soon."

At that moment the gypsy orchestra stops, the balcony doors are thrown open and Blaupot ten Cate calls for silence. As the hum of voices ebbs away, street noises and the thumping of a band invade the room.

"Pierre de Vries! May I invite you to show yourself to the people?"

In wonderment, Pierre goes towards him. As soon as he appears on the balcony, cheers rise from below. Hundreds, no, thousands of people start waving to him, men with their hats and caps, women with both arms, while the police band – drawn up in the form of a square – plays a fanfare. Pierre staggers momentarily, with surprise and emotion. Grabbing hold of the granite balustrade with one hand, he waves back, while above his head the smoky air gushes out of the foyer into the night. From the platforms of the horse-drawn trams people also wave and sing: "Long may he live!" The burgomaster, who has quickly grasped where his advantage lies (he is hoping to become a cabinet minister) stands beside him and makes demonstrative gestures in his direction, as in cabaret the beautiful girl in the short skirt points at the acrobat after his death-defying leap.

After a short while Blaupot ten Cate says, "Now you must go, Pierre. There is yet another surprise waiting for you."

He nods, waves once more and re-enters the building. The guests part to let him through. The balcony doors are closed, which gives rise to a sudden, whispering silence. After saying goodbye, in subdued tones, to the burgomaster and a few other dignitaries, he leaves the foyer amid applause – escorted by a small delegation, like a head of state.

In the corridor the theatre director asks if he may fetch his coat and hat for him from his dressing-room, but he brushes the offer aside. "You can have them sent to my house, with my other things."

"Are you going outdoors hatless, Mr de Vries . . . It is November."

"Nothing can happen to me any more."

Via the stage, at which he casts a brief glance (everything has already been dismantled) they reach the stage door at the side of the building. Again, it is the last time he goes through it.

As he steps out on to the pavement, he is dazzled by the magnesium light all around. Once again he is greeted by a large crowd, a group of students with burning torches starts singing "Io Vivat", and he is immediately jostled by people who are holding out their programmes for him to autograph. By the kerbside three open carriages are waiting; between the shafts of the first one, instead of horses, about fifteen hefty fellows are standing.

"Window-cleaners," says Blaupot ten Cate, with a broad grin.

The second carriage is filled to overflowing with the flowers he has received; attendants now also bring him his presents and his mail. Blaupot ten Cate terminates the autograph signing and introduces Pierre to the Chief Superintendent of Police, who, with one hand on the hilt of his sabre, the other touching his cap, clicks his heels. His face is virtually invisible under his beard and whiskers. In front of the theatre, music is still blaring across the square, the coachman in his long coat has difficulty in holding the unharnessed horses in check; they rear and whinny amid the noise and the jostling crowd and the constant flashing of lights that are mirrored in the gleaming lacquer of the carriages.

Pierre turns and takes leave of the theatre director, while his eye is drawn to the billboard beside the entrance:

"The Storm" by W. Shakespeare
Farewell performance of Mr PIERRE DE VRIES as PROSPERO
at the City Theatre,
Leidscheplein, Amsterdam,
on Saturday 12 November 1904

Then there is a sudden commotion. Just as the groom opens the carriage door and Pierre steps on to the footboard, on the other side of the street, at the Café Américain, where more people are thronging in front of the windows, a tumult of a different sort erupts. There is shouting, perhaps fighting, someone suddenly runs away at incredible speed diagonally across the square, a policeman pursues him, but stops at the corner and fires a shot into the air. Pierre sees the burst of fire coming out of the barrel and it is as if he can actually see the bullet vanish above the roofs in a south-easterly direction.

The Superintendent of Police does not seem at all concerned.

"Here we go again." He nods. "We'll get him by and by." Lifting his sabre, he steps into the third carriage, a landau, where he sits down opposite Blaupot ten Cate.

When the procession moves off, the incident has already been forgotten. At the head walk the students with their smoking torches, followed by the coachman holding the horses by the rein; then comes Pierre's carriage pulled by the window-cleaners, the groom in livery on the box, with his arms crossed. A cheering crowd follows the landau. In front of the peristyle of the theatre a brief halt is called. The police band draws up at the head. Pierre waves to his quests on the balcony and then they set off into the

283

city, accompanied by a resounding march.

Tears spring to his eyes. The crowds, the music, each thing on its own could make him cry, but now they are all there at once, and it is all for him; this must surely make it worthwhile to have lived and worked. That there is still something else, at this moment no longer alive, he does not for the moment acknowledge. The evening, the music, the flickering glow of the torches against the houses, where people in nightwear throw open their windows and wave, the ever-increasing cheering and singing behind him, he himself here in the carriage, alone, caught within a deep silence, the red rose in his buttonhole, beside him the high, sparkling wheels, in front of him the curved backs of the men labouring to keep up the pace, but assisted by boys in cloth caps and cavaliers in top haps, the flowers that are thrown into his carriage, the looks of admiration, perhaps even affection which he meets on all sides, even from people who have probably never seen him act, but who gather from the behaviour of the others that he who passes in that carriage is someone to be admired, yes, loved, and who therefore do so, as they do whatever else others do before them, for this is how the world has been ordained by God – Pierre lets himself sink away in it like a tired child into sleep.

In front of his house the procession comes to a halt. While the musicians stand with their backs to the narrow canal and play a slow, somewhat melancholy tune – perhaps from some Italian opera, he gets out. On the other side of the water more people are flocking. He opens the front door and the window-cleaners take the flowers and presents into the house. Meanwhile the coachman harnesses the horses, and on the doorstep Pierre takes leave of his escorts.

With slight unease Blaupot ten Cate looks at him.

"Will you be all by yourself now, Pierre, or is Etienne at home?"

Pierre nods.

"Don't worry. I don't mind being on my own."

With an air of ownership a dachshund comes strolling out of the house at that moment, walks down the steps and begins a lengthy piddle.

"Well, see you tomorrow in The Hague. There will be more

festivities there. This was only a taster, there will be sixty-four performances in all. Have a good night's sleep. I hope you are satisfied with today."

He returns to his carriage and the Chief Superintendent clicks his heels again. But just as he is about to turn away, Pierre says:

"One moment." He takes the key out of his pocket. "This is the key to my dressing-room at the City Theatre."

The Chief Superintendent looks at it, and then again at Pierre.

"Ah," he says. Then he suddenly understands that the key is meant for him, and he takes it from Pierre. "A memento. Most kind of you."

"No," says Pierre. "I give it to you by reason of your function."

The Superintendent looks at the key in his hand and then again at him, while something changes in his eyes. He salutes a second time and joins Blaupot ten Cate in the landau.

The band now plays *"Schlafe, mein Prinzchen, schlaf' ein"*, joined lustily by the students and the window-cleaners who, of course, are usually great singers. From the doorstep he waves once more to the people, who call out a last hurrah, and looks for his dog.

"Sebastian!" The dachshund jumps up the steps, he closes the door and it becomes silent.

The hall is full of flowers as far as the kitchen. He enters the front room, where without lighting the lamp he pauses and looks out. Tramping of hooves; the departing carriages. With their instruments under their arms the police bandsmen also leave; the students throw their torches into the water and start singing "Gaudeamus Igitur" on the way to their club house; the window-cleaners have to go in the opposite direction. Across the water, people linger and talk for a time but before long they too disperse, one by one the lights behind the windows go out. When it has become empty and silent outside, he climbs the stairs to his study, followed by Sebastian. Never before has it been so deliciously fragrant in the house.

He strikes a match and lights the lamp. The fullness of his possessions. With a sigh he sits down in the armchair in front of his desk and looks at the black-framed drawing of his mother when she

285

was young. On the floor, against the dark panelling, the Roman relief of a boy in profile, the same age as he was himself when the drawing of his mother was made; about it a pastel of an angel. It would be best if he now started packing at once, but instead he puts on his silk dressing-gown, pours himself a glass of port and lights a cigar. He goes to the bookcase and lets his eyes pass along the costly bindings. The gas in the lamp hisses softly. He pulls out a fine bibliophile edition of Villiers de l'Isle-Adam's *Contest Cruels*, but puts it back again. When he sits down on the couch, with Baudelaire's *Paradis Artificiels*, the dog looks up from his marrow bone and begins to whine softly through his nose.

"Yes, what's to be done with you now?" he says.

He lifts the book and snaps his fingers. At once Sebastian jumps on his lap and nestles against him, yawning with a high, contented sound at the back of his throat, his tongue curled up like a question mark.

Epilogue

First thing the next day Berta took Joost to the vet. He wasn't there but the two students who were standing in for him diagnosed that the poor thing had overeaten and had to have his stomach pumped out. Berta could not remember him having eaten too much, more likely too little, but if they said so, then it must be true. When she came to collect him a few hours later, he had still not quite come out of the anaesthetic. During the evening he began to breathe more slowly and with increasing difficulty. His jowls were pulled far to the sides while his legs and his head became colder and colder. When she turned him over on her lap, his heart stopped beating. The next morning, at the crack of dawn, she went to call the vet to account, and demanded a post mortem. Then it all turned out to be quite different. His spleen was torn, he must have been slowly bleeding to death internally for days or weeks; the last few hours he had been in a state of shock. Had he by any chance run hard into a door one day, or had anyone kicked him recently? And what had she decided she wanted to be done with the mortal remains?

She considered burying him in the garden – but why should she stay on here, all on her own in the polder? Suddenly she knew, quite certainly, she was going back to Amsterdam. Joost would have to be cremated.

When after two weeks she still had not received the ashes, she telephoned. Oh, a thousand apologies, there had been a fire in the crematorium, everything had been held up. Two days later a brown urn was delivered to the house. As the seal had not yet completely dried she prised the lid open and spread out the contents on a newspaper. There weren't any ashes in it at all.

Weeping, she looked at the little mound of grey, black-charred and yellowish fragments; bones, bits of vertebrae, grit. And three iron nails. Was this Joost, or had they simply swept together from the grate some leftover remains of all kinds of dogs and cats?

A few months later, through Michael's good offices, she found a small room with a kitchen in West Amsterdam, in a neighbourhood inhabited almost exclusively by foreigners and squatters. She paid for the move by selling nearly all she had; the portable phonograph fetched the most. She got up late and could be found every afternoon at the Tivoli, at the round table near the back, amidst young actors and actresses not only from the former Authors' Theatre but also from the new resident company at the Kosmos: the Omega Theatre. Mr Caccini had gone back to Italy, but there were new gentlemen who allowed themselves to be amused by anecdotes of her former love life. Usually she stayed until the bitter end ("Last orders, ladies and gentlemen!"), and then went, till far into the night, to the artists' club at the Leidseplein, to which she had been introduced by Vogel. Whenever she passed the City Theatre she glanced briefly at the floodlit mass of red and yellow brick (but never noticed the two empty plinths, left and right of the facade).

Often it was already light when, a cigarette between her lips, she arrived home to her increasingly squalid room. Tipsily she kissed the urn on the plywood mantelpiece, threw her wig on a chair, and when, half undressed, she crept into the unmade bed, she briefly crooned a tune,

> "Nur nicht
> Aus Liebe weinen . . ."

Yes, there are such things. Whereof one cannot speak, thereof one sings.

By way of tribute to a writer who forty years ago stood by the cradle of Harry Mulisch's authorship, the last few pages of the chapter *Last Call* contain – as is indicated in the text – a number of quotations from *The Narrative of Gordon Pym* (1838) by Edgar Allan Poe.